What people are saying about …

WOUNDED

"Poised between mystery and madness, this novel of redemption and regret is infused with the sweet essence of grace."

Siri Mitchell, author of *Moon Over Tokyo*

"This story and its characters will pull you into its spell. And the gift of salvation given to those who diligently seek Christ and humbly accept the offered gift of grace will stir your soul to long for more of Him."

—eries

"While *Wounded* is a lo ... ritty, fresh, and authentic—

Gina Holmes, au—... ...com

"Stark as life, honest as pain. Beautiful as peace. Burney's writing transcends even as it deals with the grit and ugly of a very earthly existence. I am a forever fan."

"A daring subject, ... what's not to love ... and spark convers...

"The mystery of fai... of skeptics and sinr...

"While *Wounded* is a work of fiction, the faith of many will be strengthened by reading this book."

L. Glenn O'Kray, adjunct instructor, Henry Ford Community College

"This is not a tame book, but a rich experience for the senses, a challenge to the mind, and a ministry of unique grace to the heart."

Jill Elizabeth Nelson, speaker and award-winning author of *Reluctant Runaway*

"No one tells a story like Claudia Mair Burney, and this is another installment of fearless, grace-drenched storytelling by Christian fiction's gifted Ragamuffin Diva."

Kimberly Stuart, author of *Act Two*

"Burney's *Wounded* is as fresh and vibrant as a cool autumn breeze. Her clever, needy, volcanic cast of characters responds to the important questions of faith in voices that are wonderfully authentic, rich, varied, and resonant."

Ron Hansen, author of *Mariette in Ecstacy* and *Exiles*

"*Wounded* beautifully illustrates how our Heavenly Lover goes to great lengths to draw us to Himself, demands more than we think we have to give, then proves Himself satisfying beyond our wildest dreams. This story is one I will savor again and again."

Janelle Clare Schneider, author

"Burney is among the most original and exciting authors to emerge in Christian publishing. *Wounded* is a daring exploration of suffering and redemption through broken and flawed characters."

Deborah Gyapong, freelance journalist and author of *The Defilers*, winner of the 2005 Best New Canadian Christian Author award

WOUNDED

a love story

CLAUDIA MAIR BURNEY

David C Cook®
transforming lives together

WOUNDED
Published by David C. Cook
4050 Lee Vance View
Colorado Springs, CO 80918 U.S.A.

David C. Cook Distribution Canada
55 Woodslee Avenue, Paris, Ontario, Canada N3L 3E5

David C. Cook U.K., Kingsway Communications
Eastbourne, East Sussex BN23 6NT, England

David C. Cook and the graphic circle C logo
are registered trademarks of Cook Communications Ministries.

This story is a work of fiction. All characters and events are the product of the author's
imagination. Any resemblance to any person, living or dead, is coincidental.

The poem "Marriage" on page 182 is from *Collected Poems: 1957–1982*,
copyright Wendell Berry. Used by permission of the author.
The lyrics on page 95 are from Bon Jovi's song "Bed of Roses," taken
from the album *Keep the Faith*, Mercury Records, 1992.

Scripture taken from the *Holy Bible, Today's New International Version®. TNIV®*. Copyright ©
2001, 2005 by International Bible Society. Used by permission. All rights reserved worldwide;
New American Bible Copyright © 1991, 1986, 1970 Confraternity of Christian Doctrine, Inc.,
Washington, DC. All rights reserved; *The Message*, Copyright © by Eugene Peterson 1993,
1994, 1995, 1996, 2000, 2001, 2002. Used by permission of NavPress Publishing Group.

LCCN 2008931895
ISBN 978-1-4347-9938-8

© 2008 Claudia Mair Burney
Published in association with the literary agency of MacGregor Literary.

The Team: Andrea Christian, Lisa Samson, Amy Kiechlin, Jaci Schneider, and Karen Athen
Cover/Interior Design: DesignWorks, Jasson Gabbert
Cover Photos: ©iStock

Printed in the United States of America
First Edition 2008

2 3 4 5 6 7 8 9 10

080808

To my friend, Donna Kehoe: Thanks for the chocolate, coffee, and friendship, not exactly in that order.

And to the broken beloved everywhere.

"From now on, let no one make troubles for me;
for I bear the marks of Jesus on my body."

Galatians 6:17 (NAB)

ACKNOWLEDGMENTS

As always, thanks be to God. My family members (in the Spirit and natural) amaze me with their tolerance of the many hours I spend away from them while I'm writing. Much love to my many friends who show unwavering enthusiasm for my books. No space to name you all this time, but you know who you are, especially my first readers. I'm especially grateful this time around to Kenny and Dee Mellon for being great neighbors and lifesavers, along with my mother-in-law Rutha Burney. God bless you. Glenn and Jane O'Kray have my deepest admiration for listening to my stories and sharing a few of their own. I'm also grateful to the people at Holy Family Catholic Church, a house full of friends.

Ecumenical order friends taught me much about grace and the

Franciscan and Benedictine gifts. Thank you Abbot Father Andrew Counts and Friar Dale Hall of The Company of Jesus, and Sister Paula Clare Clouse of the Order of Ecumenical Franciscans for your gentle guidance, spiritual direction, and love. Sister Max Marie, SFO (Secular Franciscan Order), I loved talking to you about stigmata and so many supernatural things. I am indebted to you. If I got anything wrong, and surely I did, forgive me.

Ron Hansen, author of my favorite novel ever, you made this lowly writer's dream come true, more than you know.

I am incredibly blessed to have such a dynamic community (family) working with me on my books—thanks all of you David C. Cook folks—but I have to give a special shout out to Don Pape and Terry Behimer. You are the *best!* My editors and friends/sisters, Lisa Samson and Andrea Christian, continue to amaze me. I want to be just like you b.a.h.'s when I grow up. Thanks Jaci, Amy, Karen, and a few who are not on my team, Melanie, John, and Steve.

I'm especially thankful for the good humor of Ken Wilson of the Ann Arbor Vineyard for engaging my "what if" story that takes place in a church a little like his own, and to Donna Kehoe for suggesting the story take place there (or someplace like it).

And thank you Regina Dolores Stinson, another queen, and my beautiful sister, for loaning me your name.

Finally, thanks for all who are willing to read this story, no matter what you believe about stigmata. I am your servant, gentle readers.

Claudia Mair Burney,
Feast of the Nativity of St. John the Baptist
Prepare the way of the Lord.

PROLOGUE

Friar John-Francis walked to the podium and stood front and center before the large expectant congregation. His nerves had frayed at the edges like the rough Franciscan tunic he wore. A knot of nausea settled like a stone in his stomach. He willed himself to ignore it. It would be the first time he'd share the book in front of an audience—for her sake he wanted it to go well. The monk had been given all the grace a man should ever need. That he stood there at all was a miracle.

Still, he stroked his scraggly beard, an anxious gesture.

O Lord, make haste to help me.

God must have taken pity. Bible verses flew like angels to his aid. He cleared his throat and inclined himself toward the microphone, clutching the edges of the cool wood. A deep breath. And another, before he prayed a few words based on Psalm 69.

"God, You know how foolish I am."

Twitters of laughter sprang up from the audience. His cheeks pinked as self-consciousness burned in his face.

"My offences are not hidden from You. Those who hope in You must not be made fools of, Yahweh Sabaoth, because of me! Those who seek You must not be disgraced, God of Israel, because of me!"

Smoothing the pages of the novel flat with his palm, he peered at his listeners. The gentle friar knew that inevitable skeptics lurked in the crowd.

God makes provisions for them, too.

The thought came to him in her voice. She would remember her enemies kindly.

He took a moment and studied the faces staring at him, some with open, eager expressions; others guarded, as if they'd come armed with a refusal to believe. He sighed. The only way in it … is to begin it. But Friar John-Francis couldn't help thinking of all the travail it took for this book to be born. All the sorrow and suffering that made it possible. If they only knew exactly how much this cost.

It wasn't Holy Scripture. Only God knew how many people would bother to read it, but to him the book was sacramental. Isaiah 53 came to mind: "Who would believe what we have heard?" No comforting answer surfaced. He'd have to trust God to convince them. It was a good story. Truthful, whether or not anyone believed it.

"Let me tell you a story," he said.

Pause.

"Ash Wednesday …"

CHAPTER ONE

REGINA DOLORES MERRITT

I was sitting in church at the Vineyard when Christ first wounded me. Minutes earlier Mike had fingered a cross of ashes onto my forehead.

Remember that you are dust, and unto dust you shall return.

Sounds like a plan. I shuffled away from him.

Throbbing pain in my knees heavied my steps—that, and the grim mood of my fellow pilgrims. You'd have thought Mike had forced us to peer inside our own caskets. We trudged back to our seats like mourners in a funeral procession, our footfalls a solemn largo on the red-flecked carpet.

For the heck of it, I pictured my tombstone:

Here lies Regina Dolores Merritt.

The world's oldest twenty-four-year-old.

Mother of Zoe.

To torment myself I filled the blank space after Zoe's name with all of the people I didn't have to love me. That made me want to throw down a punch bowl like Florida Evans did on *Good Times* when her husband died. I imagined shaking my fists to the heavens, shouting, "Dang! Dang! Dang!"

She didn't say dang, but I don't cuss.

That was my darkest moment during the whole service, and it had more to do with my life. Death would be an upgrade.

We didn't do somber much at the Vineyard West. Not that we were shallow, but let's face it, joy themes garner more enthusiasm. On Ash Wednesday, however, we cloaked ourselves in sorrow and wore our ashes like nuns wear habits.

When I arrived back at my seat in the near-empty balcony, I thought of how our Ash Wednesday service made me happy deep down in my ragamuffin soul. I could practically hear the dulcet sounds of Donny Hathaway's crooning coursing through my soul with the slow ease of an opiate.

"Take it from me, someday we'll all be free."

Amen, Donny!

Free.

One day I'd lay my pain-filled body down, along with my bipolar brain that stuttered between dancing and lying in sackcloth and ashes. I'd take off the cheap polyester dress of corruption and put on glittering incorruptible couture. Best of all, I'd be with Jesus face-to-face. That's all I wanted—all I wanted in the whole wide world.

Now seated, I closed my eyes to press the mute button on my senses and surrendered to the sweet delights of silent contemplation—if you can call our worship band softly playing Hillsong praise ditties silent. But I could contemplate with that. Mike had already darkened the sanctuary so we could focus on an image of James Caviezel hanging on the cross. The audio-visual team had projected him onto a giant screen hovering above the worship band.

I definitely wanted to avoid looking at stills from *The Passion of the Christ*. Personally, I found Caviezel way too good-looking to play Jesus, especially when he smiled—which I have to admit he didn't get to do much in the movie. And there was the fact that he was James Caviezel. Period. I mean, come on. He played J. Lo's boyfriend in *Angel Eyes*. I couldn't get that out of my mind. If I looked at him, I'd never get my holy groove on.

So, having avoided movie magic, I did what old black charismatic folks sing about; I kept my mind stayed on Jesus. Hallelu … Hallelu … Halleluuuuuuujah.

God's peace enveloped me. I hugged my arms, wrapping myself in His tranquility. It covered me like a soft, consoling blanket. Jesus hadn't healed me yet, but He always soothed my fibromyalgia-broken body. I exhaled and burrowed deep inside the solace of the Man of Sorrows. He was my true comfort. The only reason I was still alive.

Unlike the other crosses in my life, the marking on my forehead—that ironically looked like a plus sign—caused me no discomfort. The migraine headache clawing its way up the base of my neck, however, raged like the great tribulation. My limbs burned like they'd been injected with liquid fire. The way my poor knees thumped in agony you'd think they were a couple of talking drums.

I had a hard time driving to church, my hands hurt so much; an itch that felt like hives tickled my palms. I assumed it would eventually pass, or some other searing pain would draw my attention elsewhere. My fibro was so severe by then it ignored the eighteen points of pain that distinguished it from, say, lupus or arthritis. Pain showed up with no regard to protocol. And I was sensitive to all things: perfume, fabric dye, strong odors—not so strong ones. Nothing helped.

I didn't use drugs, not even prescription ones. None of them— and I do mean none—worked once the "honeymoon" period passed. On occasion I popped a homeopathic remedy under my tongue or slathered my aches in arnica gel. Mostly a few simple words kept me sane in chronic pain, if you could call a bipolar sistah with fibro who took prayer over Percocet sane.

My prayer? *Share with me, Jesus.* A breath prayer I'd come up with as homework when Mike decided to do a series on the Spanish mystics Saint Teresa of Avila and Saint John of the Cross. I dug my little prayer because it was my way of asking Jesus to bear my cross, while at the same time opening my hands to receive a portion of His.

I loved Him.

Without a doubt I didn't believe I could truly take on the suffering of Jesus, but if even the desire to give Him a modicum of relief from the agony of the cross pleased Him, oh yeah. Share with me, Jesus.

Once again I opened my eyes to see if the image on the big screen had changed. Nope. James Caviezel still looked like ground chuck. I squeezed my eyes shut again, my thoughts flying back to the real Jesus.

You could have pulled rank, being God and all, and busted up out of there, leaving the cross far behind You, but You didn't. You knew nobody would take care of our sin problem like You would. And there You hung, naked and nailed through Your hands and feet. Your side pierced by a sword. And though none could see it, except maybe Your mama, Your very heart had been impaled for the love of us.

Oh, my precious, magnificent God.

Share with me, Jesus.

I could understand what happened if there had been something special about my worship, but I didn't do anything different or spectacular. Yet luxuriant peace spread through me so profusely that I opened my eyes from the shock of it, and found Jesus, not James Caviezel, right in front of me.

Tears filled my eyes. I blinked to shy away from the blinding light of His radiance. All the colors of the prism danced within His body. I heard music, unlike anything I'd heard before. My heart stilled, and my breathing ceased. The tangled thoughts that filled my mind unraveled like a knot of thread and fell away as I found the Center of centering prayer. Awareness of anything else vanished.

Angels must have frozen and watched in stunned silence.

The Son of God Himself knelt before unworthy me. He picked up my hand and His mouth descended. Then Jesus, with the gentleness of an ardent lover, kissed me, leaving a perfect red rose in my hand.

ANTHONY PRIEST

I only went to the Vineyard that morning because my red-faced, type-A editor, Larry, threatened to fire me. Again. I'd planned to leave work to get *medicated* then show up later with a church bulletin and a testimony. If he thought the peace and goodwill I'd returned with came from God, I wouldn't correct him.

And I went for Veronica, my mother. If I didn't show up between now and Holy Week that woman would drive me bat crazy. She was holding out for an Easter Sunday appearance, but Easter was hard for me. The holiday conjured Nana in a way her nearly empty duplex didn't anymore.

Let's say I owed Veronica: my life and three hundred and fifty-two dollars. I'd stolen a few bills from her to buy some smack during a dark night of my *sin*. I'd noticed my body craved heroin whether or not it was pay week.

Not that I'm making excuses to justify my behavior. I should have said no to my impulse, but I rarely said no. Okay, I never said no. Not then. I had every intention of giving the money back, even though I never gave anything to anybody, in retribution or otherwise.

She said she didn't want money and called me a few foul names. After that she went pious on me and said I needed to come to church since I was going to hell in a handbasket. The handbasket was a nice touch. I could picture an actual handle on it. And it would be Veronica, not God, rushing me to my fiery eternal destination.

I hadn't been to church in over two years—not since the fiasco at the tabernacle of the holy and badly dressed women. Veronica dragged me to that torture chamber when she was in her scrubbed-face-and-skirts-to-the-ankles-for-Jesus phase. Those people inflicted all sorts of psychic trauma on me. They forced me into an on-the-spot baptism, just because I said I'd accept Jesus as my personal Savior.

I'm Catholic! I believed in *one* baptism for the remission of sins, and Nana made sure that had been taken care of when I was an infant. When I mentioned it, they cast a *Catholic demon* out of me. I went along with it. I *had* amassed a multitude of mortals and venials since my infant days. Perhaps in my dour reasoning I'd hoped a second baptism would pacify Veronica and make her pastor, a poor man's Billy Graham, stop yelling in my ear. The man *showered* me with spittle and tongues of fire to deliver me from satanic bondage. The experience may have damaged my hearing. It certainly made me grateful for breath mints.

If only he had used some.

And just so you know, the sound of "tongues" with a country twang will sear your brain evermore.

Why would she leave the Catholic Church for that madness?

Thinking about the experience forced me to reassess my priorities. I decided to reverse the order of my Ash Wednesday activities. I hooked up with my pharmacist-slash-herbalist *before* I went to church.

Yes, I called my pusher a pharmacist and herbalist. Those titles sounded so much more benign than drug dealer. I needed as much help as I could get to blunt reality. Coke, heroin, cannabis, *semantics*. I did what it took to get me through the day. And the nights. The awful, God-forsaken nights. So sure, I called Fox, failed makeup artist and ordained minister from the … what? Universal First Church of the Internet hacks? I couldn't remember. In not many minutes hence I stood behind my duplex—Nana's old place—while Fox watched me relish smoking a speedball for which I'd paid too much of the little money I scarcely earned.

The frigid February air numbed my bones, but I didn't want to go in the house of the Lord reeking of junk. Yes, I was concerned about how I smelled, until I wasn't concerned about anything anymore. Feeling mighty mellow, I drove the thirty miles or so to the Vineyard West in Ann Arbor and made my way inside the building.

It may not have been Easter, but the memory of Nana assaulted me at the first sign of ashes I saw on a forehead. I could almost smell the lingering scent of the Oil of Olay she'd slather on her face in the morning and at bedtime. The memory of her contralto voice as she prayed the rosary in halting Latin rushed to my ears. In my mind's eye I could see her fingers flying over the beads as she prayed in hushed, reverent tones:

Ave Maria.

Dominus tecum;

Benedicta tu in mulieribus.

Blessed are you among women.

I couldn't remember the last time I'd heard her say those words, but in that moment the Vineyard had given me my grandmother back, and there she was, wearing her uniform of all black, with a lace mantilla covering her silver coronet. I could see her wrinkled face, white as porcelain in the glowing light of the vigil candles encased in red glass. She'd light two every time she went to Mass. Prayers flickered to heaven for Veronica and for me, her little Anthony. How I missed going to church with her, watching her august form poised in unflappable tranquility on a wooden pew. Years of osteoporosis and prayer rounded her shoulders, but she was perfect to me.

She taught me, a fat, awkward, and sullen kid, to befriend the saints. After Mass we'd share—saints and all—Sunday dinner with all the trimmings in her tiny, crowded duplex. We'd break our bread without Veronica. Oh, there'd be the longing for her, Nana's mother ache, and my little boy one. Together we'd partake of the unquestionable knowing that she'd fail us, once again. Nana's love tempered the penetrating sting of her absence.

Thank God my poor grandmother couldn't recognize me now.

Pray for us sinners now and in the hour of our death.

Despite the fact that I'd blown into the church sky high off the potent blend of cocaine and heroin I smoked, I staggered over to Mike's line to receive ashes.

Remember that you are dust.

I'm not sure if self-importance or desperation drove me, but I couldn't resist going up. Perhaps the wounded kid deep down inside of me needed some sign of grace. I knew God could smite me for my arrogance, but I needed Him. Maybe I thought I'd find a hint of absolution.

It's possible that I asked for a miracle, or at the very least a sign. I don't remember. I hadn't yet been roused awake.

A black chick stood in front of me in line. If I hadn't shown up she'd have been the last one to get her cross. Thin, spiral-curled dreadlocks hung past her shoulder blades. She wore weird tree-hugger clothes, organic cotton or something completely lacking style. Black *and* green? Not a combo I saw much, but she didn't compel me enough to investigate further. Frankly, I didn't give a rat's tail about saving the planet. *I* needed to be saved! I'd noticed her. That's all.

I wasn't attracted to her. Much. I didn't even see her face until later. I noticed one or two other parts of her, but let's be honest, any male would notice those assets, even the church boys. If I had even the *remote* impression that she might be lovely I don't think I would have sat anywhere near her. No, white girl—the powdered kind—was my mistress. She robbed me of my need for a mere mortal woman.

Even when I was sober, I didn't tend to date the sistahs. I told myself if I sat by the black chick I wouldn't be distracted by *too many* dirty thoughts about her. When I thought about it, she'd be the perfect pick. She was inconspicuous enough that if, or rather *when*, racist Veronica spotted me, she wouldn't have thought I was on the make. With that occupying my muddled thoughts I determined to follow my black environmentalist to wheresoever she leadeth.

Even high I would have noticed if she smelled like roses.

Mike marked her forehead with ashes, then reminded me of my own mortality.

Remember that you are dust.

All of life is dust. At least my life is.

Vanity.

I tried to give myself a pep talk. *You're a big boy now, pushing thirty, Anthony. Nana can't hold your hand anymore, not from that nursing home, and Veronica certainly won't.*

The black dreadlocked sistah "dust" went all the way—bless her heart—to the balcony with me shadowing her like the ghost of a man I was. I parked a discreet distance from her.

We were the only two up there, and I wondered why she'd chosen isolation when she could have been on the main floor with the others.

She's broken.

Poor soul sistah. Stuck in the balcony with a junkie like me. She

looked so lonely. I actually thought—for about half of a second—
that if I had more dope I'd have offered her a hit.

Ah, but I smoked it all, soul sistah. Anthony Priest is an only child.
I never learned to share.

The journalist in me wondered what kind of demons she had. If
I weren't so self-absorbed at the time, I'd have created a story for her
in my head. I use to do that, make up stories for people. Sometimes,
I'd get their real story later and compare my version to theirs. Everybody had a story, and every story had worth. You could dive into a
life deep enough to touch bottom, and bob back up to watch the
ripples circle, achieving with the subject a type of union. Few things
stirred compassion in me, but stories did. That's what made me good
at what I did. *Did* being the operative word.

I looked down at the congregation. Like a mammoth icon, Jim
Caviezel hung on the cross on a big screen over the stage. I turned
my gaze away from the image and sighed. I'd rather watch soul sistah,
and did for a moment.

As it turns out her face wasn't bad at all, a bit roundish for my
taste, but it had an intriguing, light-amber honey color, and I found it
surprisingly sensuous. Her high cheekbones hinted at Native American ancestry somewhere in the mix. The roots of her hair that hadn't
dreadlocked yet and curled in waves maybe half an inch from her
scalp. I liked her eyes, two big brown almonds, touched by sorrow.

Don't get me started on her mouth.

If Veronica had come into my head she'd have had a massive
coronary.

But at least I'd have been rid of her.

God, that wasn't necessary. Sorry.

I turned my attention back to the big screen, though I found *no* solace in *The Passion of the Christ* images. Let's be serious. Jim Caviezel starred as some sociopath freak in *High Crimes* with a very hot Ashley Judd as his sweet thing. Mel Gibson should have known you have to hire an unknown actor to play Jesus, and then he can't be in any other movie again, ever. You can't get it on with Ashley Judd on the sofa in one movie, and then be *the Lord* on screen a couple of years later. And vice versa. You can't be the Lord, and later get hot and heavy with, say, Angelina Jolie. It's discombobulating.

And you know what the biggest affront to my sensibilities that movie image provided? That surely Veronica was somewhere on the main floor inconsolable, weeping at the celluloid image of an actor made up to look like the suffering Son of Man. And *he'd* get more sympathy than her *real* suffering son.

While I told myself, *Get over your rotten childhood, Anthony*, it happened.

The black chick screamed, piercing my drug-addled haze. An infusion of the scent of roses perfumed the air. Heavy crimson droplets fell from her hand onto her yoga pants.

I'm not sure if her scream or the fount of blood now flowing from her palm compelled me. Maybe the thought of my mother abandoning me kicked up my empathy. Or perhaps the contrast of the fake movie blood drenching Jim Caviezel with her very real blood startled me. Who can say why you act the way you do when the possibility of a miracle, or a tragedy, is in front of you?

I leapt up from my seat like a superhero, some part of me intent on rescuing her. Taking universal precautions never occurred to me. What could her blood do that I hadn't already done?

But my altered senses fought against me. I struggled to find my equilibrium as a force propelled me past my inertia. Kneeling down beside her, I caught her injured hand and cradled it in mine. Blood, like red petals falling off a dying rose, settled into my palm.

I don't know how to describe what happened next. It felt like someone had opened my head and poured sweetness and light inside of me. For a moment I couldn't think. Some kind of holy high held fast to me and killed my other buzz in an instant. I meant to say, "Are you all right?" but words failed me. I could only hold her hand while she stared at me, wild-eyed and, I'm certain, terrified.

Finally, like the prodigal son, I came to my senses.

"What happened?"

"Jesus kissed me."

She whispered the words in tones of fear and wonder then yanked her hand away and ran like Cinderella when the clock stuck midnight.

CHAPTER TWO

GINA

First He kissed me, then I bled.

I must have sat there with my hand in the air and my mouth wide open in the languid flush of feeling a woman has after she has been loved well.

Let Him kiss me with the kisses of His mouth, for His love is better than wine.

And more intoxicating.

Time abandoned me. I could have been with Jesus a second, an hour, or for an eternity. I could have died and that balcony been transformed into my heaven. Suddenly I was with Christ in His suffering. A heavy clank echoed as the first nail split my flesh, muscles, and connective tissues. The shock of pain unlike any I'd experienced before forced a scream to rip out of my throat.

Rough hands, calloused and browned at the fingertips, reached for mine. That guy's, the one who came in last, reeking of sorrow. He looked like the guy from the television show *Prison Break*. Mulatto, apparently of the tragic ilk. Head shaved like a neo-Nazi. Big crazy colored eyes that couldn't decide if they'd be blue, green, or brown. He'd been handsome, once upon a time.

He held my hand as if it were a shard of glass. All sense of the presence of God fled at his touch, as if he took my hand and God let it go.

"What happened?" he asked, eyes soft with empathy.

I had no idea.

Mike's voice reading Psalm 51 rooted me back in time. I was at the Vineyard West. Ash Wednesday. In the balcony.

> *Create in me a pure heart, O God,*
> *and renew a steadfast spirit within me.*

> *Do not cast me from your presence*
> *Or take your Holy Spirit from me.*

God was gone. My mind struggled to fathom the idea that the Lover I lived for betrayed me like Judas.

"Jesus kissed me," is how I answered before bolting from the balcony. I ran to the bathroom, leaving a trail of blood behind me.

Panting, I made it to the sink. I turned on the water and waited until it was as cold as it could get. I think I tried to baptize my hand, my panic rising like the water in the bowl. Bubbles of blood rained out of the blisters emerging from my palm and the back of my hand. The morbid sight stole my breath. When I couldn't stand to watch the macabre display anymore, I turned off the spigot and went into a stall to wrap the wound in toilet paper. Around, and around, and around I wound it, until I couldn't see a single spot of it anymore, until my heart stopped pounding so hard it thumped against my tunic.

I still smelled the flowers.

"What are You doing to me?"

Jesus didn't answer. I locked the stall, slumped to the floor, and cried.

PASTOR MIKE ADAMS

It happened maybe half an hour after the service ended. It was the middle of the week, so only a few people milled around. I was talking to one of our worship-band singers when two of the ladies from the small group Gina used to attend told me she was weeping in one of the bathroom stalls.

Nita Burton, a chunky redhead who always wore inappropriate tops and had appointed herself the surveyor of all things pathological at the Vineyard West, ambushed me right in the middle of my conversation.

She didn't say excuse me. Walked right up to me and interrupted, completely disregarding etiquette and Gina's privacy.

She announced, "Gina Merritt is bleeding in the women's restroom."

I excused myself from the person I was speaking with. "What do you mean she's bleeding, Nita?"

To be honest at first I thought she was having female problems, but we'd installed a machine in the bathroom for ladies' emergencies; they didn't even have to scrape up a quarter, just crank the handle and they'd be all set.

"Did you see if she needed help?" I hoped she'd take it upon herself to handle this like she did all those times I'd wish she *wouldn't*.

"Of course we asked." "We" meaning her and her faithful sidekick, Norah, an anorexic-looking, raven-haired parrot of whatever Nita happened to be preaching at the time.

Nita proclaimed, "She wouldn't talk to us or come out. And she wouldn't let us into the stall."

Norah said, "She wouldn't talk to us."

"And she was crying," Nita said.

"Crying," Norah repeated.

A thousand more hairs on my head faded to gray in that moment.

Nita leaned toward me, flashing what I truly did not wish to view. I turned my head and prayed my wife Lacy would rescue me soon. "There was a man standing outside the bathroom looking nervous and fidgety. He asked about her. I happen to know he followed her up to the balcony. And they were alone up there."

"A man?" I sounded as pathetic as Norah.

"They were alone." Norah nodded.

"Are you sure?"

Nita, predictably, answered first. "I watched them. If I told her once, I told her a thousand times she needs to sit on the main floor, as close to the front as possible. There's just something about being close to the anointing. Don't you think so, Mike?"

I nodded to make her happy.

Norah had an original thought. "Remember someone screamed?"

They traded places. Nita responded. "That's right. Someone screamed."

What fresh hell is this?

I'd heard the scream, but we had a few charismaniacs among us. A stray scream wasn't common, but it wasn't unheard of. A few of our zealots could do just about anything. Nothing came after the scream, so I didn't think much of it.

What in the world could be happening to Gina now?

The poor kid attracted misery like a magnet, and if Nita the Terrible couldn't lure her out of that stall, something was amiss at the Vineyard.

I didn't think anything violent had happened, not even when Nita said, "He had shifty eyes." But I allowed for the possibility of my own naivety. We'd never had any violence *at* church, and God knows, we'd had just about everything else. As a pastor I'd come to understand people suffered a lot more than they let on. Bad things could happen, even in God's house.

Not Gina, Lord. She's already had her heaping portion of pain.

I sighed. "Did you recognize the man she was in the balcony with?"

"Never saw him before in my life," Nita said.

"Never saw him," Norah repeated.

My wife, Lacy, must have spotted Nita hovering around me like my personal Holy Spirit. Thank God for my brown-haired beauty, who so satisfied me I didn't need to sneak peeks at the likes of Nita. We'd made a pact that Lacy would spare me from having to interact too much with Nita. She came up beside me and linked her arm in mine.

"Gina Merritt," I said to Lacy. "The ladies say she's in the bathroom bleeding and won't come out."

Lacy looked as confused as I must have appeared a few minutes earlier. Asked the same dumb question of Nita. "Did you ask her if she needed any help?"

Nita awarded her with a "duh-uh" look.

"We'd better go see about her," Lacy sighed. My sweetheart knew if Nita couldn't get her out of there, we had ourselves a situation.

The four of us made our way to the ladies' room, Lacy clearing it so big manly pastor guy could enter in.

Nita and Norah dogged my heels until I sent them to find the creepy guy. I told them not to say anything to him, stay clear, and keep an eye on him just in case he really was as sinister as they made him sound.

They left, and I stepped into the restroom. Lacy crept over to the stall where we heard Gina keening. Lacy had a gentle touch. She called her name instead of knocking on the stall door, probably to avoid scaring her out of her wits or embarrassing her.

"Gina," she said, in the same soothing tones she'd used on our five children whenever they hurt. "Honey?"

I felt comforted.

More crying. From Gina, that is.

"Are you okay? Did something happen today in church?"

I wanted to add, "With a shifty-eyed, nervous, twitchy guy who followed you to the balcony?" but thought better of it.

Gina wailed at Lacy's question.

Lacy tried to coax her out with her voice. "Honey, there's a trail of blood leading to you. We need to know if you're hurt."

"Yeah"—she gulped back her sobs—"I am. I think."

I tried to remain calm. I don't like people hurting my sheep, and as soon as she let me know what happened I'd go after ol' shifty-eyes myself.

She repeated, "Yeah." This time more softly than before, an anguish-filled whisper really. "I'm … hurting."

Lacy and I looked at each other.

I took over the questioning. "Did *someone* hurt you? A visitor? You sat in the balcony. Did whatever happen take place *there?*"

She sniffled. "Yeah."

This would drive me insane. Thirty years of pastoral ministry and teenagers at home, and *this* would take me over the edge of reason. Again, I gave Lacy a helpless look, but her shoulder shrug and eyes said, "You're the pastor, buddy. You get paid, not me."

I rubbed my temples and took a deep breath to have at it again.

"Nita and Norah said a man was in the balcony with you." I was loath to ask. "They said they'd never seen him, and he looked suspicious." I didn't want to hear the answer to this, but I had to ask. "Did *he* hurt you?"

"No."

"No?" I said, surprised. Lacy and I exchanged looks. "Did you say no?"

My gaze went back to Lacy who mouthed, "She said *no!*"

I sighed and addressed Gina again. "Uh … can you tell me who hurt you?"

Please don't say you did something to yourself.

The time I spent three hours on the phone talking her out of killing herself bobbled in my mind. And then the incident when I *couldn't* talk her out of acting on that impulse. I stayed with her in the emergency room while a nurse stitched both her wrists, and waited for hours until a policeman whisked her off to a facility that would find a psychiatric hospital for her.

Had the service been too much for her? All the talk about mortality and death?

She'd been doing well. She was sick a lot, but not in *that* way. She hadn't had an "episode" in two years.

She loved Ash Wednesday.

Was that a problem? That she *loved* it?

She spared me from having to think about it. Her voice punctured my worry.

"I just want to talk to *you*, Mike. Please, ask Lacy to leave for a minute."

She'd been alone in counseling with me before. I couldn't do that with some people, but Gina never posed a problem for me. However, I wanted her to know I'd have Lacy close by.

"Wait outside the door for a minute, will you, Lace?"

She nodded that was okay with her, squeezed my shoulder, and said to Gina, "I'm right outside if you need me, sweetie. We love you."

Gina managed to choke out, "I love you, too."

I called after Lacy, "If you see Nita and Norah, tell them not to stalk our visitor." I hoped I hadn't made a mistake. Maybe I needed to talk to him anyway.

I knelt at the stall, my knees popping to a burning ache, and positioned myself on the hard floor. I was getting old. Fifty-three-years young I liked to say, but I didn't feel it at that moment. All the requisite aches and pains of growing older howled inside me. Bending didn't do me any favors either, but I wanted to get down to her level. Right away the touch of bursitis plaguing me fired up.

"I'm here for you, Gina."

"Jesus made me bleed, Mike."

I closed my eyes. Not this.

I would have preferred her saying the shifty-eyed man hurt her, all day, every day, any day.

"Jesus made you bleed?"

I sounded like Norah again, with question marks.

"He kissed my hand and pierced it with His mouth."

I didn't respond right away. She'd mystified me. Jesus did not kiss and pierce at the Vineyard West. I knew this. I'd been there when we started the church. I didn't miss much.

What to do, big pastor guy? I clasped my hands, lacing my fingers together.

How to say this delicately ...

"Gina ... uh, are you taking your medication?"

She wailed again.

"I don't mean to be offensive, but I don't understand what's going on with you."

More weeping. I wanted to join her. *Come back, Lacy!*

"Can you open the door so I can see you?"

She scrambled to her feet, hesitated, then unlocked the stall. I struggled to pull myself up from the floor. My knees groaned from the effort.

I opened the door. Gina lolled in the corner. Our white industrial toilet paper circled her left hand. Crimson spotted her hippie-girl clothes. She looked every bit the kid with the world's worst luck. Wide-eyed and trembling, she begin to unravel the TP, each layer revealing a little more of the substantial disk of red in the center of her palm.

The incredulous notion of Jesus piercing her hand poked at me. I tried to empty my mind of all but what was most important: Gina was a sick girl, not a raving lunatic but someone fragile, a bent sapling with bruised shoots grazing the earth, trying to make it in a congregation of redwoods, oaks, and a few weeping willows. We weren't Eden, but most of our trees at least stood upright.

She stopped unwinding, suddenly reticent, and tried to cover her left hand with her right.

"Will you please let me see?"

Gina nodded her assent, but I thought I'd help her along. I snatched a pair of vinyl gloves from a box near the diaper changing station, and pulled them onto my hands. Cupping her hand in mine, I slowly finished the unraveling she'd started.

I thought the rose scent came from her perfume. She liked natural fragrances. Made her own blends of essential oils—that kind of thing. Once she even did a natural beauty workshop for the women's ministry.

She smells heavenly.

A fleeting image of Gina as a single delicate rose in inexplicable bloom during the endless Michigan February flashed in my mind. *Whoa, Mike. What is the matter with you? No time to wax poetic.* I finished unwinding the tissue until I got to her bare hand. "Holy mackerel" slipped out of my mouth. My stomach dropped to my shoes.

I'd never seen anything like it.

She had a wound, all right. A thin membrane of translucent flesh swollen with blood covered her palm. It was almost like a blister, but not like a blister at the same time. And it oozed blood.

"Did you try to rinse it off?"

"Yeah I did, but it keeps … leaking."

"Can I just … uh … touch it? I promise I'll be gentle."

She nodded, and I slowly turned her hand around. Same oozing blister on the back. I couldn't see well, since it was so engorged with blood, but—and I know this is crazy—I had the distinct impression that if I poked at it, my finger would go right through her.

What is this?

I pressed on it, just barely. She jerked her hand away, but not before I noticed her movement didn't change the direction of the flow of blood, completely defying gravity.

"Holy mackerel!"

Doubts assailed me. She couldn't injure herself that way, could she? Would some kind of chemical cause this effect? She wasn't bleeding when I put ashes on her. I tried to think of how much time passed between hearing the scream and Nita and Norah coming to me. Drew a complete blank.

No matter what this was, Gina Merritt needed help.

Lacy knocked on the door. "Mike, I need to come in."

"Come on, Lacy."

She burst into the bathroom with Nita and Norah in tow. Nita had what I assumed was Gina's purse in her hand. It wasn't really a purse. They were bags made of burlap and brightly colored printed fabric crafted by AIDS orphans and widows in Swaziland. We sold them to help a mission organization raise money.

Nita spoke, because that was her job. "We found him. He was rummaging through her purse."

"Through her purse!" Norah repeated, outraged.

Lacy, the voice of reason, spoke. "They said they chased him off. It doesn't look like he got any money."

All of them froze. Lacy put her hand over her mouth, and Nita shouted, "Mercy! What in the world happened to her hand?"

Norah parroted, "What in the world?" then interjected her own, "What's that smell?"

And Nita. "It's smells like jasmine or something."

It seemed that Nita grew less sure of herself the longer she stood there staring at Gina. "I called the police," she said, her voice unsteady.

Gina cried out, "No," wrapping the ruined tissue back around her hand. Lacy grabbed an entire roll out of the stall next to where we stood. She handed it, tentatively, to her.

My little sheep's distress grew as she struggled to replace the toilet paper. "I can't.… I need to go.… I don't want police."

"But someone's been in your purse," Nita said.

"And your hand!" Norah said.

I had what I thought was even better idea. "I think Gina needs to see a doctor." I turned to Gina, making an effort to speak with all the gentleness in me. "Maybe when the police get here we can sort all this out and get you to the hospital."

Gina yelled, and I rarely, even in the worse of circumstances, heard her raise her voice. "I don't *want* to go to the hospital. They'll think I did this to myself!"

"But Gina," we said, a chorus of voices, out of synch.

"I didn't do this. I *didn't!*"

She snatched her purse away from Nita with her good hand and ran out of the bathroom like a gazelle, leaving the rest of us standing there stunned.

CHAPTER THREE

PRIEST

I had no intention of stealing her money. I stole her driver's license, and I wouldn't have lifted it if those two biddies hadn't caught me, excuse my awful pun, red-handed.

Like an idiot I followed her to the bathroom, and of course she wouldn't come out. I couldn't loiter around the ladies' room like some kind of pervert. Nor did I want Veronica to waylay me.

I went back to the balcony and looked in her purse for a wallet. I wanted to find out her name. I thought she needed help.

Sure, I knew rummaging through her bag made me look like a sociopath and thief, something Veronica would have gladly proclaimed

I was, but what was I supposed to do? The two busybodies showed up, and I could tell they weren't overly burdened with reason. The way those hawks eyed me I knew I'd have to explain myself from the back of squad car.

I dashed, thanking God no big strong soldiers in the army of the Lord tackled me before I could slip off to my car. I left, but that light, buoyant feeling of well-being stayed with me.

What did soul sistah do?

I was going to find out. My inquiring mind wanted to know. She'd given me a jolt of feel-good, the likes of which I'd never experienced before. You name the dope; I'd used it.

I had no spiritual motives, at least I didn't think so. I didn't fit the profile of a God chaser in hysterical pursuit of some mystical experience. It wasn't about pursuing another high either. Wasn't even sure if what I felt was real.

Was I imagining things with what little imagination I had left?

Then again, maybe I had a little Veronica in me, as hard as that was for me to process. Who doesn't really want a miracle, somewhere deep inside themselves?

The thought that I may have had some kind of mission never occurred to me. I wasn't the guy who got chosen for *anything*. No matter what Nana drilled into me.

MIKE

After locking up the church, Lacy and I went to Gina's townhouse, since we failed so monumentally to keep her around until the police showed up. They sauntered in maybe five minutes after she left.

We filed a report anyway, citing the shifty-eyed guy who had rifled through her purse as the culprit.

They wanted to know why she didn't stick around to give her own statement. None of us had a good reason. Trying to respect her wish not to go to the hospital, we agreed before the police arrived not to mention her injury.

The officer in charge told us to have her come down to the station and file a report. We assured him, hoping against all hope that she would.

When they'd gone we talked among ourselves. None of us knew what was happening and we didn't want to race to judgment, but we did need to make sure she was all right. Lacy and I told the ladies we'd follow up and let them know.

I told Nita and Norah not to speak to anyone about Gina's hand or whatever may or may not have happened. All I needed was more craziness in the Vineyard's thriving rumor mill.

Twenty minutes later, Lacy and I headed to Inkster where Gina lived. We drove in silence and I wondered if she was thinking of what we saw in that bathroom. Whether or not I admitted it to anyone, I knew her injury wasn't ordinary.

I knew about sacred stigmata. I'd flirted with Catholicism for a long time. We were all but Anglican at the Vineyard, a mixed bag of pilgrims who'd come from a full range of church experiences to find freedom from whatever religious shackles bound us. I liked to think of the Vineyard as a stream in the desert. Our little oasis wasn't high church, or low church. We were the Vineyard West. We loved Jesus and had a passion to follow Him authentically. We tried.

I didn't lust for miracles. I was content to follow Jesus and live the gospel in simplicity. Like a good Benedictine, I believed in everything in moderation. But her hand … it haunted me.

People of God go through life believing without seeing; that's the nature of faith. It's the substance of things hoped for; the evidence of things not seen. I didn't need miracles to follow Jesus, but even the most devout followers of Christ have a little Thomas in them.

See, Thomas didn't only doubt. When Jesus told His disciples of His coming death, it was he who cried out from the deep well of devotion within him, "Let us also go, that we may die with Him." But no matter how strong we think we are, when all hell breaks loose, we want a little assurance. We want to see something as tangible as nail scars. After all, who among us can touch Christ's wounds with our own fingers and not be changed?

A shudder rippled through me at the thought of Thomas, in light of what I'd seen on Gina's hand.

Why did people get stigmata? Was it a sign? A witness? To whom? Or was it just the power of suggestion, some iron will producing physical manifestations of a faith gone crazy?

The whole thing nauseated me. The anxiety of what we'd find when we saw her churned my insides. I tried to calm myself. I flicked the radio on, and Lacy and I listened to contemporary Christian music until we pulled up in front of her townhouse in a housing project off Michigan Avenue.

This wasn't about a sign, or a miracle. This was about one of my sheep, a lamb really, in crisis. I was thinking crazy. Stigmata? Holy mackerel. I was making the whole thing into something it wasn't.

And what did that say about me?

I heaved the air from my lungs. This wasn't about me.

Gina had gone through much in her young life. The last thing I wanted was to make more trouble for her. But I had to address the bipolar thing, and the self-harming thing, and the Zoe thing. She and her little girl might be at risk, of what I had no idea.

Her car was parked in front of her little townhouse. My nausea had turned to a fist pounding my stomach. Lacy and I sat in our sedan and prayed together before we went to her door. We had no idea what to do.

I turned to Lacy, "I wish she'd never said Jesus did that to her. Anything else, including her harming herself, we can make sense of."

"I keep thinking of that little girl. Mike, what if she's really *sick*? She could have done it to herself. Maybe she used some kind of acid. She's taken a razor blade to her wrists before."

"I know, Lacy. But …" I didn't want to say what Lacy already knew. That wasn't a razor cut in her hand. I tried to move her from that line of thinking. "Why do you think Zoe wasn't with her at church?"

"She knew we didn't have nursery or children's church for the Ash Wednesday service. She probably had her at day care. If I'm not mistaken she works on Wednesdays. Maybe she took off from Subway so she could enjoy the service herself."

"Do you think Zoe is with her now?"

"I have no idea." She buried her face in her hands.

I knew my Lacy. Surely CNN images of a certain, very religious, bipolar woman who drowned her passel of kids in the family bathtub agitated her. Lacy was sick over the news story for weeks.

But I knew Gina. She wouldn't hurt that little girl. She held on to a thin thread of life when it was unbearable for the sake of her daughter. Well, she hurt herself that one time, but not since then.

"I've talked her through a lot of hard things. I don't think she'd hurt Zoe."

Lacy pressed her back against the seat. She massaged her temples, worry furrowing her brows. "She's sick, Mike."

"We don't know that. She's been coming to church more often than not. She doesn't come when she's sick. She's social, if you don't include her sitting in the balcony. Gregarious."

My voice trailed off. Was she social and gregarious? All of her behavior seemed suspect now. She hadn't stuck around after service to chat for weeks. I didn't really know her state of mind at all. Had she been hypomanic, and I didn't see it? And now she's crashed back down to the ground? Beneath the ground! But she didn't *seem* to be sick. I didn't want to color everything she did with a big bipolar crayon.

"Let's just go in and talk to her."

Lacy's mind was stuck on the munchkin. "We may have to call protective services."

"If we need to, we will, Lace, but I don't think we have to do anything that extreme."

"Mike, if something is wrong with her, I'm not walking out of there without that kid."

"Okay, Lacy, but if there's something wrong with Gina, we're going to do all we can to protect her, too."

She looked down. I think she felt a little embarrassed that she'd focused so much on Zoe when Gina was just as needy. She didn't say anything though.

I ran my hand through my hair, knowing I'd just earned myself even more gray, and said a silent prayer that all would be well, and all would be well, and all manner of thing would be well inside that townhouse, even though I didn't think it wouldn't be.

Lacy beat me out of the car. She marched up to Gina's door and knocked with the force of the police. I followed her to the porch, wondering what manner of people her neighbors thought we were, looking like we were about to pull out a battering ram to get into Gina's place.

Lord, my head hurt.

No answer.

Lacy's ire rose by the second. "We should call the police."

"*I* wouldn't come to the door if you knocked like that. Can you just relax, Lacy?"

I knocked this time. Still no answer.

"Let's call the police, Mike."

"It's possible that she's not home."

"But her car—"

"I know, honey. She could be in someone else's car. Her hand was bleeding pretty badly. Maybe she changed her mind and went to the hospital. Could be that someone else took her so she wouldn't have to drive herself."

Lacy's wrestling had etched itself in her face. "I think we need to do something. A child is involved."

"I know, but she's never hurt that child."

"Don't you think she hurt Zoe when she tried to kill herself?"

I didn't answer.

"What if she doesn't understand that something is wrong with her, Mike?"

"She was completely lucid today, Lacy."

"Do you think her saying Jesus kissed her and pierced her hand is lucid?"

"I think we need to wait before we get authorities involved. She knows how to ask for help. My gut says to wait until she asks."

Lacy crossed her arms. "I hope you're right, for that little girl's sake."

I hoped I was right for Zoe's *and* her mother's sake.

"She probably went to the hospital. She knows how to take care of herself."

Lacy let me have the last word, and we drove back home, neither of us speaking to the other.

CHAPTER FOUR

GINA

No way I was going to the hospital. I had a history in that place, medical records that said bad things, the kind of things that could get a sistah on lockdown, and where would that leave me? Or Zoe, for that matter?

What was I going to tell the ER staff? The Lord kissed me? As it was I saw the way the four of them looked at me in that bathroom: like I had a ring of birds circling my head singing, "Cuckoo, cuckoo, cuckoo!" The hospital people would be worse. They'd have me in the psych ward faster than they could say "nut job."

Jesus had pierced my hand, not my feet, and I could run like the wind. My knees might kill me for it later, but adrenaline befriended me. I zoomed out of that church to the parking lot before Nita could take me down and drove straight to CVS for bandages and Neosporin.

In the drug store I bought a bag of bandages and a few other supplies, gave the cashier a look that dared him to say something, and flew out of there before I made anybody too nervous. I bandaged my hand as quickly as possible before I headed to the day care. Dolly would be suspicious, but what else was new? She always thought I was about to fly over the cuckoo's nest.

Finally, I made my way to Dolly's center. Since that big-mouth woman couldn't mind her own business, I steeled myself to deal with her.

Miss D, or Dolly, is a stereotypical big mama who has no problem with who she is. She'd done good in day care. Kids loved her, though I doubted she did much for adults. When she saw me, she put her hand on her fleshy hip and went straight for the jugular.

"Giiiiirl? What done happened to you?"

"I'm hurt, Dolly. I need to get Zoe and go take care of this."

"And you gon' drag that baby to the 'mergency room?"

"I need to get Zoe, D."

I fumbled with the sign-out sheet. Good thing Jesus got my left hand.

"You say you hurt? Subway tryna do you in? Or somebody else?"

"I really have to go, D."

Dolly went in for the kill. "We gon' have to keep sharps away from you again, Miss Thang?"

If I cussed, I'd have blistered the walls, raging at her reference to the scars on my wrists. Dolly didn't even know me when I made that attempt! But she had commentary.

Zoe stared at my hand, tears welling in her eyes. When she said, "Mommy," her little mouth an O, I shushed her. I didn't need her pelting me with questions I'd be compelled to answer in front of Dolly. She kindly quieted for me.

"I'm okay, baby. I just got an owie."

She must have sensed Mommy's distress and didn't press me, but worry reflected in her big brown eyes, and her lips curved down in a frown.

I couldn't deal with her there. Not with D all over me. She could call protective services if she wanted to, though I knew she'd be reluctant to take such a radical step with so little information.

"I'll see you soon, Dolly. I may not be back for the rest of the week, but I'm paid up."

"I'ma check on you. I'ma call you tomorrow," she said, her voice stern. She leaned over and whispered, if you can call that whispering, "Black folks don't commit suicide."

Sometimes, I hated my life.

"I didn't commit suicide, Dolly," I said, *not* whispering. "That's why I'm standing here. Do I look like a ghost to you?"

She expected me to fold, and rankled when I didn't. "I'm just sayin'."

"Me, too. I'm just sayin'."

She gave me one last poke. "Zoe sound like she getting sick. Again. Make sure you give her something for that cold that's coming on. And don't bring her back if she get worse. Last thing I need is e'ryone here with they death of pneumonia."

Right.

Zoe and I got out of there, and despite D's nosiness, I blessed her. No, I didn't have to worry; she wouldn't call the authorities on me. That cranky old heifer would pray, in her own self-righteous way, but she'd mean it. And she'd let me be unless she felt like God told her otherwise. Even if He didn't, she'd probably be more willing than not to help me. I didn't doubt she'd find somebody to take over the kids and bring her big butt right to my townhouse, with food, and rebuking, and pleading the blood of Jesus.

And I may just need it. All of that.

Zoe asked me four times on the way home if my hand was gonna be okay. She had to be such a trouper where I was concerned. Zoe was only five, but she could make her own cereal like a pro, as long as I didn't get a full gallon of milk. She could make hot dogs on our electric stove, waffles in the toaster, and ramen noodles in the microwave.

I know that makes me a terrible mother. Does it help that all those food items would have come from Whole Foods—or Whole Paycheck? I bought organic as much as I could afford, and bulk, healthy, very expensive foods. That was the least I could do. I was sick a lot. I tried to eat healthy.

Not that it made a difference today. I was spontaneously bleeding, and Zoe was catching her death of pneumonia.

Did I mention sometimes I hated my life?

We got to our townhouse, and Zoe sneezed three or four times as I was putting my key in the door.

Great. She really was getting sick.

We got in the townhouse and locked the door. I helped Zoe

out of her snowsuit as best I could without ruining it, and when she was settled, I rinsed my wounded hand under the sink while she watched.

My poor baby burst into tears.

"What happened, Mommy?"

I knelt down and hugged her, avoiding letting the blood touch her. "I just got hurt, but I'll be all right. Jesus will take care of me."

"Like He always does?" she said between sniffles.

I taught her that. All those times I lay in bed, sick, crying in pain. "Jesus will take care of me," I'd say. Zoe was still a baby, too little to doubt it.

"That's right, baby." I kissed her on the forehead and finished rinsing my hand.

The bleeding had slowed and I examined it more closely. It looked like a thin layer of skin covered the wound on both the back and the front of my hand. The blood was fresh and bright red. And it smelled pretty.

"What did You do?" I whispered to the Lord.

"I didn't do anything, Mommy."

"I wasn't talking to you, sweetie."

"Were you talking to yourself? Miss Dolly said I should make sure you don't talk to yourself. And that you don't answer yourself."

"I wasn't talking to myself, baby. I was praying. Even Miss D knows people have to pray."

I wrapped my hand and heated up some overpriced organic version of a Hot Pocket for my daughter. In the freezer we still had collard greens leftover from Sunday dinner. I warmed those on the stovetop and boiled two pieces of frozen corn on the cob.

Zoe and I ate in silence, which almost never happened unless I was really sick. No matter how brave I tried to be for her, I knew she could tell I was in trouble. And she fretted over it.

I tried to reassure her.

"It's just a … sore." But I couldn't even say it with confidence.

"Okay, Mommy." Her tiny half-hearted smile almost broke my heart.

As soon as she finished the last bite of her food I told her, "Let's get that cold of yours taken care of."

I gave her a dose of Children's NyQuil. I hated that I gave her the kinds of medicine I didn't even take, but it acted speedier than the natural remedies, and Miss D would give me heck if I didn't get her well and back to day care fast. Zoe took her medicine like a champ. Thank God she didn't argue. I read her a story, prayed with her, and tucked her into bed for the night, even though it was only 5 p.m. or so. Before she drifted off she touched the red spot on the back of my bandaged hand where blood had seeped through again.

Odd, but it felt like something, some kind of electrical charge, shot out of me at her touch.

"Please don't do that, baby. You never touch people's sores, Zoe. That could be dangerous."

But she was smiling. "You feel good, Mommy."

"I feel good. Okay. Thanks, baby. Try to get some sleep so you can get rid of that cold."

"I don't feel stuffy anymore."

"Well, of course you don't. I just gave you medicine." I thought about the DayQuil I often took when I got colds. The menthol in it opened me up immediately. I didn't think a thing of it.

I heard Mike and Lacy at my door.

"Lord, Jesus Christ, Son of God, have mercy on me a sinner."

I couldn't deal with them yet. I needed to talk to Jesus, and Him alone. Eventually they went away.

In the next few hours I made an altar in the corner of my living room. I prayed, cried out, begged, and pleaded for some sign or sense of direction as to why I was bleeding like I was, but I got no comforting word deep down in my soul. He'd gone completely silent on me, as if His kiss, and the wound it left behind, were enough.

I thanked God for Mike teaching about those mystics. I had a book of writings of Saint John of the Cross and turned to "The Spiritual Canticle." If Jesus had left me, I wouldn't have been the first time He treated me that way.

> *Where have You hidden Yourself,*
> *And abandoned me in my groaning, O my Beloved?*
> *You fled like the hart,*
> *Having wounded me.*
> *I ran after You crying; but You were gone.*

PRIEST

I left that church and drove around for hours. I didn't even bother to go back to work, knowing Larry would blow a head gasket whenever I came back.

Whatever.

It's not like I had to fake peace now. And the tranquility that steadied my thoughts like still waters came from no drug. Drugs don't give you what I felt. Drugs give a cheap *imitation* of what I experienced when I touched her.

Ack! I chided myself. This was crazy. She was some black chick! At the Vineyard, no less.

But what the heck did she do to me?

If only I had Nana to talk to in those hours after I left that afternoon service. I wouldn't have had a conversation like that with Veronica under threat of torture. I couldn't imagine what she would say. For that matter, I couldn't imagine what Nana would say. Or worse … *I could.*

Nobody loved saints Francis of Assisi and Padre Pio like Nana. She would call soul sistah like she saw her: a victim soul, gifted with the sacred stigmata.

Could the black chick be a stigmatic?

I was out of my mind for even thinking of it. Besides, Regina Dolores Merritt—that was the name on her license—only had a single hand wound. And she went to the Vineyard. Give me a break!

But the scent of that blood. Unforgettable.

A drink would have been nice, or something a little more potent, only I didn't *feel* like having a drink because I never felt better, and what's more, I was hours past due for my next heroin nod, with or without the cocaine. And I wasn't sick. I should have been huddled over a toilet bowl, vomiting, feverish, twitching, and aching, or with a belt tied tight across my arm, popping sweet relief into my welcoming vein.

Did she heal me?

Impossible. I was bat crazy to entertain the notion.

But I had it bad. You could set a clock by my heroin use, and if

I didn't get it, I felt it. And now, here I was: bright, shiny, and feeling brand new.

I didn't make it to her house until about 10 p.m. Despite the miracle of my wellness I told myself everything was cool. I was going to make sure she was all right, and if I happened to coax out of her what kind of mojo she put on me, so be it.

If nothing else, didn't she need her driver's license back?

I had to go.

CHAPTER FIVE

GINA

I'd spent myself with my face to the floor before God, and in the end, it felt like my prayers went about as far as my voice carried. I was a little snippy with Him. Not to mention I seemed to be coming down with something. Body pains assaulted me more than usual, and all the arnica gel in my bathroom cabinet couldn't provide relief.

After I prayed, I started on the Bryonia and Rhus Tox, and popped a few tabs of under my tongue.

My pain laughed at my efforts.

Finally, I took a hot shower, washing away the ashes from my forehead. I had all the crosses I needed. Blood and water swirled down my drain.

When I came out of the bathroom I pulled out the rattiest gown I owned, which wasn't quite ratty, and kinda expensive. I'm telling you, those green companies made a sistah *pay* to be earth friendly and healthy, if you could call what I was healthy, and you couldn't. The outfit I wore to church lay in a heap on my bedroom floor, ruined. I didn't have that many clothes. I shouldn't have come home before church and changed out of my Subway uniform, but how was I supposed to know I'd be struck with love?

I dressed and rewrapped my hand in bandages with the kind of numb soldiering on that comes when you know you have to keep going no matter what's happening.

Stigmata crossed my mind. For about two seconds. That was a Catholic thing, and the closest we came to high church at the Vineyard West was our Anglican imitation, sans the real presence of Christ in the Eucharist.

But we had some awesome communion, for what it was worth. I expected Mike to fold one of these days and get his Anglican papers. It seemed inevitable. But for now, he still held out.

I told myself, *I do not have stigmata. It's only one hand anyway. It's some kind of allergic reaction. I react to everything. Now, I'm allergic to visions of Jesus.*

And speaking of allergic, I called in to work again. Had to. I was already on probation, but I didn't think I could make submarine sandwiches with blood oozing out of my palm, even with the plastic gloves.

Lord, am I gonna lose my job?

Probably, because I couldn't tell them how long before the "rash" I claimed to have would heal.

Silly, but I wondered if I should have read *Mariette in Ecstasy*, a novel about a young stigmatic nun. Initially I only read it because our book club chose it, but by the time I closed the back cover I wanted to love Jesus like Mariette did, no matter what the cost. She had an intimate, almost sexy relationship with the Lover of her soul. I mean, He really *was* her Lover.

I wanted that. His desire to be toward me, drawing His bride toward the bed He prepared for me, a bed surrounded by rose petals, scented with His longing. Oh, to hear His courting:

You are Mine.

You are perfect.

Come to Me. I desire you.

In my dreams, okay? I wasn't expecting to go *there*, even though, I'll be honest, I secretly wanted stigmata. I know that sounds weird, but it seemed nice on Mariette. Don't we all dream of an extraordinary encounter with God? Don't we all stumble about like the zombies on *Night of the Living Dead*, drunk with need of the flavor of a God who is almost close enough to taste?

Almost.

Shoot. I couldn't have stigmata. Didn't desiring it automatically keep you from receiving it?

But there was that dream I had a few months earlier.

I dreamed I bore the wounds of Christ in my hands. No details, just me surrounded by a soft white light, and my hands, palms up, as if I held in them two pools of blood. Peace woke me up that morning, and the warmth of a feeling that Christ had ravished me in my sleep.

But it was just a dream.

I went to my bookshelf and pulled out *Mariette in Ecstasy*.

Flipped pages I knew by heart to the part right after her sister, the prioress, died. Mariette held out her blood-gorged hands and said, "Look what Jesus did."

I felt dizzy. Nauseated suddenly. *Oh, boy. I'm gonna be sick.*

Somebody knocked at my door. It was almost eleven o'clock at night. I lay the book down on the love seat. I knew Mike and Lacy wouldn't come out at this hour unless I called them. Miss D wouldn't lose any sleep over me, especially when she had to deal with seventeen kids starting at 6 a.m. If she wanted to venture out to see about me she'd have come earlier.

I started to ignore my visitor, but I wanted to know who'd come-a-callin' at that hour. I jumped up and went to the door. Peeked out of the peephole.

It was the freak who stole my license! Oh yeah, I went through my bag. I knew what he took. And I knew it wasn't money he was after.

Why did he want me?

Nobody wanted me. Not even my parents.

I swung the door open without fear. Jesus had kissed and left. Maybe I felt a little fatalistic.

Or maybe not.

"What do you want?" I said. "Besides *me?*"

He stood there looking goofy, like I'd said it in Russian.

PRIEST

It didn't sound Russian at all. No, she said it in *Angry Black Woman.*

She surprised me. Not even a "Who is it?" Soul sistah threw open the door and came out fighting.

I answered with a lame, "Uh … *excuse* me?"

"You heard me. I said, 'What do you want, besides *me*?' And don't say you don't want me, because you took my license out of my purse."

She looked me up and down. "You might be tall, but you aren't that big. In fact, you look like a straight-up crackhead. I can probably take you, unless you're high, and if you are, I won't hesitate to knock you upside the head with the nearest blunt instrument."

"I'm not high. And despite your bravado, I don't really think you could take me."

"Bring it on, brotha."

"I'm not a brotha man. I'm the *other* man."

She stared at me. "Yeah, right."

"I'm not black, soul sistah. I'm as white as the driven snow."

"Keep telling yourself that. You're enough of a redbone, it might work out for you." She paused. "You know you look kinda like that guy on television—"

"Wentworth Miller. So I've been told"

"You can hardly tell what he is, either."

He had my sympathy.

"Are you going to let me in?" I said, trying to divert her attention away from my racial ambiguity.

"What do you want?"

"I came to see if you're all right."

"What do you do for a living?"

"What?"

"What do you do?"

"I'm a writer—a journalist."

"A journalist *and* a junkie, and yet you don't know how to *lie*."

"Trust me, I know how to lie, but I'm not lying *now*. I do want to know if you're okay." Somewhat.

She stepped aside and let me in, although I could tell I hadn't convinced her of my noble intentions. While she closed her door and locked it, I took in her interior design. Soul sistah's place nearly blew out my retinas. I could see the half-kitchen, dining room, and living room from where I stood in the foyer, each painted a different glaring color.

"A rainbow exploded in here."

"Too much color for you, brotha? You're afraid of color, right?"

"Drop it, soul sistah. I'm not afraid of color. You simply surprised me with all this. And I'm not black, I'm just an *ethnic-looking* white boy. I'm Italian."

"Yeah, I'm Irish. And I happen to *need* color, white-boy soul brotha."

"Is it because of all that *Africa* in you?"

"It's because I'm sick, and color feeds my soul, which in turn helps my body." She glowered at me. "I don't have much money to decorate. The color makes me feel like I have something. Took me a whole year to get it this way. One expensive gallon of paint at a time, but I don't regret it. It makes me feel better."

I wondered if whatever made her sick caused her to spontaneously bleed, or worse, hurt herself. My postulation that she was a stigmatic suddenly seemed vapid and sophomoric.

"What's wrong with you?"

"I have fibromyalgia. Real bad, among other things. Do you know what that is?"

"Yes, I do."

"Good. Most people don't. I'm tired of explaining it."

So she was in chronic pain, and probably fatigued more often than not. Possibly depressed. I'd done a piece on fibro. Interviewed a few people. Tough break. She was young.

"What are the other things?"

"I'm bipolar." She pursed her lips and stiffened.

"So am I," I confessed. Her whole body seemed to exhale, but she made no comment. We stood there awkwardly, until she finally moved into her … to her, what was it? Some kind of yellow orange? Ochre? Living room. Since we'd already broken the ice arguing, I thought I'd introduce myself.

"I'm Anthony Priest."

"Priest?" She chuckled. "I asked God to send me a sign. He *would* send a priest like you. I'm with Saint Teresa of Avila tonight. No wonder God doesn't have many friends if this is how He treats them." She gestured to her love seat. "Might as well sit down, Priest, since you're God's gift to this woman. Let me take your coat."

I surrendered my coat to her and sat down on the ashram-orange monstrosity. I enjoyed the view as she sashayed over to her closet. But her shapeliness failed to dislodge the nagging certainty that no one, other than Nana, ever described me as a gift.

But I'd take being Regina Dolores' ironic gift over being Veronica's curse.

To get my mind off my doleful life, I looked around her place. Where did she get such a kitschy love seat? She didn't have a coffee table or end tables, just an entertainment center—a nice one, definitely not cheap! Her bookshelf bulged with "Christian living" titles, more

than a few decent novels, and *Writer's Digest* reference tomes. A laptop
sat on the floor in front of the love seat. She was a Mac person.

She came back into the living room and sat down beside me.
"Peeping out my equipment."

I hoped she didn't mean that like it sounded.

*Down boy! You know you have nothing for her, or anybody else for
that matter.* "I thought you might have aspirations to be a writer.
You've got a lot of books."

"Black people can read, soul brotha, but you know that already,
don't you?"

When I replied with a censuring raised eyebrow, she elaborated.
"I have aspirations. I mean, a sistah dreams."

"What do you do for a living?"

"I'm an artist."

Her stock when up. An artist and aspiring writer. And cute—not
that I could do anything with that. "Is your work well known?"

"Sure, if you're *Jared!* I'm a sandwich artist at Subway."

Her stock plummeted, not that I could judge.

"You have nice furniture. How do you afford it?"

"I pray for bargains, and miraculously, God gives me a few now
and then. Look around, white-boy soul brotha, the place is nearly
empty. I don't have much, but I want the few things I have to be …
sturdy. You ever buy that cheap chipboard furniture? Might as well
be disposable. So I squirrel away money for something nice. I don't
have much, but I'm happy with the few pieces I have, Priest. Hey, if
you're a priest where's your collar?"

"I'm not a priest. My surname is Priest. I didn't make that up,
either."

With her sitting beside me, I realized what an *itty-bitty* orange love seat she had. Soul sistah affected me: her nearness, and that flowery smell.

I started prattling sound bites of information like I was sixteen and she was my prom date. "People used to tease me about it. Who has Priest for a last name? Well, that singer Maxi Priest does, but he may have made it up. Not that I could see the payoff for that. Actually, there's a body builder named Priest—two of them. One male, one female. And there's another writer. An Englishman. I don't even know if that was my father's last name. The space is blank where his name should have gone."

"I take it you don't know him."

"No, I don't."

"I didn't know my father either. He died last year. I mean, I knew his name. Met him a few times, but that's about it. I don't know my mother very well either. I wasn't raised by them. I was in foster care for a long time. The parents have always been a couple of unsolved mysteries to me."

"Did you get adopted?"

"I have a knack for not being chosen."

"Another commonality. What happened to your mother?"

"I don't know, Priest. I'm on my own, okay?"

Fine with me. I really didn't want to get into painful personal histories. As it was I'd disclosed far more about myself than I meant to. But her straightforward style threw me. I was used to people hiding and lying. She was as transparent as Saran Wrap.

I wanted to change the subject before she probed too deeply and touched a Veronica nerve that would leave me coveting dope.

I pulled her driver's license out of my coat pocket. "You're Regina Dolores Merritt."

"People call me Gina." She propped her legs beneath her and sat in a posture that all five-year-olds know from kindergarten, and it bothered me how cute she looked doing it. She took her license and laid it on the floor beside the computer.

"Did you know your name means 'queen of sorrows'—the Regina Dolores part?"

"I know it. I'm wondering why *you* do. You're getting kinda creepy now."

"I wasn't creepy before, when I showed up at your door, a junkie who'd stolen your license?"

"You were manipulative and scheming before, and lonelier than you might want to admit. That's different. Besides, I told you I could take you, unless you're a sociopath. If you can't *feel* you might be able to access unusual strength or endurance, in which case I'll have to stab you."

I threw back my head and laughed. "I'm not a sociopath, Queen of Sorrows, no need for violence, but I have spent a lot of my life not feeling. It never gave me strength or endurance, though. You're safe with me."

"Why don't you like to feel?"

"Why did you let me in if you thought I might be a sociopath?"

She looked unsure, like a little girl again. She shrugged her shoulders. "I dunno, Priest ... *because*. When I saw you in church you looked so sad. Nobody should look so sad. You know?"

My insides went into a flutter. I liked to think I didn't like pity, but of course I did. I liked hers a lot, not that I'd tell her.

"I'm Catholic. Regina Dolores was easy. And I happen to know more Catholic trivia than any human being should. Were your parents Catholic? That's a very Catholic name, Regina Dolores."

"Was your *daddy* Catholic? Regina Dolores can't be as Catholic as *Priest*."

"No need for defensiveness! You made it seem like you knew a little about them. I thought you might know that."

"Well, I don't."

"Fine … but I bet you're Catholic. Baptized, not confirmed."

"Which essentially means I'm not Catholic."

"That's debatable."

We glared at each other until I attacked *her* for no good reason. "You can't be a stigmatic. You're way too cranky."

"Who said I'm a stigmatic?"

"Do you even know what that is?"

"Look, I may be crazy, but I'm not stupid. I know what stigmata is. And I also happen to know saints can be cranky. We've studied a few of them at church, Mr. Encyclopedia Catholica. The mystics: Saint Teresa of Avila and Saint John of the Cross. Saint Teresa was very snarky."

"I knew that. I was hoping you didn't know so you'd be motivated to be nice to me."

She took a deep breath and placed her hands on her lap, the bandaged left hand atop her right. "I am being very, very nice to you, weird Priest. If I weren't nice to you, you wouldn't be sitting in my living room insulting everything from my intelligence to my decor."

"I'm sorry. I didn't mean to insult you. I'm an only child. My social skills leave much to be desired."

"I almost believe you."

"It's true, to a degree." One side of her lip curved upward in something that resembled a smile that quelled my heavy-handedness. "If it makes you feel any better, you're three for three, Saint Gina, crazy, cranky, and more than a little snarky."

"Maybe I can't be a saint because I'm about to *pop* you, Priest. Saints aren't violent are they?"

"I won't answer that for my own protection, not that I'm too worried. If you hit me with your stigmata hand you might heal me."

Crestfallen, she didn't affirm or deny healing powers. "I'm not a saint."

"Me either. I'm sorry, Gina. I'm being a real jerk. I want to be friends again. Can you forgive me?"

She gave me a half-smile, and we sat there exchanging shy glances for a minute until she struggled to pick up the laptop with her right hand. "So, we're friends?"

"I'm trying here."

I reached over her and picked up the computer for her, grazing her by mistake. I felt a zing, and I don't think it was God. I tried to ignore my hormones, and settled her MacBook on her lap. She went right to her web browser like I wasn't sitting beside her.

She typed "Anthony Priest, journalist" using one hand.

"You're Googling me, soul sistah?"

"I wanna find out who my friends are."

"You couldn't ask *me?*"

Her mouth opened. "Oh my. You won the Pulitzer Prize when you were only twenty-one? You really are a journalist, aren't you?"

"What if that was another Anthony Priest?"

"It's you. Nice picture, by the way, without the Nazi hair cut. You know you're looking so, *so* black in this picture with that lil' 'fro. Is that why you don't wear your hair longer?"

I ignored the hair thing.

"You look kinda *fine* here, Priest. You were a hottie before the drugs ravaged you."

"Thanks for that, Gina. May I borrow a sharp tool I can slit my wrists with?"

"I don't recommend wrist slitting." She grinned. "The *Pulitzer*. Wow!"

"The *News* won the Prize. It was a team effort. They did acknowledge my 'notable work,' however, hence the Internet idea that Anthony Priest won the Pulitzer Prize. And if it makes you feel better, my career tanked shortly thereafter."

"Why would that make me feel better?"

"You'd be surprised at how many people find that nugget quite tasty."

"What did *your team* win it for?"

"We wrote about a local school shooting that *didn't* get the coverage Columbine did. A black school without money or towheaded, blue-eyed hopes for the future sitting in its substandard, castoff-from-another-school's chairs."

"But you're not a brotha?"

"I'm for the underdog."

"Is that why you're here? You think I'm the underdog?"

I didn't answer. I wasn't sure exactly what I thought she was.

"Priest?"

"You said God sent me, Gina."

Our banter halted abruptly.

She sighed. "So I did. God sent you." She rubbed her brow, and I noticed her face had gone apple-cheeked flushed. Her forehead beaded with sweat.

Gina moaned and held her stomach. Her eyelids fluttered like bird wings. She slammed the computer shut.

"I'm feeling ill. You have to go."

As I did at the church, I reached for her.

"Don't touch me!"

I removed the computer from her lap, careful not to make contact, and placed it on to the floor beside me so I wouldn't risk brushing against her again.

"Tell me what's wrong, Gina."

"I'm just a little nauseated." She tried to stand but sank back down to that crazy orange love seat. "And dizzy."

"Is there someone I can call for you?"

"No, I … I'll be okay. I just need to sleep … and …" Incoherent muttering tumbled out of her mouth. At first I thought she was experiencing a personal Pentecost and was speaking in tongues, mercifully without the country twang. When I didn't hear the accompanying *praise the Lords* and *glory to Gods* it occurred to me that she might be having a stroke! I quickly scanned my brain trying to remember what the symptoms were: something about having trouble speaking. What else?

My panic rose. I spoke as if she'd gone deaf. *"Can you understand me? Are you having a stroke?"*

Gina froze, the only movement I could discern, a trail of tears streaming from her eyes.

I tried to follow her gaze to see what she was looking at. Nothing. Or nothing I could see. I turned back to her. "Gina, I don't know what's going on but—"

She slumped over and I caught her in my arms.

The queen of sorrows was burning up with fever. I'd have let her rest on the love seat, but it I thought it would be uncomfortable.

I hoisted her up in my arms, and tried to drag her to her bedroom. It wasn't lost on me that this was as close as I'd come to escorting a woman into a bedroom in a long, long time.

CHAPTER SIX

GINA

This time a single disc of fire as swift as a serpent's strike burned into my right hand. No Jesus anywhere, until I was there with Him as the Roman soldiers were about to nail Him to the cross.

Oh. His hand and arm were stretched taut and His veins bulged in His torn flesh. They tried to force the back of His hand flush against the rough wood. Jesus had big hands, carpenter hands, strong and sure. His fingers painfully extended, He turned His head to watch the legionnaire place a square iron nail on His palm.

My stomach lurched forcing the "Noooooooooo" I wailed out of my mouth. I squeezed my eyes shut.

Clank. The sound of metal slamming against metal. My own

hand exploding in fiery pain. An excruciating burn shot through my fingers and up my arm. Dizzying terror filled my head as I wrestled the numbness overcoming me to remain conscious.

More pounding, each swing feeling like it would flatline me. I stopped counting the blows. His pain slicing through my right hand commanded all my attention.

A scream tore out of my throat. Then I was back home.

I'd left Jesus behind being nailed to a cross! His agony remained in me. *Oh, God, they were crucifying Him.* "Where *are* You?" I shouted.

Priest, answered. "I'm here. I'm going to get you to your room."

"*No, no!*"

It felt like my lungs had collapsed. All my exhalations came out in ragged gasps. My heart hammered until it felt as though it would seize up like an engine without oil. Priest's voice aggravated me.

"You have a high fever. I just want to lay you down. I'm not going to hurt you."

"I have to get back to Jesus."

He tried to lift me, struggled, failed. I had no energy to make it easier on him. I could feel his heart pounding in his chest, afraid as I was.

"It hurts, so much."

"I know."

"It's killing me." I offered my soul to God. "I'm going to die."

"No. You're just sick."

I was crucified.

"Into Your hands, Lord, I commend ... *ohhhhhhhh.*"

"No, Gina! Don't say that."

Where was my Beloved?

"Come back, please," I said to Jesus, but only Priest responded. "I'm not going anywhere."

He pushed the door open to Zoe's room. "*Crap!* There's a little person in there."

My right hand felt red-hot. "*Ahhhhhhhhhh.* God, it really hurts."

"What hurts?"

"My right hand."

He stopped to examine it. Lightly pressed my palm. I screamed at his touch.

"Sorry, but it looks fine."

"It's not fine, Priest."

"Okay, it's not fine. I'm going to call an ambulance."

"You can't."

"Why not?"

He finally made it to the room with me, and hefted me onto the bed. I struggled to sit up. "They'll take my baby. Please don't call anybody. Just let me rest."

"Nobody is going to take your kid."

"*Please*, Priest! She's all I got. I can't let them take her."

He paced around my room, frantically. "I don't know what to do!"

I wanted to pray, but I couldn't think of anything but Saint John of the Cross's Spiritual Canticle.

O shepherds, you who go
Through the sheepcots to the hill,
I spoke aloud, *"If you shall see Him*
Whom I love the most,

Tell Him I languish and suffer, I die."
Priest stopped, whispered my name, "Gina?"
"Tell Jesus that I sicken, suffer, and die. Tell Him, Priest."
He finally relented. "I will. I'll tell Him."
And I surrendered.

PRIEST

I'd had a girlfriend, if you could call her that, two years ago. She and I were at her place about to shoot up. She'd gotten the junk from somebody I didn't know, but she wasn't choosy. I was. I only dealt with Fox, a burly black transvestite with a booming street pharmaceutical career because she said she couldn't make it as a professional makeup artist.

I don't know what it was cut with, but when I tasted it, I could tell it was ... I don't know ... off. I told her maybe we should wait and let Foxy check it out, but she was fiending for it. She got out her works and prepared to quell that vicious hunger.

I asked her one more time to wait, and she told me she couldn't. She went first.

As greedy as I was, I was afraid to try it. I was sick with need, but something in me knew. Maybe Nana was praying for me somewhere deep inside herself no one could reach anymore. Then again, she'd prayed so many rosaries and novenas for me before she got sick I probably had miracles stacked in heaven. Poor Elle didn't have a Nana. She had me.

Funny thing. I prayed for her before she took it. I asked God to protect her, and hoped He would hear my prayer for *her* sake. She seemed all right at first. After a few minutes I found a shirt and tied it around my arm. I picked up the same spoon she used to cook the dope on, prepped the same brown powder, and heated it up, ready to enjoy.

Elle's muscles started to twitch, and I set aside the needle to ask her if she was okay. She started seizing and wheezing, white foam bubbling out of her mouth. I didn't know jack about first aid. Elle's lips went blue, and I went frantic. I tried to give her CPR, but I didn't really know how. Frustrated, I jumped up and called an ambulance. That's when fear seized me, as if it locked me in a choke hold. Here's the incredible part. I was more afraid for myself than for her. As godforsaken as I was, I couldn't afford a scandal. After all, once upon a time I was Anthony Priest.

I left her. To assuage my guilt I told myself the ambulance was on its way and talked myself into the idea that they'd actually save her. When I arrived at my duplex I still had that stupid shirt on my arm.

Elle died. Nineteen years old. The police eventually found out that I knew her and interviewed me. But they didn't make a big deal of it. No headlines hit the papers about an award-winning journalist's girlfriend dying. Elle was just some junkie who OD'd, and I was the junkie who lived. They didn't even ask where we got the smack.

I believed I killed her, and I never wanted *anything* like that to happen again.

Gina begged me not to call an ambulance. That's when I realized I had no idea what I'd gotten myself into. Who was this woman? She said she was crazy, and what did that mean?

I dropped to my knees, completely overwhelmed. "Okay,

I know you don't hear from me much, but I need a little divine intervention."

Like God was going to speak to me. I yanked my cell phone from off my belt hook. I wasn't one for phoning Mom, but if Veronica was nothing else, she was a nurse. Didn't that mean she took an oath or something?

I dialed her number after I struggled to remember it. Had to call repeatedly because apparently Veronica did not want to hear from me. She answered the fourth time.

I didn't even say hello. "I need your help."

...

"*Hello?* Veronica, are you there?"

A sigh. "I'm here. *What?*"

"I don't want any money. I'm with this woman."

"Oh, Lordy."

"It's not what you think. She's sick. I don't know what to do."

"Why don't you do what you did last time and let her OD in peace?"

"Can you help her?"

"Call an ambulance, idiot."

"She doesn't want me to."

Heavy sigh. "Well, she sure as sharp doesn't! Look, Anthony, I don't want to be involved with your junkie friends."

"I don't have junkie friends, Ronnie. I'm a loner. And she's not a junkie. She goes to your church."

"What do you mean she goes to my church?"

"I went to the Vineyard today. I got in the line for ashes even. I still have the ashes on my head. I met this woman there—"

"I would have seen you if you were there. And nobody at the Vineyard would want anything to do with the likes of you."

"Her name is Gina Merritt. She's a—"

"You're with Gina? Well, I'll be switched. Not your type, is she?"

"She's sick."

"She's *always* sick."

"She's burning up. Please, tell me what to do."

"Are you doing drugs with her? She's probably got a freakin' pharmacy of prescription drugs. God! People like that make me sick."

"I don't know. I don't think so. She seems like some kind of a health nut. I just … please."

…

"*Please*, Veronica?"

She breathed into the phone. "This better not be a trick. If this is some ploy to stick my money up your arm—"

"It's not. I promise."

"Your promises don't mean jack, Anthony. Where are you anyway?"

"I'm at her place. I'll give you her address."

"I've got a stinkin' headache. This better be good."

She hung up on me as soon as I gave her Gina's addy. I didn't mind it. The fact that she'd endured the conversation was a miracle. I could only hope she'd show up.

Veronica had a way of not showing up for me, and that started way before I took my first hit of a joint.

CHAPTER SEVEN

VERONICA MORELLI

It was going on midnight, and he called claiming to be at Gina Merritt's. Drained me of any joy I could have gotten out of his darkening the doorway of my church.

The news said freezing rain had made a mess of the roads. All I could think was if I wrecked my car sliding on a patch of black ice on a rescue mission for that lowlife Anthony, I'd kill him.

I made it to her townhouse, knowing to expect the worst. What else would it be with him? I stepped out of the car and right away the wind blew my rain scarf across the street, and isn't that how things go? I'd have to set my hair again. Thinning as it was, I had to keep it short because it showed so much scalp. It looked better with a little curl, though. And I'd lost that because of him.

Before I could knock on her door—looking like a wet cat, mind you—he opened it. And I'll be switched if he didn't look clear-eyed and scared as I'd ever seen him.

"Thanks for coming," he said.

He looked awful. I couldn't lose an ounce no matter what I did, but he did dope and dropped forty or fifty pounds. I must have picked 'em up behind him. Unbelievable.

I didn't know what he was doing with Gina. She didn't seem the type to pick up stray animals, especially at church, but she was a single mother. By her own testimony she'd been promiscuous, and he was the type to sniff that kind of thing on a woman.

Or maybe she picked up something on him. He might be a mess, but he had potential. Maybe she recognized his accomplishments, though nobody else did anymore. But he'd probably be an upgrade for the likes of her.

God, I hated a nigger.

I walked in, and that had to be the tackiest place I'd ever had the misfortune to step into. All kinds of weird colors screamed at you from the walls. Like Mexicans decorate, only worse.

"Where is she?"

"In the bedroom."

"Figures."

I followed Anthony, my headache threatening to blow an aneurysm, all the garish colors walloping me on the cranium like a club. There she was in bed laid up like the Queen of Sheba, with her little girl sitting on the bed next to her. Poor kid looked more emotional than Anthony did.

I don't care what color they are, kids are kids. It would be a while before she started collecting welfare checks like her no-account mother, always pretending to be sick, the lazy cow. Poor little thing shouldn't have to suffer 'cause her mother didn't want to do anything with her life.

I took a deep breath. Walked over to the kid. "Hi, honey."

She didn't speak, poor thing. Just looked up at me with those big brown eyes. She reminded me of those kids you see on the Save the Children infomercial late at night. Not starving though, just pitiful.

"Everything's gonna be all right. We're just gonna see what's wrong with your mom."

She nodded.

"Could you tell Miss Veronica where your room is?"

The kid walked me to her room, and despite the pink explosion in there, it was kinda neat. God only knows where someone like Gina would get such nice furniture. Gleaming white Quaker-style bunk bed, and a color-block quilt in purple, pink, teal, lavender, and robin's-egg blue. Somebody probably gave it to her. I walked her over to her bed and pulled the quilt back from the bottom bunk. Nice fabric. Somebody gave it to her for sure, obviously a person of means.

I told the little girl, "I want you to try to get some sleep. It's late. You probably have school or something."

"I'm homeschooled."

Lord, that poor child. I don't mind people homeschooling, but it seemed to me you needed to have something to *teach* before you homeschooled, for heaven's sake. I'd heard her mom was a high school drop out.

"Let's get you under these covers, hon. It's chilly out tonight."

She didn't give me any trouble. I'd expect somebody like Gina to have a wild little pickaninny, but the kid was sweet. She slipped under the cover, and I tucked her in. Anthony had watched us by the door.

"Should you tell her a story or something?" he asked. Like he cared.

"I'm not here for her, Anthony. You tell her a story. I'll go see about your girlfriend."

He had the nerve to scowl at me. For a change he didn't argue, just picked up a book and went to the kid.

I went back into Gina's room. It smelled like flowers. I'd have to ask her what kind of air freshener she used. It had the nicest rosy scent … just perfect, and I thought that was about the only thing good around the place.

She'd wrapped herself in covers, and I noticed some kind of bandage on her left hand. She clutched her right wrist with it. I had rubber gloves with me, because, Lord, I certainly wasn't gonna catch anything from her. I prayed the Lord would keep me from any other kind of airborne pathogens and placed my hand on her head.

Anthony was right. His new girlfriend—or drug buddy—was burning up. I could feel it through the gloves. She had a temperature of at least 103 degrees.

"Anthony!"

He came bounding into the room.

"See if you can find a thermometer."

"I did. I couldn't find one."

"We need to get her to the ER."

"She can't go."

"Why not?"

He fixed his mouth to tell a lie. I knew it.

"Insurance."

She sure as sharp had state Medicaid. "They'll see her."

"She said she couldn't go. What if it's just a fever? If we can't get it down I promise I'll take her myself ... just ... please. Help her here."

I rolled my eyes. She did drugs with him. Had to. Both of them made me sick.

"If anything happens to her it'll be on your head. And you might not get off so easy this time."

"Nothing's going to happen to her, Ronnie. I think she's ... blessed."

What a joke. My mother said *he* was a blessing. I'll tell you what, she was wrong about the little bastard.

"Did you find any Tylenol or anything?"

"She has homeopathic remedies."

"I didn't ask for her voodoo stuff, idiot. I'm not messing with any of that New Age crap. Take her to the hospital. Or just let whatever this is burn itself out. She's probably not gonna die. Which is an improvement for you. *Maybe.*"

"Can you do *anything* for her? Please, Veronica. I'm begging you."

He looked so stinkin' pitiful. I stood there and thought about what the good Lord would want me to do. My head hurt badly. It was the middle of the night. It didn't matter what they did together, who had to suffer?

Veronica Morelli, that's who!

God, I thought, *why didn't You just let him die in my womb? He takes and takes from me, and what do I get? What do I ever get?*

I was wrong for even thinking that. I can't tell you how many "I'm sorrys" I'd said to God and my mother about my feelings over the years. Twenty-stinkin'-eight long years if you didn't count that awful pregnancy at Saint Mary's Home for Mothers.

But Gina did have a fever. Even a Samaritan wouldn't pass somebody sick on the road.

"We can give her a lukewarm bath."

"We?" he said, looking at me like he'd never heard the word.

"Don't get excited. We'll keep her dressed, Romeo. You'll have to get your jollies another time."

He didn't say a word to that.

PRIEST

To say I trusted Veronica would be overstating the matter, but I needed her. Gina was on fire, and we had to get that fever down.

I met Veronica in the bathroom, a stunning aquamarine haven. Gina had placed large stones underneath the tub; why, I had no idea. Garlands of flowers framed the mirror. She'd painted the outside of the tub an azure blue, a vivid contrast to the brilliant white inside. Near the tub on a tiny circular table she'd placed a vase full of red poppies.

Veronica scolded me. "I know it's blinding in here, but we've got work to do."

I muttered a "Sorry," not that I should have. Who were we to judge a woman brave enough to cut through her sorrow and carve a healing space to hide in? I imagined her floating in the waters of that blue womb, and the thought of it soothed me. Veronica pulled up the water stop and ran tepid water into the bathtub. "Go get her."

Once again, I went to Gina and took her in my arms. Man, where was my strength? She wasn't *that* big. In that moment I realized how much I'd damaged my body. My muscles had wasted away and the raw, blistering skin on my arms invited infection. I'd stayed too high to notice I was decaying before I died.

Gina was as pliant as Play-Doh; I was weak as water. I grappled with her until we made our way into the bathroom. By the time I reached the tub I had to rest, but I held her close to me, feeling her jagged breaths against my chest and our synchronized heartbeats.

She stirred in my arms. "What's happening, Priest?"

I stroked her dreadlocks. Looked into her eyes. "My mother is here. She's going to help you. You're going to take a lukewarm bath."

Fear flashed in her eyes. "Noooooo. I feel too cold."

"It'll help get your fever down. You're on fire, Gina."

"It's God's fire."

"Well … um … we need to take care of that God fire."

Veronica quipped, "What is she talking about?"

"I don't know. She might be delirious."

"I'm not delirious," she protested. I don't think she convinced Veronica.

"Is she plain-old crazy?"

That got even more protest, as tears spilled from Gina's eyes. "I'm not crazy." Then more softly, "I'm not."

"It's okay," I whispered in her ear. "I'm going to help you."

I looked to Veronica. "Should I just put her in the tub? She's shivering like crazy."

"Yes, *re*tard! You should put her in the tub. I didn't make the bath for you! Lower her into the water, and we'll see how she does."

"Are you sure this is—"

"Listen to me for a freakin' change."

I lumbered with Gina, trying to ease and lower her into the tub of tepid water. As soon as she touched it she grabbed me by the neck. She shrieked. Her gown rose in the water and billowed around her.

"Please, it feels cold," she begged.

"I have to, Gina."

She wouldn't let me go, so I knelt and let her hold onto me.

I'm surprised steam didn't rise off her skin it felt so hot. "Oh, man. I'm sorry, Gina."

She whined in answer.

"Shhhh. It won't be long, okay?"

Poor Gina's convulsing body troubled the waters meant to cool her. I tried to reassure her.

"At least it's not an ice bath. I saw that on *House*. He had to give it to a nun who thought she had stigmata, ironically. The whole thing horrified me. Do you watch *House?*"

Gina only quaked in my arms.

"It was only an infection she had, if that makes you feel better." I yelled at Veronica, "We're gonna freeze her to death!"

Veronica waved off my concern. "She'll be fine."

As Gina grew colder, I grew warmer from her heat. I held her more tightly until I felt her go limp. The last thing we needed was for her to fall unconscious. I disengaged myself enough to take a look at her. Gina had entered into some sort of trance state, though her shuddering never ceased. She mumbled something, her voice so low and raspy I had to embrace her again to hear.

"Though He slay me, I will trust Him," she whispered.

A warm bubble of liquid warmth seemed to burst where her hand clung to my neck. Compelled by her words, I took her by the wrist. The scent of roses lifted with her arm, even stronger than before. Once again she dropped her petals on me.

Veronica gasped. "My God, what did you do?"

I hoped she really was asking God, instead of me, or Gina.

VERONICA

I didn't know what Anthony did, so I yanked her arm away from him to see what mess I had to take care of now. Blood went flying and sprayed me right in the face.

The smell of roses smacked me. Suddenly I felt warm all over, and happy. My headache vanished. For a moment I fixed my eyes on her, confused.

Why do I feel so good?

That's when I figured it out. She was *blessed*. That wasn't expensive air freshener! She had the odor of sanctity! The odor of sanctity and I thought it was Glade. That gorgeous smell emanated from a thin sphere of blood right in the center of her hand.

Oh my stars! I grabbed her other hand and unraveled the bandages.

Anthony's whiny voice asking, "What are you doing?" grated my nerves, but even he wouldn't stop me.

Oh Lordy, oh Lordy, oh Lordy! That beautiful bathroom! Blue like the robes of the mother of God. Why couldn't my dull eyes see?

Anthony had blocked me from being spiritually in tune. If he hadn't been there I wouldn't have been suspicious. I would have known I was in the presence of a blessed one.

Her left hand! It had none of the markings of a normal wound. The blood flow defied the sure pull of gravity no matter how I moved her arm.

The Lord had granted me a miracle for my suffering—a real live, tangible manifestation of God's power. And it was right in my grasp.

I asked Anthony, "When did this happen to her?"

"At church. Right after she got her ashes."

I examined both her hands again. Unbelievable.

"Did she have some kind of vision?"

"I think so. I'm not sure."

"She's been given the sacred stigmata."

"Veronica, I know that's what it looks like, but—"

"You don't know about these things, Anthony. These are holy signs. I've been chosen to help her."

He wanted credit. "*You've* been chosen—"

"God used you to bring me to her." I laughed to the high heavens. "Glory to God."

Finally, I knew what the trial that came out of my body was for. All the suffering I'd done—all the shame and revulsion I endured having to look at him, it was for this moment.

"Praise God's holy name." Tears filled my eyes. "My soul doth magnify the Lord! Oh, Anthony! Let's get her out of the tub."

I helped him. I couldn't afford for him to be his clumsy self and hurt blessed Gina Merritt. She didn't respond to us at all, but surely she was in some kind of ecstasy. I supported her arms while he held her torso.

"Sit down on the toilet with her, and we'll dress her sacred wounds."

He obeyed me for a change, even though that motormouth kept running.

"She's still shaking."

"We'll get her warm in a minute."

I raced into her bedroom. Oh, Lordy. It looked like something out of a magazine. Wood floors made the room seem light and spacious rather than crowded by unnecessary furniture. Natural beeswax candles were arranged on all the flat surfaces, and by her bed sat a box of sand with thin taper candles like you find in church. Holy objects.

The devil made me misjudge her! The room felt consecrated unto the Lord. Demons must have attacked me as soon as I walked into her townhouse to keep me from fulfilling my destiny.

I found a box of bandages on a night table by her bed, and grabbed them to minister to her in the bathroom.

Anthony rocked her back and forth, with her head nestled into his neck. He seemed to care for her, but I knew he had to be watched carefully, even if the Lord was working in his life now, praise His name.

It was *me* who told him to come to church! If it weren't for me he'd never have been there to find her. I could see the hand of God all over this. It was as if I were blind, and the blood of His sacred wounds caused the scales to fall from my eyes. And Anthony! He was finally helping me fulfill my call instead of standing in the way.

I had a million questions. "Does Mike know about this?"

"I don't know, Ronnie."

I lifted my arms in worship to God. The Holy Spirit was all in that place. Oh, the devil wanted to deceive me. He tried to plant evil thoughts in my mind to keep me from being a blessing to God's handmaiden. He wanted to prevent me from receiving the blessing. But he was a liar. "Hallelujah, thank You, Jesus."

"Can we get on with getting her warm?" Anthony complained. "She's sopping wet."

He didn't know how to reverence the holy yet. All he could see was earthly things. I had to set him straight, once again.

"Can you think of someone other than yourself? Your precious clothes will dry."

"I don't care about my pants, Ronnie! I'm thinking of *her*. She's going to shiver to death while you worship. I think she'll be much more comfortable dry and under the covers."

"I'll take care of everything. You stay out of my way."

I knelt before her. Lifted her blessed right hand. "She bears the sacred wounds of Christ." Again, tears came to my eyes. "And it would take such a thing as this to be a sign unto me. Lord, You've sent this victim soul to show me Your passion."

Anthony looked uncomfortable with that kind of talk. The devil still had his hand on him. Mercy, Lord! But I'd deal with him later. I wrapped fresh gauze around blessed Gina's hands. Because I knew she'd need some things, I made a quick work of it. I started a list in my head of what needed to be done. I couldn't begin to imagine the gifts I'd receive for serving her.

"She's sure as sharp gonna need clean, warm linens. I'm going to look for some extra blankets. If she doesn't have any, I'm going straight over to the Super Wal-Mart to get her some."

"I can go to the store," Anthony said.

"Not with my credit card, and I'm not gonna let you shoot my hard-earned cash up your arm."

"I don't shoot money, Ronnie. You can't squeeze dollars through a hypodermic needle. Coins are even harder to inject."

I ignored his stupidity. "I'll be back as soon as possible. If there aren't enough blankets I'll need you to lie with her to keep her warm."

"Pardon me?"

"It'll be your chance to redeem yourself. Don't you see, Anthony? You can be her bed warmer, like the young wench for King David as he lay dying."

"I'm a lot of things, but I'm not a bed wench, Veronica. I draw the line at bed wench."

"I have to get her the things she needs. You will be whatever God says. Don't you see? This is not a coincidence. All of this was ordained."

I kissed blessed Gina's bandaged hands. Anthony rolled his eyes, but I paid him no mind. I hated to leave, but if I was to do God's work I had to get off my knees. I stood, albeit reluctantly.

"We need to get her in the room and undress her."

"Can't *you* do that?"

"Grow up, Anthony. You're twenty-eight years old. I'm sure you can keep your head out of the gutter long enough to help me change her gown. This is God's work."

This *was* God's work! Excitement surged like electricity through me.

I was chosen.

Not even Anthony would mess this up. He'd do exactly what I'd say.

CHAPTER EIGHT

PRIEST

I hadn't touched a female in two years. Why would a loving God call me to be a *bed wench?* But try to stop Veronica on a holy mission.

Not that I didn't owe her an enormous debt. Gina's fever had gone down. I could feel it even as I held her while Veronica bandaged her hands.

After Veronica kissed her hands with a flourish to my horror, I hauled Gina back into her bedroom. She seemed to come out of the trance, and now all she did was whimper and hang on to me. I laid her on the bed, but she wouldn't let go of my neck.

"We need to get you changed."

Veronica fetched another nightgown while I loosened myself

from Gina's grip to preserve some shred of dignity for both of us. Veronica railed at me, but I stayed firm.

"It's bad enough you're forcing me to lie with her. *You* change her clothes, Ronnie. You're the nurse. You can handle that."

Gina moaned, "Priest?"

For both our sakes I hurried out of the bedroom. I used the time to check on the kid. She still hadn't gone to sleep, so I sat on the floor beside her bed and picked up another book. I liked Gina buying books for her kid. She'd chosen critically acclaimed ones. The first time around I read the kid Mary Hoffman's *Amazing Grace*. I chose *Boundless Grace* for our second session. If anybody could use grace any way it came, it was this kid.

Her dark, almond-shaped eyes took me in as I prepared to read. Poor little … I realized I didn't even know what her name was. I placed the book in my lap.

"What's your name, kiddo?"

"Zoe."

She sounded like the saddest kid in the world.

"I'm Anthony, Zoe. And it's a pleasure to meet you." I paused and looked into those doe eyes. "Your mom's going to be okay."

"I know. Jesus takes care of her."

Good little mimic of, probably, her mom. Man, I hated to see her looking so sad. Even with Gina sick I was sure she'd feel so much more secure if strange white people weren't milling about her home, dragging her mom to the bathroom for lukewarm baths.

"Yes, pretty little Zoe. Jesus will hook her up."

Sure, I used black vernacular on occasion, though admittedly, not as well as my African-American brethren. But I lived in Detroit and spent an inordinate amount of time doing what Veronica called "running the streets." You pick up phrases. In certain parts of the city I had a vested interested in portraying myself as "brotha man" rather than the "other" man.

Sometimes I wondered if I really were black, and not the dark Italian Veronica insisted on. At least when it suited her. Nana said a child should not ask his mother about such matters. As it was, I had no father. She asked me to forgive Veronica her anger. Things were hard on her. Nana believed I should pray for Veronica and show love, and I did both, until I could do neither.

I picked up the book again and started to read.

Zoe listened, and I'd have stayed until she dropped off to sleep, but Veronica yelled for me. I stroked Zoe's hair before I stood. It possessed the same soft, downy texture of her mom's, not unlike my own hair when I let it grow. Zoe's hair was an elaborate little princess's crown of glory, a delightful crop of a profusion of plaits. Multicolored barrettes dangled off the ends of every braid. She'd look cuter than her hot mom if she had dreadlocks.

Her hot mom? An errant thought had slipped through the cracks of my subconscious mind.

Get a grip, Priest.

Priest!? I *never* called myself Priest.

I made a Herculean effort to shake off her effect on me and trudged back in the room. Bed-wench duty called. I was obliged to serve. Veronica had dressed Gina in some pretty, Victorian inspired nightshirt that shouted "virgin" even though I knew she wasn't.

"This is unacceptable, Ronnie," I said, my final remonstration, but she would hear none of it.

"Shut up, Anthony, and do something right for a change. If King David, the servant of God, could have a bed warmer, so can blessed Gina."

My futile arguments evaporated.

For a moment I gazed at her, deluged by unexpected longing. Ronnie disappeared. In my mind, her simple nightshirt transformed into a bridal gown spun into a diaphanous web of cotton lace. Gina lay on the bed, vulnerable and trembling, yes, but a woman—one I would soon wrap my arms around. I slipped out of my shoes remembering how she took pity on me because of the sorrow shrouding me. She opened her door and let me in.

I climbed under the covers, silently praying, "God, she quotes Saint John of the Cross! Help me remember that she's espoused to You."

Veronica headed out of the door, her parting words, "I'm off to Wal-Mart. I think the one by I-96 is open twenty-four hours. If not I'm going to Meijer's. I'll be back soon."

With that I took a deep breath and pulled Gina's quaking body close to mine.

GINA

In search of my Love
I will go over mountains and strands;
I will gather no flowers,
I will fear no wild beasts;
And pass by the mighty and the frontiers.

O groves and thickets
Planted by the hand of the Beloved;
O verdant meads
Enameled with flowers,
Tell me, has He passed by you?

I needed to find my Jesus, go back with Him to His passion, or wherever He wanted to take me, only I couldn't move except to tremble. My insides felt void.

The Priest He'd sent me closed his arms around me and pulled my body flush with his. He whispered, "I'm so sorry," in my ear, as if he'd been forced like a slave to couple with me.

His warmth enveloped me. I felt like I was freezing, and sleepy as a river. Priest surrounded me, stilled me, settled me. I gathered my knees curling into myself like a pill bug and let him make a protective shell of my bed linens. If I could, I'd have disappeared in that armor, even though I found no presence of God in it.

Where was my Beloved? Surely I'd die without Him. But for tonight, as I lay me down to sleep, I would accept the small comfort of this stranger like a gift.

I'd tried not to think of how it felt to be held once more. Prayed his musky, mannish smell wouldn't fill me. I gave God my weakness and hoped that even silent, He would keep me from responding to Priest's touching tenderness.

If it were possible, I would have lied to myself and said it didn't matter that I was starved for a man's affection, which *never* came to me in my bed of sickness, or anywhere else. But he felt so good. I wanted to make this right.

"Be Christ to me," I whispered to him. "His body. His warmth."

I shut my eyes and accepted his communion with a breathy prayer of thanks.

PRIEST

It was as if I held fire in my hands. And I don't mean that she was feverish. And, God forgive me, I responded by burning for her, every part of my body alight with need. I tried to use Scripture to quench the desire rising in me, but all that heeded my call came from the biblical love song.

At the very least I could focus on a passage that spoke of the Shulamite's virginity.

> *You are an enclosed garden, my sister,*
> *my bride,*
> *an enclosed garden, a fountain sealed.*
> *You are a park that puts forth pomegranates,*
> *with all choice fruits;*
> *Nard and saffron, calamus and cinnamon,*
> *with all kinds of incense;*
> *Myrrh and aloes,*
> *with all the finest spices.*
> *You are a garden fountain, a well of water*
> *flowing fresh from Lebanon.*
>
> *Arise, north wind! Come south wind!*
> *blow upon my garden.*

Those last few lines failed to benefit me.

So I gave myself to inhaling her sweet, earthy scent, a garden of delight, a profusion of roses. She requested that I be Christ to her, and her words slashed through me like a sword.

Did she know who she was asking? My own mother called me Satan.

But I couldn't have released her, not even if I'd wanted to, and I didn't want to. Something I hadn't thought about in years rushed to my mind. A song. You'd have thought hearing her say "Be Christ to me" would have brought hymns or sacred music to me. But a Bon Jovi tune bobbed into my consciousness as I savored Gina in my arms: "Bed of Roses."

I want to lay you down in a bed of roses,
For tonight I sleep on a bed of nails.
I want to be as close as the Holy Ghost is …

Oh, God. Please don't let me scandalize this woman. You know how lonely I've been. You're the only one who knows—the only one who cares.

Gina was wrong. I wasn't the gift, *she* was, and I meant that with nary a trace of irony.

Gina's Botticelli curves were yin to my yang. She was soft and full while I, plundered by drug use, had been reduced to sharp angles. Oh, oh, oh, what a ripe, round apple she was in my hands, and just as tempting as the one Adam bit into.

"Just keep her warm until Veronica gets back," I said to myself. But I'd turned into my ancient, earthly parent, in a garden, no more able to suppress my curiosity than he. I wanted to know the good and evil of her. I wanted forbidden fruit, a taste of her fragrant flesh. I desired to roll her around in my mouth until her sweet juice ran down my chin.

I'm losing my mind. See what happens when you're not on dope!

How pathetic was I? The closest I could get to having a girlfriend was lying with a feverish stigmatic, who my insubstantial body had to warm.

And she wanted me to be *Christ* to her.

I wanted her to be my manna, my sweet bread of heaven straight from God. I could only hold on to her *today*. Any thought of tomorrows would spoil our feast. I couldn't help myself. I pressed my lips to her neck and stole a single, feathery kiss.

"God, help me."

Snatches of Nana's prayers flew to my assistance, and I breathed the words into dreadlocks, soft as spun wool against my face:

Give us this day our daily bread.

And forgive us.

Lead us not into temptation.

Deliver us from evil.

I prayed those fragments until we fell asleep.

CHAPTER NINE

GINA

Crazy can happen at any time for people like me, but I've never known it to come without warning.

It begins with a delicious sense of euphoria. Suddenly I can do anything, and I *know* it! And in my twisted thinking, so does everyone else. Even at Subway I'm magnificent, every sandwich a masterpiece. Art! Exquisite in beauty and flavor.

I devour books, and when I still had credit I'd charge up ridiculous amounts of debt buying things I didn't need and couldn't afford, like orange love seats! I'd write letters and e-mails I thought were witty, winsome, and wise, only to find myself puzzled when the few friends I had left dropped away.

But wasn't I brilliant?

At first, I'm a meteor storm of light and color in this dull, insipid world. That part of sick doesn't feel sick at all—doesn't even know it's ill. But it gives way to an ocean of pervasive, all-encompassing rage, constantly ebbing and flowing. It's PMS's evil twin on steroids. Everything and everybody irritates me, and I find myself snapping like a rabid dog at Zoe over the slightest thing.

In those red, hazy days I have to take the bus to get around because I can't trust myself to drive. I'll rear end every hapless creature with the misfortune of driving in front of me. Or I can't focus on the task of getting from one place to another, and find myself hopelessly lost, even in my own neighborhood.

I become a loser. I can't find a single pair of matching shoes. My keys. My coat. My uniform for work. Appointments for Zoe and me get sucked into the gravity of the black hole of my illness. My concept of time is reduced to meaninglessness. My mind goes dead, but my body comes alive. I battle insatiable urges for a man, and any ol' man will do. But for the grace of God …

After a long while I'm propelled to the inevitable crash. I stay in bed all day convinced I'm not a Christian. I don't shower or bathe. Or brush my teeth. I want to cry but I'm too tired. Or rage, but I would have already spent every bit of anger in me. I'll feel certain I'm going to go to hell, because how could a woman in a filthy townhouse that looks like a carnival know anything about God? One year, with superwoman effort, I painted my whole place stark white again with a huge tub of flat paint I charmed the maintenance man out of. Only to take almost a year to paint it all back, in even more outrageous colors.

When I'm reduced to nil, I lay my head on the breast of the Beloved and weep.

I'm so sorry, Jesus. I'm so sorry.

Zoe makes her own cereal and sandwiches.

There used to be people—friends—to keep me accountable during these times. Most of them are gone. It's hard to be a friend to a person like me.

When I had the last few episodes I called Mike, then I seemed to have found my feet beneath me. I hadn't had any symptoms I couldn't handle in a while. And I never, ever went psychotic.

Did I?

How would I even know if I was psychotic?

I began to pick at an idea as hard as a scab, something waiting in my thoughts since my hand started to bleed. What if the thing all those doctors warned me about—my illness getting *worse* as the years went on—had come to pass? What if I was completely out of my mind, and didn't know it?

I examined my crazy behavior that fateful Ash Wednesday night. I let a man I could peg for an addict right away into my townhouse— with Zoe asleep in her room! I allowed him to lie in my bed holding me until my shudders quieted, and I was *thankful* he clung to me until the resounding clank of the nails that pierced my hands faded from my hearing.

Nails that pierced my hands? It sounded crazy, even to me.

I turned around in my sheets, triggering a sharp round of pain in my entire body, until I faced the stranger in my bed. He'd become Christ disguised as a junkie tender enough to keep me warm. The man who kissed me and didn't leave.

Priest startled like I surprised him with my sudden shift of movement. He struggled to rouse himself from sleep, just as cute as a pup when caught unguarded. I lifted my bandaged, aching hands. Took his face between them and looked into those puzzled, crazy-colored eyes.

"Are you real, or part of some delusion?"

"I don't know," was his answer.

PRIEST

What is *real?* I told her I didn't know, then told her to go back to sleep.

I was a junkie. Reality was of little importance to me most of the time. I preferred the land of dreamy dreams, and this particular stupor was a doozy.

Not that I minded it. Nosirree. She seeped inside of me like a narcotic, invading each and every one of my cells. And she was potent. Already she'd lured me like the opiate that seduced Elle to her death, yet Elle's poorly cut smack couldn't rival Gina's purity. I'd gladly go first if I could fill myself with her, and lie there on that red-stained mattress, our bodies wrapped in her covers, our burial cloths. And Regina Dolores Merritt would surge through my bloodstream like serenity.

Who cared about reality? As far as I was concerned, I'd stumbled upon paradise. I'd be reluctant as the devil to leave it.

I drew her to myself and went back to sleep.

CHAPTER TEN

PRIEST

I thought the return of Veronica would jar us out of our cozy swaddling. Not so. She *had* returned at some point during the night, and covered us with a white down comforter while we slept.

Still, early Thursday morning the distinct impression that I was being watched nudged me awake. My eyes snapped open to find the miniature one staring at me with eyes so much like her mother's.

"Hey, Zoe," I whispered, putting my index finger to my lips so she would speak soft enough not to wake Gina.

"Good morning, Mr. Anthony," she whispered back.

I peeled myself away from her mother, smarted by guilt. Didn't mean for the kid to see us like that. Not that we'd done anything salacious. Then I tried to figure out if we'd done anything salacious or not, which just goes to show you how well thought out Ms. Veronica's plan had been.

I sat up in bed and looked at Gina. After her ordeal last night I hoped she'd sleep as long as she could. However, that left it up to me to play the grown-up. I was awake after all, and oh how awake I was, more clear-eyed and lucid than I'd been in what felt like ages. I doubt if I'd have felt better if I'd shot serotonin right into my brain.

I stretched, then got up from the bed, gesturing for Zoe to follow me. "I'll cook you breakfast," I said, then blushed. "Soon as I use the bathroom."

When I'd taken care of business, I found her parked at the table in Gina's small kitchen waiting for me to be something I had trouble with on my best days: responsible.

Gina subsisted on rabbit food. How in the world could she have a Botticelli figure when she ate like my anorexic ex-girlfriends? Not an egg to be seen, not a slice of bacon. No sausages, or even real milk violated the pristine wholesomeness of her fridge. She had *soy* milk, tofu links, and a scant supply of healthy imitations of everything that's bad for you but tastes good. And fruit. Gina had acres of fruit.

If I wasn't careful, I might *live* if stayed around her. It didn't seem like a bad idea that morning either.

"All right, Little Miss Zoe. What would you like for breakfast? Keep in mind I have no idea how to make anything this healthy."

"I can make it."

"How old are you?"

"Five and a half."

"Sorry. I read *The Glass Castle*. No flaming kiddies here."

"May I have some cereal with strawberries?"

"Indeed you may." I bowed. "Even I can prepare such a light repast, my Zoe fair."

I took the strawberries out, rinsed and sliced them with Zoe directing me through the process like I'd never sliced a piece of fruit. I smiled at her precociousness, but it saddened me that she had to slice her own food sometimes. Five-year-olds should not handle a knife, even though I did when I was her age. I had to pull together some semblance of a meal too many times before I went to live with Nana.

Zoe wanted me to do it her way. She probably needed the same safety born of routine that I doggedly held on to at her age. I'd have sliced, diced, or julienned however she wanted me to.

After a while she relaxed, as she grew more comfortable with my alien presence. She prattled on in little-girl chatter about her day care, and Miss D, and her friends Najee and Asia.

Zoe's once-reticent voice had found a chord of trust and played in my ears like a happy, childish praise song. I reached for a strawberry, feeling contentment I wasn't entitled to. Never had a strawberry intrigued me like the one in my hand. I breathed it in, deeply aware of the nubby feel of its seeds puckering the satiny fragrant skin. My mouth watered anticipating the sweetness that would caress my tongue at first bite into the voluptuous ruby flesh.

I was about to pop the strawberry in my mouth when I heard a knock outside.

"Excuse me, Princess Zoe."

She giggled and I floated three feet off the ground toward the front door.

I plunged back down to earth when I opened the door, and the next best thing to Gina's *daddy* stood there, as surprised to see me as I was to see him.

"Anthony Priest?" he said.

This was going be interesting.

"Hello, Mike."

MIKE

I don't think I'd have been more surprised if Adolf Hitler had opened her door. Or more concerned. Horrible awareness of everything I'd heard from Veronica Morelli about her son filled my head. Memories of our one disastrous counseling session replayed for me in surround sound.

A slow smile crept across his face like I'd caught him with his hand in the cookie jar. "Come in," he said like he owned the place.

"You know Gina?"

"I do now."

I knew him to be a wiseacre, but his flip attitude irritated me. I nodded and smiled, making a huge effort to remain polite. "Where's Zoe?"

She came flying out of the kitchen.

"Hi, Pastor Mike!" The tyke grabbed me and locked her arms around my waist relieving one concern. I still, however, had another.

"Where's your mom?"

Anthony answered. "She's still asleep; we didn't get much rest last night."

"Really? Care to elaborate on that?"

A chagrined expression crossed his face, like he realized he'd given me more information than he meant to.

He half-smiled, "Not really. I don't think you'd want to know the details."

Now Zoe piped in. "He had to give mommy a bath and sleep in the bed with her. Is he going to be my daddy?"

Need a recipe for an instant migraine?

That was it.

PRIEST

She had me at, "He had to give mommy a bath and sleep in the bed with her." Not that I hadn't already written myself into a comedy of errors when I proclaimed to her spiritual shepherd *we* didn't get much rest last night. I probably could have recovered from that one. I may have even distracted him past the unfortunate bed, bath, and beyond reference if I could have convinced him I'd done it all for medicinal purposes. But, "Is he going to be my daddy?" sealed the deal for me. If I wouldn't love Zoe forever, I'd evermore find her dreadful timing hilarious.

Mike missed the humor though. He raised an eyebrow and repeated the question.

"Is he going to be your *daddy?* I don't know the answer to that, Zoe." He looked at me as if to say, "And what say ye?"

"I'm just the bed wench."

"Zoe," Mike said to my daughter-to-be, "may I talk to Mr. Anthony alone?"

"'Kay," she said, and hurried to her bedroom, shutting the door behind her.

"Do you mind?" he asked, stretching his neck toward the orange love seat. He sat first, and I followed, plopping down like a surly teenager beside him. We faced off like we were about to battle for Gina's honor.

"I should warn you," I said. "I already know about the birds and bees."

He gave me a tight smile. "You can save your smugness for your mom, Anthony. I'm here for Gina. Not you."

"I know what you're thinking, Reverend Joykill. My reputation might reside in the sewer, but you should have a little more faith in her."

He nodded. "I suppose you're right. Gina's a great person. But I've known good people to make bad choices. She's been through a lot; she can be somewhat delicate."

"She seems tough as *nails* to me."

"What do you mean by that?"

"Just what I said, Mike."

I guess he decided we'd dilly-dallied enough. He stripped our conversation down to the studs. "How long have you known her?"

"Long enough to want to make sure she was all right."

"You mean long enough to sleep with her?"

"If that's what it took, and maybe it did."

It wasn't right to mislead him, but he'd annoyed me. "I don't know what Veronica told you about me, but I'll tell you this before you write me off. I gave her more last night than I've given anyone in a long time."

His anger showed in the downward curve of his mouth. "I hope you used a condom, because if what your mom says about you is true, you could give her more than she wanted."

I sat back. This was Gina's pastor, and my mother's. I needed to keep my cool. I looked around at all the color surrounding me. I could see why it fed her soul. Something about her place soothed a savage beast inside of me. I'd come to appreciate her bold expressions.

I turned back to Mike. "I sat near her at church yesterday, and yes, it was the first time I'd seen her. Something happened. I don't know what. I heard her scream and responded."

He looked thoughtful. "So it *was* her who screamed?"

"I tried to help her. The blood—her blood—coming out of her hand fell on me."

He listened now, with some respect.

"I kid you not, Mike. I believe she healed me. I haven't had a craving for drugs since. It takes you being me to know what a miracle that is."

He had a faraway look in his eyes and mumbled, "My knee. I had on gloves, but after I touched her my knee ..." He seemed to snap back from his thoughts. "Why were you in her purse? Opportunity?"

"Because I couldn't talk her out of the bathroom. I went back to the balcony to see if I could find out what her name was. That's all." Mostly.

"So why did you run?"

"I'm gifted in bringing out the worst in people, as you can see. Police love to harass me. I had my hand in Gina's purse when those two old birds came after me. It looked bad. I didn't know who in your church knew about my … habits. I didn't want to go to jail. As it was I'd come there high."

"You came to my church high?"

"I find it far more interesting that I didn't leave it that way." A flicker of interest in his eyes convinced me he found it interesting as well. But he played it cool.

"So why are you here now, Anthony?" he asked, slouching against the back of the love seat.

"I was curious. She *healed* me."

"I heard you."

We were quiet for a moment, before he broached another question. "Did you see the wound? Could she have done it herself?"

I shook my head. "Negative. At least I don't think so. I've gone over it in my head dozens of times. What could she have done it with? Right there in the balcony? I was behind her in line for the ashes. No wound. And then, what, ten minutes later blistering wounds inexplicably appear?"

"Did you smell the … flowers?"

"I *still* smell them. So do you." I paused for a moment. So much had happened in the night. I didn't know where to begin, but I tried.

"While we talked last night, Gina became very ill."

"What do you mean?"

I took a deep breath. "We were talking, and her face flushed. She abruptly asked me to leave, and the next thing I knew, she almost passed out in my arms, burning with fever. I called Veronica to help me. We tried to get her temperature down and gave her a lukewarm bath. She started bleeding again in the tub. This time it was her right hand."

"Holy *mackerel*."

"Now she's got two wounds."

Mike sat open-mouthed and stunned, so I continued telling my version of the story.

"She couldn't stop shaking, even when the fever came down. Veronica asked me to keep her warm until she returned with more blankets. That's why I was in her bed. It was Veronica's idea. I held her until she went to sleep. No sex involved. No need for condoms."

But I didn't tell him how much I enjoyed it. He wasn't my priest, and this wasn't confession. I almost felt self-righteous talking to him about the altruism I'd stumbled upon, but he cut me down, fast.

"She's a young woman, and you're a young man. I don't think that was the appropriate response, no matter how well meaning."

"Nothing happened."

His gaze bore into me. "I'm not so sure nothing happened, Anthony. You are heterosexual, are you not?"

"I am." I thought about Veronica knowing Foxy. "Did Ronnie tell you …" I decided I didn't want to know. "Mike, we didn't have—"

"That's not the only thing that can happen when a man and woman are intimate. And sex isn't the only way to be intimate. I told you she's fragile."

He rubbed at his temples, and his shoulders sagged like they bore the weight of all the world's ills. He was the kind of man that aged well. But he looked the whole, what, maybe fifty years old he was that day.

After several minutes he spoke. "You're a journalist, right?"

"Yes, I am."

"What would you say was happening to her?"

I laughed. "What I'd say as a journalist would be what would sell the most newspapers. Or maybe magazines in this case. In fact, someone could make a book out of this."

"What would you say?"

"A young black urban female gets stigmata. What message does she have for the world?"

He considered that. "You planning on writing a story about her? Reviving your career?"

"I don't have a plan, Mike, and just so you know, I still have a career."

"I'd like to see her hands."

What bothered me was he didn't say, "I'd like to see *her*." She wasn't a sideshow freak for him to ogle. *I* was the Priest God sent.

I had to take a deep, cleansing breath.

Calm down, Priest. This doesn't mean he's trying to hurt her, I told myself, before I took him to her.

MIKE

He didn't act like he had anything to hide. Even if he did, I could see right through him, and I felt a little less worried.

A little.

I told myself Gina was an adult. Sexual temptation was an issue for most of our singles, but she wasn't like most of our singles. She had a certain vulnerable, childlike quality, and I protected her as if she really were a kid. As much as I hated to admit it, she was old enough to make ridiculously bad decisions, including having sex with men she'd never mean anything to. I hated to think of troublemakers like Anthony—who'd never entertain the idea of marrying her—taking advantage of her. Worse than that was the possibility some creep could come along and *marry* her, ruining her life.

God knows I'd counseled single moms like her: young, yet old, having grown up too fast with a baby or two on their hips and the kid's father nowhere to be seen. Gina had the added burdens of manic depression and constant pain and fatigue. As I followed Anthony to her bedroom, a man whose mother branded him a manipulative leech, I remembered a conversation Gina and I had in my office several months ago.

"Bipolar disorder and fibro won't kill me. They just make me wish I were dead." She sat quietly for a few minutes. I resisted the urge to fill the empty spaces of our talk with platitudes and waited until she spoke again.

"Both take a lot, but they give me something too."

"What do they give you, Gina?"

"I know things about Jesus just because I've suffered. Sometimes I wonder if suffering isn't a secret initiation into a special kind of intimacy with God."

"A lot of people would disagree. They'd say suffering was random. Evidence that there is no good God. Some believe God has forsaken them in their gardens of Gethsemane. Others claim suffering is of the devil."

"I can't speak for all suffering, only mine. Fibro and bipolar disorder are crosses. Jesus knows all about those. He enters into my suffering because He's been there, and He makes it bearable."

"What do you mean?"

"I mean, He comes to me without fail. He turns my bed of affliction into a marriage bed and loves me there."

Sometimes I'd ponder the things she said all day.

Nonetheless, I wasn't sure being confined to her bed in pain or despair was as bearable as she let on. She was twenty-four and lonely, and despite his reputation, Anthony was still a good-looking young man with a certain caustic charm. I knew from the way she laughed at *my* dry humor that he'd appeal to her.

Anthony said he held her all night, meaning, sick or no, she let him. That would be bound to affect her. She wasn't in a coma.

Anthony pushed open the door to her bedroom. We found her sitting in the corner of the room, facing the east wall. Her legs were tucked beneath her Indian style—though I don't know if it's politically correct to say that anymore. She seemed to be in some kind of trance. Never turned her head to acknowledge us.

She whispered stanzas of poetry I had taught her:

> *"Oh! who can heal me?*
> *Give me at once Yourself,*
> *Send me no more*
> *A messenger*
> *Who cannot tell me what I wish.*

> *"All they who serve are telling me*
> *Of Your unnumbered graces;*
> *And all wound me more and more,*
> *And something leaves me dying,*
> *I know not what, of which they are darkly speaking."*

My heart sank.

Oh, no. What had I done? We'd taught a whole series on Saint John of the Cross and Saint Teresa of Avila at the Vineyard. It didn't occur to me that maybe it'd be too much for her. I thought she'd find comfort in their writing.

I'd seen Gina in a bad way, on more than one occasion, but I never saw her so … out of touch. Was this some kind of spiritual hysteria?

Whatever it was, she didn't need the likes of Anthony Priest hanging around controlling things.

I crept over to her. "Gina?"

She didn't answer.

"Can you hear me, Gina?"

Anthony stood behind me. "She was like that in the tub. She was …"

Concern furrowed his brows. He fell to his knees. Placed his hand on *her* knee, annoying me tremendously. He spoke in soothing tones to her.

"I'd like to see if you're okay, Gina. I'm not going to hurt you."

He eased her leg from underneath her, and she offered no resistance. All she did was murmur, "He has made a cross of my body."

We saw the blood immediately, staining her left foot, defying the pull of gravity, smelling like she'd stood in a rose garden and a giant thorn had pierced her foot.

CHAPTER ELEVEN

PRIEST

Gina looked like a child on a time-out, only she'd gone too far out, because she'd left the building, so to speak, and journeyed to some distant place. My heart pounded, and I wondered how often she could visit before she got lost and couldn't or *wouldn't* find her way back.

I touched her forehead. "She's got another fever, too," I said to Mike, marveling. "I was with her before I made breakfast for Zoe. She was fine. She didn't feel hot at all. I thought she was sleeping like a baby."

How do you run another fever that fast?

I sprang to my feet and bumbled about until I found the bandages and began to wrap her foot. I didn't bother with washing the wound first. Not that I thought water and antibacterial oint-ment would do much for her.

I returned to her as quickly as I could and knelt before her. With the last of the bandages, I prepared to care for her. I handed Mike the empty box. He kept his eyes fastened on Gina.

"How long has she been alone?"

"Fifteen minutes, tops. She must have gotten up right after I did. Zoe came in, and I offered to prepare breakfast. I thought Gina was fast asleep."

I picked my brain to see if I remembered hearing her. Nothing. The little church mouse had drifted to the corner without a sound. No screaming this time. No crying out. And what did that mean? Progress or regress?

Mike crouched beside her next to me. "Gina?" Another futile effort. "Gina? Can you hear us?"

She didn't answer.

"Anthony, we have to take her to the hospital."

"She didn't want to go to the hospital last night. She was adamant."

"I don't think she'd fight me on this. She trusts me. Look at her, Anthony. She has to be seen."

"If she trusts you, be trustworthy, Mike. Don't take her to the hospital yet. She begged me not to, and I think she'll come out of it. You can ask her then."

Frankly, I didn't know if she'd come out of it or not. She said very little from the time she had the lukewarm bath, and now these wounds were appearing all over her body in turn, and I had a feeling we hadn't seen the last of them.

"What if she's open to infection?" Mike said. "It looks like those things are full of blood and fluid."

"Do infections smell *good,* Mike? When was the last time you got a whiff of rosy septicemia?"

"I don't understand the smell thing, Anthony. But I've raised five kids. I know fevers portend infection."

"Maybe it's not an infection, but her body thinks it is. Like, her immune system is fighting off whatever this is because it thinks it has to protect her."

"Do you know of a precedent for that?"

"I'm not an expert on stigmata."

"Stop using that word in regards to her then."

He stood. Paced the room with his hands resting atop his silvery hair. "I'm not sure she's capable of knowing what's in her best interest."

"And I'm not sure that's for you to determine." He'd ticked me off. I determined I would care for her alone. I tied the bandage off on Gina's foot but tried and failed to lift her.

An expletive shot out of my mouth when I realized I'd need his help after all. But I seasoned my words with sarcasm. "Think you can help me out here, Mike?"

He finally snapped to attention and offered me a hand. Our clumsy efforts managed to move her to the bed. Gina said nothing, her attention, without a doubt, higher than her bedroom ceiling. I lay her on the top of the covers. No spooning with Pastor Daddy hanging around. I'd have to give her a sponge bath. And even that sounded interesting to me.

Could I have been more repugnant?

I went to the kitchen to get the ice tray out of the refrigerator. The sprout queen had ice. After I located a big glass bowl, colorful as one of Foxy's ball gowns, I filled it with ice and water. I retrieved a washcloth from her linen closet and went back into the bedroom.

Mike hovered over the bed, with a pinched expression on his face. I sat in front of her, swabbing her forehead. No response to the icy water at all.

Again he paced the room, wringing his hands. "I'm worried, Anthony. She looks bad to me."

"She's probably fine. I think she's in some kind of ecstasy."

"If she's fine why are you trying to bring her fever down?"

I didn't answer at first, feeling every bit as ill equipped for the task as her pastor must. Would my negligible ministrations help? I had no idea. All of it was in God's hands as far as I was concerned. We could neither stop what was happening to her nor make it worse, but I believed we were duty bound to try to make her comfortable.

"Look, Mike. The only ecstasy I'm familiar with is the chemical kind. But I want to do *something*."

"How about if *something* is get her to a hospital? My wife, Lacy, can take care of Zoe."

"Is she going to take care of Zoe when the state takes her from Gina? Because that seems to be what she thinks will happen."

"The state won't take her. They didn't take her when she tried to kill herself."

"And when was that?"

"Two years ago. I'm surprised you didn't see the scars on her wrists."

"I guess the wounds of Christ in her palm distracted me." I set the washcloth in the bowl for a minute and lifted one of her slack wrists. There it was, a meandering scar puckering her amber honey skin, a slim pale line barely noticeable. A row of tiny white dots flanked each side of the scar where her stitches had been.

"Oh, Gina. You poor, sweet thing."

Here was stigmata of a different kind, and Gina had given herself these marks.

I'm going to take care of you, soul sistah, I thought to myself. *We're kindreds—soul mates.*

I didn't know how I'd do it, but I felt as called to care for her as Veronica said she was. Veronica, who never bothered to take care of me.

For good measure I prayed aloud. "God, give me strength," then went back to the task of bringing her fever down.

MIKE

Maybe the Lord thought I didn't have enough excitement in my life, so he gave me a rescue drug addict in a mentally ill single mother's bedroom. And she might have stigmata.

And maybe she healed the knee I'd popped sore when I hunkered down in the bathroom to talk to her. I had felt the burning pain as I tried to coax her out of that stall.

No, I'm being ridiculous. She didn't heal me. Bursitis came and went.

But not so quickly.

I stood there in that bedroom wrestling with myself about whether or not I should force the issue and get an ambulance to that townhouse immediately, no matter what Anthony said, when somebody pounded on the door like they'd bust it off the hinges.

Because he was actually helping her, *without* playing bed wench, might I add, I went to the door and opened it.

Veronica Morelli rushed in like a tsunami, and I wondered why she wasn't at work at the hospital. She carried a large vinyl tote bag packed full of God only knew what. Nonetheless, I was glad to see her. At least she had medical training. I thought she could give some meaningful input.

She didn't even bother to greet me.

She'd filled her bag with an impressive stock of prayer candles and religious sundries: holy cards, scapulars, medals, all kinds of stuff.

Veronica had gone completely Roman Catholic on me overnight.

I watch her place the items around the house, starting with the living room. She arranged prayer candles on the small bookshelf, entertainment center, and floor since Gina didn't have tables in there.

I picked up one of the candles. Since I didn't have my reading glasses with me I held it at arm's length. On the front of the candle the words *The Most Powerful Hand* scrolled across the bottom of a central image of a hand, palm facing out, with fingers extended upward. The mark of stigmata, or a nail wound, split the middle of the palm. Saints—I supposed they were saints—stood on each finger, and two angels—the one on the right hand burdened by a cross—stood on either side of the hand. Meaning no disrespect, I couldn't help but get the creeps.

"Veronica, what's all this?"

"Those are blessed prayer candles."

I didn't want to ask who'd blessed them. I honestly didn't want to know. She picked one up out of the bag and rattled off the prayer from the back of it. *"Thou who hast suffered, reach out Thy hand to me with a great blessing. Thy pierced hand with Thy saintly fingers inspires my humble prayers."*

Charleton Heston couldn't have done a better job.

She made the sign of the cross and genuflected before the candle.

Instant migraine recipe number two.

"Ronnie, do you actually use these candles in your private devotions? Before today, I mean." I had no problem with whatever she used to draw her closer to God, but she'd never mentioned anything remotely like this before, and I'd sat in counseling with her many times, not including the single session I had with her and her son.

She waved off my question. "So I've fallen away from using them; that doesn't mean it's too late for me. And these are special. They have the image of the—"

"Most Powerful Hand. So I see."

"Mike, I'm forty-six years old. I haven't seen this kind of candle since I was a kid. I found them at this dollar store off Cherry Hill, and thought, well, I'll be switched. What are the chances? It's a sign, I'm telling you."

"A sign of what, Veronica?"

"It's God's way of telling me I'm exactly where I'm supposed to be."

I have no idea why, but in that instant I thought of Pontius Pilate, the only person other than the Virgin Mary named in the

Creed. He was exactly where he was supposed to be, too. And look what happened.

She went back to her perpetual motion. Placing holy cards here and there. Burning incense, throwing holy water—where did she get a bottle of holy water? We didn't pass it out at the Vineyard.

I wasn't sure the place would be holy when she finished with it, but at least it'd look the part. I didn't need to ask, because the Most Powerful Hand candles and her overnight reversion to the religion of her youth said plenty about Veronica's stance, but I ventured the silly question. "Have you taken a look at her hands and foot?"

Her inner brakes screeched her busywork to a halt. "Her foot? Her precious foot is wounded too?"

Veronica's hands flew up in the air as she praised her way into Gina's bedroom, a decidedly *un*-Catholic response. Unless she's a charismatic Catholic now. She didn't specify.

So much for a valid medical opinion.

I followed her. She "gloried" and "hallelujahed" all the way to where Anthony sat by Gina's side on the bed. She immediately cut into her son.

"Can you move, please?!" she said icily, then put her piety right back on.

She went for her bandages but Anthony stopped her. "I just put that on, and there aren't anymore."

"Then go get her some out of my bag," she said through clenched teeth.

"I'm not leaving her."

"Anthony," she said, her voice clearly strained, "leave her to Mike and me."

Until then I hadn't realized Veronica was clergy, though God knows, I should have. At least, I should have realized what Veronica *thought* she was.

He held his ground—all the more reason for me to stick around—and gave me good reason to intervene between the two of them. "We're taking her to the hospital," I said. "Right now."

I marched over to the corner where an ornate wooden armoire stood like a sentry in the corner. I swung the door open. Gina's unmentionables lay folded in neat Martha Stewart stacks. How much should I take? *What* should I take? Would they keep her overnight, or for days—or even weeks? Doubts nagged me. I wondered if I should go to the emergency room or the psyche ward. Another cursory glance at her underthings intimidated me.

Veronica's voice penetrated my unforeseen indecision.

"We can't go to the hospital," she cried out.

She must have thought I was meditating on an organic unbleached-cotton nightgown in front of me.

"I work in a hospital, Mike. They'll never understand this mystical manifestation of God's mercy."

Anthony objected the loudest. "Forget mysticism. She's a poor black, single mother, with a history of mental illness. They'll profile her quicker than you can say 'Saint Francis.' Then haul her off to psych."

A loud sighed escaped from my mouth. "Maybe that's what she needs, Anthony."

"She's not crazy."

"Says who?" I asked him, more than a little impatient. "The drug addict?"

I closed the armoire door and rested my back against it, exhausted by this interaction. Veronica had taken over wiping Gina's forehead. She did it with such tender reverence. It's not that I didn't want Gina to be cared for. No one wanted to console her more than me, and God knows I wasn't jealous, or insecure. I knew who I was and what God had called me to do: serve. But something about Veronica's actions seemed unnatural. She wasn't a person given to displays of affection. Once she told me she'd never hugged her son.

A wave of nausea twisted in my stomach. What I saw her doing to Gina made me sick.

I don't say that to be facetious. It was wrong: Veronica cooing prayers in Gina's face as she wiped. I remembered the Stations. Each year our congregation walks the Way of the Cross on Good Friday. At the sixth station Veronica—not Ronnie, but the historical one—offers her veil to the suffering Savior.

Every year Veronica—Ronnie—weeps profusely at all the stations, but the sixth one particularly sets her off. I assumed it was because Veronica was her name saint.

The words I spoke at that station were:

Let us remember the compassion of Veronica. When she saw Jesus afflicted, with His face drenched in sweat and blood, she took off her veil and gave it to Him for comfort. Jesus took the veil, wiped His face, and left the imprint of His countenance on the cloth.

The congregation responded:

Jesus, Your face was beautiful before You started this sacred journey, but we have disfigured You. My soul was beautiful when my journey began, but my wounds and blood have made me ugly in Your sight. You alone are my Redeemer. By the merits of Your passion, restore me to my former beauty. Then do with me what You will.

Crazy thoughts, I know, but I wondered what was *driving* Veronica here, because her need to help appeared to be more urgent than her son's.

And what did *he* want from Gina?

I didn't have a single answer.

But I had my own urgent need. It behooved me to hear from God before I did anything else. I had to fast and pray. Thank God, Lenten season had begun and I'd already began fasting. It was beginning to look like I'd have to fine-tune all my spiritual antennae. Disaster brewed, and I didn't know if I'd be able to stop it. I only hoped whatever happened, the end results would be more Easter Sunday triumph than Good Friday tragedy.

Easter and Good Friday? My own thoughts were beginning to frighten me. Gina Merritt was not Jesus Christ, despite Veronica's adoration. She wouldn't be rising from the dead in three days, though I had no doubt that whatever she was experiencing could indeed be her passion—her suffering to her death.

I definitely needed to pray.

"Take care of her." I told them. "I'll be back to check on her soon. Very soon."

Both of them looked relieved.

CHAPTER TWELVE

GINA

I felt cold again so deep inside of me it felt like my bones had frozen solid. I shivered awake only to find Veronica Morelli praying over me and wiping my forehead, freezing me more.

"Stop it," I said.

"We've got to get your fever down, sweetie."

"Where's my Priest?"

"Mike just left. He's coming back."

"No, Priest. Where is Priest? Your son."

His voice saying "I'm here" caressed me. A moment later his fingers grazed my arm.

She looked at him, confused. "Why did she call you her Priest?"

"It's my name, Veronica."

"Nobody calls you Priest and she said 'my Priest.'"

"You called me Priest before she did, didn't you, Miss Morelli? At least that's what is on my birth certificate. Is there a problem with my name now? Maybe you can tell me about that. It could be quite insightful. And don't worry. Nana won't object. Not now."

Her expression fell. He'd one-upped her, and by the looks of her face, she wasn't used to it.

I didn't want them to work out their family issues in my room. I only wanted the strange comfort of being near the Priest God sent me.

My throat felt parched. Maybe I could get rid of one of them with a simple request.

"I feel thirsty."

"Oh, my Lordy," Veronica said, fanning herself. "She said, 'I thirst.' Just like our Lord."

That's not what I said.

Veronica jumped up like she'd become my servant. "I'll get you a glass of water, or maybe some juice to build your strength up. Do you have juice?"

"Water is fine. Thank you."

She leapt to her feet with such enthusiasm you'd think I'd made her day.

"Will you check on Zoe, too?" I asked. "See if she needs anything."

Veronica beamed. "I'm at your service, blessed one."

Blessed one? She had to be kidding.

When she was out of earshot, I said to Priest, "What's up with your mother?"

"Don't make me think about it."

Beneath the haggard lines on his face, I saw that he really was quite handsome. "Are you okay? Did you sleep?"

He went to his knees by my bed and rested his elbows on my mattress. He looked so tired. "I slept a little, but you don't have to worry about me. How are you?"

"I hurt. All over."

"You have a new wound on your foot."

I chuckled. "Um, yeah, I feel it."

You'd think after all I'd been through in my life I'd be brave, but I wasn't. I thought he'd identify with that.

"I'm really, really scared."

"I'm scared too, Gina."

I wished I could hold back the torrent of feelings rising in me, but they'd crested, spilling out of my eyes. "Do you think God is mad at me?"

He rubbed my dreadlocks, found one he must have liked, and curled it around his index finger. "Why would God be mad at you?"

"I don't always say my prayers. Sometimes I just think about praying, even though I have a prayer book for when I get stuck."

"I think God can handle that." He wiped the tears from my face with his hands.

I made a few more confessions.

"I don't always read the Bible. And I've never, ever read the Bible in a year. I don't care how many times I try, it never works out for me."

He raised an eyebrow. "You're going to hell in a handbasket for that."

I think I hiccupped a sob. I don't know how I looked, but he burst into laughter.

"Come on, Gina. That's not the unpardonable sin."

"Last night, when you held me ..."

He didn't rush to comfort me this time. I saw him suck his breath in. He waited for what I would say, but I couldn't now. He exhaled, his eyes flickered downward, and his cheeks pinkened at my scrutiny.

He felt it too. Oh, God. He felt it too.

His bashfulness emboldened me. "Remember what you said before, about me not being able to be a stigmatic because I'm too cranky?"

"I remember."

"Maybe I'm too human in more ways than that."

"You can't be too human. Being human is okay if you're human."

"It's not okay, Priest. Not right now. I shouldn't have too-human thoughts when this is happening to me. All my thoughts should be on God."

"Gina, whatever this is, it's *happening* to you. You're not doing it and it didn't come with a handbook, so why don't you just be yourself? Pray. Ask God to help you."

"I do! But He stopped talking to me, Priest."

"I don't know what to say, Gina. I'm not good at praying or hearing God talk to me. But you have to keep trying."

I wanted to tell him everything in my head. I smelled like roses, but I wasn't blooming; I felt as if I were withering on the vine. When I opened my mouth to tell him more I silenced myself. I could tell he wanted to say something to me. I waited.

He stammered. "About last night. When I was holding you. I felt …"

Priest faltered, which was probably for the best. I didn't know what he'd say and I wasn't sure I wanted to know. Besides, it was crazy. You don't start feeling things for a person just because you've held them. Sweetly. All night.

I needed to change the subject before I craved his confessions, which neither of us could do anything about.

"This is insane. My hands have been bleeding for reasons I can't begin to understand. And now my foot."

"I know. If you wanted to impress me you did a great job. You sure know how to get a man's attention. What happens just before you get the wounds?"

"Each time it's different. First a vision of a kiss. Then a flame, and the third time only pain, and this feeling of being lost in some … I don't know … state of being."

"You go away and then you come back."

"I go away all right. Farther than you may think."

"Are you aware of your surroundings?"

"Very. It's just that my surroundings *change* and I start seeing things that maybe nobody else can. That's not good. And you know, it makes me doubt."

"Doubt what?"

"My sanity! What little I have."

Priest rose from his kneeling position and sat on the bed beside me.

"You're not insane, Gina."

"I went to the cross, Priest. I was there with Jesus, on that hill, watching His murderers torment Him."

"When you're gone like that are you in ecstasy? Do you know what that is?"

"I read *Mariette in Ecstasy!* I know you saw my copy. It was sitting on my love seat when you got here. Did you think it was about a drug addict? *Mariette* on *Ecstasy?* It's about a young nun who gets stigmata, or at least, some people thought she did. It's got a picture of a nun with the same expression that's on the Berini statue, *The Ecstasy of Saint Teresa.*"

"I'm sorry. I saw the book. I'm not thinking straight. That's all." He shook his head, as if he were shaking his brain back in place. "Go on."

"I was trying to say I know what ecstasy is, only I thought it was some sort of pleasant, blissful state."

He thought for a moment. "The root word for *ecstasy* means something like 'to lose yourself,' so maybe it is ecstasy, and you sure look lost when you go there to me. Is that what happens to you? You lose yourself?"

"Oh, yeah, I lose myself all right. But it's not like what you probably think. It feels like I'm in some kind of *hell,* and I keep searching for Jesus in this sinkhole of darkness. I can't find Him anywhere, Priest." I paused again. "I'm not a saint. This isn't supposed to be happening to somebody like me."

"Do you think you're a stigmatic, Gina?"

"You tell me. You're the Catholic encyclopedia and Pulitzer Prize–winning investigative journalist."

"I can't tell you that for sure. I wish I could. Even if the Catholic Church sent an investigator from the Vatican to examine you—and they won't—you couldn't be declared an authentic stigmatic until after your death."

"I'm going to die from this, aren't I? I can feel it."

His eyes cast downward and he didn't answer.

"This can kill me, can't it? Tell me. You know the answer."

"Not necessarily," he said.

"How long is the shelf life of a stigmatic, Priest?"

He blew air from his cheeks. "Varies."

He was trying to spare me the truth. I sighed. I desperately needed somebody to tell me, or help me figure this whole thing out. God sent me a Priest. I needed him to teach, guide, and protect me like all good priests do.

"Help me understand this, Priest. I have to be causing this somehow myself. I can't be a real stigmatic. I don't fit the profile."

"You *absolutely* fit the profile."

Priest scooted up on the bed until he was beside me.

"Come here," he said. He rested his back against my headboard and gathered me into his bony arms. He said to me, as I sank into his warmth, "Let me tell you a story ..."

PRIEST

"Cloretta of Oakland, California"

How's this for a girl-in-the-'hood tale, soul sistah?

Imagine it's 1972, Oakland, California, before the drive-by shootings and the John Singleton movie.

Think of a little girl, say, Zoe, at ten years old. Bright-eyed and brown-skinned, she's from a big Baptist family. She lives with her mom, a dental assistant, and her stepdad, brother, and a sister with four, count 'em, four kids. A crowded house, yes, but a happy home, even though a few of them partook of the bread of sorrows somewhere along the way. They all went to church, perhaps with some notion that their patchwork family could stay together if they prayed together.

Now, little Cloretta was an ordinary kid, pretty and pleasant, friendly, with unremarkable grades. She was at her desk in school one day, drawing pictures of Saint Francis of Assisi—must have been a Catholic school, even though she was Baptist—lost in little-girl reverie.

Or perhaps not.

Her left palm began to bleed, right there in the classroom. She experienced no pain, only blood, which washed off easily revealing no lesion on her unblemished skin.

She wasn't crazy. Maybe a little impressionable. Four days before she bled she watched a television show about the crucifixion.

Cloretta was in excellent health, and neither she nor her family had a history of bleeding disorders, prolonged bleeding, or psychiatric illnesses, unless you count the fact that after she saw the program she heard voices, voices that told her to pray for people. Their message was straightforward: God would answer her, and He did. Every prayer. Jesus healed them all. Unlike you, loved ones whisked her to the hospital, and all they found was dried blood crusted in the palm of her lesion-free, ordinary hand. She went back to school with a clean bill of health.

I'd like to know what kind of curriculum they had at that school, because within three hours of the first bleed, while she was in school, Cloretta's right palm began to bleed. Five days later her left foot bled, and within twenty-four hours of that, her right. The day after, she bled from her side. Mind you, I didn't say she was *wounded*; I said she bled.

Maybe there's a difference.

On the fourteenth day of this strange, pain-free passion, Cloretta Robinson bled in the middle of her forehead. This happened seven days before Easter.

Little Cloretta Robinson bled for nineteen days in all, sometimes as little as once every two days, and up to five times in a single day. Her hands bled more than any of the other sites. Teachers, the school nurse, the hospital staff, her family, both at home and at church, all bore witness. She bled without lesions, or reasons.

On Good Friday, the nineteenth day, Cloretta announced that she felt like, "It's over." Though blood oozed from every site, by the day's end she bled no more.

One of her doctors said although she was normal, she possessed unusual piety. Here was a kid who spoke of Jesus in reverent detail, at only ten years old, and boy, does that sound familiar to me.

Do you know what else doctors noted? That she was preoccupied with Christ's suffering. She thought her life was dedicated to alleviating the suffering of others.

The next Easter her family watched her carefully, but it never happened again. Or if it did, they didn't let on, and I can't blame them for that. She was a kid. You protect the defenseless.

Cloretta Robinson drifted into obscurity. Like the high school I wrote about years ago, few people cared about a black juvenile stigmatic. But sometimes I wonder what became of the little girl who was marked with the passion wounds of Christ one Eastertide. I imagine she wondered why she was chosen, questioned both her sanity and sanctity, and maybe when she was older, and those years were far from her, she wondered if she made the whole thing up.

Then again, she could have died young, and her family let her rest in peace without the stain of stigmata to prick her eternal rest. Or perhaps she lived the rest of her life quietly healing the suffering and alleviating the pain of others through her prayers, knowing God so loved the ghetto, that He gave His only begotten Son, and left His mark on Cloretta to prove it.

GINA

I looked up at this man, this crazy storytelling junkie who appeared in my life, like an angel with broken wings and a tilted halo. But he was an angel just the same.

"Did that really happen?"

"Absolutely. I read about her in a book. Everyone knows everything in books is true."

I found his sarcasm, even though he'd used it gently here, to be a coat of armor to shield what I sensed was an essential innocence in him. He may have been a mess, but in some ways he saw more clearly than most, believed more readily, maybe in everything good except himself. Something about the way he said "absolutely" touched me to the core. Tears sprang to my eyes again.

He whispered, "Don't cry, soul sistah. Everything will be all right. I promise."

"It doesn't feel like everything will be all right. It feels terrible, Priest. I feel terrible."

I needed help. Only his.

Wrapping my courage around me like a shawl, I took a deep breath and asked him for what I wanted—what only he could give me.

"I can't get through this alone. I need you. Will you please—"

Veronica blew back into the room with a pitcher of ice water and a glass. She poured it in front of me, all the while blathering about Zoe.

"I checked on her. She's in her room with a coloring book of Saint Francis of Assisi I bought for her."

"Did you say a Saint Francis of Assisi coloring book?" I shrieked.

"It's just Saint Francis."

Priest squeezed me. "Just go with it. You've filled your stigmatic quota. Only one per household."

Veronica scowled at Priest. "Move ... talking crazy again."

Like a wounded dog, Priest slunk away from me. She dropped down onto my mattress and placed her hand under my head and lifted it, still talking about the dollar store. "I thought it was run by Arabs, but they must've been Catholic. Had all kinds of kitsch: plastic saints' bracelets, cheap sacred heart pictures. I'm telling you, you just never know about those people."

I resented the way she said "those people." It made me choke when I tried to drink. The icy water spilled on my chest. I abruptly sat up. I'd have tried to take the glass myself, but my hands were wrapped like a mummy's.

"Priest, will you help me?"

"I'll see if I can find you a straw or something. I think I saw a sippy cup that must be one of Zoe's."

The muscles around Veronica's mouth tightened. She muttered, "At least you're good for something."

Her demeanor had completely changed. She turned as cold as the water. I wasn't sure if I wanted to keep getting help from her at all.

PRIEST

She said she needed me. I had no idea what she meant, but I was going to find out. And I was going to help her.

Veronica posed the most obvious obstacle to me helping Gina. I determined on the way into the bright sunshine of Gina's kitchen that there was no way I'd allow Veronica's spiritual gluttony to stand in our way.

Our way?

Man, you hold a woman, and the next thing you know you're an *our*.

We couldn't be an *our*. I could serve her, but I couldn't be anything more than a friend. I could kill her with my love. She had enough problems than to be a martyr for my sake.

VERONICA

Oh, Lordy, forgive me, I prayed.

I never meant to be so sharp with Anthony. But he always managed to bring out the worst in me. It was that obnoxious, arrogant way of his, all smug and sarcastic. I couldn't believe his nerve, trying to hang on to a woman of grace like she was one of his two-dollar crack whores. I asked him to do one small thing that may have saved that miraculous lady's life, and he thought because he kept her warm he could hang around like a puppy on her heels.

Why had he even called me if he thought he could do it all?

Because he couldn't do anything. He was inept. The only thing he'd ever been good for was stringing pretty words together, and he couldn't even do that anymore.

He called *me!* And the next thing I knew he wanted to take over. Well he was out of his element. I was the one who'd spent my whole life seeking God. It was Ronnie, dragging herself from praise team to prayer ministry, small group, women's ministry, the divine hours, you name it. I don't care what kind of church I went to, and I've done 'em all, I've been faithful.

It was my time to be a part of the mystery. My reward was due me. I sure as sharp wasn't gonna let him keep me from maybe the biggest thing I've ever seen God do.

She had a message with the gift of stigmata she'd been given. The wounds themselves were a message, I just knew it, and people like her needed somebody to get them ready for the world.

That's why God purged me in hospitals, and He'd use all of my training to serve His purposes! I lifted holy hands and prayed in the Spirit.

When divinely inspired tongues finished flowing out of me, I sat guard at her bed. My head itched. I reached up to scratch and found a thin downy layer of fuzz covering my entire scalp. I fell to my knees in worship.

God healed me! Even my hair! Through the blessed one.

Oh yes. I had to watch over her to make sure he wouldn't ruin this, 'cause sure as sharp that Anthony could ruin anything.

CHAPTER THIRTEEN

MIKE

Lacy knew right away something was bothering me. She put her hand on her hip as soon as I walked into the house. I shut the door behind me and leaned against it like I could keep all the ills in the world out by the strength of my back.

I knew what Lacy wanted to hear.

"Zoe's fine. Looks like she got a new dad," I said, hanging my coat in the closet. I kicked off my sneakers.

"Do I even want to ask?"

"No, you don't. But she is fine."

"What about Gina?"

I sighed from deep in my chest. "Not so fine."

"What do you mean, Mike?"

Lacy laid her hand on my shoulder, eliciting another heaving sigh from me. "Mike?" her gentle voice prodded.

"I need to pray, Lace. I need God's sure guidance on this one. This isn't your run-of-mill pastoral crisis."

"She's mentally ill, Mike."

"We've got mentally ill people in our congregation, people suffering from depression, addiction, bipolar disorder. None of them have spontaneous bleeding wounds."

"Wounds. As in plural?"

"She's got three now, Lace. Both hands and a foot."

"Mike, that sounds crazy."

"I know."

"She did it herself. Somehow. What else could it be?"

"A miracle?" I looked at her sheepishly. She looked back at me, incredulous.

"You don't mean that," she sighed. "Even if you do mean it, whatever their cause, bleeding wounds need the attention of a doctor."

"You haven't seen her since church, Lacy. It's amazing. I've never seen anything like it. I can still smell that flowery scent." I shook my head, trying to find a way to rationalize it all.

"Mike, people have been calling the house. Somehow it's been leaked. I guess Jesus' concept of 'tell no one' is lost on Nita and Norah. You're going to have to do something."

"The concept of 'tell no one' is lost to more than those two if the Bible is any indicator. This is going to get completely out of control, and I don't know how to stop it. Any ideas, Lacy? Because I'm fresh

out of them. There aren't any handbooks I can pick up at Family
Christian about what to do when somebody in my congregation gets
the wounds of Christ."

I think she saw in my face how serious I was. She took my head
in her hands, stroking my temples. "Oh, honey," was all she said
before we held each other.

"I'm going to go pray."

Mostly I spend quiet time in my study. This time I went straight
to the bedroom and lay down on our bed. My thoughts felt too scattered to utter a coherent prayer. I closed my eyes and mostly let my
sighs speak to God, with the exception of my saying, "I'm listening."

The only comforter I experienced was the one spread across the bed.

GINA

Priest and his mom had locked horns in a bloody battle of wills. She
wanted him to leave, and he wanted her to do the same.

My vote would have gone to him staying. Veronica was creepy.
She was one of those people who never gave you a second of her time
unless she benefited somehow. I remember once I went up for prayer
and she swooped down on me.

She's such an odd woman, squat and heavy, more than just
spiritually. That terrible haircut. And she wore those fat-lady clothes,
made to look like deplorable floral tents. Those were just outward
things. Veronica reeked of desperation.

That day at church she prayed for me, spouting off what I guess
she thought was a "word of knowledge." But everything she said was
wrong. All wrong. And her eyes? Her eyes are what I remembered

most. They looked kinda crazy, and she kept searching my face for affirmation for what she was saying, like I could prove with a nod of my head that God really spoke to her.

I gave her that nod, I'm ashamed to say. The whole scenario was painful, at least to me. And now she was taking over my house. Burning candles. Asking for *my* blessing. Trying to pry a "message to God's people" out of me that I didn't have. She wouldn't let Priest near me, and I couldn't get out of bed except to hobble to the bathroom. For an hour she lay prostrate on my bedroom floor.

God forgive me, but I prayed she would leave, and soon.

PRIEST

I spent most of the day with Zoe. Apparently I'd forgotten the intricacies of Candy Land and Chutes and Ladders. I wished I had my Xbox, but it went the way of Foxy three months before.

When she got bored with board games we watched Nickelodeon on her Mickey Mouse television—the speakers were shaped like mouse ears. Cute. As much as I enjoyed being with her, I felt like a kid myself, banished to my room by my mom.

Who was I kidding? I always felt like a kid when it came to Veronica. A rotten little scoundrel she hated at that.

Zoe fell asleep watching Sponge Bob. I had to face my life eventually, so I took a few minutes to check the messages in my cell phone's voicemail.

Fox: "Where you at, baby? You feeling all right? Foxy is getting worried about you. You need your medicine, baby. Don't you worry, if you ain't got the money right now—"

I pushed the delete button to spare me having to hear the rest. It would be the same story. She would take care of me if I took care of her. I'd done a lot of dirt to get junk, but I hadn't yet resorted to being a smack ho. And I certainly wasn't interested in meeting the needs of a six-foot-three transvestite drug dealer. I didn't care how good her dope was.

How I rued the day she failed as an Internet minister and makeup artist.

Larry's voice bellowed out at me, the next one in the queue. Come back into the office. He had something for me. This was my last chance. If I didn't come up with something better than the drivel I was turning in—

Delete. But I did take a moment to call him.

"I'm on something, Larry," I said before he could rage at me. I meant a kid's floor, but that was confidential.

"What? What are you on, Tony?"

"I can't get into it now," I stage whispered. "Somebody might hear."

"You serious?"

"I'm totally serious. This is something big." Zoe's bedroom floor was quite substantial for a townhouse in the 'hood.

"I'll call you in a few days, or a week or two. I promise."

I hung up before he could scream profanities, and turned the phone off. Better to have as little of my life as possible invading.

Watching TV in Zoe's room was more fun than my life anyway. But how long could I stay with Gina? Everything I felt yesterday seemed to be dissipating in the cold of Veronica's shadow.

My thoughts must have conjured her up. Ronnie marched into

the room and announced she needed to do a twelve-hour shift at the hospital.

Was that the "Hallelujah" chorus I heard? I couldn't be sure. I was so overcome with gratitude, everything went all warm and fuzzy. Of course, she couldn't leave without a last strike.

"Don't do anything stupid."

"Would I do that?"

"I won't dignify that with an answer."

She turned her nose up, spun on her heels, and headed on out to her real job.

GINA

I think I heard the "Hallelujah" chorus when she walked out of my townhouse. I would have leapt out of bed if I hadn't known my foot would cry out in pain. But I did manage to drag myself out of bed and make my way to the bedroom door, which she'd closed. Made me wonder if she didn't do it to create another obstacle to me getting at her son. I didn't know how I'd manage to turn the knob with my bandages.

Everything, even the simplest act, was a challenge to me. And I thought I knew something about disability! I was *so* lonely in that bed all day. I mean, Veronica, when she wasn't driving me crazy trying to take care of me, talked on and on, spitting venom about Priest.

He seemed so … *reduced* … in her presence. Not the same sparring partner who showed up at my door. And the way she talked to him! One reason I got up was to see if he was all right. I kinda missed him.

As I pondered how I could possibly open the door with my elbow, it swung open and Priest stood there. We both laughed, but he immediately went into help mode.

"Can I get you something?"

"Your mom took care of everything I needed, and then she took care of things I neither needed nor wanted." I scrunched up my face when I said this. "I thought she'd never leave. Don't hate me."

"Don't hate you? Like I didn't beg God to take her away."

We didn't laugh that time. We stood there at that door, neither of us moving. We were like a couple of teenagers with a crush on each other, finally alone—almost—and not knowing what to do.

I was so aware of him. Just a few inches stood between us. I felt a little shy in front of him, and my gaze went to my foot. Veronica had wrapped it tightly. I didn't have to worry about dotting the floor with my blood. But it did hurt. Priest must have noticed me wince, but every wound hurt, constantly, even when they weren't bleeding.

"You look like you're in pain," he said. "Let me help you."

"I need to lose twenty pounds so you can pick me up, and you need to find them."

He laughed. "You stay just like you are. You feel good to me."

"Excuse me?"

His cheeks reddened. "Did I say feel?" He chuckled. "I meant look."

"Do you ever write fiction?"

"Is that a trick question?"

"You don't know how to lie."

"I can lie. Believe me, and I can write fiction too. Or I used to."

He put his hand on my waist. That was a bad idea. Butterflies fluttered around my belly. "Oh" slipped out of my mouth.

"What?"

"It's nothing."

"You're not a good liar either, Gina."

I lifted my face and we gazed at each other. He was as affected by me as I was him.

He cleared his throat. "Put your arms around my neck."

My heart pounded in my chest. "Why?" I thought he wanted to kiss me. And maybe he did.

"So you can put your weight on my shoulders and off your foot."

I felt silly. "Oh."

"That 'oh' wasn't as much fun as the first one."

He told the truth about that.

I slipped my arms around him, and he drew closer to me. Now my heart hammered like *it* wanted to wound me. I felt giddy wrapped around him. I tried to pull away.

"Wait," he said.

So I waited. For him to kiss me, but he didn't. For him to pull away, but he didn't do that either.

All he did was hold me for the longest time.

PRIEST

Veronica was going to kill me.

For a few moments—okay, more than a few, I didn't care—Gina was exquisite in my hands. I don't think I could have let her go if I tried. At first.

I knew I was wrong. She was vulnerable just like Mike said, but so was I.

Man, when am I going to stop being so selfish?

I knew I didn't have some whirlwind romance straight out of a grocery-store paperback to give her. The best I offered was a cheap thrill—if I worked hard at it—and a premature grave.

"Time to man up," I told myself. Sure, I held her longer than I should have, but I let her go, eventually.

"Let's get you into the living room."

I supported her while she limped, tottered, and lurched into the living room and then hoisted herself onto the orange love seat.

"Do you want me to get something to prop your foot up with?"

"No," she said, shyly.

Her heart beat with such intensity I could see it thumping through her gown. What a jerk I was.

I gave us both time to collect ourselves, and was glad when she finally broke through the tension between us and got down to business about exactly what she wanted. It wasn't what I thought it would be—or maybe hoped it would be despite the fact that I knew we were hopeless.

"What's a gonzo journalist?" she asked.

Gonzo journalist?

My heart hammered inside of me. I didn't know where she was going with this. Nobody had called me "Gonzo" since I was twenty-two.

"You can't believe everything you read about me on the net."

"I didn't see it on the net. Your mom told me that was your nickname. She said it was a journalism thing."

"Back in the day it was."

"Back in the day?"

"I'm entitled to use the vernacular. Didn't you insist I was black?"

"And you insisted you weren't."

"I'm sorry. I had the impression that I have freedom of speech."

"You do, Priest. You can say whatever you want. I just want you to be yourself. And maybe tell me what gonzo journalism is."

"I'm not into that anymore."

"So what is it?"

"Why do you ask, Gina?" The edge in my voice was sharp enough to give her another bleeding wound.

"I'll get to that; just tell me." She stared at me with those doe eyes of hers. "Please," she said, looking just like Zoe. Like I could deny her anything with those peepers.

But I didn't speak too soon. Memories pummeled me, nearly taking my breath away. I stared ahead at the entertainment center while she waited, patiently. Finally I took a deep breath and dived into my glorious past.

"Gonzo journalism is a way to tell stories. Bottom line: The journalist weaves factual events into a fictional tale. He plunges himself right in the middle of the story, and gets down and dirty in it, whether or not he belongs there."

"Sounds pretty subjective. I thought journalism was all about being objective."

"Not gonzo journalism, baby. The fact is, no matter what the story is about, the writer can put himself, in a very personal way, into the context of the piece. You have to be a little crazy to do it, with some big stones. It's all about style—gritty, earthy style. And it kicks the cool veneer of 'polished' journalism in the teeth with its filthy boot."

"So, you just make up stuff?"

"It's truthful. Maybe more than the factual content. It's like fiction. Or maybe you could call it *friction*. Good fiction always tells the truth, but gonzo has a heckuva bite. I was an expert at it, but I don't write like that anymore."

"Why not?"

"I don't know, Gina. I sabotaged myself. Maybe I just didn't know how to be successful. I'm back to the status quo now. I am wildly, magnificently, brilliantly unsuccessful. No one remembers Anthony Priest, except a few die-hards on the net."

That wasn't completely true. Larry kept trying to give me a chance. I kept letting him down. "Why do you need to know about me as a journalist?"

She hesitated.

"Spill it, toots."

"Veronica thinks maybe you should do a story about me."

"Veronica thought I should be your bed wench."

"Was that a problem for you?"

Yes. I was thinking of her in Song of Solomon terms. But I didn't let on, even though her face fell at my silence. She was a real soldier though. Plowed right through.

"I want you to help me find *my* story. You can get deep inside of it, dirty boots and all. I want you to see it, hear it, feel it, taste it, touch it, smell it."

Why did that sound as hot as being her bed wench? But the idea sparked, flickered, and flared in me.

"You want me to write a story about you?"

"That's not what I said. I said I want you to help me *find* my story. I want you here, in my life, living through this with me. You can find out stuff. Help me figure out why this happened to me."

I tried to talk both of us out of it. "Besides the fact that gonzo journalism has nothing—and I do mean nothing—to do with spiritual mysteries, I'm not gonzo anymore."

"Yes, you are."

I wished I were. I couldn't even stand up to my mother.

"I don't understand what you're asking me for, Gina."

You know how preschool teachers look at "challenging" kids? That's the look she gave me, which felt more than a little patronizing since I wasn't Zoe's age.

"Priest, I'm asking you to approach what's happening to me like you were gonzo. If you were gonzo, and writing a story about me, what would you do? What kind of research? What kind of anything?"

"You don't understand what that will cost."

She sighed, her face downcast. "I don't have money, Priest. I'm a *sandwich artist* at Subway. Part-time because I'm sick so much, and I don't know what's gonna happen with that now. I'm not sure the health department wants people with blood-soaked palms preparing submarine sandwiches. I'm so fired in about five minutes."

"I know you don't have money. I wasn't talking about paying me cash."

Her brow rose slightly to punctuate the suspicion in her voice. "What *did* you mean?"

"Remember how we spooned?"

She paused. Glared at me. Her postured stiffened and she bit at her lower lip.

"We'd have to get closer than that."

I knew what she was thinking. She was wrong.

"How close is closer than us spooning?"

Close enough for me to be sprung. As it was I'd made her my Shulamite. It wouldn't be long before I was reading the Song of Songs to her and declaring my love, but could it be *after* knowing her at least forty-eight hours? Please, God?

Reflecting on my pathetic juvenile emotions gave me some modicum of strength. I rolled my shoulders back, resolved.

"I can't help you, Gina." I didn't expect her to play hardball.

"You're *already* in my story. Filthy boots and all. What's going a little deeper going to hurt?"

Me!

Or *her.*

But she was right. I'd been in her story since I got behind her in line to get ashes on my forehead. We were a Möbius strip twisted together, and I could tell if only by my reactions to her, and hers to me, we could get more tangled in a very bad way. As tempting as her request was I couldn't let that happen.

"It'll expose too much about you. Think about it, Gina. Your story has everything: God, mental illness, a kid, a junkie, racial profiling." I snickered. "It has Veronica! By necessity we'd have to reveal what's happening to you to public scrutiny, and that'll be a bear."

"Only if you write and publish the story. You don't have to do that. "

"I write to publish."

"Then publish. By then it won't matter. I'll know what I need to."

"You don't even want to go to the doctor, Gina, scared they'll take Zoe from you."

"Then you have to help me protect her."

"Me?"

"That's what you've been doing for the last twenty-four hours."

"I've been playing Romper Room with the kid! Did you have a single conversation with Veronica? Surely she told you everything about me. I lie. I steal. I manipulate. She probably told you my rear end stinks, and everything else you didn't want to know about me."

"She gave me an earful, but all I can see is the guy that keeps showing up."

"You can't really afford to be that naive. I've been here a day. Anybody can show up for a day. A lousy, stinkin' heroin addict can show up for a day."

She needed a reality check. I tugged at the button of my shirt cuff, freeing it from its constraints. Shoved my sleeve up and showed her *my* stigmata.

"Look at this, Gina. I want you to see my needle tracks and these sores and scabs marking my arm. These are *my* I-tried-to-commit-suicide scars, only there are a lot more of them than you have. I try to take myself out every time I shoot up. Mine aren't holy. Jesus didn't kiss me and leave those."

Her eyes filled with tears. She reached for my arm, but I drew back.

"You can't touch mine. My blood doesn't heal people."

"Neither does mine."

"Apparently it does, Gina. You healed Mike. His knee. You healed *me*. My drug hunger is gone, and I haven't had a single withdrawal symptom. I couldn't go three or four hours without using. Right now I should be rolled in a fetal position, shaking, sweating, and hurting, with my entrails coming out at both ends. But none of that is happening. *That's* why I showed up here. I wanted to know what you did to me."

I added, so there'd be no question about the matter, "And I can't be gonzo for you because gonzo is dead. I killed him myself."

CHAPTER FOURTEEN

GINA

He lifted his shirtsleeve and revealed a roadmap of misery. His skin was so disfigured from sores and lesions I'd have thought he had leprosy if I didn't know better. Some of the sores, thick as boils, had crusted over with pus. Others were fresh, angry red swellings. If you looked in his face, you could see how his fair skin was touched with a hint of gold and red, like a Jonathan apple, but on his arms there were spots void of color coexisting with the red, black, and blue of needle tracks.

I didn't heal Priest. I'd have started right there if I did. And then I'd have healed that place inside of him that didn't remember he was irrevocably the *Imago Dei*—made in the image and likeness of God, no matter what he did to himself. I'd heal his mother hunger, and put in my healing touch all the love he'd ever need. I'd heal his confidence and restore what the locust hadn't eaten of his career. Then I'd go for his anger and his sarcasm, and the rift between him and God. After that I'd stand back and watch the blessings flow.

Maybe I'd heal Gina after that, laying hands on my own manic-depressive brain. And then I'd wipe out the fibro. Go back to school and get a real job I could actually take care of my daughter on.

Healer? I couldn't even feed my child on my own. I'd heal my need for food stamps. And I'd keep healing Gina. I'd get those pesky scars off my wrist, because sometimes in the oddest moments, like when I'm waiting for the cashier to give me change in the grocery store, I glance down at those scars, and I'm always surprised to see them. I wonder if they're not glowing like I'd painting them in Day-Glo yellow and everyone can see them, and they all judge me as crazy. Crazy enough to try to off myself.

Or pathetic.

I whispered, "I didn't heal you."

He seemed angry that I denied it. "Oh, yeah, Gina? Then why aren't I sick?"

"Maybe you are sick, Priest, deep in withdrawal as we speak. But it's been so long since you've acted like a human being and cared for somebody other than yourself that you've got some kind of benevolent euphoria going on, and you haven't come down from acting like you could love somebody yet."

He threw his head back and laughed. "I don't think so, dear."

"Don't be so quick to deny it. Think about it, Priest. You came, you saw, you stayed! Took all the abuse your mom shoveled on you all day long, and waited it out until she left. You could have booked up out of here like you did with Elle. Veronica told me about her."

He blanched and withdrew into a full-blown sulk at that, resting his chin on his hand. He wouldn't look at me now.

I crossed my arms across my chest again. "I offered you something. Something I know you can use, and something I can tell you want. I saw the excitement leap into your eyes when you talked about it. Yet you didn't say yes. Why not, Priest?"

We sat there, him staring at the entertainment center, my eyes fixed on him until I finally said, "Are you gonna help me?"

Now he turned to face me, his expression grim. He raised his voice, "No." His expression, with his tight-mouthed smirk and side-long glance, struck me as arrogant.

I don't know why I was surprised, but I was.

He would get no more of my time. "I guess you'd better go then."

Priest didn't have to think about it. He stood. "Can I help you back to your room?"

"I'll manage. Bye."

"Fine. Good-bye, Gina."

Zoe ran out of her room and planted herself in front of him. My baby's sweet little voice brimmed with concern. "Are you fixing to go?"

Her eyes darted from Priest to me and back to Priest.

If I cussed, I probably would have done it right then.

PRIEST

I didn't want to care about Zoe, or her mother. It hadn't occurred to me that the kid might care about me, but clearly she did.

The little moppet looked up at me and all I could see was little Anthony at that age hoping Veronica would stick around instead of locking me in the bathroom while she went God only knows where.

Where was Zoe's dad? What kind of fool would leave them alone, and I know he wasn't around because Zoe's father hunger was almost palpable.

Crouching down to her level I spoke to her. "Hey, kiddo. I thought you were sleeping."

"I heard you and Mommy talking. Are you about to go?"

"I haven't been home since yesterday. I have to change my clothes and have a shower."

"Then you're coming back?"

I looked to Gina for help, despite the fact that I was an animal and had just told her no to something she wanted. She was kind to offer some.

"He's busy, honey. He's really been nice to spend so much time with us already. We'd better let him get going."

"Is he coming back?"

"We'll see."

Her little arms crossed. "When you say, 'we'll see,' that means no."

"That's not true, Zoe."

Kids are so transparent. She stomped off into her room, wailing. I moved to go after her but Gina stopped me. "Don't you dare!"

"But, Gina, she thinks—"

"And she's right. I'll deal with my daughter. You go. At least she won't have to see you walk out the door."

I wanted to protest. I wanted to tell her Zoe didn't deserve for me to just waltz out of her life without even a good-bye, but Gina was right. Prolonging our good-bye would only make things messier.

Gina didn't even look mad. With the way she'd drawn her knees up, hugging her arms around her legs, with the downward slope of her shoulders, I'd have said she was disappointed, a more grown-up version of Zoe. To put us all out of our misery I pulled my coat out of the closet and left.

GINA

He walked out the door, and I fell into a chasm of loneliness. No matter that I had been foolish. I trusted that man *way* too fast, as if I really believed that God sent him. I remembered what people told me after I left Jesse. "Don't fall for the first person who's nice to you. You'll think they're something that they aren't."

I trusted the first one, and the one after that, and a few more. I finally figured out how to protect the wilted flower of my virtue, and despite man cravings that drove me to my knees, I hadn't been so stupid in years.

Drug addiction hadn't stolen Priest's pretty smile. His multicolored eyes at times were a well of such depth that I wanted to dive into them and swim in their dark, tear-salted waters. His gentle touch belied the roughness of his calloused hands—hands with fingertips likely burned on crack pipes and cocktails from joints smoked down to nothing. His caresses never revealed—not in a single meeting with my flesh—that they were made for anything other than touching me, even if he had succumbed to the dope.

Zoe whimpered in her room. I could imagine her, prostrate on her bed, crying into the quilt that I will be making minimum payments on until old age creeps in.

I stared at my mummy hands, so sore and weak that I couldn't hold my own darned cup. I had a little girl who'd need dinner very soon. What was I gonna do?

He might not be very talkative, but I didn't doubt God would listen to me. So I sat there on my love seat in the quiet, with only the muted sound of Zoe crying in the background, and spoke to the Spouse who should have been the only One I trusted after I realized Jesse would kill me if I stayed with him.

"Jesus, tonight I'm Hagar by the spring beside the road to Shur. I'm not sure of anything. I'd run away, but I don't know if I can make it to the water right beside me with this foot. Even if I could, I can't hold on to the cup to dip into the spring."

Tears stung my eyes. "Lord, I'm tired of that baby in there looking after herself. I can't stand myself anymore. You revealed to Hagar that You are the God who sees her. Look at me. Protect me. I'm poor and needy, Jesus. Save me."

I wiped my eyes, and let my tears mingle with the bloodstains on my bandages.

CHAPTER FIFTEEN

PRIEST

Foxy's familiar pink Cadillac was parked in front my house. After I pounded on my steering wheel with my fist and released a stream of bad words, I knew I had to man up and get out of my car.

Fox stepped out of "Pinkie" as soon as I got to my porch. She wore a miniskirt with red heels and topped her ensemble with a bad blonde weave she once told me made her look like Mary J. Blige. She looked like a hooker on steroids.

Her mouth curved into a smile. "Hey, baby."

I hated the lecherous way she called me baby, or sugar, or sweetie pie.

My greeting, a curt nod and, "Fox."

She sized me up, no doubt calculating where I could have gotten some junk. "You look like you had your medicine."

"Looks deceive. You of all people should know that."

What was I saying? Foxy fooled no one in her woman's clothes. She looked like the man she was, with fake breasts and big bad hair.

"I ain't seen you since yesterday. You had something, didn't you? I know my boo. Who you getting yo' pharmaceuticals from?"

"What do you want, Foxy? I didn't call you."

"You don't have to call me. I told you I'd be here for *you*."

Despite the fact that I was freezing, I didn't want her in my house tonight. "Thanks, but I really don't need anything. It's been a long night. I'm going in."

I didn't put the key in the door yet. If she wanted an invitation, she'd wait in vain. I could outwait her. I didn't mind the cold like she did.

She rubbed her arms. "Brrrrrrrr." Acted like she was trembling. "You gon' invite Miss Foxy in?"

"Not tonight."

She reached into the pocket of her massive Baby Phat jacket and pulled out two packs with her brand stamped on the paper; a black mudflap girl with an afro. On the street we called it brown sugar. She extended them to me.

"I don't need any H. Okay?"

Didn't need it, but I sure could use it. The not-so-distant memory of the first burn when I pop a vein and the flush of it easing through my blood called to me. I tried to resist, but the thought of its comfort seized my attention and pilfered my vocabulary. I could only find a couple of leftovers to string together.

"No money."

"I don't want you seeing anybody else but Foxy, baby. Foxy is the woman for you. These are a gift. We been together a long time, Tony. I don't want to lose you."

Always talked like we were some kind of couple. Crazy man-witch! Sober twenty-four hours and I realized how much she sickened me; but in the wake of walking away from Gina and coming back to my own destitute life, the drug she offered did not. At all.

She stuck the packs in my coat pocket. Blew me a kiss. "I'll call you tomorrow. I told you I'll take care of you." She winked. "Maybe one day you can take care of me." Then she turned on her high heels and sashayed away.

I went into my grandmother's old duplex alone. As I closed the door behind me I thought, for the millionth time, *Nana would be so disappointed in me.*

I'd tried to banish her convicting presence the way most junkies do. I sold anything she had that had any value. Only a few reminders of her dotted the desolate landscape, like the crucifix on the living room wall. I'd gotten rid of the others. St. Vincent de Paul's Thrift Store gladly took them in. All I had left were her Sacred Heart of Jesus picture and a few of her rosaries.

I went straight to the kitchen drawer where I kept the beads, grabbed a set, and settled on the cheap futon I'd bought to replace Nana's couch. No need to even remove my coat; how could I with the heroin burning in my pocket?

Once Nana told me when Marian devotion reached its peak in Europe they begin to call the circlet of beads a "rosary." The name was in honor of Mary favorite flower, the rose, and this was her bouquet.

Gina's bouquet clung to my shirt from when she bled all over me during the bath. I fingered the beads, smarting on the inside that I had the gall to leave her alone with Zoe.

Zoe would be hungry soon, if not already.

I tried to pray, but I couldn't. Having failed, I made a lame effort to meditate on the joyful mysteries: annunciation, visitation, and nativity. But it was Lent. Gina had been graced with the passion wounds of Christ. I was almost sure of it. Nothing but sorrowful mysteries came to mind.

Again I tried to pray. Got through the sign of the cross, the Apostles' Creed, and the "Our Father," then quit to mumble a weak request to our lady, to whom Nana had given me when my own mother couldn't stand me.

"Hail Mary, full of grace, the Lord is with thee, blessed are thou among women, and blessed is the fruit of thy womb, Jesus."

Gina's grace stabbed at my consciousness.

"Holy Mary, mother of God, pray for us sinners, now and at the moment of our death."

The words sounded hollow coming out of my mouth.

"Queen of heaven, Nana always said you were my mother. Pray to your Son for me. I need help. I'm weak. I don't want to use, but I'm tempted. If you have any suggestions now would be a good time to share."

Then, odd, but something from the gospels came to mind. The words of Jesus in Matthew 5:23 and 24. Nana had me memorize this Scripture so that I'd remember to forgive Veronica her trespasses when I prayed and try to reconcile with her.

"Therefore, if you bring your gift to the altar, and there recall

that your brother has anything against you, leave your gift there at the altar. Go first and be reconciled to your brother, and then come and offer your gift."

What do you know about that? I stayed so faded I couldn't remember my name sometimes, and now Scriptures burst to life in my head like they were on fertile ground. For the first time in many years, I felt like God had given me a bit of guidance. Amazing.

Somehow I didn't think it was Foxy that God was asking me to go to.

I took the smack out my coat, tossed it on my ratty futon, and grabbed whatever clothes passed the smell test enough for me to throw in a bag.

I left my hovel to go be reconciled to my brother, like the Holy Scriptures said.

Brother Gina.

GINA

Zoe came out of her bedroom after an eternal hour that left me glued to the love seat, ashamed that I allowed Priest to hurt her. She lumbered over to me without her usual pep. My poor little pumpkin had exhausted herself, but I saw forgiveness in those baby browns. She could have been a little old lady with those wise, healing eyes, looking right through me, seeing all my lack, and loving me anyway. I was *so* grateful to her for that, even though she was only five.

She didn't ask about Priest.

"I'm hungry, Mommy."

"I'll make you a sandwich."

"That's okay. I can make it myself."

She could, but why should she have to?

Lord Jesus, give me strength.

I stood up. A shaft of pain ripped through my wounded foot all the way up to my thigh. I swallowed my moan and staggered to the kitchen, nothing but prayer holding me steady. If Jesus could walk the stations of the cross, I could make it into my little kitchen.

"Jesus," I prayed under my breath, "if these wounds are what You want to give me, I'm going to take them. I want whatever You want me to have. But if this isn't from You, take them away. Zoe doesn't have anybody but me. Help me be a real mother. Forgive me for failing her completely."

I got to the fridge, bit the inside of my cheek to get my mind off the pain in my hand, and pulled open the door with my elbow. But I'd have to use my hand to grab the box of Not Dogs.

"Do you want me to help you?" Zoe asked, so tenderly her words hurt.

"No, baby. Jesus will help me."

"Mama, why are you bleeding like that?"

What was I supposed to tell her? How could I make a five-year-old understand what I didn't understand myself?

But I tried. "Priest—" She looked like she didn't recognize the name. "—I mean Mr. Anthony told me I may have a special gift from Jesus."

"A special gift?"

Her eyes lit up, like I was going to tell her I got a Christmas present early … or late, depending on how you thought about it. This was no nativity gift. This was all Easter. Good Friday, actually.

"It's not a present like a toy, or a new outfit. It's a way to teach me, and maybe other people, like Mr. Anthony, what Jesus suffered on the cross for us."

Bad move. I saw the terror in her eyes. The crucifixion happening to *Him* was one thing; *I* was her mama.

I started to reach for her but thought the bandages would scare her. I tried to backtrack, ease the horror of this.

"It's not the same as He suffered baby. You know Mommy's breath prayer? Share with me, Jesus?"

She nodded, still unsure.

"I think it might be a way of sharing a little of Jesus' sores. And He takes mine, too, a lot more of mine than I take of His."

I'd asked her to be strong, but she was five! She hollered. So, I sat my big behind down on the floor and held her like Priest held me. Zoe cried and cried and cried, too much groaning coming from one so young. It tore my heart into pieces.

What have I done? What have I done?

I assured her, my sweet baby, against all evidence to the contrary, that Jesus would take care of me like He always did. Somehow I knew He would.

When she'd calmed down, I forced myself to my feet. I grabbed the Not Dogs with my fingers poking out of the bandages. The holes in my hand felt like repositories of raw, stinging pain. I released the container, shocked by the fierce agony cutting through me.

The room went fuzzy, full of soft light.

"Dear Jesus."

A creature appeared before me with wings spread over its entire body. Each wing flared with plumes of golden fire. A sword of light emerged from the flames, and the creature lifted it high above its head.

I felt myself being plunged into a vision of Calvary. I was standing before the True Cross, my lowly Jesus nailed upon it. Then I bled on a cross beside Him, my hands already nailed to the wood. My body felt as fiery as the seraph in my vision. The words I prayed earlier came out of the mouth of crucified Jesus. "I want whatever You want me to have."

Jesus wept.

The seraph thrust its sword into my foot. A plaintive howl ripped from my throat as the fiery blade burned a hole in me. I slumped to the kitchen floor, and the room went black.

PRIEST

I was back at her townhouse in about an hour. I'd have brought her flowers, but God already saw to it that she had some.

Though I felt bad that she'd have to get up to answer the door, I knocked, hoping the ordeal wouldn't be excruciating. I tried my little-used patience. Waited. One or the other of them would let me in. At least I hoped so.

That's when her scream slammed into me, making my heart stutter. I cursed. Banged on the door.

"Gina!"

I tried the doorknob, cursing myself for locking it before I headed out. More curses spewed from my mouth as I threw my weight against the door to bust it open like I had the kind of weight or strength to accomplish that.

Desperate, I searched for a way to get in. Her neighbors had a few sizable rocks in their yard, part of an ill-advised landscaping project. I grabbed one hoping to God nobody would call the police on me. With all my strength I hurled it into Gina's picture window.

Zoe screamed, but not her mother. Glass showered the floor and I waited until the rain of shards stopped and pushed the remainder of the pane out with my elbow. A jagged edge ripped through my thin coat and sliced my arm.

It's taken more abuse.

I pulled myself through the window, yelling, "I'm coming, Gina!"

The icy breeze seemed to blow me in the rest of the way. I fell on glass, but only a few superficial cuts stung my hand.

Gina had the worst injury. Her bare foot bled a small puddle on the kitchen floor.

I told Zoe to go in her room and pray. I needed her out of the way, and God bless that child, she obeyed, eyes as wide as the lunch plates most likely she'd set on the table. "It will be all right, honey. I'm here now. It will be all right."

I made quick work of washing my hands and put on a pair of gloves Veronica had tossed in the bathroom wastebasket. I could touch Gina's blood, but I wouldn't let mine mingle with hers.

In the next ten minutes I cleaned and bandaged Gina's foot. I settled her in her bed, and while waiting for her state to pass, nailed the big comforter up to catch the wind flowing through the broken window. Exhausted, I comforted Zoe, fed her, and settled her in front of the television assuring her that Jesus and I would take care of her mom.

At last, sitting up in bed with Gina shivering in my arms, I waited for her to come back from wherever she was. I hadn't looked forward to something so much in years.

PRIEST

She woke up swaddled like a newborn in blankets. I sat on a chair by her bed. "Hey, you," I said.

A weak smile crept across her face. "My mouth feels parched so badly my lips hurt. Everything hurts, Priest. What happened? Why are you here?"

"I came back because Jesus said I couldn't pray if I didn't."

"Jesus spoke to you?"

"His words did. That's about as good as it gets for the likes of me, and I'm glad to get that much."

"It feels cold in here."

"Besides the fact that you probably still have a fever, your window is broken and maintenance hasn't come to fix it yet."

Her brow furrowed. "What happened to my window?"

"I told them some crazy person must have broken it trying to get in here. I didn't give any details."

"You have Band-Aids on your hands. Would you be that crazy person?"

"I've got a 'don't ask, don't tell' policy. Be glad. At least you don't have to pay for it yourself."

She tried to sit up. I eased her back down with my hand. "No can do, baby. You need rest."

"What time is it? I've got to get Zoe something for breakfast."

"It's one in the afternoon, Gina. I gave Zoe breakfast when she woke up. You'd have been proud of me."

"Well, she must be ready for lunch."

"Negative. I'm sure she ate at Miss D's."

This time Gina did sit up, pushing my hand away with her forearm.

"Stop it, Priest! How did she get to D's?"

"Mike took her, if you must know. I didn't want to leave you alone, and he thought it'd be good to get her out of the house and around some kids, just so she'd have some sense of normalcy."

She hugged her arms to herself, looking pitiful and small in that full-sized bed. "Mike was here again!" A statement, not a question. "How long before I'm at the hospital? And then Zoe goes straight into foster care?"

"Nothing's going to happen to Zoe."

"How do you know?"

"Because I'm not going to leave you alone again. No one's dumping a kid in foster care, sick mom or no, if the mom has help."

"You can't help me, Priest."

"I have to help you, Gina."

She sank back down on the mattress, and I pulled the covers over her shoulders. An idea had been stirring inside of me for hours. "I've been thinking," I said. "I've got a plan."

She cackled, an irksome sound. "Thinking? A plan? That sounds scary coming from you, Priest."

"You didn't think I was scary when you begged for my help."

If an entire face can frown, hers did. "I didn't beg, and as I recall you said no to me."

"Before you gave me my walking papers, prematurely might I
add. But fear not, Gina full of grace. I'm back. Maybe all of this is
happening for a reason."

"I'm not convinced."

"Do you know *anything* about stigmata, other than what you
read in *Mariette in Ecstasy?*"

"No, but I'm sure you do."

"I'm not an authority on it, but I picked up more than a few
facts. My Nana had extraordinary devotion to Saint Francis of Assisi.
She made pilgrimage to Assisi on three different occasions, one of
which included me."

She shook her head. "I cannot believe that."

"Believe it. And odd, but it was *I* who sat near you when this
happened. Coincidence or providence?"

"How 'bout negligence?"

"Somehow we're connected, Gina. I want to find out how as
much as you do."

"So what's your plan?"

"I don't want to say right now. But I'll tell you soon. One thing I
can assure you of is that Zoe will benefit as much as you will."

"Is this going to be a gonzo thing?"

"I'm afraid it'll be more radical than that."

My recklessness scared me almost as much as her slow crucifixion did.

CHAPTER SIXTEEN

MIKE

Someone had to check on Gina, despite the fact that Anthony was there. Maybe especially since he was there. I went myself. This was no task for the Sick and Shut-In Ministry to handle.

When I arrived I noticed the broken window. I knocked on the door and who should answer but the drama king, looking so refreshed I wondered if he got to play bed wench again.

He let me in and ushered me to Gina. He'd wrapped her tightly in blankets, and she slept as peacefully as a newborn.

"Reminds me of how Lacy used to bundle our kids."

"She was cold."

"It's drafty in here. Did you make sure Zoe stayed warm?"

"Of course. You can check on her. She's in her room similarly bundled."

I did, and she was, but I couldn't resist taking a shot at him. "Glad to know you didn't obligate yourself to being Zoe's bed wench." I regretted it as soon as it came out of my mouth.

Anthony snorted. "If you think I'd do something like that, you're the one who's sick."

The situation needed no added sarcasm. "Sorry, Anthony. That was uncalled for."

He shrugged my apology off.

We left Gina to rest and again sat on that crazy-colored love seat to have a man-to-boy chat.

"How long do you plan to hang around here?"

"Still trying to figure the plan out, Mike. You have to admit, the situation is a little unusual."

"It's not *your* situation."

"*Au contraire*, my friend. I'm neck deep in it. And so are you. Only I don't have to explain myself to anybody. I don't have to worry about what the church people are going to think, or question every decision because it'll affect somebody else. I have nothing to lose, which means I'm more available than you are."

The little twit ticked me off, but I couldn't deny the truth of *some* of what he said. "You're right, Anthony, whatever I do will be like a pebble in a pond. It'll send ripples through my church, but believe it or not, I care about what happens to her."

"Believe it or not, so do I."

"Your mom says you're one of the most self-absorbed people she's ever known."

"Veronica will tell you a lot about me. Keep in mind that most of it will be colored by her disdain."

"I've dealt with addicts before. I find as a whole when they're using they're mostly about themselves."

"Without turning this into an NA meeting, let me ask you one question: Why do I have her blood all over my clothes? Let me answer for you: Because I'm here. Helping her. These stains are evidence that even I can recognize grace in my midst."

Now I had to ponder things *he* said. Disturbing. But I'd do that on my own time. I wanted him to know he didn't have carte blanche to go sniffing around a single woman in my congregation twenty-four-seven, no matter how rosy she smelled.

"I understand grace. I'm a pastor. I preach it, and I live it. But word is spreading about Gina's condition. People are throwing around the S word, if you know what I mean."

"Are *you* spreading the good news, Mike?"

"I asked the three people who saw her hand to keep it to themselves. I only told my wife, Lacy, about the other wounds, and I know she isn't broadcasting the news. And then there's your mother. And you. What about you, Anthony, are you spreading the news? To create interest in a story maybe?"

A half-grin crept across his face. "I'm assuming the word is spreading among the *Vineyard* faithful. I don't happen to have your church directory. Try again."

"Gina has one. You've been here since Wednesday. That's more than long enough for you to find it."

"Maybe the Vineyard could use a boost. I didn't see that many people on Ash Wednesday. Big day for Christians. Maybe a miracle is just the thing a pastor needs to get his numbers up."

I needed to work on my long-suffering. If he said one more smart-alecky thing to me I'd strangle his scrawny neck.

If I don't end this chat I'm going to end up doing something I'll have to repent for.

"I'm going to say this again, Anthony. Gina needs to see a doctor for whatever this is. I'm going to give this a few more very prayerful, days, but you'd better make sure she's in church. If she isn't doing better by Sunday morning I'm ending this, and you can find some other woman, preferably not a woman of God, to slither around."

"She's an adult. And she's asked for my help."

"She's my spiritual daughter. I'm going to round up a group of ladies I trust to take care of her until we figure this out. Then you can leave."

"You have no idea what this is about."

"I don't have to. I know the Word of God says to avoid the appearance of evil. You're not going to bring reproach on her, I don't care how sincere you are."

"Veronica will be back. We won't be here alone."

"That's good. For now."

I didn't think I could trust Veronica either, but at least she'd protect her, even at the expense of her son, until I could find more reliable help.

Without a doubt he'd fail to get her to church. She rarely came to church ill, and this was as ill as I'd ever seen her. I left Anthony feeling a little triumphant.

On the way to my office, I remembered praying on my bed about this situation. I've known Christ as my Shepherd most of my adult life and, like John 10:4, I've followed His voice. Now I was salt-and-pepper-haired and in my fifties. I may have been wrong about many things, but not the guidance the Lord had given me. Jesus told me He had Gina in His hands and to let Him take care of her. That didn't mean I'd stop doing my job, however.

Not at all.

PRIEST

God upped the ante. I suppose that was the only way He'd get me to act. Mike made clear his intent to get me out of the way. We had to get this party started.

I considered the who, what, when, where, and why of the situation. Who: Gina. And me. What: She's got stigmata. I've got to protect her. Where: Here, where'd she'd be the most comfortable; my place isn't colorful. Now the big one. Why: God only knows, literally. "Why" for Gina meant we'd have to go deep into a mystery that wasn't cozy at all. For me the why was about a calling, a purpose, and if I wasn't called, I was *driven* to help her.

Zoe had her own set of the five Ws.

Sure, Mike could get a host of Vineyard sisters, my mother included, to go on casserole-and-prayer-chain duty. The thing was, he was bent on treating this as if it were a medical condition. Two days now, and Gina's wounds had no sign of infection, or healing. This wasn't an ordinary medical condition, though I knew sooner or later she'd have to go to the doctor. She'd need to go if only for evidence, to prove to herself and to the world that there was no natural explanation for the wounds. But she couldn't go in as vulnerable as she was.

The more I thought of my plan, the more logical—in a twisted way—it seemed. It could work all the way around. She needed some-one to run interference for her. She also needed someone everyone would have to go through to get near her. She needed a dad for Zoe.

I couldn't be Christ to her, but I could be Joseph. Gina needed a husband. And I needed Gina. Like I told her, my plan was more radical than gonzo. But it was the only way I could help her.

CHAPTER SEVENTEEN

PRIEST

Her fever had broken. Brave woman, she'd tottered all the way into the living room where the television watched me. She'd moved so stealthily I didn't hear her. Or maybe I was absorbed in my thoughts.

Perspiration beaded on her face from her effort. "Zoe's going to need something to eat soon. I'm going to make her dinner."

"No, you're not."

"Yes, I am."

"Why, Gina? I can feed her. You, too. You've got to be starving."

Her gaze went to her feet. She opened her mouth to speak; nothing came out but a sob. "Oh, Priest. I can't take care of my child."

I went to her. "Come here." I made the mistake of taking her in my arms.

Gina's arms went around my neck, and the dizzying gesture made me ache with want for her. I cradled the back of her head with my hand. At my touch she lifted her face to me, and I lowered mine to hers.

I knew then I'd fail. In everything.

Her lips grazed my cheek. She was so sweet I could consume her whole, but she couldn't be my manna. That was only a fantasy born of crushing loneliness and momentary sobriety.

"This is just a dark night," I whispered into her ear. "You are not lazy, or ill, or crazy. I know you need consolation, but you don't need this kind, and even if you did, I can't give it to you."

She tried to pull away from me, but I held her firmly. "It's okay that you feel like you do. I'm honored, but I have to protect you from me. I'm not rejecting you."

"Let me go," she said, trying to squirm away from me. I remembered showing up at her door and her telling me she'd knock me upside my head if I tried anything. She was wrong, however. I wasn't as weak as she thought I was, ironically, because of her. I was growing stronger by the day. She couldn't take me at all. I squeezed her.

"I'm going to hold you until you relax. I'm not rejecting you. I'm going to marry you, Gina. You're going to be my betrothed and my beloved."

Now she pushed with earnest, crying out from the pain of forcing her hands against me. "No."

"I'm going to marry you, and I'm going to take care of you and Zoe."

It was as if my words breached an interior levee in which she'd stored years of hopes, dreams, and tears. Some part of her protective barrier crumbled and rushed down a slope toward me. I couldn't take it—her—that soft, lovely brokenness.

I took her face in my hands and kissed her. My actions stunned me. I hadn't planned the kiss. The passionate moment swept me away. I said I'd marry her. I'd never uttered those words to anyone, not even Elle.

What surprised me was that she kissed me in return: passion for passion, weakness for weakness, and want for want.

I released her. Her head dropped, and it occurred to me that she might have felt ashamed. Neither of us spoke. I helped her to the love seat—she let me—and I seated her until she was comfortable.

"I'll fix you a late lunch," I said.

"I'm not hungry."

"Then I'll start on dinner for Zoe."

I headed into the kitchen, trying to convince myself of what they'd told me at the health department two years ago.

I couldn't spread it with saliva.

I told myself one kiss shouldn't hurt her. *Please God, don't let her catch it because I was stupid enough to kiss her.*

But just in case. I couldn't let it happen again. Ever.

GINA

Priest was crazy! He said he couldn't kiss me, but he did. He said he couldn't offer me that kind of consolation, and promptly told me he would marry me. He really *was* bipolar!

Jesus, have mercy, I thought I'd made a terrible mistake. My face burned with embarrassment. I don't think I could have been more mortified at my momentary weakness. I curled into my love seat, sick with shame and my raging desire.

You have to come back to me, Jesus. 'Cause that is a hot steaming mess, and my decisions are going from bad to worse. I can't do this—any of this—without You! I just wanted to share with You. You weren't supposed to leave me alone.

Every rejection I'd ever experienced collided into my thoughts: My own parents didn't seem to want me, and neither did Zoe's father. Oh, sweet Jesus, man after man turned his back until I was reduced to this sick, sad shell, like the fragile, dried-out carcass of an insect scattered in the wind.

"Why have You forsaken me?"

I squeezed my eyes shut, the canticle surging within to rail at my soul's true Lover.

> *Why, after wounding*
> *This heart, have You not healed it?*
> *And why, after stealing it,*
> *Have You thus abandoned it,*
> *And not carried away the stolen prey?*
>
> *Quench my troubles,*
> *For no one else can soothe them;*
> *And let my eyes behold You,*
> *For You are their light,*
> *And I will keep them for You alone.*

Reveal Your presence,
And let the vision and Your beauty kill me,
Behold the malady
Of love is incurable
Except in Your presence and before Your face.

I couldn't think about anything else.

I am leaving here. I have to go.

My thoughts were as dangerous as those that compelled me to drag razor blades across my wrists on another impossibly lonely Godless night.

PRIEST

When I returned to her with a plate of real-food imitations in my hand, I could tell something was wrong. She was leaving me again.

I don't care how many prizes I'd won, or how many articles I wrote, seeing this happening to her was like standing too close to fire. The staggering fear of it caused my breath to stall, a flame that burned to ash my words to describe it.

Gina really was the queen of sorrows, and she didn't need stigmata to prove it. He'd pierced her hands and feet. Not much left now. If she got all five wounds, He'd pierce her heart. I didn't know if this was going to happen before my eyes with me standing there holding tofu cutlets in my hand or not.

I set the plate down on the entertainment center, knelt before my Gina, and spoke. "Can you hear me?"

She didn't respond, but she hadn't gone away to ecstasy or

whatever it was, either. I'd hurt her. I didn't mean to, but I did. She was ignoring me.

I didn't know what to do with her. See, I'd learned all about the saints and how they loved God, but what I didn't know was who the people who *loved* the saints were, the ones closest to them. Who were the people God called to take care of saints? Not people like me; I was sure of it.

I felt so much for her, and I'd all but forgotten how to feel. So pardon me if I wrecked a few things.

Our clashes reminded me of a poem by Wendell Berry, ironically called "Marriage."

> *It is to be broken. It is to be*
> *torn open. It is not to be*
> *reached and come to rest in*
> *ever. I turn against you,*
> *I break from you, I turn to you.*
> *We hurt, and we are hurt,*
> *and have each other for healing.*
> *It is healing. It is never whole.*

That's what we were like. I never meant to hurt her, but inevitably I did.

GINA

I wouldn't eat.

The only hunger churning in me now was for Christ.

Priest didn't mind that I refused to talk or look at him but took issue when I wouldn't eat.

"You need your strength."

"It's Lent. I can fast if I want to."

He tried to guilt me into it. "So, is this a hunger strike? Are you going to do something else to hurt yourself?"

When I didn't respond he continued. "Let me ask you a question."

"As if I have a choice."

"Who's going to take care of Zoe if something happens to you? Your best friend?"

The pause must have been for dramatic effect. "Where is your best friend, by the way?" The smirk on his face amplified his maliciousness. "Oh, you don't have one, do you? Maybe your mom will take her. Oops! She isn't around either."

If my hands weren't wounded already I'd have socked him, and he kept going.

"Maybe Veronica can raise her. If she does as good a job as she did with me, Zoe will be a drug addict and a failure in short order. But at least she'll be able to cut her own strawberries. Microwave her own food."

Then the twist of the knife he plunged into me: "Wait. She already does those things. Go ahead and kill yourself. She doesn't need you at all."

Maybe I should have punched him with my blessed hand, but there was something in me that heard the painful truth hidden deeply in what he said. I sank deeper into myself.

Surely God would have spoken up then if He were going to at all. He didn't say a word.

PRIEST

I wasn't going to force-feed her.

The truth be told, my appetite had disappeared too. I felt like scum. Even though everything I said was true, I found no comfort in being right. I'd failed to speak the truth in love. Not that my actions should surprise anyone. What did I know about love?

Like her, I found myself in a story, only I was the bad guy, and a little confused about my character. I was a bad guy trying to do good, but all the signs pointing to my wretchedness were there. I was the junkie, the liar, the thief, the narcissist.

She'd mistaken me for the romantic interest. I didn't play that role so well. My own love story ended in tragedy, if you could call what I had with Elle love. Then again, maybe my *true* love waited at home for me: two packs of brown powder on my futon.

Most of us know what we hate about ourselves, but we find a way to forget about it to make it bearable. Heroin, crack, meth, but especially heroin—they made me forget what I hated about myself, if only for a short time.

God appeared to be Gina's drug of choice, and that seemed to be working out for her better than it had for Veronica.

Good for her. Maybe He would help her forget what she hates about herself. But He'd have quite a task on His hands. I'd given her a heckuva reminder.

I had the nerve to pray for her.

CHAPTER EIGHTEEN

VERONICA

I was happy when I got to Gina's, even after a twelve-hour shift at that godforsaken hospital. I hated nursing. It was a job and a woman could do it, but there was nothing about it to love. I was never meant to be a nurse. I had a higher purpose. I always knew that. I counted all those years as the refiner's fire, purgation to make me the woman of faith I am. And finally, something big was happening.

When I arrived at Gina's, Anthony was morose, as usual, in the kitchen sulking. He picked at some health food blessed Gina must eat for spiritual sustenance. She lounged on the love seat refusing to talk or eat. I didn't know what he'd done, but the idiot had done something.

She'd eaten for me before. Never gave me a minute of trouble. I knew I should have called off work. She was too delicate for him to run roughshod over. You can't just approach the sacred like a bull in a china shop. I'd be switched if I'd give him the chance to be alone with her again. I may as well have cast my pearls before swine.

I let him have it but good. "What did you do, you *re*tard?"

He tried to ignore me, and I'd be switched if I'd let him.

"I *said* what did you do to her?"

Once I read Anthony the riot act I planned on asking her how she fasted for Lent. I wanted to make sure she had whatever she needed. She was like a child in a lot of ways. Somebody had to take care of her and keep the riffraff away.

Since he wanted to act as mute as she was I made that horrible sound those poor deaf people make when they try to talk, and I pretended to sign it out. "Antwaanee! Whaaa nid n'you n'do?"

He rolled his eyes. "I'm going to go get Zoe from day care."

"Come here," I said. No way was I gonna let that kid get in the car with him if he was stoned out of his mind.

He stopped. Grimaced at me like I was being unreasonable. "Why, Ronnie? Why do I need to come to you?"

"I want to look in your eyes."

He mumbled, "I'm not high, Veronica."

"Yeah, I'm sure. So let me see already."

He tried to walk away from me, and lemme tell you, I sure as sharp wasn't gonna let that scrawny little jungle monkey get outta there without answering to me.

I snatched his arm and pulled him back, then grabbed his face.

I looked right into his eyes, but his pupils weren't constricted, for a change.

"Hurry up and get back here, and next time don't take Zoe *anywhere* without my permission. Or Mike's."

He looked at me like he was up to something even then.

Hmmph. Not if I could help it.

PRIEST

Stigmata: wounds of Christ, or marks corresponding to the marks left on Jesus' body after the crucifixion. Seen as a special grace in the Catholic Church, a favor of God granted to those of extraordinary piety who identify with Christ's suffering.

Stigmata: a mark of disgrace associated with a particular quality, circumstance, or person.

Gina had the wounds of Christ.

Me, I just had drug addiction as my stigmata. I wasn't revered, and didn't want to be, truth be told. I can't even say I wanted my mother to respect me. I'd let go of that dream when I was twelve, long ago, when I was still innocent and wanted to be a Franciscan who wrote great books about God. Now all I wanted was to be treated like a human being.

But nobody loves a junkie.

I trudged inside of Miss D's and Zoe ran to me, wrapping her little arms around me like she did Mike. It was the only moment during that day so far, except for when I'd locked lips with Gina, that I felt some semblance of happiness.

In that moment I understood why Jesus said unless we changed and became like children we couldn't enter the kingdom of heaven. Zoe loved without reservation. She didn't mind that I was lousy with wounds.

Not so Miss D. Upon seeing me her lips poked out in a frown and she put a hand on one of her cow-flank hips. Her eye flickered up and down my body. I don't think an MRI could have scanned me more thoroughly.

"What you doin' here?"

"I'm Anthony Priest. Mike told you I'd probably pick Zoe up."

"He told me somebody name Anthony Priest was comin' if he didn't. He ain't tell me enough, I see."

I wouldn't mind if she wanted to cream me. But I didn't want her to do it right in front of Zoe. "Would you like to see some identification?"

"I'd like to see more than that, brotha."

I wasn't going to do the "brotha" thing. Not now.

She wanted to see something. I pulled out my driver's license and press card. It was from a major newspaper. She took them both, and scrutinized them.

"Go get your coat, Zoe," I said.

But Miss D stopped her. "Wait a minute, baby." She searched the sign-in sheet. "I'ma see if yo' mama's pastor left a number I can call."

She couldn't find a number and actually got the telephone book and looked up the Vineyard. When she couldn't find a listing in the Wayne County Yellow Pages—and why would an Ann Arbor church be in the Wayne County phone book—she called directory assistance.

I stood there red-faced with embarrassment and anger. At myself, mostly.

Miss D couldn't see the scars on my arms. I wore a coat. No, she saw the less obvious ones I bore on my body. My gaunt appearance, the dark cast shadowing my skin—something I only saw on other addicts, and am, for all my words, hard pressed to describe. She looked like she could see through what was left of the body I dragged around like a cadaver into the dead soul rotting on the inside. It would have been easy to hate that shrew, or disregard her in the way I cut everybody off so I didn't have to feel, but she'd turned a harsh microscope on me and forced me to take a look at myself, the same way I brutalized Gina with "the truth." Only I'd treated Gina worse.

Miss D quite effectively made me hate myself a little more.

Zoe asked Mike if I was going to be her daddy. Not a chance, lucky kid.

Miss Dolly finished her phone calls. She never reached Mike. She called Gina's house. I stood there listening, not hearing what Veronica said, but knowing every contemptible detail.

She turned to Zoe. "Take yo' coat off, baby. Miss Dolly gon' take you home soon as I close. I'ma let you have a special treat for waitin'."

Zoe cried, and Miss D shooed her off to play with the other kids.

She leaned close to me and said, "Looka here. That baby's mama ain't wrapped too tight. She don't need no trouble. You hear? You stay way from Gina and Zoe Merritt. They don't need yo' kind."

I felt so low. I thought I might as well yell, "Unclean! Unlean!" before I came into a place. Clanging my bell of indignity with every step like any other leper.

CHAPTER NINETEEN

GINA

Veronica was answering my phone since I couldn't hold anything. I heard her talking to Miss Dolly.

I wondered what she would say if she knew I never met a Percocet I didn't love. Nobody, not even my doctor, knew that one of the main reasons I stopped with the 'scripts was because I'd become hopelessly addicted to them. He'd have kept feeding them to me. He thought I was a nice girl. That I'd caught more than a few tough breaks. He found my need for pain relief valid.

But what is pain?

First I took them when my physical misery had peaked. Oh, the waves of pleasure they gave me. Zoe loved it when I took my medicine, because I laughed and played and hugged and kissed her so much more. And God, how it killed me when I realized I was a better mother high as a Georgia pine.

Pretty soon I needed to take one every eight hours. Then every six. Several times I took them every three hours. By then I had become very generous with my definition of pain. All it took was a little blues coming down on me and I'd reach for the little football-shaped pills. I took them to help me sleep. On those hard days—and weren't they all hard?—I used them to chase the edge off the day.

I'd tell myself I had to stop, then fill another prescription too soon.

The doctor said I needed to deal with pain. He said if I didn't, it would alter the path of my neurons or something brainy, and that I'd damage myself beyond repair. I'd have a lifelong struggle because my body would become impervious to relief. In short, I would have taught myself to be in pain, and my brain wouldn't know how to do anything else.

I didn't have the heart to tell him nothing helped me manage pain anyway, and I was just an addict. Oh, I couldn't really call myself an *addict*. Such a hard word to speak regarding myself, *addict*. I was "tolerant" of the drug, "habituated," and concerned for my liver.

No, I was concerned for my *soul*. If I kept up the pace I was going, I'd never feel anything again.

That's what I thought as I lay on the love seat, listening to Veronica diminish her own son to my day-care provider. Later, after her acid tongue had practically melted my telephone, she turned on some Gregorian chant she bought to elevate the spiritual vibrations now that Priest was gone. As much as he wounded me with his malicious little speech, I felt sorry for him. I knew Miss D's wrath. Her bold assessments and graceless judgments. She'd already condemned me for my first stigmata in her eyes: attempting suicide. When she found out I was bipolar—I was dumb enough to tell her—she nailed me to a tree in her mind.

I prayed for Priest, that God would be gentle to him, and reveal Himself, even though He hid from me. I also prayed that he'd come back.

I thought about him telling me that I was not lazy, crazy, or sick because my hands and feet had holes in them. And I always felt lazy, crazy, and sick, whether or not I was.

He seemed to be, for better or worse, the only person who could see me for who I really was.

It was hard to hold anything against him.

PRIEST

I didn't exactly burn up the road trying to get back to Gina's. I'd have been glad to see her; it was Ronnie who was at risk of having me bludgeon her to death with one of those candles she'd brought. I'd show her the most powerful hand, all right.

Okay. Unnecessary. But anger is an engaging, absorbing friend to shield you from the grief threatening to break through your pores. Not as pleasurable as drugs, but an effective barrier between you and crushing sorrow in a pinch.

I missed Gina. I wanted to tell her all about what happened at Miss D's and how it made me feel. In return I'd hear her smart-mouthed replies that covered her own grief, but she'd talk to me. She'd listen.

Gina would make me laugh, delight me with a turn of phrase that I in my arrogance wouldn't have expected from somebody … like her, which goes to show you how little I saw.

At the rate things were going, I would probably want to touch her. I would definitely want her to touch me, and perhaps, if God was good to me, she'd heal more than my withdrawal symptoms.

What is a miracle? Why does God heal somebody from cancer and then they get killed by a drunk driver a year later? Why do some people go to the healing crusades to fill the coffers of swindlers who are no more moral than the worst pimps I know—sick, broken people who slog to their meetings, dragging two-ton bags of mustard seeds of faith—along with their generous offering—only to walk away as sicker than before because God didn't heal them?

Gina healed my drug sick, but I didn't know if she could take care of my love sick; God knows I had a serious withdrawal from *that* drug. And it started long before I met lovely Gina.

If I couldn't have Gina's brown sugar, the afro-mudflap girls on my sofa would do. I'd be home in ten minutes, and the brown powder twins would relieve me of my existential pain, or so I told myself before I changed course and rode to my Nana's old church. Hopefully my old friend Father Alessandro would be around. I'm sure he'd hear my confession.

CHAPTER TWENTY

FATHER ALESSANDRO DIAMANTE

Il mio fratello. My brother.

Anthony and I used to sit for hours at his Nana's—a blessed woman if ever there was one. She wasn't one for a lot of television, no, but we never needed it. I've met few souls who possess Anthony's imagination. Oh, we must have been eight years old. My dear mother, God rest her, worked so hard, as we'd lost my father to cancer when I was just a *bambino*. Nana often cared for me.

Anthony and I would sit on the floor for hours in his little room, sorting through stacks of holy cards for trade. He would tell me saint stories. Even then he loved stories.

I always thought he'd go to seminary. The holy gospels say, "A little child shall lead them." It was Anthony who fueled my love for God, the saints, and our lady in that tiny room when he was just a boy, my poor friend.

Without a doubt I was surprised to get his call. I must confess, when he'd told me of his illness and I hadn't heard from him for two long years, I feared him dead. Always I lit candles for my friend. Always. And suddenly there was his voice on the telephone like a gift.

I often left the rectory to enjoy a respite before evening Mass, but having received his call I waited in the sanctuary for him.

The gospel of Saint Luke says, *There was a man who had two sons.* Surely Anthony and I were our Father's children: Anthony the prodigal, and I the dutiful son. *After he had spent everything, a severe famine took place ... and he began to be in want.*

That's what I heard in his voice: want.

So he set off, and went to His father.

You can't imagine my anticipation. I saw him when he walked into the nave, his coat draped over one of his arms. Blood stained the collar of his shirt.

But while he was still far off, his father saw him and was filled with compassion; he ran and put his arms around him, and kissed him.

Our Father is very, very good, and I believe this gospel offers to all a fine example. I wanted to do as our Father would.

It was I who joyfully ran to meet my brother. I put my arms around him and spoke the words of grace to him before he could utter his "I am not worthy" speech.

"This brother of mine was dead, and is alive; he was lost, and is found."

I kissed both his cheeks, and let my own tears fall upon his face.

"Come, *mio povero*, we must go to the Father for the sacrament of reconciliation. We must dress ourselves in the garments of sons of God. We must eat of the fattest calf together."

My brother wept in my arms, and I noticed, despite his having slept among swine, Anthony bore a faint scent of roses.

PRIEST

Oh, my God, I am heartily sorry.

The words had never felt so true as they did that evening. It took us a while. I'd wracked up more than a few mortal sins, venial ones, and probably some that hadn't been named yet.

I told God everything, holding nothing back, and Alessandro listened—father, brother, and friend.

Why did it take me so long? I sat alone in my little hovel and in the darkness of my mind believed the whisper of demons that I had no friends, no family, no one who cared. And love was ten minutes down the street.

I could have chosen what Alessandro did all along; life over the liquid death I pumped into my arms, and the comfort He gave me:

"God, the Father of mercies, through the death and resurrection of His Son, has reconciled the world to Himself and sent the Holy Spirit among us for the forgiveness of sin; through the ministry of the Church, may God give you pardon and peace, and absolve you from your sins in the name of the Father, and of the Son, and of the Holy Spirit."

I came into that church a sad, lost boy; I left it a man again.

Forgiven.

CHAPTER TWENTY-ONE

PRIEST

Having experienced a spiritual awakening, I wanted to spread the love. I went to the Saint Anthony of Padua Nursing Facility to visit my Nana.

It had been several days since I'd gone, but I never let too much time pass. I can't say I was altogether unselfish. I wanted Nana to remember me, each and every time I walked into her room, but she never did.

How I prayed, to God, to Jesus, even to Saint Jude, patron saint of hopeless causes. I begged Saint Anthony, my name saint, and patron saint of the elderly and lost things on her behalf, chanting a childhood rhyme Nana taught me.

"Tony, Tony, rally 'round. Something's lost and can't be found."

What I couldn't find was my Nana in that shell of a woman sitting in that nursing home.

"Saint Anthony, intercede to our Lord that He bring her back to me, if only for a moment."

I'd show up dutifully, all my hope resting on that scant request.

The staff greeted me, as per usual. I nodded in answer and walked briskly down to the hallway to her room. I gathered my nerve and prayed again. In my unworthiness I begged Saint Anthony to intercede. Finally, I opened the door and braced myself.

My heart felt weighted with chains as I took off my coat and placed it on the chair across from her. Nana lay in her hospital bed, infantile and unresponsive. Compassion surged in me for her. In a way, I had no choice. I'd been given a miracle. Sobriety. If the closest thing I had to a miracle in a long time had changed me, I had to see if Nana, lover of stigmatics, would respond to Gina's graces.

I took off my blood-stained shirt and lay it on top of her, the scent of roses rising from it like incense. I'd used the sleeve of it so many times to tie around my arm before I shot dope into my vein. I thought of the words to a rosary Nana was particularly fond of. One that reminded me of Gina.

"O Jesus," I said, "Divine Redeemer, be merciful to us and to the whole world.

"Strong God, Holy God, immortal God, have mercy on us and the whole world. Amen."

Tears came to my eyes, and I could barely choke out any more of the words.

"Grace and mercy, O my Jesus, during present danger; cover us with Your precious blood. Amen. Amen. Amen."

I wiped my eyes and took a deep breath, hoping this prayer would encompass Nana, my worthless self, and my sweet Gina. I offered it up, wiping her face like Veronica, not my mother, but Veronica of the stations of the cross. Her glassy blank eyes stared out at nothing. I hoped like Christ, His image would imprint Himself on that cloth of mercy, and Jesus would heal my Nana.

"Eternal Father, I offer You the wounds of our Lord Jesus Christ to heal the wounds of our souls." I added in my mind, *And bodies, too, Lord.* "My Jesus, pardon and mercy, through the merits of Your holy wounds."

I waited, but nothing happened.

Finally, I kissed my Nana on the forehead, put my shirt back on, and went on my way.

GINA

The story of the prodigal son …

When he came to his senses, he said, "I am starving to death!… I will set out and go back to my father and say to him: 'Father, I have sinned against heaven and against you. I am no longer worthy to be called your son.…'"

So he got up and went to his father.

Priest returned to me changed. Literally. He even had on different clothes.

He came to the door with a loaf of bread in his hand and a burden off his back. Veronica let him in with her usual barrage of verbal abuse at the ready.

"Where have you been?"

He responded by hanging up his coat in the closet.

Veronica ripped into him again. "I hope you weren't out getting high and coming back here with your tail between your hind legs like this is some kind of halfway house."

He smiled, a small, gentle smile. "I went to see Nana. And Alessandro; he said tell you he said hi." Priest held up the loaf. "They had some raisin bread left over from donations. He didn't want it to go bad. I thought Zoe would like some."

Zoe shot out of room like a rocket launched her. "Mr. Anthony!" she exclaimed. "How come *you* couldn't take me home?"

"I wasn't ready. Maybe next time, moppet," he said. "Want some raisin bread?" The generosity in his smile eclipsed his sweet gift of bread.

Zoe said, "Yaaaaaaay."

On the inside so did I.

Veronica stood there with her hands on her hips. Maybe she was trying to figure out what to do now that Zoe's unconditional love had sucked the poison out her venom.

"Excuse me." Priest stepped past her. "I'm going to wash my hands and give Zoe a snack."

She trailed behind him. I couldn't see them but heard every word.

"I hope you don't think getting religion is going to change you. You'll need to go to NA meetings. Everything."

"Good thing God has everything."

"You're not serious."

"Sorry, Veronica. It's not the kind of thing you talk about."

A moment later the two of them came back into the living room. Zoe must have stayed in the kitchen to eat. He came over to me, with a saucer of bread cut into eight small squares. He sat with me on the love seat, Veronica behind him harping.

"She's not gonna eat. Don't you think I've tried?"

He attended to me as if she wasn't there at all. He leaned forward. "I am so, so sorry for the things I said. Will you please forgive me?"

Veronica flipped. "What do you say to her, idiot? What did you do, you little foul-mouthed weasel?"

"I forgive you," I said. And I meant it.

She kept going. "You can forgive, but you'd better not forget. Honey, I told you he's dangerous."

Anthony sighed, but kept most of his attention on me. Veronica finally quieted, hands still on her hips. I'm sure she was waiting for me to reject his offering.

He lifted the plate toward me. "Would you like some? We can call it the bread of sorrows and partake together."

What a sweetie.

"I've had my fill of the bread of sorrow," I said, "but I'll take a few squares anyway."

"Father Alessandro is my friend. We grew up together. I told him all about you, and he wants to meet you."

Veronica tore into him. "You told somebody? How do you even know if you can trust him? He's a Catholic priest, moron! They might come in here with their Vatican miracle detectives and try to claim she's a fraud."

I'd hoped I could handle the bread—sweet, nourishing and kinda nutty, just like Priest—but it felt like I was swallowing glass. I tried to force it down, but it wouldn't go. He held the plate close to my mouth.

"Are you okay?"

"I can't eat. I'm sorry."

"When is the last time you had any food?"

"Fat Tuesday. At work. I wanted to fast on Ash Wednesday."

Priest shook his head, "You haven't eaten anything since Tuesday."

"I'm hurting. I just don't feel like eating."

Veronica went off on him again. "She's a stinkin' mystic. She probably has to live off the host."

"Which would be great if she were Catholic! She doesn't partake of the Eucharist at the Vineyard, Ronnie, and you'll excuse me for saying, but if they don't believe the 'this is My body, this is My blood' thing, in a very real sense, it probably won't be as nourishing to her."

Anthony frowned. I tried to reassure him.

"It's just fasting for a few days. Christians are supposed to fast."

"But Gina, you didn't drink much water, either. You can't hold a cup by yourself. I doubt if you drank while I was gone."

"So what?" Veronica said. "She'll drink when she's ready."

"She can die, Ronnie. She has to eat and drink."

"Living miracles aren't subject to the laws of nature."

Priest shook his head, but he kept his eyes fixed on me. "Living miracles die. You've got to have something. Please."

"No."

Veronica started in on Priest again, and while the two of them argued, I thought about my lack of desire for food and what he said about me dying. The words "she can die" watered the fertile ground in which the seed of my death had been buried. I really could die, and true to form I didn't mind so much.

God would find somebody to take care of Zoe if He took me away. If it was *Him*, not me, doing the taking.

PRIEST

I said I knew some facts about stigmata. I also knew what it wasn't. The books with the accounts of authentic stigmatics also threw in a few frauds for good measure. Then there were the books that question if anyone was a stigmatic at all and not merely a hysterical zealot. In other words, a crazy.

I let Gina rest and went into the living room to do some research on her MacBook. Ronnie lit into me right away.

"What are you doing now?"

"I just want to look something up."

"What?"

"Can you back up off me, Veronica? I'm not going to steal Gina's computer. I want to research something so maybe I can help her. She needs to eat and drink."

"Just how do you think the Internet is going to help you, genius? This is an act of God. It goes against the laws of nature."

"I believe we're dealing with a miracle too. But all stigmatics die. Saint Francis died. Saint Catherine of Siena and Saint Padre Pio. The only person with those wounds who didn't die was Christ Himself, and even He died. He just rose from the dead."

She raged on, but I tuned her out, intent on finding the site with the medical information I was looking for. After a few minutes I found it and read:

*Scientists and scholars alike argue that mystical experiences
are a biochemical reaction to severe fasting and self-denial
(holy anorexia). Serotonin levels drop and the brain misfires,
causing shifts in both personality and perception. A person can
experience auditory and visual hallucinations, and in severe
cases, stigmata, spontaneous bleeding of the skin* (psychogenic
purpuras). *One can truly believe he or she is encountering
God during these "ecstatics," which are likely dissociative or
schizoid states.*

The words sobered me.

What if Gina was completely out of her head? And I was out
of mine along with her? Veronica, too, all of us caught in a grand
delusion because we wanted to see some evidence of the God who so
often eluded us?

What if we were doubting Thomases in reverse, seeing so that
we could believe?

The truth is, I didn't want Gina to be *that* crazy. I needed her to
be what I wanted her to be: chosen. That way I could hang on to the
idea that since God had brought us together He must still love me,
was with me, and wouldn't give up on me.

That's a whole lot of *me*, but at the time I didn't see it that way.

Sure, I thought about talking to Mike about what the fasting could
do to her, but what if she wasn't crazy at all? What about the aroma of
the wounds? The fact that they neither healed nor putrefied?

I decided I'd find a way to get her to eat and drink. Somehow.
And then I'd see. Even if she wasn't a stigmatic and hadn't healed me
at all, something about her was healing.

That would be enough.

As I stared at that computer screen, deep in thought, my cell phone rang. It was the nursing home. I wasn't the primary contact person, but the staff knew me well enough to call *me* instead of Veronica if something went wrong. I supposed they'd also call me in case something went miraculously right.

I answered promptly.

"Mr. Priest," a cautious voice said.

"Yes." My heart swelled with faith.

"I'm calling from Saint Anthony's, the nursing home where your grandmother is."

"Yes, how may I help you?"

"I'm afraid you need to come in, right away. Your grandmother, Mrs. Morelli, has passed away."

I almost dropped Gina's computer I stood up so fast.

VERONICA

Anthony looked like he saw a ghost.

"What now?" I said. Could have been anything with him.

"Nana." He paused. "Mom," he said. He never called me Mom. I didn't let him. "Nana's gone."

"What do you mean she's gone? Am I going to have to go down there and tell somebody off? What a bunch of incompetents, letting her wander off. I told you she didn't belong with those Franciscan freaks."

"She died."

I froze. For a minute I felt a little confused. I hate to admit it, but I'd wished that woman dead so many times when I was young it wasn't even funny. The burdens she forced me to bear! To go to that God-awful maternity home, pregnant with the baby of a nigger I hated. To bring that little bastard home and then force me to raise him when I couldn't stand to look at him. She took my life away. She ruined me for white men and I sure as sharp wasn't gonna get one that wasn't white. And now I had to bury her.

Then it hit me. She was my mother.

Oh, Lordy. Oh, Jesus.

I sank down on Blessed Gina's orange love seat, stunned, until understanding dawned on me.

Oh, Jesus, my mother is gone. My mother is gone.

PRIEST

I thought I killed my Nana.

For the second time in my life, someone I loved had died because of something I did or didn't do.

Yes, my opinion of myself was wholly self-important. It didn't even occur to me at the time that death may have been a relief to her. That finally, after years of being diminished, she could cast off her useless body. I missed the idea that being with Jesus, face-to-face, may very well have been the healing I prayed for.

It was all about Anthony.

I could have sat there wrapped up in *me* for hours, but Veronica's wails pricked my very soul. She'd become a fount of sorrow. Veronica—who rarely went to check on her mother, who seemed to hate that kind, God-fearing woman without a cause—was grieving.

Gina sat beside her, offering what consolation she could. Every effort brought her pain. I could see it in the agony of her face, and yet she tried to comfort her. My mother. Not hers.

I'd pondered the meaning of miracles that week almost obsessively, when I wasn't fixated in my thoughts on Gina the woman, not the saint. I don't think I thought much of what miracles require.

I looked on that love seat and saw huddled together two incarnations of Christ: a stigmatic showing me the Suffering Son of Man, the Man of Sorrows, acquainted with grief. And that incarnation of Christ was giving comfort to another; a wounded child—still a teenage girl in many ways. Petulant. Angry. Sad. Unfinished. And she, as blessed Mother Teresa of Calcutta would say, was Jesus in one of His distressing disguises.

Seeing them forced me to act.

The words Christ said to Saint John came to me, and in that moment, I became John, beloved disciple, and Jesus was speaking His words to me.

"Behold, your mother."

And I could see Veronica as God wanted me to, for the first time in my adult life.

I went to her to offer up my love.

GINA

We were all wounded, and I wasn't speaking of the wounds of Christ on my body. All three of us had mother aches.

I couldn't imagine that call. Sometimes, I prayed that I would die before my mother to spare me whatever chasm of grief I'd fall into when I heard of her death, even though I scarcely knew her.

Sorrowful mothers made me think of my own baby. I wondered

if Zoe would grow up to hate me for being bedridden, depressed, crazy, and now this.

What a tangled mess of humanity we were, interacting with one another and interconnected in ways we could never fully understand. We loved. We failed in love. We protected ourselves. We harmed ourselves in a myriad of ways.

We had regrets.

We wept.

We held on to one another until we had to let go, which would be all too soon.

VERONICA

So what. I let Anthony comfort me. But I comforted him, too. It was like it always is when somebody dies, you come together with a bunch of people you can't stand, but before the first handful of dirt is thrown on the casket none of you are speaking again.

He told me he'd take care of all the arrangements, but I'll be switched if I'd let him near real money. He'd been slick enough before to get a check I wrote out to *somebody else* cashed. Nossiree. I'd take care of things myself, and he'd lounge around all sad-eyed sucking up sympathy, blessings, and the intercession of Blessed Regina Delores.

And he wanted Alessandro to do the funeral. His friend! I smelled a rat. Nosirree. Mike Adams was going to officiate over my mother's funeral at the Vineyard West. It was the only way to keep everything from going to hell in a handbasket.

I know. Jesus said for us to let the dead bury their dead. But He didn't have to deal with Anthony, who could be worse than Judas Iscariot, if you asked me. Even the dead have more going for them than Anthony. No, Ronnie was gonna have to bury the dead. And isn't that just how it is?

I've always believed Martha got a bum deal. She loved Jesus just as much as Mary did, and I could just see her, lemme tell you, working her fingers to the bone, and what did she get? Worse than bony fingers, I'll tell you that much. She got rebuked.

All she wanted was a clean house for Jesus. Everybody's more comfortable when the house is clean. I read that story over and over, and I didn't see what was so wrong with that, but that stinkin', lazy Mary gets the praise.

She *benefited* from Martha's nice clean, comfortable house, and Martha's cooking, too. Does anybody talk about that? You're not gonna have Jesus Christ sitting in your midst someplace the health department is gonna shut down.

I wanted to be Mary, but if I were her, all I'd get was a dirty house falling down on top of me, and isn't that just how things happen?

But I'd make sure Anthony wouldn't be able to do too much damage while I took care of funeral arrangements. And I had a few more things in mind. Big things. I had to make something happen fast, now, or it would all fall apart.

I believed that.

So, yeah, I made a few calls. I did it all for Blessed Gina's protection. Honest to God, I did.

PRIEST

I suppose I should be grateful Veronica and I had a moment, and I do mean a *moment.* Then she turned back into Veronica and I her loathsome scourge. Gina's presence in my life made all the difference, along with Alessandro, who took over an hour to talk me through the shock of it all.

Veronica ordered pizza for dinner that night, which she ate with gusto. Zoe enjoyed it too. I didn't touch it, and neither did Gina. Unfortunately, I was a too disjointed to force the issue, and too selfish to upset her, which could deny me her sympathy. I did get her to drink an eight-ounce glass of water, which she took in an ounce at a time over a several hours.

While I didn't think God was mad at me for making Gina drink, He may have taken issue with my attempt to heal Nana with Gina's blood. He took Nana away from me like He'd take Gina, perhaps sooner than I wanted to believe.

I didn't understand a thing that night. *Nothing.*

Afro-mudflap girl called out to me with her soothing, sultry voice. But I resisted her.

When I'd finally tucked Zoe into bed, I sat with Gina on the love seat. I felt as if my feelings for her would spill through my skin, but I had a habit of fatally wounding the women in my life. In my state of mind I could scarcely discern miracle or madness, not even when it was right in front of me. I began to doubt my ability to help her.

I was so tired. *I* wanted to lie in a bed of roses. Let Gina be as close as the Holy Ghost is.

"Gina," I said, "be Christ to me."

She opened her arms and held my head in her wounded hands. And like the disciple John, I laid my head upon her breast.

CHAPTER TWENTY-TWO

GINA

I didn't expect him to be all right, but he was more than just grief stricken. He was dangerous. I recognized the symptoms.

He'd withdrawn somewhere inside of himself, to a place I couldn't reach, because he no longer wanted to be reached. I knew that kind of poverty, the kind blind to abundant generosity right in your face. But to his credit, he stuck around. He helped with my daughter, which I felt so guilty about I thought it'd kill me. He needed to be served, but he served me. And I was too incapacitated to do much but murmur my pity in his ear with my aching arms wrapped around his neck.

But Priest didn't know how to be loved. He pulled away too quickly, and my feet were too wounded to chase after him.

After he got off the phone with his friend that evening, the other calls started. The zombie that looked like Priest had to answer them since I still couldn't pick up anything without shards of pain slicing through my palms.

According to him, most of the callers, even the ones who'd offered both of us condolences, were so much like Miss Dolly sitting in judgment about our tragedies, but their own troubles they could ignore. It was the trials and tribulations of others they made sure to have a hand in, whether or not said hand was needed.

Well, maybe some callers were sincere. Priest didn't say. Like I said, he still hadn't learned that love could be all around him; he simply missed it because he assumed it wasn't there. I understood those kinds of pain-filled, futile thoughts. I had enough of them myself.

I decided to see the callers through a filter of grace. I was bleeding spontaneously, and Priest's grandmother had died. People would call. There was no cause, despite Priest's sullen insistence that people were watching our tragedy unfold like vultures, for either of us to be paranoid. Or so I believed.

I thought Veronica might have told one or two people, and maybe they told one or two. In my mind, nobody was going to see this as anything but Gina Merritt snapping again and that poor junkie, now having something awful happen to him, going back to dope that much faster. And I thought they might be right about both of us. I still wasn't sure.

I mean, what did I know? In some ways, I was such an innocent.

PRIEST

I learned a long time ago that things aren't always what they seem to be. Take all those urban legends for instance. How many e-mails about atheist Madalyn Murray O'Hair's petition to ban religious broadcasting does a person have to get before they realize the woman was missing since the nineties and was discovered to have been murdered in the year 2000? I think I got one of those three months ago.

People love to be hysterical. Doesn't take much to rouse them. The truth makes little difference when they're in such a state.

I knew that as a journalist. I tried to tell her that when the calls started something wicked this way was coming. How could I be so stupid not to spirit her away immediately? We were about to walk into disaster, and I was too caught up in my misery to protect us, or rather, her and Zoe.

CHAPTER TWENTY-THREE

GINA

Sunday morning, and my four wounds wept blood profusely. Despite the crippling pain, after Priest washed and bandaged my wounds, I made a big effort to totter around the house, failing miserably. Priest, thankfully, seemed to have no problem continuing to serve me, even with the vacant look in his eyes.

"We should go to church," he said, flatly.

"Are you sure? It's been a rough night. I don't think God will mind if we take the day to collect ourselves."

"He'll mind."

"Priest, I'm chronically ill. I've missed church before."

"You can't miss this Sunday."

I didn't understand it. He'd been so tender and kind. And now he seemed to be forcing the issue of going to church.

"I'd like to stay home."

"If you do, it'll all fall apart, Gina. You have to trust me on that. I'm not quite myself. I can't protect you like I could if … if I wasn't hurting so badly. I told you, I'm not used to feeling. I'm having a hard time here, but I have to take you to church. Maybe God will do something for me while I'm there too. But I have to take you. You *have* to go today, and I promise, after that we'll do … or not do … whatever you want."

I didn't know what was going on, but I could tell this was important to him.

"Okay, we'll go to church."

I tried.

I showered *myself*, thank you very much! My pain may have been increasing, but the more time I spent with him, the more my affections for him grew. He wasn't going to weaken me again with his soft touch and those pitiful opal-like eyes melting me.

I dressed myself too, no matter how difficult the task. I'd pulled out a long shift—one of the few pretty dresses I owned—and wrestled it on. If I do say, I was one hot mama, even though I felt like Priest *looked*.

There is some benefit to being chronically ill. I make it my business to use the best means available to me to make myself comfortable. Sometimes it hurt to have anything touch me, including clothing. The absence of prescription drugs meant the presence of natural, breathable, wonderfully touchable fabrics.

I wore sensible shoes too. I had a pair of Børn clogs, two pairs of Birkenstocks—one for winter, and one for summer. And some Ugg boots.

The Uggs were out. The clogs were a bit narrow for my feet, swollen, sore, and bandaged. I went for the Birkenstocks. They were nice and wide, and with socks they'd keep me warm.

It was Priest who put my socks on for me. He was gentle, but the experience was not without pain. I tried to hold my breath and just endure it but punked out early on. At one terribly tender spot I shrieked.

"I'm so sorry," he said, just like the first time he held me, the bed wench.

"It's okay. But I'll tell ya, those crucifixions are *murder*."

He laughed at my stupid joke. "I'm sure Jesus is nodding ..." He fashioned his voice into a thick Jewish accent. "Tell me about it! Oy!" His joke was worse than mine, but he laughed, and that was good.

Priest put my socked feet together. Held them between his hands. He lowered his head and touched his forehead to them, surprising me with a blessing.

"How beautiful on the mountain are the feet of the messenger announcing peace."

I shrugged it off. "I don't know about that. I don't even want to go out and use these feet today." I looked into his sad eyes. "I know this is important to you, and I want to be there for you in the same way you've been here for me, but I'd be lying if I didn't say I wasn't discouraged. I know Mike thinks I'm having another episode. Maybe he's right. Maybe I should just go to the hospital, for crying out loud."

"That'll make matters worse right now, Gina."

"Maybe. I don't know, Priest. I don't even hear God anymore. Maybe that's a good reason to listen to my spiritual shepherd instead."

"I'm the shepherd now, Gina. I'm the Priest. Listen," he said "a story ..."

PRIEST

"Saint Mary Frances of the Five Wounds"

Sometimes, it's the people closest to you who give you the most trouble, and God knows I know the truth of that statement.

Anna Maria was born to a middle-class family in Naples. Her family had the high hopes all parents have for their daughters— that she'd be happy and marry a man as rich as sin. Her father had secured her as intended, and all was well except for one thing: Sixteen-year-old Anna didn't want the rich man. In fact, she didn't want any man. She had her own intentions, and they included staying a virgin for life, giving herself to God alone, and becoming a Franciscan sister.

Yes, she had a thing for Saint Francis. Remember what happened to Cloretta Robinson, who only colored pictures of him? Saint Francis tends to give people ideas, and the next thing you know they're being crucified, or at least radically changed.

Her family did not appreciate Saint Francis of Assisi.

When her father realized that she'd have nothing to do with the eighteenth-century Donald Trump he'd chosen for her and was talking about becoming a Franciscan tertiary, renouncing sex *and* money, he locked her in her room. He spared her not the rod of his wrath. After he beat and threatened her to no avail, he finally gave up and let her join the order, but only if she lived at home.

Oh, joy.

Actually, Saint Francis would have called it *perfect* joy, for she would suffer.

She took the name Mary Frances and gave herself to living the gospel way of Francis in poverty, chastity, and obedience. Her brothers, sisters, and father treated her horribly for years, knowing she was a "turn the other cheek" kind of girl. Even her father confessor—her *pastor,* so to speak, completely misunderstood her, and that's true to how life is for many, many gifted special souls, fair Gina.

It must have been so hard for her to be despised, and maybe they thought she was crazy. I don't know if she felt God's silence, but she had to feel her family's disdain for her and her pastor's disbelief. Yet she continued in good works, helping the helpless, loving the loveless.

Sister Mary Frances devoted herself to the passion of Christ, and this was no movie. She lived the way of the cross daily, following Him into both His death and His favor. And not only for herself. Like little Cloretta Robinson, this teenage girl and Franciscan sister continuously prayed for the healing of needy souls everywhere.

The little poor woman, Sister Mary Frances, took her sufferings and gave them to God as an offering: the beatings, neglect, persecution, and misunderstanding. God accepted her sacrifice— her bloody, painful sacrifice—and He allowed her to share in His passion by placing the stigmata on her hands, feet, and finally her side. Every year until her death she experienced the passion ecstasies. And Gina, there are *still* people who don't understand her.

You're in good company.

GINA

"Way to cheer a sistah up, Priest," I said, hoping he didn't miss my sarcasm. "Thanks."

"What?"

"Now I'm thinking I could get the side wound too. And ow!"

He laughed. "Come on, Gina. I know you count it an honor to suffer with Christ."

"What if it's *you* that's misunderstanding me, and I really am crazy?" Truthfully, the thought was never far from my mind. "And this silence. How am I supposed to know this is of God when He won't share with me?"

"He *is* sharing with you. Just not in the way you're used to. Be glad He's sharing with you at all. Some people never get a sense of God. Mother Teresa suffered the dark night of the soul for decades. The point I'm trying to make is, whether or not we feel Him, God is present."

"But I'm Pentecostal! We charismatic folks need a God we can *feel*."

"I'm not expert on spiritual things, so take everything I say as regurgitations of the spiritual masters I've stored in my head." He sighed, heavily. "We feel, or we try not to feel. God doesn't change. Maybe we should trust He has His best interest for us. I don't know, Gina. I'm not that ambitious. I'd be happy if I could do right. He doesn't have to speak to me. If I could do anything with integrity I'd know God was present."

"Can you feel Him? Now?"

For a moment he didn't answer. He looked down at my hands and feet, then back up and into my eyes.

"Let me tell you something, queen of sorrows, I know these wounds are hard for you to understand. I don't understand them. They are firmly planted in the land of mystery. Let's say you are crazy. By some act of will you've caused this to suffer with Him. That alone would impress me. Or how about if you did this to yourself on purpose? You burned, or stabbed, or did something unimaginable to yourself. If you did it to suffer with Christ, that is amazing devotion. It's a very medieval expression, and certainly ill-advised, but it's devotion. What else would it be? I don't see you trying to get attention, or any secondary gains. Are you still with me?"

"Yeah. I am. Go on."

"Now let's say God orchestrated it all. Maybe this thing that happened to you wasn't for you, but for me. Maybe I'd forgotten how real what Jesus did on the cross was. How bloody, and painful, and horrible it all was. So I see your hands, but they don't speak to me of you. They speak to me of Him. They point me back to Calvary. You understand what I'm saying?"

He looked as if he struggled to find the words to express himself. Tapped his fingertips on his thigh. Finally: "I think it's real, Gina."

He paused for a long time. "Remember when you said, 'Be Christ to me'? You were Christ to me *first*, Gina, when you opened your whole being, for whatever reason, and said like the blessed mother you were named after, 'Behold, the handmaiden of the Lord; be it unto me according to Thy word.' You received this gift, and now when I look at your hands and feet, I see you giving Christ to me. Like she did."

He put his hands on my shoulders. "I couldn't be Christ to you the night you asked me to. I was too afraid and maybe too tempted by what my own flesh both wanted and needed, so let me be Christ to you right now, the voice of His mercy toward you this morning."

Priest touched his hand to my chin, then cradled my face. "Gina, Christ says to you with the assurance of His Word, 'Lo, I am with you always, even unto the end of the world.'"

And if that wasn't enough, he added the words of my second favorite mystic, Saint Teresa of Avila. He'd paraphrased it, but I liked his version:

> *"Let nothing disturb you.*
> *Let nothing frighten you.*
> *Everything passes.*
> *But our God never changes.*
> *With patience you can obtain all things.*
> *You who have God lack nothing.*
> *God is enough for you.*
> *Christ has no body now but yours,*
> *No hands, no feet—none but yours.*
>
> *"Yours are His eyes to look with love on the world.*
> *Christ has no body now but yours."*

I gathered him into a hug, and cried all over his clean shirt.

PRIEST

I was so depressed my most compelling reason to rejoice that morning was that I didn't have to arm-wrestle Veronica to take Gina and Zoe out with me.

Gina made a brave effort to be more independent. Even after Ronnie left to handle Nana's affairs, Gina put on the strong-girl act. She'd grown weaker and her pain had increased, but she was unrelenting in her courage, though I doubt if she'd see it that way. I admired her for her fortitude, but maybe the fact that I had to fight my own weakness so diligently bothered me. I still thought about the dope I left at home, I still wanted Gina in a very sensual way, I also doubted my decision to ask her about marrying me—if I could bring myself to ask her at all. I was bat crazy to think she'd give it a thought, even after I'd gone to confession and had my soul cleansed.

We drove to the Vineyard West, all the way in Ann Arbor, sister church to the Vineyard East in Detroit. Why did she go to church in Ann Arbor? The Detroit church was actually closer, but I didn't ruminate too long on it. Gina stayed quiet as we rode, and Zoe prattled on about little-girl matters.

I fretted about what would happen with Veronica and me now that Nana was gone. I worried about the changing dynamics between us if I stayed clean. Recovery, the few times I'd actually tried it, taught me that the balance shifts when an addict gets sober can be unpleasant affairs, often damaging a relationship worse than the addiction did. Codependent relationships are woven together as tightly as Chinese finger cuffs. What once bound people when they pulled against one another could begin to slowly ease them apart when the addict becomes sober.

I thought about Veronica's phone calls. Did she tell people how she sobbed upon hearing her mother had died? I wondered, could she have honestly felt as lost about Nana's death as I did? I wished I knew for certain if, between making calls, she stewed like she had always done, or was what appeared to be her devastation real? I didn't know; she went suspiciously quiet on me. Though I hated to think so, I knew her well enough to know she was up to something. What was it?

Yes, I had glimpses of God's presence now in a way that eluded even Gina. I was moving faith muscles that had gone flabby or atrophied, but Veronica still had the power to grate at my serenity. Her assaults bothered me more than I wanted to let on. And the loss of Nana? How would I bear it, and how long before I succumbed to my fatal flaw and went home to get that brown sugar?

I cast off such gnawing thoughts, and prayed that my little reunion with God, even with my grief about Nana, was going to last.

Nana, my lovely Nana, pray for us sinners, now and at the hour of our death.

Amen.

CHAPTER TWENTY-FOUR

PRIEST

The Vineyard was packed solid. I didn't know if this was an every-Sunday occurrence or not. It wasn't unusual for some people to skip the midweek services, but that was a heckuva contrast.

A sinking feeling hit me.

"Why don't we go to Father Alessandro's church, Gina?"

"But it's ten o'clock! We can't drive to Detroit now and make it in time."

"Then we'll just chat him up at coffee hour. He's a great guy. You'll love him. Let's go."

"I want to go in, Priest."

"Don't you think it's crowded? No way you'll make it all the way up to the balcony with those feet."

"I'll sit on the main floor."

I wanted to tell her something was wrong. I knew something bad was going to happen, but I didn't trust myself. I didn't know how to say it.

So I took her inside.

Yes, I know. Pathetically weak.

GINA

Nobody gave us a bit of trouble going in, maybe because we were already late. Most people were in the sanctuary, and praise and worship had already begun. Everyone was singing, or should have been, and my heart lurched unexpectedly inside of me. I thought it was because I was glad to be in God's house.

I held onto Priest's arms as I made my way, unsteadily, toward the door to the main floor. An usher greeted us, gazed at my bandaged hand, and started a bit.

Here it comes, the crazy-Gina-hurt-herself-again thing, but the worship band was singing, "All hail King Jesus, all hail Emmanuel. King of Kings, Lord of Lords, bright Morning Star." Ah, yes, an oldie but goodie. I wanted to praise Him throughout eternity, like the song said. I wanted to get to my seat, relax, and get my praise on.

The usher asked, nodding toward Zoe, "Are you going to take her to children's church?"

"He'll take her after we find our seats," I said. I thought it was obvious that Priest would have to help me. But I said nothing.

At first I thought the noise I heard was singing in the Spirit, but I turned to look at the congregation and realized waves of whispers were spreading through the people, and with every step we took, we parted the gossip like the Red Sea.

Were all those people whispering about me?

Even I wasn't that paranoid, or arrogant. But I whispered to Priest, "Can we sit in the back?"

"I think we should sit anywhere but this church," he shot back, and I expected him to act that way. But no, I walked lamely, holding on to him, to my seat. Heads craned around to look at me. I wasn't imagining it.

"Take Zoe to children's church," I said, no please or thank you. I caught myself. "Sorry. Will you please take her? It's near the ladies' restroom."

"Why don't we let her sit with us, Gina?"

"Because she needs to be in children's church," I snapped. Now he was irritating me. I wasn't sure why she couldn't sit with us. I just knew I wanted her out of that sanctuary. Now! I softly chanted Saint Teresa of Avila, encouragement to calm my burgeoning nerves. "Let nothing disturb you, let nothing frighten you. Everything passes," but the words, so meaningful to me less than an hour ago, sounded hollow coming out of my mouth.

Priest heard my mumbling. "Not leaving you," he said tightly.

I took a deep breath. I'm sure a few worshippers held up phones to take my picture.

"Just take her away, okay, Priest?"

"Not a good idea, Gina."

"Please," I said, as evenly as I could.

He finally sighed. "You're making a mistake," he whispered. "We need to leave. Something is up."

"Mike won't let anything bad happen to me. Not here. Not in church."

What was I saying? Not in church?

"Not anywhere, Priest." Mike had saved my life. Stuck by my side on my worst day.

Priest got up and took Zoe by the hand, leaving me alone in a room full of people. I glanced around. Many of the looky-loos turned away when I caught their eye, but a few were rude enough to keep on staring with no regard to how I felt. I tried to focus on the big screen. Now the band was singing, "It's all about You, Jesus." I closed my eyes and focused on the words:

And all this is for You, for Your glory and Your fame.
It's not about me.

I felt nothing but a knot of fear inside of me. *Hurry back, Priest. Come even sooner, Lord Jesus.*

I wanted to lift my hands but I thought the bandages would draw too much attention. The song didn't seem to be doing anything for me—not that I could hear the band singing it. Not with the talking people were doing now.

I kept my eyes closed. The words of a psalm came to me and I prayed them to find comfort. That was the thing about the Psalms. You didn't have to clean up to pray them. You could be down and dirty in the muck and mire, but if you were practiced enough at praying them, those vertical prayers would shoot heavenward propelled by your suffering. I couldn't even think of a whole one with my heart beating so fast, and any cohesive thoughts were jumping ship.

"I am poor and needy," I prayed, "but the Lord hears me."

Not long after I heard Mike's voice. "May I have everyone's attention?" He repeated it more firmly this time to the protests of the congregation. "I *said*, 'May I have your attention?'"

I froze. God knows I try not to be too wrapped up in Gina, Gina, Gina, and that's a challenge being chronically ill, but like I knew my name meant "queen of sorrows," I knew his next words would be about me.

My eyes snapped shut, and I waited for somebody's wrath to fall on me.

PRIEST

The woman in the little classroom kitty-corner from the ladies' room eyed me as suspiciously as Miss Dolly had. I was sober as a judge, I didn't care what I looked like, and I wasn't going to let her bully me with a look of contempt. I'd grown up with a mother who loathed me; why, I didn't know. I could certainly stand a few moments of this wispy blonde taking names.

She gave me a fake smile, "Uh, what's your name?"

"Uh, Anthony Priest."

"Where's Gina?"

She must not have known I was son of Veronica, now mourning her dead mother.

"She's sitting in church. Do you honestly think if I were up to no good I'd be checking the kid into children's church? You don't know much about criminals, lamb. That's okay. I don't mind it. I would, however, like for you to take Zoe now, and teach her about

Jesus like you're supposed to. Best if you did that without troubling yourself with unnecessary precautions. If you want to check out if Gina's here, do it after you check Zoe in, and I'm back to my seat, right next to her."

"Why didn't she come back here herself?"

"My guess is that she isn't as paranoid as you are, and then there's her inability to walk very well."

The annoying children's church lady's eyes lit up. "Is it true?"

"What?"

"That she's got Christ's wounds."

I gave her my best withering glance, until I realized she didn't wither from it. "Is that all I need to do, sign her in?"

She wrote a number on the clipboard, and pulled the corresponding number from behind the sign-in sheet. The number three was printed on a paper shaped like the universal sign for female, a skirted kind of stick figure. She held it out, but not out for me to take.

"Is it true? Or do you think she's faking it?"

I snatched the number-girl from her hand and stormed off, not caring if I was as rude as she was.

MIKE

Holy mackerel!

All I could think was that I should never have insisted she come to church. The last few times I'd gone to her house she was asleep, or in some kind of stupor, or ecstasy, or whatever Anthony Priest decided. I wanted a sign it was time to end this and involve some medical professionals; I still believed she needed something beyond pastoral care.

Honestly, I never thought she'd show up, walking like that, and hanging on him with those glaring bandages on each hand.

The calls started as early as Thursday. By Saturday night Lacy was at her wit's end and I was ready to take up drinking—and I don't mean communion wine, not that we used wine. I answered the questions as best I could.

"All I can tell you is that she isn't feeling well right now, and we're not sure what she has. To my knowledge she has yet to go to the hospital. We've asked her to, but it's her right to refuse for her own reasons, and we want to respect that. No one on the Vineyard West staff is qualified to diagnose medical conditions. We've never had a case of stigmata at the Vineyard, and there's no reason for us to believe we're dealing with that now."

It felt idiotic to say, but I had few options. I wanted to be cautious. Had to be. If I had said she had stigmata, and she didn't, I could damage my church beyond anything I'd be equipped to repair. On the other hand, I couldn't denounce stigmata, or Gina. If I did, and by some miracle—and it truly would be a miracle—she actually had stigmata, it would bring unnecessary pain to Gina, and damage my congregation as well. Far be it from me to withhold a sign from God because I failed to discern it.

The calls continued, some from people who didn't attend our church. When the press began contacting us, I told them I had no knowledge that a member of my church was a stigmatic. That was the truth as I knew it.

I knew I had a problem on my hands when I saw all those people. There were too many strange faces. I watched the congregation as the worship band sang, and it seemed pretty obvious many of them had no idea what to do. I could tell our worship style was foreign to them. They weren't ours. Not at all.

When Gina sat down, the whispering escalated. People stood up to snap their camera phones at her. I couldn't let that go, not in the house of the Lord. Sunday morning was about worship, corporate prayer, and strengthening one another for the week ahead, and it was turning into a sideshow.

Gina didn't seem to be doing anything to draw attention to herself. She didn't even insist on coming! I forced the issue. I had to fix this.

I stopped the worship band and asked if I might have the people's attention. That only made matters worse. Veronica ambled up to the stage, and what was she doing there when her mother had died Friday? We hadn't even bought her flowers yet. She'd draped that awful red vinyl tote bag on her arm, and I had the distinct feeling there was something funny about her, and it wasn't just grief because she'd lost her mom.

Holy mackerel! Had her bald spots started filling in?

I couldn't deal with it. Not at the moment.

I tried to chase her away with a stern look, but of course she missed my cues. She held up her hands as if to quiet the people and oddly, they responded, and why not? That's when I knew.

So, Veronica spread the word. Great!

She should have been telling people she'd lost her mother.

People were watching her, sympathetic folks who knew her mother had just died. She wanted to say something. If I didn't give her the mic I'd look worse than I already did. I handed it to her, burning mad, but I stayed on stage, anticipating when I'd have to take the mic back from her, and regain control of my sheep.

What a nightmare.

She took the microphone, breathed into it, and tapped it a few times. I didn't have much patience for her. The audio was fine. Get on with it, already.

She cleared her throat, grabbed the podium, and looked around the room. The drama was excruciating. "My name is Sister Veronica Morelli, and I represent the Blessed"—she pronounced it in two syllables—"the *Bless-ed* Regina Dolores Merritt. For those who don't know, Regina Dolores means 'queen of sorrows.'"

No, no, no, no, no. This was not good. *Sister Veronica?*

She went on. "We are truly blessed"—one syllable for blessed this time—"to have a victim soul in our midst."

Victim soul! I didn't even know what that was! And I spent the weekend on the net reading up on stigmata. The books I ordered off Amazon hadn't arrived yet.

I held out my hand for the microphone, but wouldn't you know it, Veronica didn't want to give it back. I wasn't going to play tug-of-war with her, and until our board of directors appointed someone else, I was still the pastor.

One of the worship band singers saw my dilemma and handed me a different mic. I gestured to the sound guy to turn Veronica's mic off, which he did without hesitating.

The people went nuts. They popped up from their seats like popcorn firing questions at whoever would answer them: me, Veronica, or God help her, Gina.

Is she or isn't she a stigmatic?

What evidence do you have? Has anyone from the Catholic Church confirmed?

Is it true that she's healed several people, including your janitor who cleaned her blood?

Is this a fraud?

Did you do this to yourself? Let us see the wounds.

People around her started calling out.

She smells like roses.

I see fresh blood coming through her bandages. Dear God!

Can she raise your mother from the dead?

And who would ask a question like that? Nobody in my congregation.

"Ladies and gentleman, brothers and sisters in Christ, please. Gina isn't making any claims of being a stigmatic." I looked at that poor girl. She'd hunched over and rocked, back and forth, her hands together in her lap. She appeared to be furiously praying.

I've never wished we had security in our church until that moment.

Lacy, who always sits on the front row, took off. I had no idea where she was going.

Veronica, with no mic at all, pulled some papers from her tote bag. "I have information about the sacred stigmata of Blessed Regina Dolores right here, and information about how you might hear her message and obtain healing."

Anthony must have had taken Zoe to children's church. He entered back into the pandemonium just as people started to rush her. Now they pulled out real cameras, not just cell phones. Voices rang out in the sanctuary.

Can the blood heal me?

Can you heal my child?

Blessed Regina Dolores, pray to God for me.

My people didn't talk like that. We had our jargon, but that wasn't it.

People closed in around her. Anthony yelled, "You're scaring her. Back off."

I admonished them from the platform. "Please! Gina is no miracle worker. She's a young person who's having a hard time." Nobody cared about that.

Veronica dug in her tote bag and yanked out a fistful of tiny plastic baggies, like she was pushing drugs or something.

"I have swatches of Blessed Regina Dolores's stigmatism blood for a small donation. The donations are only to continue the work and for the care of Blessed Regina Dolores. She is no longer able to work, having received the wounds of Christ."

I intervened. "Let me make this clear. The Vineyard is in no way endorsing or condoning Miss Morelli's actions today. Our official position is that we have no evidence of Gina Merritt being a stigmatic, and no evidence that her blood has healing powers."

Gina stood unsteadily. Anthony took her by the waist like he was holding her up.

I'm sorry, but I had to ask myself if they hadn't planned this. Of course it wasn't Gina's idea. She wouldn't orchestrate anything like this, unless she'd become really confused, and that wasn't impossible if she'd started sleeping with the guy. And Veronica! As off center as she had been, I just wouldn't have seen this coming. But Anthony seemed just as appalled as I was by what was going.

She had on some kind of simple, un-dyed organic-cotton

dress—the kind of thing she always wore. The red spreading across her ribs was unmistakable. A collective gasp sounded in the sanctuary. People started clapping wildly.

I'm telling you, I'd never seen anything like it. It was so dramatic I had to ask myself if it wasn't staged. People started grabbing her hands now, and even Anthony couldn't keep them at bay.

She seemed to be in some kind of daze, and a few people were kneeling in front of her, as if they were waiting for blessings.

My own people shouted at me. "What's going on, Mike?" Some of them got mad. "Jesus said, 'It is finished' on the cross. His blood is what saves and heals. Not hers."

Blasphemy!

Heretic!

Spirit of delusion!

The way I saw it, I now had two really big problems on my hands: how to keep a full-blown riot from ensuing, and how to get our Gina safely out of the building.

My head hurts right now, just remembering it.

VERONICA

I'd lost my mother. Things happen to a woman when she loses her mother, no matter how bad their relationship was. When God brought me to Blessed Regina Dolores, I thought my destiny was to serve her. When my mother died right after that, I knew for certain that, even though she was younger than me, she would be my *spiritual* mother.

It was as if when Mom died, Jesus looked at me, pointed to Blessed Regina Dolores, and said, "Behold, thy mother." But she still needed my help, spiritual mother or not. And I'd be a holy terror making sure her message to the world got out—heck, making sure she realized she had a message.

I didn't care what anybody thought. I'd had to take care of my own mother for years after she got Alzheimer's. That self-righteous Anthony thought *he* took care of her because he went to see her, sitting at her feet, the little monkey. But who made sure the bills were paid? Not that junkie.

And don't think I didn't *get* the fact that Mom died right after he went to see her. The boy was cursed. I always told her that.

I had to take control, even in my grief. I had to go on.

Had to.

I didn't think I was wrong for that.

PRIEST

Veronica actually said that: "I have swatches of Blessed Regina's stigmatism blood." For a small donation! Let's not forget that. Oh, I knew Ronnie to be shrewd, but she'd outdone herself this time. And I was sure she'd find a way to justify it.

When Gina's side began to bleed, people started stuffing bills into Veronica's hands in exchange for *what*? Cut off squares of Gina's discarded bandages. And what did Ronnie mean she had information about how people could hear her message and obtain healing?

Worse than Veronica's brazen exploitation antics, people stormed Gina, begging, "Touch me. Please!"

I had to get her out of there before people tore her apart. Thank God she made me take Zoe to children's church so the kid didn't have to see it. Gina started tuning out again, and I grabbed her arms and shook her. "Gina. Stay with me here."

She snapped out of her trance, and her eyes filled with tears. "Hurts."

People laid themselves at her feet.

"We have to get out of here." But I couldn't pick her up because we'd both have fallen, and she couldn't run.

I scanned the room. Now, people were surrounding us, begging for her intercession.

"Get out the way!" I shouted. "I've have to get her out of here." Nobody moved.

Is that my…? My editor Larry is here! And a few people from rival papers I recognize. I cannot believe she called the media. And my senior editor!

Mike jumped off the stage and came running toward us, several men following him. I could only hope he was going to help. But just in case he wasn't, "Lay hands on a few of them. Hurry!" I shouted at Gina.

If I could just get her in the car, we could escape the madness. All of it! But I had to get Zoe. Oh, man.

Gina started touching people, crying out with pain each time. But they'd fall away when she touched them, some of them looking suspiciously slain in the Spirit, which I knew about from following Veronica's spiritual antics for years, not to mention watching more Benny Hinn broadcasts that a good Catholic boy should.

Of course, I wasn't a good Catholic boy.

Never mind. They could fall in multitudes as long as they weren't in the way.

Mike and his boys started clearing people out, and I took that as my opportunity. Veronica stopped being a moneychanger long enough to try to get my attention.

Her shrill voice vexed me. "Stop, Anthony! Don't take her away. She belongs to the people. She's a gift to the world."

Not today.

I grabbed her arm and pulled her through the still gathering crowd. "Hang on, baby."

People shouted at me, "Who are you? Do you represent her? When will she come back?" Others shouted "Heretic!" and worse.

Two of the men who ran down with Mike trotted up to us. "We'll get her to the car. You go get Zoe."

At least they cared about Gina. They didn't seem to be opposing me, trying to get her on the sly to the hospital.

I shoved my keys into one of the men's hands. "It's a gray Ford Probe. Racing stripe in the front, and illegally parked in a handicap spot right in front."

I wasn't sure how illegal it was now. Gina was collecting handicaps by the day.

I ran out of the sanctuary to the children's church area and thrust the number-girl at the woman who was questioning me earlier.

"She's not here," she said, looking smug.

"What do you mean she's not here?" I demanded.

"Lacy took her."

"Lacy?"

"Mike's wife. The first lady."

"Why would you give her to somebody else?"

She shrugged. "She's Mike's wife."

I let out a torrent of bad words those good Christian kids had likely never heard before, and never would again, before hunting Lacy down like an animal in hot pursuit of its prey.

CHAPTER TWENTY-FIVE

PRIEST

I'd find Lacy Adams and Zoe if I had to tear that building apart, brick by brick, even if I had to build it again. I'd be like Francis. Gina was like him. We'd make a good couple.

Somehow I'd found courage. I wasn't afraid of us being an "our" anymore. I knew we couldn't have a normal relationship, but we'd be together, for whatever time God would kindly give us. And I'd make it good for her. I meant that with everything in me, even though I was scared to death for feeling that much.

The crowd in the sanctuary spilled out while I opened any door I thought would take me to Lacy and Zoe. Some people in the throng wanted her for healing and deliverance while others sneered their contempt, no doubt intent on crucifying her. She was getting Palm Sunday and Good Friday at the same time.

I opened a closet, a conference room, and finally Mike's office where I hit pay dirt. Zoe was on the floor playing with some Legos, and Lacy sat at Mike's desk.

I didn't bother with any pretense. "Let's go, Zoe." She lit up when she saw me.

"Mr. Anthony!"

Lacy countered, "Don't move, honey. You're going to stay here with me." That's when it dawned on me—she was on the phone.

I didn't really care who she was yakking with, however. That is, until she told Zoe, "The police are coming to talk with Mr. Anthony, and you're going to stay with me."

"The police are going to have to catch Mr. Anthony. *And* Zoe."

Lacy shrieked, "I will personally make sure you do time if you walk out of here with her. Kidnapping, Anthony. And I'll tell them all about your habits."

"Whatever, Lacy."

I went over to Zoe and picked her up. "Your mom's waiting in the car."

I tossed back at Lacy, "They'll have to find us before we can have that little conversation, won't they?"

"If you take this child we'll find you, and I promise you Gina Merritt will never get this little girl back again!"

"I'll take my chances."

With Zoe in my arms, I ran outside to my Probe.

GINA

It was as if my heart had burst within me.

What do you do when you are completely vulnerable? In that moment I was the girl in the dark alley about to be raped, hair raised on the back of my neck, intuition full throttle, with an insidious stranger's hand about to grab my throat just because I wasn't quite fast enough, or maybe smart enough, to escape. I was the automobile accident victim watching with just enough time to see the Mack truck that would barrel into me in a moment, knowing without a split second of doubt that this was the end, 'cause I couldn't get out of the way in time.

Stares and whispers crowded around my chair while menacing speculations suffocated me.

Heretic!

Blasphemer!

You are of the devil!

The voices of the slanderers and accusers mingled with the desperate hope of those who believed I was evidence of Emmanuel. And God was with us, and He'd pour out grace through my open wounds.

I was scared to death.

Even the Psalms abandoned me. I rocked my body back and forth, becoming a ball of pain, and all I could say was, "Oh God, oh, God, oh God, oh God, oh God."

There was so much … suffering in that room, and all of it slamming into my heart. Someone had cancer. I could smell the rotten stench of tumors eating away at his body. I felt the palpable desperation of mothers whose children had any number of needs. There was a young girl with cerebral palsy, and a boy who'd been dabbling with drugs, a teenage girl depressed and suicidal. I knew their thoughts, all of them—everyone present; I *was* them. Some had come, hoping against hope that a wonder-worker would show up and fix it all. Most of them didn't think it was really possible, but they wanted to believe. I knew that. Their sorrow and anger made a stomach-churning combination.

Every bit of the faith, pain, aches, hopes, moans, and curses jabbed at me like a spear. I wished I could take them all, wrap a big red ribbon around them, and present them to Jesus, but I'd been reduced to one big lesion.

My entire chest cavity burned like it was on fire. I stood, a task that felt impossible now, because every gash on my body—hands, feet, deep recess of my heart, had split open wide, grieving the losses of everyone in that building.

And still, I did not love them. Not yet.

Blood gushed from my right side, soaking my dress.

A ragged breath tore out of me; I thought it'd be my last.

I think Priest steadied me, but I'm not sure. My attention was on the woman. She wore all white, except for a bloom of crimson at the front of her dress. She took my hand, and led me back to Calvary.

She was His mother. And I stood beside her while she wept beneath the towering shadow of His instrument of execution. He was already dead. The sun grieved.

The woman sighed and wept, sad and afflicted along with her Son. Those of us gathered, the beloved disciple, and His dear friend Mary Magdalene mourned and trembled, but we could not stop looking at the bloody mess He'd become.

Why didn't I love Him? What was all that high talk of mine, about Him being the Lover of my soul? My Beloved. My Prince.

Oh, God. Like He came to the Shulamite, He'd come to me, countless times, knocking on my door, and I would lie sleeping, reluctant to let Him in. Making excuses.

Now, I stood at the foot of His cross, and I still didn't know how to love Him. I smelled the acrid, coppery scent of His shed blood. Could almost taste the sharp metal of it on my tongue. His blood pooled on the ground right in front of me, and I did not yet love Him.

I turned to His mother. The stain on her dress had grown, covering every inch of fabric with blood. His blood. Her blood. She spoke to me. "My heart has been pierced by a sword."

And I wanted to love Him like she did. But I didn't know how.

"I want my heart to burn with love for Christ our Lord, that I may please Him," I said. "I desire God to grant the wounds of the Crucified be scored deep in my heart, and share with me, like He has with you, the pains of your wounded Son."

She squeezed my wounded hand. "Stand with me and share my grief. Weep with me and grieve for the Crucified as long as you live." And then that gracious lady said to me, calling me by my name, "Little Regina Dolores. You were born to share in His sufferings."

Did you ever wonder what the apostle Paul meant when he said these words? Listen carefully: "Now I rejoice in what I am suffering for you, and I fill up in my flesh what is still lacking in regard to Christ's afflictions, for the sake of his body, which is the church."

I hadn't wondered either. I believed the atonement on the cross, just once, was enough to redeem the world. So why did he say he filled in his body what was lacking in Christ's afflictions?

There wasn't anything lacking.

That's what I thought. But things aren't always what they seem to be at first glance. You really have to dig deep enough to pierce a vein to find out some truths. And don't be afraid to make a bloody mess of things.

I realized right there at the foot of the cross, having pledged to share in His suffering for the rest of my life, that Good Jesus was so kind, that when I offered up my paltry suffering, He accepted it.

Oh! Amazing grace to all who suffer, no matter what the wound.

The Scriptures tell us though Jesus was in the form of God, He did not count equality with God a thing to be grasped, but emptied Himself, taking the form of a servant, being born in the likeness of men. And being found in human form He humbled Himself and became obedient unto death, even the death on the cross.

Christ offered up His Godness and became man, showing us what it is to sacrifice, and He allows us to imitate Him. He commanded us to take up our own crosses, oh, but He is our Simon of Cyrene helping us to bear the terrible weight of them, each and every time we pick up our cross.

Every time we act like Him and offer up our sacrifices—all our sufferings, great and small—they rise like incense before the throne of God. That's what Paul meant in Colossians. We make up in our bodies what is lacking in Christ's suffering when we suffer, but only when we give it to Him. And He'll take it. He'll take it all and give us back abundant gifts in kind. Incredible gifts.

Ask me how I know.

CHAPTER TWENTY-SIX

PRIEST

The only thing that kept Lacy from tearing behind me was that she was already on the phone with the police. I saw her leave the sanctuary. I knew they'd be there any minute.

I might not be able to hold Gina, but I sure as heck could hang on to Zoe. We pushed our way through the crowd, my arms tightening around her little frame, my voice telling her everything would be okay.

Police sirens wailed in the background. Mike's henchmen stood guard like sentries around my car where Gina sat. Gina was gone again. Lost in ecstasy. The men couldn't have known I'd had a run-in with Lacy, because if they did, it would have been all over.

The man at the driver's door moved aside. I thrust Zoe inside that vehicle as quickly as I could get her in there without hurting her. She slammed into Gina, felt the blood on her dress and screamed bloody murder. Gina was totally out of it. I tried to soothe her, but I had to focus on the task at hand, getting out of there. I buckled Zoe in on Gina's lap, and yes, I know it was crazy, but I didn't have time to disengage her. Then I slid over to the driver's seat and shut the door behind me. Whoever got Gina in the car had started it for me, purchasing precious seconds for me. But people had crowded around the car.

The men tried to run them off, but they were outnumbered by the multitude that spilled out of the church.

I was going to get her out of there if I had to run somebody over. I started banging the horn, but only a few responded. Finally I shifted the gear into drive with my foot on the brake and eased off a little just to let them know I was serious.

That's when Lacy came running out of the church screaming, "Stop him."

The police pulled into the parking lot.

I said one more desperate prayer before I peeled out of there no matter what. How I freed us without plowing over several pedestrians or getting busted was a miracle. Not that I wasn't beginning to feel like I had more of those than a man could take.

I wasn't up for this. I asked for grace in my deficiencies.

GINA

I don't know how long I was gone, transported to some quiet place of wonder where I worshipped God, no matter that I did not feel His presence. His Word had comforted me and given me a bit of faith to face the present dangers.

When I awoke I looked over at Priest. I don't think he could have appeared more wild-eyed and crazy if he were high. He must have been driving ninety miles an hour, burning up I-94. I bumped and shook along in that little car he was pushing past its limits, and each time I got knocked around, pain ripped through me.

He shouted obscenities. I didn't want Zoe to hear all that, but he was so upset. Not that she heard him. She cried her little eyes out, strapped on my lap with my blood all over her little blue dress.

She was five! As forgiving as she was, I think she'd grown a little tired of seeing holes poked in her mother.

I would have kept holding her, but Priest continued driving like a maniac. "Unbuckle the seat belt, Zoe."

"Nooooo, Mommy," she wailed.

"It's okay. We can't sit like this. It's not safe. We can get hurt even more."

That got her attention.

I made her crawl in the back and buckle herself in. And not for a second did she stop crying. And I couldn't even click her seat belt on, but maybe she'd survive the car wreck Priest was intent on killing us in because she sat in the back buckled up at my command.

"Priest!" I said. "Slow down. I don't have a seat belt on, and besides, if we don't crash, the police are gonna come after you for speeding."

He didn't slow down. His adrenaline drove us onward. Either I could sit there and add my own crying and screaming to the chorus

of his blistering cussing and Zoe's wailing, or I could try to talk him
off his ledge.

It's bad if I'm the one who's the voice of reason.

But a girl's gotta do what a girl's gotta do.

"Tell me a story," I said.

"What?"

"You said you know all kind of saint stuff. Tell me a saint story.
Make it a good one."

He shook his head. "I can't tell you a story right now. We're …
on the lam!"

"You're gonna have to stop watching those Turner Classic Mov-
ies, Priest. Why would we be on the lam? What did we do wrong?"

"Lacy called the police. She was trying to keep Zoe."

"But what was our crime? Taking Zoe to church? Or would it be
leaving church early with her?"

"People were coming after you. They'd have torn you apart."

"Most of them just wanted some help. They were a little
confused."

"No, Gina. People who thought *The Da Vinci Code* was based on
facts are a little confused. My drug dealer, a transvestite who has a crush
on me? She's a little confused. *I'm* a little confused because people keep
thinking I'm black, and frankly, I'm inclined to believe them despite
what my birth certificate says. Those people at the Vineyard weren't
confused. That lynch mob was going to crucify you for real."

"Your pusher is a transvestite?"

"You focused on the wrong point."

Zoe's wailing slowed to a whimper. Our talking must have comforted her. I kept it up.

"And you call ... that person ... a she? Did ... that person ... ask you to, or did you do that on your own?"

"Again. Wrong point."

But he was slowing down.

"I think I'd be confused about what to call him. Or her."

Laughter exploded out of him.

"Tell me another story, Priest. Please."

I don't think he was good and convinced it was time to start the story hour yet, but he was a journalist; he loved a story. I knew it from the two he'd already told me. I nudged him a little more.

"We Protestants mostly go with Bible stories. I mean, we might stretch out now and then and somebody will tell us about Corrie ten Boom, or Dietrich Bonhoeffer. One day Mike got really crazy and taught us about Etty Hillesum."

"I'm seeing a real Holocaust theme here, Gina. Any reason for that?"

"Probably, but don't make me conjure it. Anyway, I love Bible stories. They strengthen my faith and beef up my Bible knowledge, but I know next to nothing about the saints. Or even stigmatics. So tell me a saint or stigmatic story or something."

He sighed and watched the road ahead. "I'll tell you about Saint Padre Pio."

"You mentioned him before. He was a stigmatic, right?"

"Sure. Bore the wounds for fifty years."

"Fifty years?"

"Yup."

"Maybe you shouldn't tell me *his* story."

Priest laughed again. I think we'd slowed to seventy or so. I'd get his blood pressure down yet.

"Okay. Padre Pio it is."

I settled back, as achy I was, and let Priest spin a saintly yarn for me.

PRIEST

"Saint Padre Pio"

Some people are born poor in spirit. Padre Pio was one of them.

He was the fourth child of a poor farmer and his wife in Pietrelcina, a mountain town in southern Italy. His parents named him Francesco—wonder who they had in mind when they called him that? Could they have known when they first laid eyes on him that he'd be a true spiritual son of another Francesco, the one you may know as the birdbath guy, but to those of us who love him, he's know as *Il Povello*, little poor one.

Little Francesco Forgione was one sick kid. And he was a little screwy too. Perhaps because he had a gaping father wound right after his dad took off to America to fund a proper education for all the little Forgiones. Young Francesco must have taken his father grief to God. He told his mother he wanted to be a monk. Makes you wonder if the kid wasn't trying to find a replacement papa. After all, it worked for the *other* Francesco.

But Mama and Papa Forgione were smart. They told little Francesco he could do what he wanted to do, as long as he went to school first. And so he did, but he didn't thrive there.

He was just too much for ... pretty much everybody. Always fasting and praying—and I do mean always. He was into kiddie mortification, sleeping with a big rock under his pillow until Mama Forgione found out and put a stop such self-denial.

He survived, despite himself, and at the age of sixteen he became a novice in the Capuchin Franciscan order. He took the name Pio, which means *pious*, and he was one person who could pull the name off. But young Pio had funky lungs and after seven years of praying, fasting, and trying to breathe they got him out of there. A month later, in the solitude of a reed hut Pio built in his family's fields, Christ and His mother appeared to him, and Pio received the sacred stigmata in his own flesh—all five wounds!

That's gotta hurt!

I don't have to tell you how much pain and embarrassment the wounds caused him. He prayed that they would become invisible, and his request was granted.

Don't get too excited though. I know what you're thinking. But I'll get back to that.

During the First World War, Pio was drafted. They had no idea how sickly he was. He spent so much time on sick leave the army had to discharge him. The brass sent him to Our Lady of Grace Friary, and doesn't that sound like the place to go? The air was supposed to be really good there. Apparently it was. On the eighth anniversary of his receiving the stigmata, his now invisible wounds were pierced with rays of light from the Crucified Christ as he prayed before a crucifix after Mass.

They became visible again and stayed that way for half of a century, until just before he died from that same lung condition. He wore half-mittens to hide the wounds in his hands. A sash absorbed the blood on his side.

Padre Pio walked through the trials and tribulations of life with pain as his constant companion, but he wasn't one to complain about it. Maybe because he smelled so good, like another saint I know. Some people thought he smelled of roses. Others tobacco. I guess it depended on what you were into.

And don't be cute. You smell like roses to me. It was one of the first things I noticed about you. Hey, I said *one* of the first!

A humble, unassuming man, he wanted to hide his stigmata, but you may have noticed it's a little hard to keep the wounds of Christ on the down low. His notoriety spread, and Catholics came from the world over to have him hear their confession. He could read souls like I go through *The New York Times* book review, and he had the gift of healing. Padre Pio could also consort with angels and had the habit of bilocating when he just had to be in two places at once. Demons beat him mercilessly all the time, but come on, with all that other stuff? What's chronic pain and demons constantly trying to kill you?

His gifts did draw devotees to him, including my Nana, but sometimes he could be the object of hysteria, the likes of which you saw today. In 1968 he died, with a body unmarred by the scars of crucifixion he so patiently carried.

Padre Pio inspired pilgrims to love whatever cross God gave them. He once said to his spiritual children:

> *Religion is a hospital for spiritually sick people who want to be healed. To be healed, they must submit themselves to suffering, to bloodletting, to the lance, to the scalpel, to the fire, and to all the bitterness of medicine. In order to be spiritually cured, we have to submit to all the tortures of the Divine Physician.*

Don't laugh. He was serious about that.

If you ever feel all alone, you can pray his prayer for Jesus to stick around:

Stay with me, Lord, for it is necessary to have You present so that I do not forget You. You know how easily I abandon You.

Stay with me, Lord, because I am weak and I need Your strength that I may not fall so often.

Stay with me, Lord, for You are my light, and without You I am in darkness.

Stay with me, Lord, to show me Your will.

Stay with me, Lord, so that I hear Your voice and follow You.

Stay with me, Lord, for I desire to love You very much and be in Your company always.

Stay with me, Lord, if You wish me to be faithful to You.

Stay with me, Lord, for as poor as my soul is I want it to be a place of consolation for You, a nest of love.

You might want to memorize that one.

GINA

I knew who Saint Francis was. I even knew his name in Italian was Francesco. Don't sleep at the Vineyard. Mike slips in all kinds of knowledge, just when you think you'll run for the hills if the worship band croons "I Can Sing of Your Love Forever" just one more time. Priest astounded me. All that from the top of his head.

His voice, and the engaging way he told a story, put Zoe right to sleep. I didn't happen to think that was a bad thing. When he was done he asked if we could stop and get gas. "I wasn't expecting we'd have to keep riding."

"Knock yourself out. We're fine, especially since you stopped driving like a lunatic."

"I'm concerned that we still don't have enough distance from Ann Arbor, but the tank is demanding a pit stop."

We pulled off the freeway in Belleville.

"There's a Mobile up ahead on Belleville Road," I said. I thought maybe I should get a snack for Zoe for when she woke up, but for the moment, my mind was still with Padre Pio, and Priest's way of telling a story. "Do you have a photographic memory?"

"I don't know. I don't think about it that way. I remember things, but I fried a lot of brain cells. Sometimes it surprises me the information that pops into my head that I haven't thought about in years. I can remember whole quotes. Long ones, sometimes with perfect recall. Helps with the journalism thing."

"Amazing. I'll bet you're a formidable Scrabble player."

"Hey, where you been all my life, Gina? If I had you to beat in Scrabble I may not have gotten in so much trouble."

"Who says you'd beat me?"

He found that funny too. We pulled up at the Mobile station, and Priest chose the pump farthest from the building. He put the car in park, and his whole body seemed to exhale.

"I'm not trying to amaze you. I'd be happy to help you in any way I can to make peace with what's happening to you." He gazed at me with those soulful multicolored eyes. "Maybe we've begun your story in earnest now and I'm foraging for parts of it amid all the other stories in my head's database. Like you were always there, somewhere."

"That almost sounds romantic."

He thought for a moment. "Not romantic. Connected."

Next to the Mobile sat a McDonald's and a dollar store. Outside his little gray Probe, everything looked so normal. Every*body* looked as regular as unleaded gas—87, but what were their stories as they milled about? Were we all intertwined in one big God yarn He was still spinning?

"My story somewhere in all the stories in your head? It does sound connected, but why does that sound scary to me too?"

"I think we both know why. Can we salvage the little self-esteem I have by acting like you didn't just ask me that?"

"Why did you park so far out?"

"You've got blood all over you. I don't want anybody thinking we're spree killers or something. I don't want to raise any suspicions."

"You might want to try not driving like a bat out of hades then." I hadn't thought of how I must look. I guess I was getting use to bleeding from all kinds of extremities. And now my side. Wow. But at least it had slowed, I could tell, which made me wonder if being around all those people hadn't made it worse. "Where are we going, anyway?"

"To Alessandro. He'll help us. He's a Franciscan and a priest. Stigmata won't make him want to sick the authorities on you."

I'd trust him because Priest did. Besides, I always wanted to meet a real Franciscan. Plus, Priest had already told me he said he wanted to meet me. Nobody had looked forward to meeting me in a while.

But I wanted to probe Priest further about the stories. He seemed to be merging us in a way that intrigued me. And it didn't sound so gonzo, either. It was different, and I couldn't quite place what made it so.

"Do you really believe it? That you have my story already, I mean, on some level? That they're tied together in some way?"

"I already told you I thought our meeting was providential. Do you believe it, Gina? Do you want that?" His thoughtful gaze caressed me. Nothing harsh or painful about how he touched me with that look.

"Want what?"

"Our stories to commingle."

"Do you want it?"

"You tell me first."

"No, you first; you're a girl."

"Are you some kind of sexist? I was starting to like you. Are you going to go all macho man on me now?"

"*Now?* What do you mean *now?* I've been rescuing you since Wednesday. Not half hour ago, I stormed through a church carrying our kid. Didn't that speak to you of my valor?"

"Not really, I was preoccupied thinking I'd have to heal or be killed." I froze. "Did you say 'our' kid? Have you made us an 'our' in your mind?"

"I didn't say 'our.'"

"Did too."

"Did not."

"You cannot lie to me, Priest. Don't even try. You made us an 'our,' didn't you?"

"Would that be okay with you?"

"I suppose I've already accepted it. We are on the lam together."

"No, you were right the first time. We're not on the lam. It just feels like it."

He unbuckled his seat belt. "What do you want from inside? I don't think they have Tofurky."

"Can you just get me some orange juice?"

"What about *our* growing girl? She needs more than orange juice."

"Get her something healthy."

"You do realize this is a Mobile gas station, not Whole Foods."

"Healthy, Priest."

"Fine. One more thing, since we're on this business of being an 'our.'"

"Technically we were talking about buying snacks."

"Let's talk about getting married."

I froze. We were waaaaaaay off topic now. Before I could shut my open mouth he opened the car door and headed to the store.

CHAPTER TWENTY-SEVEN

PRIEST

Back at the car I acted like I didn't drop an M-bomb on her as I slid back into my seat holding a brown paper bag full of Karr's trail mix and assorted Veryfine juices.

I didn't shut the driver's side door. The better to escape through, my dear.

I shoved the bag at her. "This was the best I could do. Consider the source."

She still had the bewildered look on her face that asked what *she* did a moment later. "Did you say you wanted to talk about getting married?"

"I have to pump the gas. Time is money, Gina. I'll be right back. Hang on."

I had a few minutes to think as the cold air bit through me. Easter would be here in three weeks or so. We'd turn a corner and stumble into spring, slowly sure; this *was* Michigan. Prince could have been singing about the Great Lakes State when he wailed, "Sometimes it snows in April. Sometimes I feel so bad."

I began to feel bad all right. Pumping gas and buying time away from Gina's rejection, I felt every bit the idiot Veronica branded me. I had some doubts, sure, but protecting her at the Vineyard felt right enough to make my courage swell. My visions of us being like a holy family of sorts, fleeing persecution, seemed attainable. I liked the idea of being her Joseph, and she a maiden mild, with child. So the child was five. She was small. We'd make it work.

I thought if we talked about it somehow it would be possible.

I finished pumping gas. Man, did I ever want to stand out there and smoke a cigarette before I got back in the car. Whatever conclusions we came to, she'd say yes, or she'd say no. I leaned heavily toward no.

But I had to face her. I couldn't stand out there and freeze to death. So I opened the driver's side door and got back in. Before she could say a word, looking at me with those dark eyes, I laid it out for her.

"If you marry me, everybody who wants to get to you will have to come through me. I know I'm suspect. You have no reason to trust or depend on me, but I am in this story. You asked me to come into it yourself. I'd like an upgrade to hero if you can stand to take a chance on me. I'll do everything in my power not to let you down. You need me. Zoe needs me, and I need to be needed. This can work out for both of us." I added, without the bite of my speech on Thursday, "If there's anybody—any human being—in your life you think will take better care of you, I'll take you to that person. But I might be your Joseph. This must sound insane, but don't forget God chooses the foolish things of this world to confound the wise, and I'm the biggest fool He's got. Maybe He's got big plans for us."

She didn't speak for the longest thirty seconds ever. Finally, she said, "Think you can hold the juice bottle for me?"

Sounded like a yes to me.

And just so you know, she never took a sip of that juice.

GINA

Neither of us was much for conversation after the proposal. All I could think about was Zoe. What if something had happened to me at church? What if some people in that crowd were as malicious as Priest thought? And since I was bleeding from five wounds, what if this thing killed me? I wasn't sure about the life span of stigmatics, but with my luck it'd be pitiful short, Padre Pio notwithstanding. Who would take care of Zoe if I died?

My mother? Who knew where she was, or what she was up to. She didn't even raise me, and it's a good thing, because if she had I'd have to take Priest to meet her. "Meet the son-in-law, Mom, a washed up junkie who used to be Anthony Priest, prize-winning journalist."

I didn't see him that way, but she probably would, even if she was in worse shape than he.

The whole idea was crazy.

I've been in the 'hood long enough to know that most addicts stay addicts. They might be clean for a short run, but most go back. Someone told me once a recovering addict is just a junkie waiting for his next fix.

He seemed changed, but it had only been five days. What if he fell away so fast it astonished me? And what was all that talk about him never being able to give me what I wanted in a relationship? Did he think marriage would make him some kind of bodyguard with benefits, benefits he'd already told me he'd opt out of?

Where would his relapse leave Zoe if I were gone?

But I couldn't *hold* anything. I could hardly walk. It was Priest running through that mob with Zoe in his hands being the hero. It was he who had given the two of us the tender, loving care Zoe's own father denied us.

And wasn't I a recovering addict, too? I just didn't wear the title like a badge of honor.

I hated to admit it, but he sounded like God's best offer.

Because I had to, whether I felt God was speaking or revealing Himself to me or not, I prayed. I did it in the spirit of the lady who stood beside me at her Son's crucifixion, and told me I'd share her grief always.

"I am the Lord's servant," I said to God. "May it be to me according to Your Word."

And that was all. Priest had delivered what seemed to be God's plan to me, as crazy as it was. I just hoped he was more angel than devil.

I didn't even feel up to prolonging our agony.

"Priest," I said, as we drove down Woodward Avenue headed toward Father Alessandro's parish.

He said a very quiet, defeated sounding, "Yes, Gina?" I think he was expecting a different answer.

"I'll marry you."

His face lit up like someone had turned a light on inside of him. I took that as a sign.

"Let me tell you a story," he said.

PRIEST

"Saint Francis of Assisi"

Blessed are the poor in spirit; theirs is the kingdom of heaven.

Everybody thinks he's the happy birdbath saint, and it's true, he had a special affinity for nature, but there was more to the little poor man than preaching to birds and bargaining with wolves to stop terrorizing villagers.

I'll admit, the poor little rich boy used to be the life of the party. He was a true wayward son, no doubt the person who kept his pious mother Pica on her knees, and grayed his father, Pietro Di Bernadone's, hair. Papa was a wealthy cloth merchant who got rich off some of the very fine things in life he loved. Francesco blazed through his money like a prodigal with riotous living—wine, women, and song! Lots of song. And he did it big. He was well known among the youth of Assisi for his wild parties, fair-haired beauties, and for strolling the streets in the middle of the night singing the love songs of a troubadour.

He was glorious.

Wanted to be a knight in shining armor.

Fresh out of his teens, Francesco's country went to war with their neighbors in Perugia. He mounted his horse and sped off to battle expecting to return with tales of valor and courage, but instead he found that war is hell, and he was taken as hell's prisoner.

Francesco languished for months in a dank disease incubator. When his father finally bailed him out, Francesco staggered home, ravaged by malaria and his own shattered spirit. His fevers may have burned the bad boy out of him. Or maybe they made him crazy. Maybe his sickness germinated into a garden of prayer like Gethsemane that would lead him to the death of his old self.

In not many days, he had traded his fine clothes for a rough cloak. Like the poor, he wore no belt, and possessed no pockets to fill. He spent his time kissing lepers and begging for stones to build God's house because a crucifix told him to.

Once, when he had stolen cloth from his father's wares and sold it—far below market value, might I add—he tried to give the money to a priest who knew of his reputation for being bat crazy. The priest wouldn't take it, and speaking of people who wouldn't take it, Dad had a little problem with his son's action too. He didn't care how big of a nut job he'd become. This was about money!

Pietro Di Bernadone demanded justice and dragged Junior before the bishop. Maybe Francesco didn't know what he'd done wrong. Weren't they one big happy family? What's mine is thine?

Perhaps his dad just wanted to show him the extreme nature of his actions. He could have been tired of all of Francesco's antics: feeding the poor and living like he was one of them. The boy was a disgrace.

I think that may have been when the little poor one knew exactly how poor he was. He didn't really own anything. Nobody did. Everybody was poor as dirt. Might as well make his stance official.

Francesco stripped down to the skin and renounced his father to the laughter of the jeering crowd. He laid the last of his fancy clothes at his father's feet. No longer will I call you my father. I will call our Father in heaven mine.

His Father in heaven would be all that he had as he embraced radical poverty and let her become his lady. But it was not all joy and praising Brother Sun and Sister Moon. No, he suffered. He remained imperfect. Sometimes he lost his temper. Sometimes he lost his mind. He'd ask his brothers to do crazy things like preach in their drawers, then, feeling badly that he'd been so harsh, he'd strip down to his and preach a rapturous sermon by his brother's side.

Saint Francis of Assisi, in living the gospel with authenticity, offers good news to the bad boys of the world. You can be who you are, fall, get back up again, fall, get back up again, and still recommit yourself to God.

And God will receive you, very human you.

Two years before his death, partially blind and wracked with illness, Saint Francis asked two graces of Christ before he died: to experience personally and fully the pain of His passion, and to feel for Him the same love that made Him sacrifice His life for His friends, even though they weren't very friendly.

God granted him what he asked for, and for the next two years he was a walking sign of Christ's love that was tough as nails. He gives me hope that anything is possible, especially if you do it with love—and a little sacrifice.

Do you know what I'm saying?

I hope you do, because I can't tell you any other way right now. All I have is a story. God must have made you just for me.

PRIEST

We arrived at Sacred Heart parish, a historic church in the heart of the Motor City, and I didn't have any clue what Alessandro could do for us, but I knew he loved me enough to do something, and by default, he'd love Gina and Zoe, too.

Not by default. Love didn't come hard for him, and he wasn't stingy with it.

About Alessandro. He was a tenderhearted kid. I was roly-poly at eight. He was frail and sickly. We were a couple of rejects growing up in a mostly black neighborhood. I was an outcast because of my weight and my insistence that I was white. He existed on the outskirts because he was Italian and talked like a little old man, even then.

I wanted to prepare Gina for him, to offer him to her like a gift. Both of us were impoverished of people. She could use a Father Alessandro.

"Okay. About Alessandro. He's going to tell you an appalling thing we used to do when we were kids."

"Uh oh. Am I going to have to see you through therapy when we get married?"

"You may, but it probably won't be for that. Or maybe it will be. He's going to tell you that when we were kids, when other boys were playing with action figures, we played with holy cards while I regaled him with stories about the saints."

Gina gave me a sidelong glance. "Holy cards and saint stories, huh?"

"Yup."

"No wonder he became a priest."

I nodded. "The next logical question is, what happened to me?

I didn't want to be a priest. I wanted to be a Capuchin Friar of the Renewal, all about poverty, chastity, and obedience. No bling. No sweet thing. Christ my King."

She smiled at that. Then she took me in with those big brown eyes. "I'm not sure that would have been my next question. I know what happened to you. You kept telling stories."

"But they weren't saint stories."

"Maybe they were. Maybe we all have a little saint in us. You told good stories, right? I mean, wasn't the Pulitzer about a school with a tragedy nobody wanted to pay attention to?"

"Well, there's *that*, I guess. Anyway, Alessandro, or Father Alessandro now, is still Italian."

"Some things never change, except for when they do, uh, *soul brother*."

I ignored that.

"And he talks like he's a little old man, even though he's only twenty-eight. There's just something geriatric about him, always calling you dear one, precious, and things that make you feel enfeebled."

Gina smiled at me and made my jaded little heart flutter. "I won't feel enfeebled, any more than I am. I love him already."

"With the exception of a few days ago, I hadn't been around him for a long time. My loss, but I trust him like a brother. I should have gone to him a long time ago."

"You're going to him now, Priest."

"I'm going to ask him what we should do."

"About getting married?"

"Among other things."

"What else are you going to ask him?"

"Where we should go, Gina. I saw no less than three newspaper reporters at the Vineyard West, including my own editor. I'm not going to be the only one trying to find your story now, and they won't all have honorable intentions."

She studied me for a while. Laid her head back against the headrest.

"Why would Veronica do that to me?"

"She's on a mission. You're her job now."

"But I never did anything to hurt or exploit her. I never asked for her help."

I hated to get to the sad core of my wretched life with my mother, but she needed to know. "I don't think this is about you, Gina. It *is* about you in the literal sense because she couldn't do this at all without you. But she's probably on the rampage because you liked *me*, even preferred me to her. She couldn't stand that."

"Why does she treat you so badly?"

"That's a question I've been asking myself for years. I can speculate, but I really don't know. I'm not sure I want to find out."

She reached for me, and her healing touch surged through me like an electric current. At least that's what I told myself it was—her healing touch. But even if it wasn't healing, it was *healing*. Being near her made me better.

"I'm going to do whatever he tells us to. I need help, Gina. And I want to make sure we have God's blessings."

"You trust him that much?"

"I do."

"Well, let's go meet him. I trust him too."

My heart filled to overflowing. I had to ask myself how long could it last. It seemed too good to be true, which most the time meant it probably was.

FATHER ALESSANDRO

My brother underestimates the value of playing with holy cards. With images of our friends on the front and prayers on the back, they were like windows into heaven. I never felt quite alone when I had my friends and my dear brother Anthony.

Those cards taught me to see that heaven is always nearer than it seems, and more people love you than you can possibly realize. I needed that.

Anthony called when they'd arrived in the parking lot, and I went outside to meet them.

My dear brother stepped out of the car first, and once again, I offered him my deepest sympathy. I drew him into an embrace, which he shrugged off too quickly. This worried me, I must admit, but I convinced myself he only needed time. Then I took in his lovely Queen of Sorrows, and what a scandalous beauty she was.

When he'd visited before, for the sacrament of reconciliation, he told me she had but four wounds. Now, a large and most terrible bloodstain flowed down the front of the thin cotton shift she wore. My heart leapt within me, for immediately the odor of sanctity overcame me. It was quite cold, and she had no coat. The poor girl, she could not even walk without assistance and what appeared to be great pain.

Anthony helped her out of the car and held her by the waist, and she'd circled her arms around his neck. Blood stains had crept

through the barrier of bandages on her hand. I rushed to their
assistance and placed my coat over Regina Dolores and together we
helped her and her darling little girl into my home.

Oh, the burdens I foresaw that Regina Dolores would bear.
She was not even a Catholic. Who would honor what she had been
given? As far as I knew, there was no tradition in her Protestant
denomination—the Vineyard, did he say?—to support this grace.
The holy Catholic Church could not help her. There was scarcely
time for the church to investigate the lives of those within its own
ranks. They would not take the time to examine this dear child.

Even if she were Catholic, the authenticity of her wounds would
never be confirmed in her lifetime. No stigmatic had received such
confirmation while he or she was still alive. They were but human,
even with such extraordinary graces. There was the risk of these dear
souls falling from God's grace at any time before their death. The
church could not honor such souls for exemplary lives of virtue and
piety if even the potential for a falling away were present.

And it was present. I saw the way they looked at one another.
Anthony did not tell me he was in love with her, and she with him.
What would become of it?

I was afraid for them, for life could be difficult enough without
such remarkable circumstances.

We had clothing stored in our pantry. Not much; we mostly
made room for food, personal care items, and diapers and such. But
there was some clothing. I dug out a few pieces for Regina Dolores
and her Zoe, thankful that the ladies of Sacred Heart had dutifully
cleaned what we had available.

I was concerned about calling upon any of the ladies to help bathe her. I wished to protect her privacy. I wanted her to feel safe within our care. We helped her to the bathroom, ran water, and heaven help us, sent the child in to assist her. It broke my heart. Where was this girl's mother? Did she have sisters? A trusted friend? Anthony said no. No one should be that alone.

While Regina Dolores bathed, Anthony retired to my sitting room, a simple room; the furnishings are unimpressive but comfortable. I'd made a fire after Mass and planned to spend the day quietly reading and meditating until evening Mass. He sat near the fire. He needed to bathe as well. Her blood and scent were all over him.

I spoke frankly to him. "You are in love, my friend."

He neither confirmed nor denied what I said. I don't think he could deny it—not to me.

"I want to marry her, Alessandro. I'm talking to you as my friend, not my priest."

"Anthony, I am friend and priest. I must speak to you as both."

"I've asked her, and she's agreed."

"I can see the two of you have fallen in love."

He opened his mouth, surely to deny it, but closed it again and waited for me to speak.

"You said you've only known her for a short time. Less than a week."

"She has no one."

"Lots of people have no one. You cannot marry everyone who is lonely."

"She needs a Joseph, Alessandro. God provided our lady with a husband to keep her from reproach."

"Does she know of your illness?"

"I said I'll be her Joseph. It won't be that kind of marriage."

This concerned me. "Anthony, you are in love with her. She looks at you with love in her eyes. Do you truly believe you can have a marriage without physical intimacy?" A blush crept to his cheeks. "Anthony, have you already shared intimacies with this dear sister?"

He shook his head vigorously. "No. That's the truth." He seemed to doubt his own words. "Well, I've touched her." He laughed. "This isn't coming out right. I'm not used to talking to you about women, Al."

"You spoke to me about Elle."

"What I had with her was different. She was like me. She was an addict. She was lost. She was …"

I waited for him to say it. He needed to speak it for himself, but I helped him.

"What else was she, Anthony?"

"She was HIV positive."

"You must tell Regina Dolores you carry the virus if you plan to marry her. And I urge you to wait, my friend. Marriage is not child's play. It is a lifetime commitment. A sacred vow and a sacrament."

"Maybe she healed my HIV, too."

"Then it should not be a problem for you to be tested and confirm such a lovely miracle. Will you take an AIDS test, my friend?"

He didn't respond immediately. I did not believe he thought she'd healed him at all, even if God had been so merciful to use her that way. I believe my brother did not think he deserved such grace from God, but that is the wonder of grace. We do not deserve it.

"Anthony?"

"The vultures are already sniffing around her. I have to protect her."

"Who will protect her from you?"

I know my words stung him. It was not my intent to cause him pain. He stared at the flames flickering in the fireplace. I did not wish for him to shut me out. I wanted only to speak candidly. I did so with love.

He turned to me again. "I want to do what you say, as friend and priest. But I'm set on marrying her. I'll do it with or without your blessing."

"Anthony. She is not a Catholic. You are. You know a civil marriage is not the same as the sacrament of holy matrimony. You must marry in the church, or you will not truly be married."

"I won't sleep with her, Al. I wouldn't do anything to hurt her."

"You are not yet strong, dear one. You are not ready to take on a wife and child, even if you have the most honorable intentions. What is happening with your career?"

"Apparently, I'm working on a story about a black Protestant stigmatic."

"And that will enable you to care for them?"

"I have a job, Alessandro."

I stood and walked over to where he sat, placing my hand upon his shoulder. "I say this with great love for you. You will make a grave error if you marry Regina Dolores. You have not learned to be responsible. Nor are you accountable."

He looked up at me. I'd never seen him so sincere. "Please, please help me, Alessandro. Marry us before God. I promise you I'll take care of her."

"It is not God's timing. Perhaps if you were to wait. I'm not saying that you may never marry her, but surely you know … it was only Wednesday that you were in the house of the Lord, intoxicated from drugs. You need time, Anthony. Your beloved Nana has died. You are still grieving. You mustn't be selfish because you hurt. Let me find a place for her. You can trust me."

"I know I can trust you, but I don't need to send her somewhere. I'll take care of her."

"Where are her parents, Anthony?"

"Not here. Or she wouldn't be with me, but since she is, I'm going to marry her."

"What is driving you when I am certain you know that she can be cared for by others—a community of people, not just a single, struggling young man who is reeling from a very painful loss?"

"I need her!"

His back curved into my chair. I knew he was discouraged, though it was never my intent to cause him to despair. I believed in him. I always did. I wanted my dear friend—my brother—to be prudent in matters. A vulnerable woman and small child were involved, and marriage was a holy sacrament before God.

For just a moment, I saw my dear brother as the eight-year-old boy full of sorrow and saint stories, mourning the rejection of his mother. He did not want to let her go because he was afraid she wouldn't return to him. My poor dear friend.

"She appears to love you, Anthony. You must trust in love."

"Love has never been good to me."

"You are mistaken, my friend. Love has been exceedingly kind to you."

"I'm not sending her away."

"She is not an object for you to possess."

"I won't be able to do this without her, Alessandro. She's like the soul of this poor man that I am. I need her to need me because without her I'm lost."

"Anthony, God will not forsake you."

"It's me that will forsake God without her help. I'll marry her with or without your blessings, Alessandro."

My heart felt heavy within me. I was so very sorry. "You will marry her without them, my dear friend. But please, I beg you, don't do this."

From there on I began to pray fervently for the three of them.

PRIEST

I don't know if it was the whole addict thing that made me so manipulative, or if it was plain old selfishness like Alessandro said. I'd decided I was going to marry Gina, and nobody was going to stop me.

I thought I'd heard from God; I was supposed to be her Joseph.

How do you even know when God is speaking to you? Alessandro was a priest. I didn't hear him saying things like that. "God spoke to me. God told me." Those were the things Veronica said, as if God Himself were that approachable, babbling endlessly to whomever would listen.

Even Gina did it. She told me God stopped talking to her. That He seemed to disappear when the wounds started, like she had Jesus on the main line. She spoke of Christ as if He was her Lover, and she was a bride forsaken. And something about my talk with Alessandro made me resent such lofty talk.

I knew perfectly well the Bible as well as tradition supported her claims. The church as the beloved bride of Christ was a thread woven through both Testaments. I knew the Scriptures spoke of Christ as a Good Shepherd who spoke tenderly to His sheep.

But I wanted her. I wanted it all, and I didn't want Alessandro, or even God, standing in my way.

So when she finished bathing and dressing and called to me to come help her, I went to her. She wrapped her arms around me and I whispered in her ear, "We have to go."

She stared at me with those almond eyes. "Why?"

"We just have to move on, that's all. You didn't think we'd stay here did you?"

She grazed her fingertips across my face. "Why aren't you being straight with me?"

"Come on, we're going to have dinner with Alessandro before we go."

"Wait."

She'd stopped trying to walk. I kept trying to pull her forward.

"I said stop!"

I forced an exhalation from my lungs. "Why, Gina? I can't *carry* you. Why won't you just keep holding on and walk with me?"

"Are we being metaphorical here?"

Man, she charmed me.

"No, we want to get out of this steamy bathroom to make you comfortable."

"What are you afraid of, Priest? What's going on?"

"I'm hungry. Can we just go to dinner?"

Gina didn't argue, for a change. She let me help her into the dining room where Alessandro waited with strips of cloth diapers he'd fashioned into bandages.

GINA

Funny, I'd spent so long in relative isolation, and now all kinds of people were trying to protect me. Mike thought I was sick. He wanted to protect me by seeing to it that I got medical attention. Even Veronica, in her own strange way, wanted to protect me. She saw me as some chosen vessel that had a message to share with the world. And she wanted to make sure the higher purpose for what was happening to me was fulfilled. I honestly believe a part of her thought that. The fact that she could benefit was a secondary gain.

And then there was Priest. I think, despite him not saying it, he was motivated by love. He was more altruistic than he realized. But even though he'd returned to his heavenly Father, his faith was as tenuous as mine. I wanted to protect him, and believe in him.

I could tell he'd spoken to Father Alessandro and things had not gone like he expected them to. I didn't know the specifics, but I assumed Father Alessandro said our getting married was ridiculous, and it was. And he would have said that to protect me. Priest, too.

In the book of Matthew there's a story about two blind men. I love to read this one in *The Message*. It says these two blind men cried out to Jesus, "Mercy, Son of David! Mercy on us!" They followed Jesus all the way home, and when they got to where He lived, they

followed Him inside. And Jesus asked them, "Do you really believe
I can do this?" I liked that question, "Do you really believe I can do
this?"

Well, sure they did. They wouldn't have been following Him
home begging for mercy if they didn't.

There are so many miracles in that story, and some aren't so
obvious. Like, how do two blind people hook up? They can't see!
The story doesn't say they had anybody but each other. I mean, did
they have Braille classes back then? Support groups? I don't think so.
Maybe each heard the other begging in the dark, and somehow they
found their way to one another.

That had to be a rough journey, full of falls and bumps and
bloody hands and knees. But they found each other. Linked arms
and made a plan. They would find Jesus together. Stick with Him
until He gave them mercy. They weren't too proud to beg. Life
hadn't been kind. So, it wasn't about pride. You can't have too much
pride when you're blind and dependent, even if it's on another
blind person. It was about the need. They needed each other, and
they needed Jesus. And He healed them. Jesus healed them both.
Another miracle. He told them, "Become what you believe."

Yeah, Priest and I were blind, but I believed we could work. The
idea of us together against the world ignited and burned within me,
and it felt as warm and comforting as the fire we sat by in Father
Alessandro's den after dinner. I felt the tension between them, but I
believed in the end we'd be all right.

Isn't that how it is for all Christians? I don't care what hell breaks
loose, we get our happy ending.

I knew as the three of us chatted over dinner, saying a whole lot of nothin', that I'd go with Priest. That I'd marry him. I wanted to be happy. I wanted to be with him. I figured we might be blind now, but we could make our way to healing together.

You ever wonder why Jesus told those two formerly blind guys right after He healed them not to tell anybody? He told a few people that, and I never understood it. I mean, He'd come to do His Father's work, right? Wasn't that good news? Shouldn't every testimony draw more people to Him? Thy kingdom come, and all that? But Jesus said, "Don't let a soul know how this happened."

Maybe it's because, a few passages later, the now-sighted men were telling everybody they knew, and the Pharisees were trippin'. "Hocus-pocus," they said. "He's probably made a pact with the devil."

That just goes to show you, even Jesus was questioned.

And we just needed to keep what we were doing to ourselves.

CHAPTER TWENTY-EIGHT

PRIEST

I took her home to my apartment. I'm surprised Alessandro didn't stop us. He'd pulled me aside.

"Leave her here, Brother Anthony. I promise you I will put her in excellent hands. You may stay too, until I've secured help. Don't rush into anything."

But I'd made up my mind. We were getting hitched.

I settled them inside the duplex, and man, it was no place for Gina and Zoe. Gina told me she'd make it to the futon and I didn't think anything about it. I was worried about hiding the car, because when Veronica didn't find Gina at home, this was the first place she'd come.

I parked it on a street a few blocks over. Doubts assailed me.

What was I doing? That's when something occurred to me, and I took off like I'd been shot out of a gun to get back home.

I'd left my "works," my drug paraphernalia, strewn around, and two packs of brown sugar on my futon! I should have known right then and there to take her back to Alessandro as fast as my Probe would carry us.

So, there I was, panting and looking crazy when I burst back into my duplex, and the needle's on the floor, and the smack is where I left it. Zoe's parked in front of my television, remote in hand, surfing like she's in my place watching television every day, and Gina's eyeing me like my face just flashed across the screen on *America's Most Wanted*.

Then Zoe breaks my heart by saying, "I'm sorry you're sick, Mr. Anthony."

"What?"

"The needle," Gina said. "She thought you might need some kind of shots, and I told her you were sick. She didn't touch it."

I snatched it up myself, along with the packs of heroin.

"I used to be sick, Zoe. I'm better now," I said feeling like the wretched of the earth. I looked to Gina to see if she'd discovered my "medication."

"If I could have picked it up and done something with it I would have."

"I'll take care of it, Gina."

"I hope so," she said, her voice as cold and hard as steel.

I wish I could tell you I was strong, but I didn't have the nerve to throw the smack out. I tucked it away on the top of my closet, syringe and all. Gina couldn't go looking for it. Not on her own.

I slogged back to the living room and plopped down beside her.

She looked into my eyes, and I couldn't hide my guilt. I started in with excuses. "I haven't had time to clean up that part of my life, all right? I'm sorry I don't have the place childproofed." She looked away from me. Crossed her arms across her chest, her lip poked out.

"I moved it out of her reach, Gina."

"You'd be surprised what a child can get into. Why didn't you throw that stuff away?"

"I will. You can't just toss a dirty needle in the trash."

"Why not?"

"Because it can poke through. It's a biohazard. What do you think?" I don't even know why I felt angry with her, but I did. And she kept at it.

"Is there something wrong with your blood, Priest? Something that would trouble you inordinately if you put your little kit in a regular garbage bag?"

"What? Do you think I have … hepatitis … or something?"

"Do you?"

"I don't share needles." Anymore.

"Is there anything I should know about you, healthwise, before we"—she lowered her voice and stole a look at Zoe who paid us no mind—"get married?"

Why couldn't she just leave it be? Let me tell her in my own time? I'd given her hints. You don't just blurt something like that out. "I'm not going to give you anything, okay?"

I'd be careful. We wouldn't be making passionate love. I hoped. I almost wished she'd fought me on it. Demanded to know, but she didn't. She just put her arms around me.

"I don't want to see anything like that again."

"Sure thing, Mrs. Priest."

"If I do, I can't do this."

"Yeah. I know. You don't have to worry."

"Throw it away, Priest."

"I will."

"Now."

"Not right now. I'm tired now. But I'll do it."

My heart thundered inside of me like I'd stolen something and narrowly escaped the repercussions.

I still believed we'd be all right, despite myself.

GINA

I knew what he looked like when he came to me: haggard appearance, needle tracks, and the scars marring his arm. He'd said it was his own stigmata. But now, confronted with the harsh, in-my-face reality … watching him snatch up a dirty needle and *not* throw his stash of drugs away … I was scared.

He didn't offer me any real assurance. I needed to make a decision, and I opted to go with him, blind, hoping he was looking for mercy from Jesus as much as I thought.

And here's the other thing. Didn't he say I'd healed him? I didn't want to be arrogant. Let's be for real, *I* didn't heal anybody. If somebody got healed it was an act of God. I hadn't even laid hands on him. But whatever was going on was happening through me. I couldn't make it happen on my own. At least I didn't think so.

I wanted him to be healed. Why not? Why couldn't God heal through me?

Priest said he had no withdrawal symptoms. That was compelling enough for me. If God could heal that, He could heal everything he had.

I let him lead me inside of his place. And if I thought my townhouse was a study in minimalism, Priest had a jail cell. Futon. Television. Crucifix. Not much more than that.

Lord, have mercy! Where were we going to live? And *how* were we going to live? I didn't have to get a call to know I was so fired from Subway.

But no, we were just a couple of blind folks, stumbling toward Jesus. Love would find a way. It had to be true.

He ordered in, and we ate in the dark. We did everything in the dark that night. Veronica came by, banging on the door, but we ignored her. She couldn't be sure we were in there. The only sign of life in his place from the outside was that the flickering light of the television. People leave their televisions on, even if nobody's home, and it's a total waste of energy.

Lots of things are a waste of energy. We just pretend they're not.

PRIEST

Gina and Zoe retired blissfully early for the night, and the two of them slept on my futon while I sat on the floor letting the television watch me.

I'd steal long, luxurious looks at her now and then. I wanted to reach out and touch her so badly I could hardly stand it.

I should have been a gentleman and slept on the floor, but I wasn't a gentleman, and I wanted to lie with her again. I told myself it was innocent. I just wanted to put my hand on her: her bare arm, her back curved to cuddle with her little girl, the soft mound of her hip.

I crawled on the futon and lay behind her. After all, I didn't have Veronica to regulate me. I wouldn't have tried anything with the kid there. I wouldn't have tried anything *without* her there. Or so I let myself believe.

This was all about honor, protecting her and keeping her beyond reproach, but my honor was slipping fast.

I whispered her name. She didn't answer. Zoe snored softly.

I placed my hand delicately on her hip, willing myself to explore her no further. "You are Psyche, my love. I have no soul but you. And I am Cupid, desire burning for you. I love you, but I can't show you what I really am. It will hurt you if I do and ruin everything. This will have to be enough."

I moved just a bit closer to kiss the top of her head. Her dreadlocks tickled my chin. And I fell asleep praying for strength.

GINA

You didn't really think I was asleep, did you? In truth, I slept a little while, but my body hurt more often than not, and I felt so odd. It wasn't unusual for me to wake up in the middle of the night. What was unusual, however, was having a man crawl in bed with me, telling me I'm a goddess.

Once again, he'd underestimated just how well read a girl with barely a high school diploma could be. I knew the myth of Psyche and Cupid, or Eros, depending on who's telling the tale.

Let me tell you a story. It won't be as good as the ones Priest tells, but I think you should know this, because that moment, alone, knowing we were going to get married and no one was going to stop us—that's where things became even more complicated.

Psyche was one of three sisters, and all of them were incredibly beautiful, but Psyche was most beautiful of all. She had garnered so much admiration that Venus—not the planet, but the goddess— became insanely jealous. So, she asked her son Cupid to go poke her with his Golden Arrow and make her fall in love with the ugliest creature that walked the earth, ever.

Mama's boy went to do her bidding, but whoops! She really was fine. Cupid ended up falling in love with her himself without having to poke her at all! And don't even get me started on that symbolism.

Everybody continued to think she was gorgeous, but nobody wanted to marry her. This frustrated her parents. After all, she was getting a little long in the tooth and they had two more to marry off as well. They wanted to get the show on the road, especially since everybody dug her anyway. They were so concerned when nothing happened they consulted an oracle, who told them she was so beautiful she was destined to marry a god.

I'm sorry. I have to stop here. The thought of marrying God, when I think of it, even now, is too much for me to bear.

PRIEST

The story goes that the oracle told her parents to abandon her to a mountain, and there she would be taken care of. So they sent her away.

Sent her away. Mountaintop. I'm seeing a real Gina theme here. But I digress.

So, Psyche—you can call her Soul for short—headed for the mountaintop, but the west wind got, uh, got wind of her journey and on its gentle breath carried her away to a picturesque valley where a magnificent mansion of her very own awaited her.

Invisible servants ministered to her every need, and then night fell, and in the darkness her bridegroom came and consummated their union. It was the love she had waited for all her days, and she gave herself completely to him, and he to her.

The bridegroom, Cupid, had but one demand: that she never light a lamp when he visited her—when he loved her. She had to remain in the dark.

He didn't want her to know who he was.

Here's the thing about myths. Their scope is universal. You can almost always find yourself in the story. You can find your true love. You can even find God. It was all right there.

I didn't know she heard me. I didn't know that she'd surprise me. It wasn't supposed to happen that way.

CHAPTER TWENTY-NINE

PRIEST

I made it through the night without ravishing her. That Monday, if I could pull it off, would be our wedding day. I awoke before my girls and immediately set about to plan my work and work my plan. There were obstacles to my wedded bliss, however.

Instant wedding obstacle number one: We didn't have very much money. It would take money to procure items such as a wedding license, services rendered by a minister, and miscellaneous items that my blushing bride may want, such as a cheap wedding ring, a cheap—preferably free—wedding dress, flowers maybe.

Instant wedding obstacle number two: We had to get married today, or we'd officially be shacking up—whether or not we were living in sin—until I'd obtained a wedding license, which was not instantaneous in Michigan expect under exceptional circumstances. If I could manage to talk the state into the idea that we actually had exceptional circumstances, I could obtain our marriage license when I applied, but the minister officiating over the wedding must provide—and faxing was okay—a letter on official church letterhead of his or her intent to marry us on that very day.

Since Alessandro had said no, I'd have to find a minister who'd agree to marry us today *and* give me the letter. I couldn't think of a single other person who'd me help with this.

Instant wedding obstacle number three: My bride was limited in her activity as she bled from the crucifixion wounds of Christ.

It was going to be a long day.

Gina woke up a little after nine. I helped her to the bathroom, ran a shower for her, and gave her the rare commodity in my house of a clean T-shirt and sweatpants. She came out an impressive fifteen minutes later, cleansed, looking terribly cute in my clothes, and predictably smelling like roses. When she ambled with her awkward gait to the futon, refusing my help this time, and sat down, I told her what I was working on.

"I'm trying to get us hitched today. Not having much luck."

"Anything I can do?"

"You might want to ask God to help us. I think He's fond of you."

"I ask God to help us every day, Priest."

"Then maybe we'll be okay."

I told her about the instant wedding obstacles and watched her face to gauge her emotional responses. She seemed genuinely discouraged, which told me, and I hoped I was right, that she cared.

There we were sitting on my futon, Zoe still curled in a fetal position on the left side, and Gina and I on the right. The house was nearly empty of the things that make a home. This painful reminder only served to underscore my soulless existence. And here was Psyche before me. Would her color, her natural fabrics—would her beauty, which surpassed that of even her fair sisters—touch the stark black and white of my life?

I had it bad, but I was getting discouraged, too.

We'd waited an hour for any delivery place to open and bring us food. "I hate to leave you, Gina."

"Zoe will help me."

"You know that bites, right?"

"I've known that for a long time, Priest, but she got stuck with me as a mother. She doesn't seem to mind it nearly as much as I do, but I'll make a big effort to do things for myself. Maybe I'll manage holding my own cup, today. I mean, I got from the bathroom all by myself.

"How are the wounds?"

"They aren't so bad today. That weird protective covering—that is so strange—seems a little thicker today." She held out her palms for me to see, and sure enough, the thin membrane appeared to be thickening, revealing the twisting lines of the road map of her palm print.

"Amazing. Do you think they're healing?"

"You mean, like it's going away?"

I shrugged. "I don't know."

The look of dejection that crossed her face was enough to force my hand of its own accord to caress her face. "Would that be okay with you?"

Now she shrugged. She made a few failed efforts to speak on it, faltered, then I watched her pull her courage out of some deep well within her. "There's a part of me that knows as long as this is happening God is with me. Despite the darkness, the maddening silence, and the withdrawal of His sweet consolation, as long as these marks are here, so is He. You know what I mean?"

"I do, Gina."

"You have a great imagination, right?"

"I have my moments."

"And the stuff you told me about you and Alessandro growing up. You felt close to God and the saints then, didn't you?"

"Yeah, sure. What about it?"

"I came to Jesus when I was a teenager. And this was no quiet, say-the-prayer-on-the-back-of-the-tract thing. It was big, Priest. And I don't know, almost violent. It turned me on my ear."

I watched her without interrupting, once again examining her palms. There was no big show of blood today, and she seemed to be as puzzled by the lack of it as she was by its appearance in the first place.

"What if I made the whole thing up? Not intentionally. But what if everything I've ever believed about God somehow I fabricated? Maybe because I needed God. I needed a mother, and a father, and someone who wouldn't leave or feel disgusted or run away if I was sick. And I needed a lover who wouldn't fail me, and God could be all of that. Mother—the Holy Spirit, Father, Son, who became Lover. And what if I made up these wounds, as terrible as that sounds, because it was Ash Wednesday? I didn't mind dying, and if I crucified myself, maybe I thought it'd be okay?"

"Elaborate."

"That's it, Priest. There's nothing to elaborate. It's really very simple. What if I made the whole thing up?"

"How would you have done it? I was with you in the balcony when you got the first wound."

"Were you watching me the whole time?"

Couldn't say that I was. And I was high. I could have missed a lot.

Her eyes seemed to brighten with the possibility of it. "Did you actually see me get any of the wounds?"

"In the bathroom, when I was helping Veronica give you the ice bath, you got one then. It wasn't bleeding before."

"How can you be sure?"

She had me. How could I?

"What about at the Vineyard?" I said. "Your side bled in front of everyone."

"Or did it just seem like it did?"

Now I was frustrated. "What are you saying? That you faked it all? How is that possible? You couldn't even hold anything in your hands. I saw every wound. Washed them. Smelled them. If you were doing this, how'd you make the strange, gravity-defying flow of blood happen? How could you make a wound stay fresh with no signs of healing? If you could pull that off you're a wonderworker, even if you were some kind of magician."

For some reason my heart began to race. I could feel my blood pressure rising, and it made me a little dizzy. She pressed on.

"And what would that say about you?"

I took a few deep cleansing breaths to steady myself. Waited a few beats before I'd even attempt to answer her. "I guess it would say that somewhere, deep inside of me, I wanted to have faith, and at the same time, I wanted a sign. A wonder. And I went about, consciously or not, looking for one until I found you."

"And …"

"My story merged with your story. And here we are."

"Do you think we could have made all of it up?"

"We could have. Mind over matter. Heart over mind. It doesn't matter now. I told you. I believe in you—in you, Gina."

"If it makes you feel any better, I'm not faking it. Or if I am, I'm not aware of it and am far crazier than even *I* think I am."

"If it makes you feel any better, I don't think you're crazier than you think you are. I think you're a miracle, Gina. But you'd be that to me even if you didn't have stigmata."

"Would you still marry me if the wounds went away, and I could go back to Subway and build achingly beautiful submarine sandwiches capable of making the whole obese world lose weight?"

"I think I would."

"Do you think God would leave me because I needed help?"

"I hope not. He wouldn't be a very loving God, would He?"

"Would He leave me if I belonged to Him, and maybe He just doesn't want anybody else to have me?"

All that and now she gets to the point. She was scared of losing her true Love. And it certainly wasn't me she was all bent out of shape about.

"I can't answer that for you. Gina, you know if you believe in God by faith, or if you made up God. I think deep down inside, we all really know. If nothing else we have the testimony of creation to point to a Creator. I'm not a theologian, but it seems to me God always used … marriage … as a way to tell us something about how He wants to relate to us. It's not supposed to take you further away from God."

"What if a part of me wishes the wounds would go away so … someone … would see me as I really am? A woman. Just a woman, Priest. Far from a saint. Don't you think that's selfish?"

I sighed. "Selfish? I don't know. But let me tell you a story."

PRIEST

"Saint Catherine of Siena"

Baby Catherine di Benincasa was born to a family who knew moderate wealth, and lavish heartache. Her mother, Lapa, was the daughter of a poet, and her papa a dyer and tradesman. Lapa bore an astonishing twenty-five children, and Catherine was the next to the youngest. Only twelve of Lapa's kids lived beyond infancy, so she kept her hopes for her daughter simple: She wanted her girl to have a normal childhood, snag a husband of adequate means to provide for her, and live a happy, quite predictable life.

Poor Mama di Benincasa.

Catherine was so not normal, and it started early. When she was but a little grasshopper, one day she and her brother walked about the rolling hills of the Italian countryside. She looked across the wide fields of green beauty toward the cathedral of San Domenico, and there in the bright expanse of azure sky Jesus was looking right at her with His immense and loving eyes. He smiled at her and blessed her with the sign of the cross.

Her brother, however, could not see the Lord. All he saw was his nutty buddy sister stopped in her tracks and looking like she was falling in love with the sun. He couldn't force her to move. Finally he said something to the effect of, "I'm telling mom and you're gonna get it."

Young Catherine replied. "If you could see what I see, you would never try to disturb me."

Not that anyone really disturbed her. She could write the book on homegrown mysticism—not many people would buy it, but she could do it.

Little Catherine from that day forward abandoned her Barbies to play nun. Her family's garden was her convent, and she instructed the neighborhood kids in the ways of God. The miniature saint prayed for hours at a time and began to mortify her flesh before it even had time to show her it was going to be a problem!

She got worse (better?) as she got older. She cut her hair to ward off male suitors, and once, when her mother sent her to a fancy day spa she purposefully burned herself on the vents so that she could identify with the poor souls in hell.

Mama fought back and Papa joined in too. They forced Catherine to do all the household chores, essentially making a slave of her. Only one day, her father saw a dove hovering over her head. He took it as a sign. It may have been just a crazy bird that got loose in the house and really liked Catherine's hairdo; nonetheless, her father freed her, and even gave her a cell of her own with only a crucifix on the wall, a table with a lamp to illuminate the cross, and a couch that she insisted on covering with planks so she wouldn't be comfortable on it. She often hurt herself. Her body was covered with deep gashes she'd put there, which she called her "flowers." She'd made a bouquet of her self-inflicted suffering.

When Catherine was nineteen she went ahead and married her Beloved. He vowed to her, "I have determined to celebrate the wedding feast of your soul and to espouse you to Me in faith as I have promised." Jesus' mother officiated over the ceremony. You've got to love that she had the full approval of a Jewish mother. John, the beloved disciple, John the Baptist, Saint Paul the Apostle and Saint Dominic—she was a Dominican nun—were all witnesses. King David was the wedding singer. He did the music too.

Jesus said to her, "I marry you to Me in faith, your Creator and Savior," and put a ring on her finger only she could see. After that she went out into the world inflamed with passionate spousal love. She didn't keep Him to herself.

Despite the fact that she celebrated Mass and took the blessed sacrament daily, she couldn't shake her own humanity. She agonized over her temptations, so much so that one day Jesus came to her, showing her His five wounds. He invited her to have a long refreshing drink from the wound in His side, and she did and gained strength to endure her ordeals. Later she had a vision. She saw the Lord coming to her in a great light. Five rays of blood came toward her: to her hands, her feet, and her heart.

She begged her Beloved, "Do not let these scars show outside of my body!" The rays of blood-tinted light became invisible, and when they touched her, she received stigmata that, like her wedding band, no one else could see.

She gave herself flowers but didn't want the flowers from Christ to show. Who can understand it?

Was she crazy? Some say she was. A holy anorexic who died at the age of thirty-three most likely because she'd abused her body so badly. No matter what you say of Saint Catherine of Siena, mystic or lunatic, you couldn't deny that she loved God. What she did or did not do to her body didn't diminish that love. And God loved her. What she did or did not do to her body did not change His love for her.

She was the bride of Christ. Nothing would change that. Nothing at all.

Do you understand what I'm saying to you?

GINA

I understood all right, or I thought I did, and I awarded my sweet storyteller with a kiss. Not a deep kiss. Not a lover's kiss. A peck of gratitude. I thought lover's kisses would come later.

Priest reluctantly left Zoe and me alone. He gave us stern warnings to stay quiet and not let anyone inside, no matter who they were, or what they said. And people came. Veronica. We knew it was her by the yelling. Others we couldn't identify came to his door and to the window, but Zoe and I laid low. She watched television, cuddled with me for a while, and asked why we had to hide and be quiet. I told her we were playing a game, and it would be over with very soon. I could only hope I was right.

I missed my colorful little ghetto townhouse. I missed my orange love seat and my books. Though I had it memorized, I missed holding my Saint John of the Cross book in my hands. I missed holding everything in my hands.

I lay back on Priest's funky black futon thinking of Saint Catherine seeing the eyes of Christ when she was just a little girl. I never saw Jesus but, oh, the times I felt His gaze on me. I thought of The Spiritual Canticle:

> O crystal well!
> Oh that on Your silvered surface
> You would mirror forth at once
> Those eyes desired
> Which are outlined in my heart!

My heart hadn't changed so much. I still loved Jesus the most. I mean, I was feelin' Priest, but God knew how lonely I was for a flesh-and-blood love. He wouldn't punish me for that, I told myself. He sent Priest. Didn't He?

Even Saint Catherine had temptations. That didn't mean God would abandon her. I thought. Maybe. That was the whole point to the story, wasn't it? It didn't mean God would abandon me for wanting Priest to love me.

I hoped Priest was right, but I prayed God would give me the teensiest peek at His eyes just to prove it. I mean, if He could give me the wounds of Christ, that shouldn't be a hard thing.

CHAPTER THIRTY

PRIEST

The crowded, bustling office of *The News* was a flurry of activities. Writers of every station huddled over computer monitors, the clicking of their keyboards a robust and vibrant pulse.

I strode into Larry's office and found him poring over pictures with a photographer. I stepped closer to his desk and found, among other images, a black-and-white photo of Gina.

"She's much more interesting in color."

Larry looked up at me. "Tony, you son of a gun, if your mother hadn't have called me—"

"What exactly did she say?"

"She said she had a story for me. I asked her why you weren't calling yourself, especially since I hadn't seen you since Wednesday when you said you were going to church!"

"She said she had a story?"

"That's what I said, Tony."

"Did you get Veronica's story?"

"Are you kidding me? Of course I did, but when I saw you joined at the hip to stigmata girl I thought your story might trump hers, though I did find the bloody bandage fragments available for a small donation hilarious."

"I can't stop laughing, Larry. What'd she tell you?"

"Not as much as the *Free Press*," he said. He picked up the rival paper strewn across his desk and tossed it at me. It was opened to a page featuring a bad picture of Gina that could have been from her driver's license, and an even worse shot of her laying hands on a young woman at the Vineyard.

"Great," I said. "Just great."

"Read it," he said.

I braced myself for somebody else's take on Gina's story:

Monday, February 11, 2008.

Stigmata in the City:
Could an Urban Black Woman Bear the Wounds of Christ?
By Mary Beth Michaels

Free Press Staff Writer

Ann Arbor—Sunday morning services at the Vineyard in Ann Arbor were interrupted yesterday when a mysterious black woman and her unidentified companion joined those gathered for worship.

Unidentified companion, huh? Mary Beth looked right at me!
She knows exactly who I am. Witch!

The woman, confirmed to be Regina Dolores Merritt of
Inkster, a former employee of Subway in Inkster, claims to
be a mystic with healing powers who bears the crucifixion
wounds of Christ.

What!? And just when did she make these claims! And to
whom!

Pandemonium ensued when Merritt stood as the
congregation sang hymns—

Hymns!?

—and spontaneously began bleeding from her side with
no apparent cause. She appeared to be in *ecstasy*, a supernatural phenomenon in which the senses are temporarily
suspended and absorbed, allegedly, in God. By all accounts
when she stood she appeared to be unaware of her surroundings. Some members begin clamoring for her healing
touch, while others vehemently claimed she was a fraud.
    Several reliable sources report that Merritt, a single,
never-married mother, has a troubled past, including a
history of mental illness and psychosis. According to these
sources, who wish to remain anonymous, Merritt has
allegedly mutilated herself before to get attention.

According to her spiritual adviser and caretaker, Ms.
Veronica Morelli of Canton, Merritt, whose first and
middle name, Regina Dolores, means "queen of sorrows,"
attended the Vineyard service Sunday to share her message
of healing and forgiveness of sins. Ms. Morelli stated for
the record: "Blessed Regina Dolores is a victim soul. Her
gifts have appeared as a sign to an unbelieving church that
Jesus is real, and He's still with us. Anybody who thinks
she's a fake can stuff it."

Ms. Morelli had fliers available that explained stigmata,
and for a nominal donation, swatches of bandages which
she claims have been saturated with the miraculous blood
from the wounds. This reporter noted a strong odor of
roses emanating from the fabric.

Carol Letterman of Ann Arbor claimed to be healed of
sciatica on the spot when Merritt laid hands on her as she
was leaving the building. Other claims of healing have yet
to surface.

Stigmata has been a troublesome subject throughout
history. Conflicting theories regarding its validity abound.
Some claim stigmata is a miracle and sign from God, and
others, including popular miracle debunkers, claim the
paranormal phenomenon has either psychogenic origins—
mind over matter—or is an outright fraud.

Vineyard pastor Mike Adams declined to comment.

I tossed the paper on Larry's desk. "I can't believe this made it to
print. Her facts aren't accurate, and it has no heart. No humanity."

"Can you do better?"

I didn't answer.

He sat at the edge of his desk. Larry enjoyed toying with me, and I deserved it. I'd earned every bit of contempt he could heap on me and more. "Wanna see your mom's flyer?"

"Not really."

He handed the rose red flyer to me, and I grudgingly took it from the weasel. "Nice touch, the red paper," I said. "Ronnie went all out at Kinkos, didn't she?"

"Read it to me aloud," greasy Larry said.

I hated that I had to jump through these hoops with him, but he had something I needed if we were going to celebrate our nuptials that day. I read:

THE PASSION OF BLESSED REGINA DOLORES "QUEEN OF SORROWS"

God has graciously graced us by placing in our midst
a contemporary victim soul for the expiation of our
sins. The Blessed Regina Dolores Merritt has been
endowed with ~~four~~ five of the wounds of Christ.

For over seven hundred years specially chosen Christians (a
little more than three hundred) have exhibited the physical
marks of Christ's suffering. The first known stigmatic
was Saint Francis of Assisi. Other famous ones include
Saint Padre of Pio of Pietrelcina, recently canonized, who
bore the wounds for half a century; Teresa Neumann of
Germany, who bled profusely from her eyes whenever

she meditated on the crucifixion; and even a little black
Negro girl, ten years old, from California who received the
wounds during holy week. Blessed Regina Dolores is also a
black Negro female. Her wounds have the odor of sanctity
and she is actively involved with working miracles. She
personally helped my hair grow, and is involved in one-on-
one ministry to drug-addicted indigents. Blessed Regina
Dolores will be available to counsel and advise suffering
Christians. She is available through her spiritual adviser
and caretaker, the servant of God, Ms. Veronica Morelli.
A donation for services rendered is recommended or we
cannot guarantee an audience with the Blessed Stigmatic.

Veronica left her cell-phone number at the bottom.

"Nice," I said. "Veronica's in rare form. She's managed to outdo
herself, and that's a feat. Give me a bucket so I can hurl."

Larry quipped, "Veronica told me herself God was raising up
the queen of sorrows to change the world. A real sin eater, she, and
through her suffering she'd expiate the sins of many."

"Do you even know what 'expiate' means?"

"I've got a fact-checker. And I've got you, Tony. You can tell
me what *expiate* means when you write your future award-winning
story."

"Expiation is atonement for some wrongdoing. A person offers
themselves to God to satisfy the punishment of others. I assure you
Gina is doing no such thing."

"Gina? So you're diminishing names with her now. What's she
calling you?"

"Priest, which is not diminutive."

I never said I'd write a story—not for *The News*, just so we're clear.

"I need money," I said.

"You just got paid, Tony."

"I had expenses. Prize-winning stories take time. I'm going deep, Larry. Gonzo lives."

"Are you serious?"

"Sure. I need money to take care of Gina and her little girl while I work on …" I wanted to say finding her story, but he'd want to know what I meant. "While I work on it. I need more than my miserly salary pays."

"You don't deserve what you get."

"I'm not asking for me."

"She staying with you, Tony?"

"What do you think?"

"She giving it up? To you?"

"That's an offensive question, Larry."

He laughed. "Who are you? What have you done with Tony?"

I waited for his amusement to pass.

When he'd had his laugh he plundered through my silence. "How much do you need?"

"Five hundred. For now."

"You're crazy."

"Go with your Veronica story then. Make sure you mention to Ronnie that black and Negro, in the context she used the terms, mean the same thing." I knocked on his desk. "Hey, you should try the blood-stained bandages. Might get a little zing out of 'em. Can't hurt."

"I hate you, Tony."

"Go get me a check, Larry. I don't care if it comes out of your personal account. They'll reimburse you."

God, what was I doing? Where was I going to get the money to pay him back? I had no intention of delivering any sort of product to him.

Just as I thought, he had a check for me within five minutes. It came from his personal account.

"Make me proud, kid. This could turn everything around for you."

"Sure thing," I said. And headed to the desk of an old friend.

CHAPTER THIRTY-ONE

PRIEST

Julie Carboni was sweet on me back when I used to be Anthony Priest, hot stuff. We did each other a few favors—not that kind— and I knew she was connected to all kinds of people. People who could help you get things you want.

She was seated at her desk, twirling a lock of her long blonde hair around her fingers. Oddly I thought, *I'll never be with a white woman again. I'll never be with anyone other than Gina for the rest of my life.* I had to remind myself that we weren't going to have a "normal" marriage. I wondered if everybody thought stuff like that before they got married. Not the "We're not going to be normal" part, the "This is it. This woman I'm going to marry is as good as it gets from now on" part. Then I wondered if anybody thought their marriage would be normal.

"Julie," I said. She looked up at me, and her eyes lit. I don't care how much I disappointed her, in her mind I'd bounce back and be Anthony Priest again. Why didn't I remember that when I was shooting up? That not only Larry but Julie Carboni believed in me.

"I need a favor."

She grinned. I never asked her for money, so she didn't have to guard against that. I kept our favors business related.

"What's up, Tony?"

"I need a marriage license. Today. I don't have a minister yet."

She raised a perfectly groomed dark brow, which betrayed her true hair color. "*You* need a marriage license. Are those wedding bells I hear chiming around you?"

I leaned toward her, drumming my fingers on her desk. "Can you help with that?"

"Stop making that irritating noise," she said.

I stood upright.

"That'll be hard," she said. "You have to prove you're getting married by someone who's qualified to officiate over the ceremony."

"I know that, Julie. Which is why I'm speaking to you. If I can come up with a license, maybe I can show up at City Hall and hope somebody takes pity on me and my beloved."

"Who is she? I thought you were a lone wolf."

"I'm just a wolf."

"Is it the girl with the stigmata? Larry said you seemed … close."

I hoped I'd distract her by moving the conversation forward. "How do I get out of the proving it?"

"You wait. Or find a minister in a hurry. Listen, you can fake the letterhead, but you need a real, live minister."

"I'll keep that in mind. Thanks, Julie."

Before I could get away she nailed me. "Is it her, Tony?"

"She's not a sideshow freak, Julie."

She folded her arms and smirked. "You really are in love. Who'd a thought it? Tony Priest and a wonderworker."

"Everybody needs a little wonder, Julie."

"Well put. But don't let love keep you from writing a good story."

"Love is what made me write the few good ones I wrote, and I do mean few."

"I stand corrected."

Her voice trailed behind me when I turned and walked away. "Any old minister will do, Tony. Be creative."

"Creative?" I repeated, turning more than a few dismal ideas around in my head. I turned back to her. "Thanks." I walked away to the sound of Julie's best wishes.

I spent the next half-hour calling wedding chapels and independent ministers only to find a remarkable number of people don't answer their phones on Monday. *Be creative*, I reminded myself. Just when I was about to give up I my cell phone chirped.

Fox.

I knew I shouldn't answer it, but I guess I wasn't as ready to let go of the comfortable-as-blue-jeans familiarity of my old life. I answered the phone.

"Hello there, Foxy."

"Hey, baby? How you? Foxy misses you. Where you been?"

"Busy."

"You must need yo' medicine real bad. I can't believe you makin' it on just that lil' dab I gave you."

"I still have it, Foxy. I'm not really interested in using right now."

"What happened, baby? You always interested in a little feel good. You found Jesus?"

"Maybe I have, Reverend Foxy."

I know. I shouldn't have even damaged my brain cells considering it. I *know* this.

But ... he was *virtually* a minister.

Don't make me say it, okay? I was desperate.

GINA

The first thing I thought? *Oh no, he didn't.* But he did. He came home several hours later with a ring, a marriage license, and a flaming queen. I don't mean a dainty little girly man in drag. I mean a big, hulking Ving Rhames queen with a capital Q from that television movie *Holiday Hearts* with Alfre Woodard.

He or she came promenading into the living room with, "Umph, baby, something sho' does smell good in here."

I don't think I could have spoken. My mouth was one big O.

Because I didn't have bandages on, my wounds—at least the ones on my hands and feet—were completely visible. Priest must not have mentioned that detail to his friend. He got a gander at me, and froze.

She put his or her hand over ... *shoot* ... *his* heart and dropped to his knees screeching, "Lord Jesus! It's that the girl I read about in the *Free Press*."

Foxy grabbed my feet with his/her massive hands. "Oh, sweet Jesus I needed a sign. Lord, have mercy on me. Jesus help me!"

"Priest!" I yelled.

"She's ordained."

Foxy went on. "Mercy, Jesus. I need a miracle. Thank You, Lord for sending me to the Bless-ed Regina Dolores for the healing of my soul."

Heavenly (I think) language poured out of his (her?) mouth.

Foxy began to weep. "I'm so sorry for my sins, Jesus. I was just trying to make a lil' change on account of that makeup artist school was a scam. Jesus, I ain't mean to hurt nobody."

I looked at Priest, horrified.

"Just go with it," he said. "We all need to be cleansed from our sins."

"Bless me, sister Bless-ed Regina Dolores, queen of sorrows." He stopped his flood of tears and lifted his head. "Um, baby. What kind of queen are you?" He scrutinized me with keen interest.

"Not that kind."

"Oh," and he went right back to crying, which led to flushing the impressive stash of dope he carried down the toilet as he renounced his sins.

After a half-hour of this, he finally calmed down, and that's when Priest sprung on me that he was completely serious about his *drug dealer* performing our marriage ceremony.

I really didn't want to get into how appalled I was by the notion in front of Zoe or Foxy.

Priest said, "We don't have many options, love. We need to do this *quickly* so we can get on with our life. And now that Foxy has asked Jesus to come into his heart, you shouldn't have any objections."

"Priest …"

"I checked out the Universal Life Church, or Life Universal … whatever it is. It's legit enough for him to do this for us. So can we get on with it?"

"We can't," I said, beaming. "We don't have any witnesses. Zoe's too little."

"Baby, you can get your neighbor—that ol' man and his wife. They don't never go nowhere."

"Thanks for that, Foxy. Wow," I said.

Priest ran his hand through his hair and heaved a sigh. "Fine. I'll be right back. Foxy, you stay saved, and Gina, you stay. Period."

He went out to his duplex neighbors and fifteen minutes later came back with a curmudgeonly old black man he called "Mr. Glenn" and his wisp of a wife whom Mr. Glenn called Mu'deah.

Jesus, please help me. This can't be my life. I'm in a Tyler Perry play.

But it was my life, truly.

They all gathered around the futon, and there I sat in a T-shirt and sweatpants. Foxy asked, "Bless-ed Regina Dolores, queen of sorrows, you want me to put yo' dreadlocks up and give you a lil' gloss and rouge?"

"Nah. I'm going in just as I am."

"Awww right then, baby. Let's do this."

"Can we speak alone, Anthony?" I begged.

For a man in a rush to be my husband he looked reluctant to be alone with me. But Foxy excused himself to freshen his makeup, and I spoke to Priest.

"What are you doing?"

"I'm getting us married."

"Is this really how you want to do this?"

"I just want to do it, Gina."

"What are you afraid of?"

His shoulders rounded. "I'm afraid it's all going to go away. At least if I marry you, when everything falls apart I'll still have you. I need you, Gina, so much."

What was I supposed to say to that? I was afraid it would all fall apart too, but in the end, I'd have him. That was more than I had before.

I knew we were wrong. I knew it.

Heaven help us. We let Foxy of the Universal Church of the Whatever marry us.

PRIEST

I should have straightaway taken myself to an NA meeting. I had hit rock bottom resorting to such antics, but that's how much I wanted her. I wanted to close the deal. More than I realized.

I got those people out of my house, begging them not to tell anyone about Gina's whereabouts. I had no idea how long we were going to last at my place. I had very little money and had to keep a wife and child out of harm's way.

Oh man. I was a husband and a father, completely ill equipped for both. I did a lot of praying that day, with my new wife and alone. I wanted hope, but I felt like the walls were closing in on me.

We had a quiet evening, the same setup as the night before, only this time, while Zoe became vegetated in front of the television, Gina and I talked.

We shared a lot of secrets. A lot of hopes and dreams. We had the kind of hours-long conversation a man and woman have when they're falling very deeply in love. Finally, we got Zoe ready for bed. Since Gina's wounds weren't actively bleeding, she was a little more independent, though still in pain.

I'd bought her a nightgown of her own, a little wedding-night trousseau—and I truly did mean little. I thought it would make her feel better since she got married in sweatpants. It certainly would make *me* feel better.

She told me she was tired and wanted to shower and get some sleep. I chuckled, because she made sure to say "get some sleep" instead of "go to bed." Gina showered and hobbled out of the bathroom wearing the gown.

All I could say was, "Wow."

Scrubbed face and dreadlocks pulled back and held in place by, of all things, one of her dreads, my wife was a masterpiece: a golden Botticelli maiden, with crucifixion wounds. Lust and reverence wrestled within me, but surely lust would lose. She was, for better or worse, the Blessed Regina Dolores. And me, I was the king of sorrows, knowing I could never know her as *all* of me desired to.

GINA

I wasn't trying to seduce him by coming out of the bathroom dressed only in that gown. I mean, what were we going to do with Zoe lying there sleeping? I wanted him to see me in the present he bought for our wedding night. He'd chosen something pretty. Natural fibers. Soft, like he'd paid attention to the things around me—the things I said were healing to me. But it had a little sexy to it, and I believed he chose that gown for a reason.

If someone were to ask me that night what I wanted, I don't think my answer would be any different than it is now: I wanted to be loved.

I looked boldly into his eyes as he watched me standing before him, and what I saw was a man gazing upon his Psyche—the most beautiful of all. The look in those opal eyes of his made me hungry for more.

Yeah, for a moment I was weak. I closed my eyes, took a deep breath, and said, "Be Christ to me again, Priest. Christ my Lover."

Turns out I didn't want a Joseph after all.

PRIEST

I did a little Bible study looking upon Gina in her bridal gown.

> *How beautiful you are,*
> *my beloved,*
> *how beautiful you are!*
> *Your eyes are doves …*

> *Your lips are a scarlet thread*
> *and your words enchanting.*

> *Your two breasts are two fawns,*
> *twins of a gazelle*
> *that feed among the lilies.*

You are wholly beautiful,

my beloved,

without a blemish.

Except those wounds.

A Veronica hit parade played in my head. Her telling me I'd ruined her. Her telling me I was cursed. Blessed Regina had a divine destiny, but I was a stain on her white gown of righteousness. She'd called me monkey and ape baby. And then she'd run off to church to her Lover Jesus. She'd leave me locked inside of our tiny apartment. And I would wait, afraid, sitting in front of a television after I'd exhausted myself with tears. And hours later she'd return, happy that she had spent time with Jesus.

Ever hear the saying, some men marry their mother? That we try to work out what we missed with this new person that's just like the person who hurt us so much?

Elle was like Veronica; when she was sober she lacerated me with verbal abuse. And I followed her like a lost … child. She was only good to me when she was nice and mellow, and only dope made her that way.

Veronica was only nice to me when she was nice and mellow too. When Jesus had visited her.

Jesus *really* visited Gina.

I knew dark nights of the soul didn't last forever. Her wounds were already changing. Maybe they'd go away. What purpose would I serve then?

What would she do when she found out I was scared to death I'd infect her with HIV?

Gina was my beloved.

I wasn't hers. I knew that. I couldn't be. I wasn't Christ.

In my haste I underestimated what our farce of a marriage would do to us. I wanted to love her in the way she wanted to be loved, but I was no more capable of taking her into the heart of the mystery she was asking to be initiated into than I was of truly protecting her. I knew she didn't want to make love that night with Zoe there, but she would, and so would I. Even considering it—a love story between a junkie and a stigmatic—was outrageous.

Miracles. Were they real? What about the miracle of at-long-last love? Did I make all of it up because I wanted somebody to love me?

Was what happened to Gina psychogenic? Could she heal? What if you believed she did, whether or not she actually could? I wondered if Blessed Regina Dolores healed my HIV status as effectively as she healed my drug cravings and withdrawals. Then again, she hadn't healed the craving at all. Afro-mudflap girl had grown as seductive as my luscious wife before me asking me to love her as Christ would love His church.

I asked myself the question she'd asked me earlier. What if I just made it up because I *needed* to? What if I made her a living placebo?

All I had to do was go get tested and put my fears to rest, or tell her everything and let her opt out.

I was afraid. Afraid to know if she'd healed me or not, and afraid to lose her in case she hadn't. The last thing I wanted to be was the HIV-infected junkie who stumbled, high, into her church.

Afro-mudflap girl was so much easier. She demanded nothing, and I couldn't disappoint her.

I had to protect Gina, my *wife*. In my own way, I was looking out for her, even though my foolishness got us into such a predicament in the first place.

"Get dressed. I have to take you away from here."

An endless pause, then a shy, uncertain smile. She tried to blink away her confusion. "Get dressed?" she repeated. The words came out of her sounding like a question and some penance she'd regrettably resigned herself to.

God knows I wanted to shield her from the humiliation I knew she had to be feeling. I wasn't trying to hurt her. I was trying to save her, which was about as Christlike as I could muster.

"I should take you to Alessandro, Gina."

Maybe if she'd argued with me, raised the roof with her rage, I could bear the crushing heaviness weighting my heart.

"Baby," I said, "my love, if I don't take you now, I'm going to literally love you to death. And I can't do that, no matter how much I want to."

She struggled with herself. Stumbled over her words, "Ha— How? How can you love me to *death?*"

"I'm an intravenous drug user, Gina."

"Not anymore."

"Things happen when you live that life, Gina."

"But you're not a—"

"Don't make me say it, Gina. I've given you enough hints."

She paused, as if she were choosing her words carefully. "Anthony ..."

She never called me Anthony. I wouldn't let her finish. It didn't matter what she was going to say I couldn't ... I couldn't.

"I'm HIV-postive, Gina."

"You're not."

"I *am*. Listen to me! Making love to me could be a death sentence for you."

And then she did the darndest thing. She laughed and held up her hands.

"I've already got a death sentence, Priest. And it didn't come from you." Then she did another thing I marveled at. Gina laid her hand on my forehead. Blood began to seep in earnest out of all her wounds. She cried out in anguish as warmth spread through me, even more intense than what I felt the first time I touched her.

Then she fell forward into my arms.

CHAPTER THIRTY-TWO

GINA

Quench my troubles,
For no one else can soothe them;
And let my eyes behold You,
For You are their light,
And I will keep them for You alone.

Reveal Your presence,
And let the vision and Your beauty kill me,
Behold the malady
Of love is incurable

Except in Your presence and before Your face.

That was the beginning of the end for me. I gave up. On Priest. On Gina. On everything except the God I couldn't abandon, though it felt like He'd abandoned me. He wouldn't love me, and He wouldn't let Priest love me.

Nobody thrives without love. Saint John of the Cross had it right. The malady of love really is incurable. A desperate pursuit of God was all I had left.

Even if it killed me.

PRIEST

So two blind people try to make their way to Jesus. Immediately, there are problems because they're *blind,* which makes everything harder, and I do mean everything.

I called Alessandro. It was him, Veronica, or Foxy! I hoped my friend could see better than I could.

Thank God he believed in miracles. He didn't insist we take her to the hospital.

We washed her, dressed her in another gown from her trousseau, wrapped her wounds in bandages, the essence of roses filling the air. Alessandro scolded me the entire time.

Zoe, mercifully, slept.

"You have done a terrible thing, my friend," Alessandro said.

"I know."

"You knew you desired her. You knew it, Anthony."

"Right. I understand."

"And now you have wounded her."

"I didn't mean to. How was I supposed to predict she'd pass out like that?" Man. I still tried to justify my actions. "Just ... keep her away from me and she'll be all right."

"I will, my dear brother. I am afraid I must, not that I did not try to prevent this earlier. I blame myself, my friend. She is God's. She is not yours. I should have insisted you leave her with me."

Tell me about it.

"This isn't your fault, Alessandro. I should have listened to you."

Then he said something I found so strange. "Even in the best of circumstances, Lent is not a time to marry. It is a time of penance. It is a time of dying to the will. It is about the cross, not the reward. This you know, my friend."

He was right. It's all about death. Sure, there's Easter to look forward to, and a joyous resurrection, but you don't get Easter without a betrayal, an unfair trial, a few denials, a cross, and death. That's just the basics.

Somebody has to die. Nobody likes to think, sitting in their pews wearing their Sunday best, that Christianity will kill you. But it will. Jesus called it right:

"In all truth I tell you, unless a grain of wheat falls into the ground and dies, it remains only a single grain, but if it dies, it yields a rich harvest. Anyone who loves his life loses it; anyone who hates his life in this world, will keep it for eternal life."

Whether it was symbolic or literal death it was still death. And we have to go there, all of us who believe in Christ.

That's the truth.

He took her away. And wouldn't even tell me where'd he'd taken her, which is what I deserved, and despite all that, I remained all about me.

I thought I knew what would happen. She'd get around some real men and women of God and she'd see, in short order, everything lacking in me. I wasn't the only guy who could tell a saint story. And I certainly wasn't the only man who could love her—if a mere mortal man could love her at all, and truthfully, I had my doubts.

I read The Spiritual Canticle and several other works by Saint John of the Cross. I knew what the ending would be. She'd taste the sweetness of the real Christ, her true Beloved, and she'd realize I how very disappointing I was. In that bliss-filled place of union she would sing:

> *"And there I gave to Him*
> *Myself without reserve;*
> *There I promised to be His bride."*

Ultimately, according to the song, her sole occupation would be love. And I would never hold her again. I would never taste of her sweetness. She would be all His.

I was jealous of God.

But once upon a time, I actually thought she could be just for *me*. Then again, maybe she was.

Two blind people go after the loving lowly Jesus. He asks them, "Do you believe I can do this?"

What if one of them *says* yes, but he really doesn't believe He'll give him a miracle at all. He believes a miracle can happen for *her*, but not for him.

That changes the whole story.

CHAPTER THIRTY-THREE

GINA

I woke up in an apartment I didn't recognize, with a very cute ragamuffin—mahogany hair streaked with blonde—standing over me. I ached
all over, but I was bandaged, and warm, firmly tucked in a comfy bed.
The room looked like I could have decorated it, only she had a large
wooden San Damiano cross hanging on the wall—the same cross that
spoke to Saint Francis and told him to go and rebuild His house.

The ragamuffin girl, who looked about my age, grinned at me.
She wore a brown tunic over blue jeans she'd embroidered a funky
design on. She accented her hippie look with beaded earrings that
looked like they were made of some kind of seed, and a silver crucifix
with two medals on either side of it. Her feet were bare.

A girl after my own heart.

"Hey," I said.

"Hey, hey, girlfriend," she said. "I thought you'd never wake up, and I couldn't wait to ask you about this stigmata thing." A hearty laugh followed her bold statement.

"I don't know what I can tell you. I'm no expert."

She laughed again. "You look pretty astute to me."

"Don't believe the hype," I said, and was rewarded with another throaty laugh.

She unnecessarily fluffed my pillows. "Sorry, my friend. I'm a believer. You smell like—"

"Roses. I noticed," I said.

"It's incredible. Father Alessandro thinks you're the real deal. And you're not even Catholic. Awesome!"

"Father Alessandro? Is that how I got here?"

"You know it."

"Where's my daughter, Zoe?"

"She's at the Detroit Science Center with Father Alessandro. He's a doll, and so is Zoe. He thought she could use a diversion."

"I'll say. Is … uh …?" I was a little embarrassed that I wanted to know where Priest was. She seemed to intuit what I thought.

"He's not with them. He doesn't know where you are. Father Alessandro thought he needed to bake in God's oven a little longer. He's not quite done yet, my friend."

My face fell. "Oh."

She laughed again. "Don't look so glum. Father Alessandro is a marshmallow. He'll let him know where you are when Anthony's ready. You'll see him again."

"I'm not so sure he'll ever be ready for me."

But she paid my doubt no mind. "As beautiful as you are? He'll be back, and he'll be ready for you. You'll get to live happily ever after and all that, but man, you might wanna rethink the romance thing. I mean, what you've got going on with Jesus is spectacular."

"You can have it."

A throaty laugh burst out of her. "Me? I'm a big baby. I howl if I stub my toe!"

"Me too!" Both of us laughed.

"They're pretty awesome," she said, shaking her head at my wounds. "A real stigmatic in my room. Just like Saint Francis. I'm a Franciscan," she said. "I'm Franny."

"Short for Francis?"

"Totally, though it's not only for Saint Francis of Assisi. I have to say, I never met a Saint Francis I didn't like, and there are a few of them."

"Where are we, Franny?"

She sat on the bed beside me.

"You're in the Motor City, sister. At the humble monastery of the Companions of Jesus. We're a neomonastic apostolate along the lines of the Capuchin Friars of the Renewal. No bling. No sweet thing. Christ our King. Okay, we can have a little money, but we stress simplicity. And we can have a sweet thing, but we still honor our chastity vow. It's *modified* chastity vow, but we make it work. We've got a married monk and his wife. I guess you could say she's a monkette."

She giggled. "That sounds like a sixties girl group, doesn't it?"

"Anything else I need to know about the Companions of Jesus?"

She thought for a moment. "Well, we're not just Catholic anymore. We're ecumenical now."

"Now?"

"Starting last night when you got here. Welcome home!"

I laughed. "Priest would love it here."

"He'll join you and Zoe. Don't you worry about him."

She went right back to talking about the community like we never mentioned Priest at all.

"Anyway, we rent this apartment here in the belly of Cass Corridor because we're all about social justice, and sister, Cass Corridor has the poor. But we're artsy too, and you can get away with saying we're in the heart of the Cultural Center instead of Cass Corridor on a good day. You can walk to Wayne State, the Detroit Public Library, the Science Center, and the Detroit Institute of Arts from here. Who can ask for more than that?"

"I suppose that's great if you can walk on your own, which sometimes I can, and sometimes I can't."

"Oh, pshaw!"

Pshaw? I hadn't heard that in ages.

Franny went on like she wasn't feeling my self-pity.

"Our community happens to have two patron saints, Saint Francis of Assisi and Saint Benedict of Nursia, and each member has to choose which saint's rule of life he or she will live by. If you ask me, we're *Francidictines*. To Brother Dave or his wife Sister Bea we're Beneciscan. Most people call us Francidictenes. Those Benedictines always seem to let me have my way." She looked chagrined for a moment. "Well, not when it comes to sloughing off on my chores around here, or being lazy about my prayers, but stuff like naming I totally get away with."

I liked the Companions of Jesus already. Any group that could come together with a patron saint driven by excess, even in poverty, and another by moderation, had to be interesting.

The community only had three fully vowed members, the married couple, Brother David and his beloved Sister Beatrice, and Franciscan Franny. According to Franny the middle-aged couple she lived with was Benedictine through and through. Rooted to their crowded apartment monastery from which they made a habit of welcoming the stranger, they were almost comically moderate in everything from politics to diet.

Franny assured me the three of them would go out of their way, using whatever cloak-and-dagger methods necessary, to keep my presence there a secret. I had to admit, Franny and company felt a heckuva lot safer than Veronica. And even Priest.

Franny must have seen my expression change. "I'm so sorry you're hurting, my friend. Physically, and in your heart."

"I don't understand any of this. These wounds. My feelings. God's absence. Nothing makes sense."

She touched my shoulder. I had a feeling she'd have held my hand if it weren't bandaged.

"Regina D," she said, "your little girl is at the Science Center with one of the most loving, amazing, whimsical priests I know. You can't see her, and you can't hear her, but she's around. And she loves you."

She looked into my eyes. "God loves you. You can't see Him. And you can't hear Him, but He's totally with you. You've been given a gift very few people get. If that's not a sign of His favor, I don't know what is."

"But what about the fact that in some religious traditions this doesn't happen at all? I know some people think this is a spiritual delusion, and sometimes, I'm not so sure it isn't. I mean, maybe I just wanted to identify with Jesus and I'm making this happen somehow."

"That's some skill, sister! I'd be impressed with that, unless of course you were faking it. These wounds aren't fake, my friend. And they aren't normal either. So, let's just come off that idea and get with the program."

I shook my head. "I still don't get it, Franny. I'm not even Catholic. I'm in no way a saint."

"Saint *schmaint*. You know what Dorothy Day said when people called her a saint?"

She didn't give me time to answer, even if I did know, and I didn't.

"She said, 'Don't call me a saint. I don't want to be dismissed so easily.' Isn't that a riot? Listen, what you've got going on is all God. It's a sign to us and a big, fat affirmation of Christ crucified. You know what Saint Paul said. 'Those who belong to Christ have crucified their flesh with its passions and desires.' You're a living testament to the fact the we all need to crucify ourselves."

"That can't be true, Franny. Because I've got flesh. And passions and desires."

"Hey, I said you were a sign. Not the Lord Himself. You can learn from this too, you know."

But I had my doubts. "Priest's mother thinks I have some kind of message for the world, but I how can I tell the world a message I don't even get yet?"

"Maybe you get it more than you think." She scooted a little closer to me on the bed. "For instance, think about the wounds in your hands. How do they affect you?"

"I can't hold anything."

She grinned. "That's an amazing metaphor for poverty. Spiritual poverty. And that's a good thing, no matter what the television preachers say. You can't hold on to the things of this world, and God's kingdom is that much closer. It's awesome!"

I was beginning to believe her.

She touched my feet. Delicately. Reverently. "The wounds in your feet. What do they do for you?"

"Besides hurt like heck, they make it hard to walk."

"Don't think of it like some kind of disability. Think of it as a strike against pride. And selfish will. You can only go where God wants you to. It's all about obedience. And you have to rely on your brothers and sisters in Christ to help you get around. I'm thinking, lucky you! You're learning interdependence on community and total reliance on God, and not from a book! You're way ahead of us here in the COJ."

"And my heart wound?"

"That's the best one of all. God has opened your heart up wide. You can be totally about love. Real love. Not impostors of love that lead us astray. So, the heart wound is about chastity. With your heart wide open you can avoid using your beautiful, precious sexuality to satisfy your own lusts. The heart wound is a witness to perfect love, which ultimately drives away all our fears."

That's when I broke. I wasn't chaste at all. I knew I wasn't truly married before God to Priest and yet …

A tear rolled down my cheek.

"Hey … hey. Don't cry."

Franny wiped my face. "Nobody said you weren't human. So you fell in love. Anthony is a doll. He's a little rough around the edges, but he looks just like that guy from *Joan of Arcadia* the second season. Remember him? He totally played the devil. What's his name?"

"Wentworth Miller." I laughed through my tears. "Priest really does look like him. Kind of ambiguous racially, if you know what I mean."

"He's biracial. Isn't he?"

"I'd say so. But he doesn't seem clear on it. He doesn't know who his dad is."

"I think his mom may have liked a little chocolate, and who can blame her?"

We giggled like girls.

"Glad I got you laughing. Listen," she said, "Anthony knew it wasn't time for the two of you. And so did you, I think. You're here. Nothing happened. God is good, and let's just focus on that."

"I feel like I'm dying, Franny. Dying, body and soul."

"I know. But in the kingdom of God, that's a good thing. You'll be all right. I promise."

She crawled in bed with me and held me like a child. And then that white girl began to sing the Beatitudes with her smoky alto voice like she was a soul sistah in Sweet Honey in the Rock:

> "Blessed are the poor in spirit;
> for theirs is the kingdom of heaven.
> Blessed are they that mourn,
> For they shall be comforted …"

But I didn't feel comforted. I felt weak and wounded, and a whisper away from death.

GINA

All night I thought about what Franny said. About the wounds being kind of a witness to poverty, chastity, and obedience. That Franciscan thing was beginning to look good to me. All night the words to the song she sang haunted me.

I also thought about Veronica believing I had some kind of message. I didn't have a message, but if I did, I'd want it to be as close to the words of Christ as possible.

Despite what was happening to me, I didn't want to cause anyone to stumble. I didn't want to spend fifty years, or even fifty days, being Blessed Regina Dolores. I think every person who truly loves the Lord, faults and all, wants Him to be lifted up, so that all men may be drawn to Him.

It was possible I might not live through this experience. If I were to die, maybe a few people would ask what my message had been. I figured maybe it'd be my last chance to testify. And it wouldn't be about my wounds at all. Or maybe it would, but it would be about every wound I had: the mental illness, the fibro, the addiction, the promiscuity, every mistake I've ever made, and every heartbreak I bore that never healed. I would want people to know that God never stopped loving me. I couldn't do anything to make Him love me more or less. He just loved me. Even when I couldn't feel Him.

My message? It was the same as Jesus', and it could heal any brokenness. It was THE message for the walking wounded, and the wounded who couldn't walk at all. And listen. The world is never gonna tell you this. Here goes:

You're blessed when you're at the end of the rope. With less of you there's more of God and his rule.

You're blessed when you feel you've lost what is most dear to you. Only then can you be embraced by the One most dear to you.

You're blessed when you're content with just who you are—no more, no less. That's the moment you'll find yourselves proud owners of everything that can't be bought.

You're blessed when you've worked up a good appetite for God. He's food and drink in the best meal you'll ever eat.

You're blessed when you care. At the moment of being "carefull," you find yourselves cared for.

You're blessed when you get your inside world—your mind and heart—put right. Then you can see God in the outside world.

You're blessed when you can show people how to cooperate instead of compete or fight. That's when you discover who you really are, and your place in God's family.

You're blessed when your commitment to God provokes

persecution. The persecution drives you even deeper into God's kingdom.

Not only that—count yourself blessed every time people put you down or throw you out or speak lies about you to discredit me. What it means is that the truth is too close for comfort and they are uncomfortable. You can be glad when that happens— give a cheer, even!—for though they don't like it, I do! And all heaven applauds. And you know that you are in good company. My prophets and witnesses have always gotten into this kind of trouble.

That's it. The Beatitudes as given in *The Message.* If you can believe them, and live them, you'll have everything you need.

I didn't care what happened to me. I couldn't hold on to anything.

I let go.

CHAPTER THIRTY-FOUR

PRIEST

I missed Nana's funeral. I needed to protect Gina, and if I went around
Veronica she'd ambush me. And I missed Gina. I'd gone three days
without her. Three never-ending days. I worried if she was eating.
Father Alessandro assured me that she was with Benedictines and they
would surely offer her food. But I didn't know if Gina would take it.

I stayed away from afro-mudflap girl, though I hadn't yet removed
her from my home. I guess I couldn't picture my life without heroin,
even though I wasn't using it anymore. Classic junkie behavior.

Did I go to any NA meetings while she was gone? No. Nor did
I work on helping her find her story. I was too busy feeling sorry for
myself, my selfish nature battling grace in me.

I'd been careful at first, but as the days chipped away at me, I found myself slipping. I didn't hide my car after a few days. I kept the lights on, and as Veronica would say, she sure as sharp found me.

She banged on my door hurling insults. By then I was fool enough to answer, even though I knew better.

"You didn't come to the funeral," my mother said.

"I couldn't, Ronnie." I left her to decipher what that meant. Not that she cared. She was after Gina.

The smell of roses lingered in my little duplex. She noticed.

"Where is she?"

"She's not here, Ronnie."

"You're lying. I smell her. That certainly isn't *you* smelling so sweet."

"If you haven't noticed, I'm wearing a shirt that has her blood on it. Even though I washed it, the smell doesn't come out."

She stormed past me into the house and began going through the rooms. She actually cursed, then demanded, "Where is she, you stupid nigger?"

Maybe I was just tired of her. I challenged her.

"Why do you call me things like that, Ronnie? My birth certificate says I'm white. You tell everybody I'm white. It's what you told me, but when you're mad, I'm a nigger. Why is that?"

She tore through the virtually empty rooms, me trailing behind her. "You look like a nigger."

"And why is that? In fact, why don't you tell me who *Mr. Priest* is?"

She recoiled but kept searching: in closets, even in the kitchen cabinets, like I could actually have stored her there.

"Priest is nobody. Like you." She stopped her furious motion and screeched. "Where is she, Anthony? Where is Blessed Regina Dolores?"

"She's gone."

She went Veronica on me. "You'd better get her back here right this minute, or I'll call the police. I don't know what you did with her, but—"

"I married her."

Her face fell like an avalanche of sorrow. "What?"

"I married Gina. And you know what, Ronnie? Nobody can get to her unless they go through me. So you can take your little mission, whatever it is, and be gone. It's over. I'm not letting *anyone* exploit her."

Including myself.

It felt like a year passed in the moment that she stood there, and then she threw back her head and laughed. But it wasn't a hearty, pleasant laugh. It had a sinister bite, and when she looked me again with a sneer, she simply said. "You're a lying little demon. You came straight from the pit of hell, and as soon as you die you're going right back. Where is the Blessed Regina Dolores?"

I should have stopped it right there. Something about her expression froze my bones. I knew something was wrong. I'd faced a lot of the wrath of Veronica, but I'd never seen the look she had in her eyes. But it was as if we were both driven by some insidious evil. Neither of us could escape it.

I should have been praying, but I wasn't. I pulled out the folded marriage license I had in my wallet and tossed it at her.

"See for yourself. Here's our marriage license."

I shouldn't have done that.

VERONICA

I knew he was telling the truth, and wasn't that just the kind of thing he would do to hurt me? And I was hurt. God, I was hurt.

Everybody has a dream. My dream? I just wanted to be part of something bigger than myself. I didn't think that was too much to ask. When I was a little girl, I wanted to do something beautiful for God. And then that man, that hateful, awful nigger, stole my dream.

My dream died right there in that kitchen I grew up in. Just like it did the day I told my mother I was pregnant by the man who raped me, and she insisted that I keep it.

At that moment I told his wicked little offspring the truth. I'd never told him before, but I was so angry I spat out the evil that he was.

"Your father wasn't a priest. My mother made me give you that last name because I sure as sharp wasn't gonna give you mine. You want to know who 'priest' is? He's what your grandmother thought *you'd* be. She thought you were a gift. She said she discerned a religious vocation in you, before you were even born. But I knew you weren't a stinkin' gift. You're the foul, corrupt, filthy seed of the black nigger who raped me. And every day of my life I've wished on that ape man suffering like he made me suffer. And I wish him dead. Every single day.

"I hate you. I've always hated you and I always will. And now you've taken away the one thing that could have redeemed you for me."

He stood there with this stupid, stunned look on his ugly face. Looking like he was going to cry.

I couldn't stand him. Honest to God I couldn't. But I had one more question for him. "Did you defile her? Did you put your rotten seed in her?"

He looked up at me like I was joking with him, then he smirked. And do you know what he said? Do you know what he had the unmitigated gall to say to me?

"Sure. And you know what, Veronica? It was good."

I picked up a knife he had in his sink, and I tried to kill him.

PRIEST

She got that knife so fast I could barely react. Lunged at me and would have gotten me right in the chest but I turned and she plunged the knife into my arm.

I don't know why I turned because a part of me welcomed that knife. Another part of me, however, rose up. Maybe I didn't want to give her the pleasure of doing what I was more than capable of doing myself.

We struggled, and Ronnie was like a bulldog charging at me again and again. Finally, as painful as it was with my injury, I hit her. Knocked her to the floor and she lay there wailing like some kind of wounded animal. I'll never forget that sound, as long as I live.

I called the police.

They came and took her away without incident. She went like a lamb to the slaughter. They tried to get me to go to the hospital, but I told them I wouldn't go. In fact, I told them she was the one who needed to go to the hospital.

I hit her pretty hard.

God, I am so sorry.

When they left, I tried to clean my wound and stop the bleeding by tying a shirt on my arm.

A shirt on my arm.

It was a no brainer after that. I was almost there. I really didn't see a reason not to go all the way.

I got my "medicine." Sat down and got ready for the sweet relief of brown sugar in my veins. The fact that it didn't look like Foxy's usual junk didn't even phase me.

I'd stopped caring. Why should I? Gina was gone, and probably wouldn't come back. Not for the likes of me.

What did I have to lose?

CHAPTER THIRTY-FIVE

GINA

I wouldn't eat or drink. Not even Franny, and what a charmer she was, could talk me into it. I'd given myself to Christ. I just wanted Him.

For three days I took nothing.

There was talk of force-feeding me. I was slipping in some hazy place between life and death now that almost felt like God's presence. It felt so close, but I couldn't quite reach Him.

Father Alessandro fretted over me. Brother David and Sister Beatrice set up a twenty-four-hour prayer vigil. I could hear people all day and evening chanting their prayers, and I prayed with them.

I clung to the canticle. That Friday evening I lay in bed, saying the verses aloud.

> *My Beloved is the mountains,*
> *The solitary wooded valleys,*
> *The strange islands,*
> *The roaring torrents,*
> *The whisper of the amorous gales;*
>
> *The tranquil night*
> *At the approaches of the dawn,*
> *The silent music,*
> *The murmuring solitude,*
> *The supper which revives, and enkindles love.*

That whole "supper which revives" thing must have spoken to Franny. She came back, maybe an hour after she heard me, with a chalice and something wrapped in cloth she seemed to handle with particular care.

She came to my bed and sat down on it as was her way.

I had grown so weak, but I managed a smile. "What's up, Franny?"

"I brought you what you want to eat."

"I don't want anything but Christ."

"That's what I brought you," she said. She sighed. "Look, I'm what you call an extraordinary Eucharistic minister. I take the most blessed sacrament to sick and shut-ins. Catholics. I'm not supposed to do this, but we're a little desperate here, and this is looking extraordinary to me. I'm hoping God will work with me on this.

So, for the moment, you're Catholic, okay? Father Alessandro said Anthony thought you were probably baptized Catholic with that name of yours. And if you weren't, we're going to make our definition of Catholic very generous this evening. Were you baptized in the name of the Father, and of the Son, and of the Holy Spirit as far as you know?"

"Yes, I was. I got saved in a Church of God in Christ."

"Fabulous. Now, about the Catholic thing, think of it as meaning *universal.* I'm going to take you through the world's fastest Rite of Christian Initiation for Adults now. Okay?"

I nodded.

"Do you know the Nicene or Apostles' Creed?"

"Yes."

"You believe it?"

"Yes."

"Groovy. That's about it, but I'll add Jesus loves you, and He wants you to partake of His body. It's a John 6 thing. So you'll have life in you like He said. You still with me?"

I nodded again.

She removed a white round wafer from the red cloth.

"This is His body. And in the cup is His blood. I didn't consecrate these gifts, Father Alessandro did, so it counts. You still with me?"

"I'm still with you."

She took the wafer and held it up. "His body was broken for you. Take this and eat. It's Jesus, my friend. Trust me on this. Take Him."

A tear slid down my cheek. I opened my mouth and took the Christ that Franny offered into my mouth.

"And this is the blood of Christ. Take it and drink all of it."

She'd given me a pretty good-sized cup of His blood, but I drank every drop of it without choking.

Franny started to cry. "This is a great mystery, Gina, but it's what you've longed for. You have received the body and blood of Christ. This is the supper that gives life." She wiped her tears. "Be at peace, my sister. You have everything you need."

We held each other. We cried a lot. Peace settled over me and strength surged through my body. I fell in a deep and restful sleep.

GINA

I awoke later that evening, and everything was beautiful. I still had the wounds, but the difference was I sensed God's nearness. I had thought that feeling would never return.

All I could do was praise the Lord. I felt so happy. I began to laugh and sing, an old Fanny Crosby hymn I knew from when I went to a Methodist church back in the day:

> *I am Thine, O Lord, I have heard Thy voice,*
> *and it told Thy love to me;*
> *but I long to rise in the arms of faith*
> *and be closer drawn to Thee.*

> *Draw me nearer, nearer, blessed Lord,*
> *to the cross where Thou hast died.*
> *Draw me nearer, nearer, nearer, blessed Lord,*
> *to Thy precious, bleeding side.*

I spent hours with Jesus, enjoying Him, and in His kindness, by the Holy Spirit, He spoke to me. Not audibly, but in a knowing. Just ... a knowing.

"Go to your Priest. He's in trouble."

He said it gently, but I sensed an urgency in this prompting. I called Father Alessandro and told him I had to go.

FATHER ALESSANDRO

Regina Dolores asked me to come to her new home, insistent. She told me my poor dear brother was in trouble and she must go to him as soon as possible. I was reluctant. I didn't think my brother was ready to see her, but Regina Dolores persisted, growing more distressed the longer I waited.

It was a difficult choice, beloved, for she bled as if she had been in truth nailed to a cross. I had never seen the likes of it. It was terrible. Absolutely terrible.

Zoe cried profusely at the site of her mother. The poor dear could not be consoled. Oh, this was a grave burden. Regina Dolores begging me to take her to Anthony, and her child begging to go with her mother. Sister Franny offered to keep the child, but Zoe has the temperament of her dear mother. I took them both, unwilling to further upset either of them.

My dear brother had given me a key when I took his beloved Gina to her new home. Together Gina, Zoe, and I slowly, and painfully for her, made our way into the duplex.

Oh, how she must have hurt, leaving a trail of roses behind her. But his home had its own roses. Blood in the kitchen and living room.

I was afraid at the sight of it. I prayed God's mercy.

"Anthony," I called out, and he did not respond. I sought him out, fear having taken hold of me now. If he was sick, I would find him in his Nana's bedroom—this I was convinced of, and that is indeed where he hid. He'd tied a dress shirt around his arm. Oh, dear Lord. I couldn't bear it. I wanted to spare Regina Dolores this misery. I shouted for her to stay behind with the child who was already terribly afraid, but she would not. She was going to lumber her way up the stairs after me. This I knew, dear ones.

I wanted to spare Regina Dolores this. But she would not listen.

GINA

I should have listened, but I had to make it up those stairs to reach my Priest. But dear God, it felt like it would kill me.

I counted the stairs before I headed up. Thirteen. I could make it. I knew I could. No matter that I bled like crazy. Father Alessandro bounded up those same thirteen stairs like Priest was *dying*, then pleaded with me not to come up. I knew Priest was up there, and I was going find him, so help me God.

It was only thirteen steps. The stations of the cross were fourteen. I could do thirteen.

"God, I don't know what's going on, but I've got a real bad feeling. Help me. This is a real short journey, Lord. Help me."

I grabbed the rail. Pain shot through my hand up my entire arm. I gritted my teeth. "Jesus, I love You more than I love myself. Help me." I placed my foot on the first step and thought my knee would buckle when I put my weight on it.

Now, the second step. "I'm so sorry, Lord. I embrace all the suffering You destined for me." The pain was dizzying. I began to sweat and pant, and all I could think of was Jesus carrying His cross. For me. For Priest. For Foxy. For the whole wide world. "Jesus, my Love, I beg of You, help me to bear my cross with perfect patience."

On shaky legs I lurched forward—a misstep that toppled me forward. I hung on to the rail with one hand—one deeply wounded, bleeding hand. I could see Christ in my mind, falling at the same time, the weight of the cross bearing down. The weight of my sins.

"Oh, God. I'm so sorry. Keep me from falling. Jesus, keep me from falling. Please."

I'd told Zoe not to move from the bottom of the stairs, but now I heard her little feet brave a stair to come toward me. "Mommy, Mommy!" she screamed, weeping.

"Don't try to follow me. Go back, Zoe."

"Mommy, let me help, you," my baby cried.

"You can't help me, Zoe."

I thought of the mother of Jesus, the sorrowful mother, and the image of her heart joined to her Son's came to me. Two hearts joined, both aflame with love. Thorns crowned His heart, and roses hers. His mother's was pierced with a sword. Zoe's cries slashed through my heart, but I had to keep going.

I tried to think of the words of the rosary, though I never prayed it.

"Holy Mary, mother of God, pray for us sinners, now, and in the hour of our death." I didn't know how far into that hour I was.

I made it to the fifth step, and Zoe came behind me. "Please, Mommy, let me help you." She held on to my waist. I could feel her trying to give her little-girl strength to me, and I was moved by her compassion. She was my little Simon of Cyrene, helping me to bear my terrible burden. Through her kindness I made it to the sixth step, but I did so weeping.

Zoe wiped my tears with her bare hands.

Gentle Jesus. How many times have I neglected this child, completely self-absorbed? Forgive me. I keep falling and You keep forgiving me. I call on You with all my love. Forgive me, and bless my little girl.

I tried to move forward. The next step was the seventh. I had more steps behind me than before me now. I could hear Father Alessandro praying, "O God, save him."

With everything in me I tried to move faster. The blood on my foot wounds poured out of me, making a slippery, perilous mess of the stairs. Once again, I fell. My head hit the stair in front of me, renewing all the pain in my body. Indeed the Lord had made a cross of my body, and I could not bear it. Burning, aching, stabbing raw pain crucified me.

"Lord, I keep falling. Give me the grace to persevere in Your love. Greater love has no man than this, that he would lay down his life for a friend. I can't do this on my own. It's killing me. I call upon You, Jesus, my Love."

Zoe followed behind me. Slowly. Step by step, my poor baby wailing.

"We're going to be all right, Zoe. I promise. Jesus will take care of us."

I heard her repeat through her tears, "Jesus will take care of us."

Oh, Jesus. Gentle Love, I give myself to You.

Lord, have mercy, I fell a third time. This time I stumbled back.

Zoe tried to grab me and caught my T-shirt. I thrust myself forward with all my strength, but she held so fast to me that my shirt ripped. I grabbed hold of my baby and held her and let her cry in my arms, but it hurt so to have her in my lap.

"Zoe, go back downstairs before you get hurt."

She pleaded with me, "Please, Mommy, no."

"Go downstairs, Zoe."

Almost there. I hoisted myself forward, bloody and aching, and dying on the inside. Christ carrying His cross with me and through me.

Alessandro's voice pieced through me. "Oh, my brother has died. He is not breathing. *Ohhhhhhh.*"

"No, no, no, no, no, noooooooooo."

I could hear an ambulance in the background. "Jesus, You gave me the stigmata. Don't take him. Don't take him, Lord. Please. Let me have his suffering."

Jesus reminded me that Priest had his own stigmata.

For a moment I wanted to ask Jesus to take me, but Zoe didn't deserve that. *Lord, have mercy.* But I was dying in some way, every second I couldn't reach him. What could I do but surrender this?

"Thy will be done."

I crawled up that thirteenth step with what felt like two-ton anvils weighting all my extremities. Made my way on my elbows and knees following the sound of Alessandro's weeping until I reached my husband.

He wasn't breathing. Spittle had foamed white at the corners of his mouth. I didn't care. I didn't care if he had hepatitis A, B, C, or X. I didn't care if he had HIV because I had G-O-D.

Father Alessandro moved aside so I could get to him, and I opened his mouth and blew the breath of all the life I had in me into his lungs.

I took my scarred and blood soaked hands and pumped his chest though, God, it hurt so bad to do it.

I called on Jesus. Asked Him for a miracle.

FATHER ALESSANDRO

I could not bear the sight of Regina Dolores trying to revive my brother when I knew he had gone on. Oh, a priest sees many sorrows, but my heart was truly broken.

The images would stay with me always; Anthony so covered in Regina Dolores' blood it appeared he bore Christ's wounds rather than she. The stairs looked as if someone had died on them instead of in that empty bedroom. And the child downstairs, the poor dear, was beside herself with grief.

I'd given my dear brother, my friend, his last rites before he took his final ragged breath and touched the unction oil I'd brought with me to his closed eyes. I said through the veil of my tears, "Through this holy unction and His most tender mercy may the Lord pardon thee whatever sins or faults thou hast committed by sight."

I moved my hand to touch and anoint my poor lamb's nose. "By smell." Now his mouth. "By taste." And my poor brother's hands that had shot this poison into his veins. "May the Lord pardon thee whatever sins or faults thou has committed by hands." I anointed his feet, believing, despite his weakness, that my dear one—he would soar on mercy wings to heaven.

The ambulance had come, and I went to meet them. To my knowledge, my dear sister had given up.

I told the emergency medical technicians that they would find him upstairs, and that he'd overdosed.

They rushed up the stairs, and I stayed with the child. I could hear a commotion going on, and one of the technicians hurried down the stairs.

"Which one is the patient?"

"It is the gentleman. I believe he is gone."

She shook her head. "The … uh … gentleman is sitting up holding the lady. What happened to her?"

I charged upstairs two or three steps at a time, beloved. What they spoke was true.

I do not know what happened in that room. Anthony was alive, Praise God, but my dear sister, oh, my dear suffering sister, had fallen into a coma.

CHAPTER THIRTY-SIX

PRIEST

Alessandro said he's sure I died. I only know I was asleep, a dreamless sleep, which I awakened from.

I didn't feel high anymore. My eyes fluttered open and I looked around me. My Gina, my queen of sorrows, lay far too still beside me.

She was covered with blood. I couldn't find her pulse and she didn't seem to be breathing. I tried to wake her but she didn't respond. I thought she'd died. I held her, thinking the last thing she'd done was find her way upstairs to be near me.

Oh, my queen. My beautiful soul. My Psyche.

I did not deserve whatever sacrifice she made for me. I just held onto her.

Slowly I began to piece together what must have happened. I got high, but something was wrong and I knew I didn't feel right. How did they find me? I didn't want them to see me that way.

I thought I was going to die, with a long-sleeved T-shirt sleeve tied across my arm and a needle in my wrecked arm.

Alessandro somehow made it to me, but where was he now, and how did Gina come to be in the room?

I supposed it didn't matter. I thought I'd lost her for good. I thought she was dead. Then I heard my doorbell ring. In moments EMTs ran up the steps and found us.

Gina had not died. Something was very wrong, but she wasn't dead.

They took my dove away, and I knew I had to do one thing. I had to be a better man: for Christ, for Gina and Zoe, for me.

No turning back.

FATHER ALESSANDRO

It was only after all the madness had died down, and Gina and Anthony had both gone on to the hospital—he went in the same ambulance as she—that I held the child Zoe until she feel asleep.

I asked Franny and Beatrice to come get her, and they handled her from there. I thank the Lord for that.

It was Sister Franny who discovered another miracle. She went to the crucifix—the one in the living room. The one that his Nana—the dear woman—had cherished. Sister Franny said to me, "Father Alessandro, you gotta see this. It's awesome!" And I did go to see what she spoke off. For I loved that crucifix.

And our precious Savior, laid out on the cross, wept. His tears streaked down the wall and pooled in tiny puddles on the floor.

CHAPTER THIRTY-SEVEN

PRIEST

Gina languished in a coma for weeks, but nobody took Zoe away. Gina had a husband. They might have looked suspiciously at me, but I was hers. And she was mine. At least on paper.

Miss D even resumed taking care of her at her day-care center. She didn't give me a hard time anymore. I guess she saw how dedicated I was to Gina. A little late, but it was all I had.

Once she came to the hospital and we prayed together.

"I'm believing God to raise her up," she said matter of factly.

"Me too, Miss D. But even if He doesn't. I'm going to stay right here until He does whatever He'll do."

She rebuked me. She was good at rebuking. "Don't you go talkin'

like that, boy. You gots to believe. Jesus said all thangs is possible if
you believe. Now don't you go doubtin'. That baby need her mama.
And she been through enough. I know you like to be all long-faced,
but sometimes folk do get a happy ending."

"I stand corrected." But she actually made me feel better.

They did a variety of tests on her, including examining the stigmata, which remained. Yes, the medical professionals called what she
had stigmata. It's a valid medical diagnosis used to described unex-
plained bleeding that corresponds with the crucifixion wounds of
Christ. What they refused to say was that it was a miracle. They went
with the theory that prolonged fasting may have caused an unusual
physical response. I wouldn't allow them to release any information
to the press, and Veronica remained in a psychiatric hospital none
the wiser. The doctors said she had a psychotic breakdown and was
having delusions of a religious nature.

I thought she was just telling her story. Unfortunately, it wasn't a
very credible story. And I told them so.

I didn't have to convince them.

Just before Holy Week I had Gina transferred to our home—or
rather, our new home with the Companions of Jesus. I still held out
hope she would emerge from the coma. She was a fighter. She was
amazing.

On Good Friday Gina's eyes fluttered open as I was praying noon
prayers over her. She looked at me and smiled, and I took her in my
arms where she promptly, and peacefully, died.

She loved Him most. Her Beloved had come to her. Received
her. Loved her, and she went drunk with love. She would say, like her
beloved John of the Cross:

In the inner cellar
Of my beloved have I drunk, and when I went forth
Over all the plain,
I knew nothing,
And lost the flock I was following before.

There He gave me His breast;
There He taught me a sweet and living knowledge;
And I gave myself back to Him,
Keeping nothing back;
There I promised to be His bride.

And finally, my beloved wife would say of her Lord, her Love:

If then, I am no longer
Seen or found on the common,
You will say that I am lost
That stricken by love,
I lost myself, and was found.

That's all I have to say about that.

When I announced her death to the media many brought her roses. Thousands of roses came. In dozens. Single roses. Rose buds. And people wore roses pinned to their hearts in her honor until Easter.

The newspapers had a field day. Stories about her ran for weeks, but eventually it died out. All the players, with the exception of Veronica, engaged in a conspiracy of silence. All of us. Me, Mike,

Alessandro. For whether we believed or not, we recognized Gina's dignity. And her privacy. We happily allowed her to rest in peace.

She was healed. Finally. And I am healed. Finally.

I'm certain of it.

May God grant you peace.

EPILOGUE

"May God grant you peace."

It was done. The audience stayed quiet. He broke the silence by asking, "Are there any questions?"

A man raised his hand. Friar John-Francis nodded for him to speak.

"Uh, Mr. Priest, I mean, uh, Friar John or Francis, or whatever your name is now, what happened to the little girl, Zoe?"

"Zoe is doing great. She's loved, and mothered by a few women in our community, including one in particular, who she's very close to."

"Are you still HIV-positive?"

"No, I'm not. I have a very strict vegetarian diet now and take a number of supplements. Doctors have suggested that caring for my health so aggressively could have reversed my status. The jury is still out on that."

"So you don't believe Gina Merritt healed you?"

"Gina Merritt would say God healed me, not her. I'm certain of that."

A woman stood up. He recognized her. Mary Beth Michaels. The journalist who wrote the initial story about Gina after the Sunday fiasco at the Vineyard.

"Did you ever remarry?" she asked, an eyebrow raised.

He grew nervous and hoped it didn't show. "Uh, I did. I married the woman Zoe is so fond of. I am very fortunate to be with her."

Mary Beth fired another question at him.

"Friar John-Francis, rumors have persisted that Regina Dolores Merritt did not die, and that she has a secret identity somewhere. It does seem odd that she awoke from the coma and died. Seems to me she could have just slipped away unconscious. It doesn't make sense. Is she really alive? Are the rumors true?"

Friar John-Francis smiled shyly at the woman. His cheeks pinked. "I've heard that rumor as well. I'm afraid that it's pure foolishness." He picked the book up, a bit of a nervous tremor in his hand.

"But there was never a funeral."

"I'm sorry. That's all the questions I will answer. Again, thank you, and may God give you peace."

He walked away, trying to hide the effects of the rush of adrenaline surging through him.

She always said that he couldn't lie, his Mary-Francis. She laughs at him and teases, "And to think it's you who wrote the book." But he didn't lie to the nosy reporter. He was a storyteller. He may change a fact or two, but he stayed truthful.

He simply said it was foolishness.

Everybody knows that God always takes the foolish things of this world to confound the wise.

Mary Beth Michaels was the last in line to have her book signed. She held a dozen red roses in one hand and the book in the other. She handed him the book. He scrawled the Chi Rho symbol for Christ on the title page and handed it back to her.

"No autograph, Anthony?"

"John-Francis now. And it's not about me, Mary Beth. I'm just a guy who helped someone I love find her story."

She looked him in the eyes. "You know, I had first-stage cancer when I showed up at the Vineyard that day. I didn't believe in any of it. I got one of those swatches from your mother. I thought it was a joke. I was going to take it to be analyzed to find out why it smelled like roses."

"Did you?"

"The lab said it was blood. They couldn't explain the smell."

"Is that so?" he said, but he wasn't surprised.

"These are for Gina," she said. "Or whatever she calls herself now."

He took the flowers giving her a cautious look. "Gina's dead."

"I get it. Crucified with Christ, and all that. I hear you. I'm not going to rat you out."

A smile tugged at his lips. "Why would I be concerned you'd rat me out, Mary Beth? I've told her story. It's all there in the book."

"I know. You made it clear. Tell her I went to the doctor and I didn't have cancer anymore. All traces of it were gone. The doctors couldn't explain it. I never told a soul what happened to me. Not a soul."

"Thanks for telling me, Mary Beth."

"Congratulations on your son. He's two now?"

"Not quite. Getting there."

"That's terrific, Anthony. Really terrific."

"God bless you, Mary Beth," he said. "You're quite an extraordinary investigative journalist."

"I never won a Pulitzer Prize, Anthony."

"Me, either, Mary Beth. And I'm not Anthony. I'm John-Francis."

"I know all about it."

He tucked the roses under his arm and headed home to his little family. Sister Mary-Francis would appreciate the gift. Christ still sent her roses on Ash Wednesday, roses with thorns so fierce you could plait them into a crown. Their petals sweetened the air until Easter when they'd fall to the ground to die. And Mary-Francis would scoop those petals into her wounded hands and spread them across an altar, their clinging scent ascending to the heavens with her prayers.

"My Jesus, pardon and mercy," she'd intercede, "through the merits of Your holy wounds."

Her Jesus would grant pardon and mercy every single time.

... a little more ...

When a delightful concert comes to an end,

the orchestra might offer an encore.

When a fine meal comes to an end,

it's always nice to savor a bit of dessert.

When a great story comes to an end,

we think you may want to linger.

And so, we offer ...

AfterWords—just a little something more after you

have finished a David C. Cook novel.

We invite you to stay awhile in the story.

Thanks for reading!

Turn the page for ...

- **Discussion Questions**
- **A Spiritual Canticle of the Soul and the Bridegroom Christ**
- **The Sorrowful Passion of Mary Rose of Inkster**

DISCUSSION QUESTIONS

1) Stigmata is traditionally granted to those of extraordinary piety who identify with Christ's suffering. Does Gina seem to be someone who is extraordinarily pious? Why, or why not?

2) Gina says: "I know things about Jesus just because I've suffered. Sometimes I wonder if suffering isn't a secret initiation into a special kind of intimacy with God." How does Gina's suffering bring her closer to God? Have you seen this in your own life?

3) When Mike goes to visit Gina he finds her "out of touch." In what ways is she actually more aware than Mike?

4) Veronica has a great deal of self-loathing. How do her feelings of self-hatred affect the way she views others?

5) Gina views her condition as an opportunity to share in the sufferings of Christ, yet Veronica looks at her as a "victim soul." Do you think this label is more about how Veronica sees herself?

6) Do you know people who, like Veronica, seem spiritually arrogant? How do you typically respond to these types of people? Did understanding Veronica's story give you compassion for her?

7) Gina asks Priest to help her find her story—why this happened to her. In what way does Gina's search become Priest's?

8) Do you think Gina's condition is trivialized once it becomes a production? Can you draw any parallels to the church today?

9) In what way is Priest still judged within the church? Do you think there are times in your life where you see what you expect rather than what is? How can we guard against this?

10) Do you think that love inevitably leads to suffering? How has love caused you to suffer in your own life?

A SPIRITUAL CANTICLE OF THE SOUL AND THE BRIDEGROOM CHRIST

St. John of the Cross

Translated by David Lewis with corrections by Benedict Zimmerman, O.C.D.

Prior of St. Luke's, Wincanton

June 28, 1909

Electronic Edition with Modernization of English by Harry Plantinga, 1995

This electronic text is in the Public Domain

SONG OF THE SOUL AND THE BRIDEGROOM

I

THE BRIDE
Where have You hidden Yourself,
And abandoned me in my groaning,
* O my Beloved?*
You have fled like the hart,
Having wounded me.
I ran after You, crying; but You were
* gone.*

II

O shepherds, you who go
Through the sheepcots up the hill,
If you shall see Him
Whom I love the most,
Tell Him I languish, suffer, and die.

III

In search of my Love
I will go over mountains and
* strands;*
I will gather no flowers,
I will fear no wild beasts;
And pass by the mighty and the
* frontiers.*

IV

O groves and thickets
Planted by the hand of the Beloved;
O verdant meads
Enameled with flowers,
Tell me, has He passed by you?

V

ANSWER OF THE CREATURES
A thousand graces diffusing
He passed through the groves in haste,
And merely regarding them
As He passed
Clothed them with His beauty.

VI
THE BRIDE
Oh! who can heal me?
Give me at once Yourself,
Send me no more
A messenger
Who cannot tell me what I wish.

VII
All they who serve are telling me
Of Your unnumbered graces;
And all wound me more and more,
And something leaves me dying,
I know not what, of which they are
  darkly speaking.

VIII
But how you persevere, O life,
Not living where you live;
The arrows bring death
Which you receive
From your conceptions of the Beloved.

IX
Why, after wounding

This heart, have You not healed it?
And why, after stealing it,
Have You thus abandoned it,
And not carried away the stolen prey?

X
Quench my troubles,
For no one else can soothe them;
And let my eyes behold You,
For You are their light,
And I will keep them for You alone.

XI
Reveal Your presence,
And let the vision and Your beauty
  kill me,
Behold the malady
Of love is incurable
Except in Your presence and before
  Your face.

XII
O crystal well!
Oh that on Your silvered surface
You would mirror forth at once
Those eyes desired
Which are outlined in my heart!

XIII
Turn them away, O my Beloved!
I am on the wing:

THE BRIDEGROOM
Return, My dove!

The wounded hart
Looms on the hill
In the air of your flight and is
   refreshed.

XIV
My Beloved is the mountains,
The solitary wooded valleys,
The strange islands,
The roaring torrents,
The whisper of the amorous gales;

XV
The tranquil night
At the approaches of the dawn,
The silent music,
The murmuring solitude,
The supper which revives, and
   enkindles love.

XVI
Catch us the foxes,
For our vineyard has flourished;
While of roses
We make a nosegay,
And let no one appear on the hill.

XVII
O killing north wind, cease!
Come, south wind, that awakens
   love!
Blow through my garden,
And let its odors flow,

And the Beloved shall feed among
   the flowers.

XVIII
O nymphs of Judea!
While amid the flowers and the
   rose-trees
The amber sends forth its perfume,
Tarry in the suburbs,
And touch not our thresholds.

XIX
Hide Yourself, O my Beloved!
Turn Your face to the mountains,
Do not speak,
But regard the companions
Of her who is traveling amidst
   strange islands.

XX
THE BRIDEGROOM
Light-winged birds,
Lions, fawns, bounding does,
Mountains, valleys, strands,
Waters, winds, heat,
And the terrors that keep watch by
   night;

XXI
By the soft lyres
And the siren strains, I adjure you,
Let your fury cease,
And touch not the wall,

That the bride may sleep in greater
  security.

XXII

The bride has entered
The pleasant and desirable garden,
And there reposes to her heart's
  content;
Her neck reclining
On the sweet arms of the Beloved.

XXIII

Beneath the apple tree
There were you betrothed;
There I gave you My hand,
And you were redeemed
Where your mother was corrupted.

XXIV

THE BRIDE

Our bed is of flowers
By dens of lions encompassed,
Hung with purple,
Made in peace,
And crowned with a thousand shields
  of gold.

XXV

In Your footsteps
The young ones run Your way;
At the touch of the fire
And by the spiced wine,
The divine balsam flows.

XXVI

In the inner cellar
Of my Beloved have I drunk; and
  when I went forth
Over all the plain
I knew nothing,
And lost the flock I followed before.

XXVII

There He gave me His breasts,
There He taught me the science full
  of sweetness.
And there I gave to Him
Myself without reserve;
There I promised to be His bride.

XXVIII

My soul is occupied,
And all my substance in His service;
Now I guard no flock,
Nor have I any other employment:
My sole occupation is love.

XXIX

If, then, on the common land
I am no longer seen or found,
You will say that I am lost;
That, being enamored,
I lost myself; and yet was found.

XXX

Of emeralds, and of flowers
In the early morning gathered,

We will make the garlands,
Flowering in Your love,
And bound together with one hair of
    my head.

XXXI
By that one hair
You have observed fluttering on my
    neck,
And on my neck regarded,
You were captivated;
And wounded by one of my eyes.

XXXII
When You regarded me,
Your eyes imprinted in me Your grace:
For this You loved me again,
And thereby my eyes merited
To adore what in You they saw.

XXXIII
Despise me not,
For if I was swarthy once
You can regard me now;
Since You have regarded me,
Grace and beauty have You given me.

XXXIV
THE BRIDEGROOM
The little white dove
Has returned to the ark with the
    bough;
And now the turtle-dove

Its desired mate
On the green banks has found.

XXXV
In solitude she lived,
And in solitude built her nest;
And in solitude, alone
Has the Beloved guided her,
In solitude also wounded with love.

XXXVI
THE BRIDE
Let us rejoice, O my Beloved!
Let us go forth to see ourselves in Your
    beauty,
To the mountain and the hill,
Where the pure water flows:
Let us enter into the heart of the
    thicket.

XXXVII
We shall go at once
To the deep caverns of the rock
Which are all secret,
There we shall enter in
And taste of the new wine of the
    pomegranate.

XXXVIII
There You will show me
That which my soul desired;
And there You will give at once,
O You, my life!

That which You gave me the other
   day.

XXXIX
The breathing of the air,
The song of the sweet nightingale,
The grove and its beauty
In the serene night,
With the flame that consumes, and
   gives no pains.

XL
None saw it;
Neither did Aminadab appear
The siege was intermitted,
And the cavalry dismounted
At the sight of the waters.

THE SORROWFUL PASSION OF MARY ROSE OF INKSTER

One Friday during Lent. I walked into a fish fry at my parish, which I'm compelled, for no good reason, to go to. I had no money, nor real inclination to buy a fish dinner. I simply felt I *had* to stop at the church. I didn't think much of it. I figured my mother-in-law would be there and if nothing else I could enjoy chatting with her and her friends. This faith community was new to me. It was always a pleasure to get to know people and have them welcome me into their communion.

I had no idea what I was about to walk into.

I spotted Mom as soon as I made my way into the fellowship hall and found a seat with her and a couple who looked vaguely familiar to me.

According to Mom, she'd practically conjured me. Only moments earlier had she mentioned me in the conversation she was having with John and Katherine. She made introductions, and as it happens, I knew this couple after all. I'd gone to school with their daughter. Those were good times for me. With delight we caught up on what had been going on in everyone's life throughout the years and of course they asked what I'd been up to.

I told them about my books, which my mother-in-law had already piqued their interest in, and I also shared a few of my personal struggles. This led to a discussion about *Wounded*, my most personal book of all. I'd given Gina Dolores all my "issues," past and present. She was bipolar, suffered from fibromyalgia and chronic pain disorder, and had made many mistakes, despite the graces she'd been given. Like my fictional alter ego, once, in a particularly harsh season of pain, I dreamed I had the wounds of Christ in my hands. I had no idea what the dream meant, but I am certain, even now, the dream was from God. I placed Gina in my own hometown and made her what I would have been like with my current struggles if I were her age.

John looked thoughtful after I told him about *Wounded*. He sat back in his chair, his chin resting in the cradle of his thumb and index finger. He regarded me with great interest. Then he and Katherine began to tell me a story.

Katherine met Joseph, a simple, yet extraordinary man in a church theology class. He was one of a half-dozen people who'd come to know more about the Catholic Church. He struck her as a very sincere, devout, and humble Christian—salt of the earth. One of the most gentle, caring, open, and faithful Christians she'd ever met. Joseph seemed always hungry to know more about the faith.

As the class progressed, he'd never brought up his wife, until one day he mentioned that every Sunday he drives for hours to put flowers on her grave. Katherine asked him why he drives several hours every weekend to put flowers on her grave when she wasn't there anymore. Just her body remained. Joseph told her that his Mary Rose was very special. Then he told her a story.

He began his tale with a shy and solemn testimony that his wife suffered the wounds of Christ for many years. I asked Katherine what she thought of what he said.

"I didn't disbelieve him," she said. "He was not the kind of person that would say something that wasn't true. But I was astounded. However, as a child, I had been familiar with Padre Pio, the stigmatic in Europe. My parish priest, growing up, had gone to see Padre Pio, and my mother had written to him. So, I didn't think it was impossible, but I'd never met Mary Rose, even though we went to church where she was a member. I still never recall meeting her."

Katherine's husband, John, had a different reaction to Joseph's declaration. He says, "Initially, I thought the man's wife was probably hysterical. I didn't believe it. It was only when I met Joe and saw his piety—his holiness—that I thought, *I believe it because he said it was true.*"

Later, they recounted, after weeks or months had passed, Joseph bought them a book, saying he wanted to share his beloved Mary Rose with them. This was an exceptional privilege. He'd kept his wife's condition quiet from most people, and for good reason. Only a few good, prayerful friends, and the priest who bought her communion, knew.

When I heard this story, of a stigmatic, living in the very city where *Wounded* takes place—this story of a real woman who literally lived down the street from where I placed Gina's home in the story, I, too, was astounded. And there was a record of this, faithfully (and secretly) kept for years, first by Joseph, and later, entrusted to John and Katherine after Joseph's death.

John and Katherine had me in their home sometime later to talk about Mary Rose and Joseph. They showed me the book. I must admit I had a visceral reaction to it. My heart began to palpitate when I held the simple green photo album.

On the cover of the album Joseph had placed strips of luminous gold-embossed labels, with these words:

THE HAND OF GOD AMONGST US
MARY ROSE MASTERS
WIFE
MOTHER
STIGMATIC-MYSTIC

With reverence I opened the book to the first page. There I found Mary Rose's death certificate, and these words on a red, embossed label, as if to stress the importance of them:

TO PROMOTE AND STRENGTHEN FAITH—YES—BUT—

And now, the color changes again. Yellow gold-embossed labels, with a flourish of orange swirls:

THIS IS NOT TO PUT DOWN ANYONE'S RELIGION
FOR MARY ROSE HERSELF SPRANG FROM PROTESTANTISM
WHICH WE BOTH RESPECTED AND EACH FELT
THAT WHOEVER HAD SINCERE FAITH AND PRACTICED IT
ACCORDINGLY
MUST SURELY POSSESS THE KEY TO HEAVEN
NOR IS THIS TO PROCLAIM MARY'S SAINTLINESS
FOR SHE HAD NUMEROUS PROBLEMS—
AND REACTED TO THEM MUCH THE SAME AS ANY OF US
HOWEVER—WHAT MY EYES HAVE BEHELD
LEAVES NO ROOM TO DOUBT—
THAT GOD WAS PRESENT HERE IN A SPECIAL WAY
—JOSEPH MASTERS

The second page was labeled:

The Sacred Heart of Jesus
The Subject of Mary Rose's Visions

Beneath the words a five-by-seven image of Christ stared at me with blue, mournful eyes. His sacred heart illuminated His chest, fire beneath a cross on the top of it, and a crown of thorns wrapped around it. His heart had been pierced with a sword and bled.

I turned the page and found on the left-hand side Mary Rose's death certificate. She died ten days after Vigil of Ascension, in 1972. Cause of death, coronary heart disease. On the right-hand side there was her picture, smiling serenely, a slight woman, with a childlike, innocence in her face. "Mary Rose in Spring of '71," the gold label said. No visible wounds that I could see. She looked happy.

On the next page I found a copy an excerpt from a log the priest who'd brought her communion kept of Mary Rose's ecstasies. He, too, had passed on. Besides his remembrance card and obituary, was the priest's chronicle of this event:

```
March 23rd, 1958


    In the early part of March, Mrs. Mary Rose
Masters of this parish wanted to confide in me
about some spiritual experiences she was having.
Hitherto Father N., the assistant, had been her
counselor and confessor. At this meeting Mrs. Mas-
ters insisted on taking me into her confidence and
```

revealed to me that she had visions of our Lord (Sacred Heart) for the past several years. Same month He appeared to her and told her she would "suffer." This frightened her and caused her to seek my explanation. I assured her that no one could surmise what our Lord had in mind by this suffering. It could mean one of several things. It could be constructed as mental, such as pain from sickness, it could be grief by talk of others and then again of any such form. To this she replied perhaps it would be another attack of heart seizure from which she was currently suffering.

He would go on to record several passion ecstacies, in which Mary Rose bled profusely with severe pain. The next page of the book has a photograph of Mary Rose in ecstasy. She is wearing a white gown, and her hands are clasped together as if in prayer. Her eyes appeared to be glazed over. These sober words accompany the photograph:

SUFFERING THE PASSION—LENT 1969

And beneath the picture:

FROM ANY POSITION THE BLOOD FLOWED AS IF FROM THE UPRIGHT POSITION—OFTEN COUNTER TO GRAVITY.

Another page from the priest's log says:

At about 1 P.M. Father L. was called to the Masters' residence, Mrs. Masters was bleeding more profusely than any other time. Her blouse was red from where blood was coming from her back. The heavy padding and towels on heart and feet were blood soaked. She was offering her suffering today for a fallen-away priest.

According to Mary Rose's own testimony, written on scraps of papers she wrote on which her husband added to the album, Jesus told her to suffer in silence. Though she was doggedly committed to secrecy, she never suffered for suffering's sake. There were so many stories, interwoven in this book. So many people she touched. Mary Rose, like Gina, my character, offered up her suffering for others, including a priest—don't miss the irony here, and the strange patterns—who had fallen away from the faith and his vocation.

Her husband fills in the details. Mary Rose sought this priest out, her scarred hands hidden by gloves. She never let on about her gifts and suffering for him in her visits, yet she was able to pray and plead and lead him back to a restored relationship with God. This once-fallen priest went into a monastery to do penance and not much later was killed in a boating accident. Who can say what influence Mary Rose had on his eternal destiny?

I turn the page and find another log from the priest. He writes Mary Rose's words. My stomach clenches within me.

Good Friday, March 27, 1959

Passion

Don't let Him do it! ----- He can't! He

can't----. Don't let them do it to Him.-------No
more strength to carry the cross----- Oh! No!
No! No! -----If I could only take Your place!
-------Please! Please! Please! I will suffer
again. Close by your side, blessed Mother, to
share your grief."

The words chilled me. So much like Gina's in my fictional account. It was as if somehow I, like Priest, found Mary Rose's story. And how could that be? How could something so unusual, whether or not one believed in the miracle of it, have happened, so quietly, in a six-mile-square city that would attract little attention in this world?

Her husband records in his own handwriting:

Because of the message, "to suffer in silence" Mary Rose so often received, she was always reluctant to let others know of the many and reccurring manifestations that had filled her life during the past fifteen years or so, and the thought of pictures during these times gave her considerable worry that her secret might be exposed. Except for a couple of occasions, I respected her wishes.

I am sorry now that I do not have shots of all the many different things that did occur. I thank God for the few of them I have and pray that He will so guide my use of them as to best promote His honor and glory according to His will.

In recent years, Mary Rose walked through life as two persons. Most knew her as an ordinary individual, with many of the difficulties that confront us all, and having just as great a problem to avoid life's pitfalls. A select few knew her as an instrument of God attempting to abundantly fulfill His will.

Many will be more astounded because they were so close but yet had no idea of the other Mary Rose, and it will seem that such could not have happened without their knowing.

The following page has a poignant photo of a very disappointed Mary Rose and the label:

MARY ROSE'S FACE SHOWS DISAPPOINTMENT WHEN SHE LEARNS OF THE PICTURES I'VE BEEN TAKING.

Mary Rose and Joseph had two children, a boy and a girl. They faced tremendous hardship with her condition. They did not have other children over to visit and play as normal children do. They considered her sick and were embarrassed by her. Her daughter renounces these experiences to this day and is not willing to have her mother's identity revealed. I have purposely changed the name of all the people in this account, out of respect for their wishes.

But Joseph Masters believed in his wife's passion. He wrote:

There are those who would claim—work of the devil—but could God permit His passions to be used by the forces of evil for entrapment? I think not!

As I read the book and listened to the stories Katherine and John told, I could almost palpably feel Mary Rose's extraordinary sufferings. Yet she had such surrender. She prayed:

My dear Jesus, I am Thine and Thou art mine. To be surely united to You, I consecrate to You this day my ears, my eyes, my heart, and my whole being, guard them as Thy property and possession. Not my will, but Thine be done. My God, I love Thee with all my heart. Teach me to love Thee more and more.

The last two pages of the book display a holy card, a memorial from Mary Rose's funeral and another of her prayers. On the holy card, there is an image of the sorrowful mother—an image on a medal I've worn around my neck since I started writing *Wounded*. On the back of the card the words from Matthew's gospel, "Blessed are they who mourn, for they shall be comforted." And finally,

"My Jesus have mercy on the soul of Mary Rose Masters."
Amen.

Joseph Masters finished the very last page of the book with bloodred labels:

> Mary Rose's stigma included
>> The crown of thorns
>> Nail punctures of the hands
>> Nail punctures of the feet
>> Lance marks of the chest
>> Lash marks of the back
>> Bruised knees and elbows
>> Bruised right shoulder
>> Bleeding from all places

> The occasions of Mary Rose's experiences followed the church calendar and were most prominent during Lent & often disappeared as instantaneously as appearing. Her last suffering—vigil of ascension—May 11, '72.

Mary Rose died ten days after her last suffering, on the Feast of Pentecost.

Two stories here. One made up, of a stigmatic in full bloom in Inkster. Another of a stigmatic, suffering in silence in Inkster for fifteen years. Only her story is real—a story that came to me on a Friday in Lent, a day in which Mary Rose suffered her passions most.

John said to me, as we pondered these mysteries after he and

Katherine entrusted the special book to me. "In a way, I feel like I've been preparing for this day all my life."

I feel the same way. So many strange coincidences, so much of what my characters said and did, and who they were right in the pages of my novel, lived in truth in Mary Rose's life. Whether you believe it happened or not, you have to admit it certainly is mysterious. And I still don't know why I told either story. I had at first some vague idea that I wanted people to know that it was okay to suffer, and that is true, but I have to wonder if God isn't saying something more. And I am straining to hear what that could be.

And now as I sit here, Mary Rose's book beside me, a strong odor of roses rises from the pages. I stop and turn to the book, lift it and smell, and suddenly the scent is gone as quickly as it appeared. And in silence I wonder if the story of Regina Dolores, queen of sorrows, was the one I was meant to tell at all. Maybe the real story I was to find was the one of the real stigmatic in Inkster, who may, wherever she is, still be interceding for all of us who hear this.

My Jesus, have mercy.

I wonder.

Who can know?

—Claudia Mair Burney,
April 29, 2008,
Feast of Saint Catherine of Siena